BOOK ONE

BETWEEN TWO MINDS:
AWAKENING

D C WRIGHT-HAMMER

To Emily, Cameron, and Avery for being amazing
even when I am between two minds.

WARNING!

Chapter 15, Hope's Funeral, may be uncomfortable
for some who have experience with suicide.

Please read with caution.

PROLOGUE

HEARTS AND MINDS

"Bravo Company, rough turbulence ahead. You are cleared for takeoff, but proceed with caution. HQ out."

The endless night sky was clearer and darker than I could ever remember. All the constellations made their presence known. Orion's Belt and the Big and Little Dippers shone bright against the black sky, but the Gemini grouping was particularly apparent. Filling the sky to our left, a super moon provided the only light we had. Strangely, the limitless black space above provided a wholesome comfort in its simplicity, and it was then that I became aware of the warm, growing sense of peace emerging from my core. With all of our preparation, things had felt fairly routine up to that point. We'd done it a hundred times before, and I had no reason to believe this night would be any different. At that moment, the journey ahead seemed like it would be a successful one.

Then my perfect view of the abyss above became obscured by a thick, black cloud of smoke. The intense stink of gunpowder followed, burning my nostrils and making my eyes water a little. The echo of gunfire and explosions in the distance killed the calming silence of the previous few minutes, and in an instant, my serenity was obliterated. The inner warmth raged from peace into hellfire, and an unquestionable certainty popped into my mind.

No one will return unscathed from this mission.

Backs against the wall, Bravo Company and I readied our weapons for battle after receiving the go-ahead from HQ. There was almost a rhythm to the clicks and clacks of the loading of magazines and the pulling back of operator pins as we prepared for the enemy across the street. Our heads all turned to our scout, who took the cue to inch toward the edge of the wall. Deliberately peering around the corner to gain a view of our target, she turned back to us.

Thumbs-up.

In unison, the rest of the squad slid behind the scout and waited for the final confirmation signal. Unlike the firefights raging on the other side of the city, it was deadly quiet at our location. If I hadn't known better, I'd have thought we infiltrated that deep into enemy territory undetected and the hostiles would be caught off guard. Maybe we would be in and out in no time, and all of us would be back at base later that night, celebrating an easy victory. But no. I definitely knew better than that. Something was off.

In those final moments, with sweat pouring down my neck and onto my back, I was anything but confident. Looking over at all my squad mates, I saw that familiar look of conviction stretched across each of their faces. They were all tough as nails in their own way, and it was always an honor to go to battle with them. But through the face paint and sweat and behind their calloused, defensive exteriors, there were hints of something very different—uncertainty, doubt, and to some extent, fear. After a few moments, it was clear that I looked the same.

The scout raised her hand up high and extended her thumb, index, and middle fingers, then dropped them one by one.

Three...two...one...

Backs down, we all slipped around the corner, across the street, and toward the factory. The aerial scans had brought back an 80% chance that it was being used to manufacture and house illegal drugs and possibly munitions, but it was grunts like us who would provide confirmation.

Reaching the outer wall of the building, we gently eased our bodies against it and pointed our rifles to the sky. Again, the scout took initiative and headed for the door, placing a small amount of plastic explosive with precision while half of us looked outward in case she needed cover. The other half were the battering rams preparing to kick down the blown-up door and engage the enemy. Normally a scout, I was more than happy to be a big gun for this mission. The tension grew thick as the minutes ticked by while the scout did her work.

With all of my mental power, I was focused on the mission until I felt a movement next to my left boot. It took all of my years of training and missions not to jump out of my skin as the scarlet death, a scorpion with fatal venom, started its ascent up my pant leg.

Shink!

It will forever be burned into my memory, the grin on my squad mate's face as he lifted the stabbed and flailing arachnid to my face before dropping it the ground and crushing it under his boot. The audible crunch was the loudest noise we'd made all night. Knowing I would get shit later for the incident, I quickly came to peace with it and focused back on the task at hand.

The scout finally put her hand in the air again to move the mission forward.

Three…two…one…

Pow!

The battering rams and I led the way, launching the door inward, followed by a barrage of muffled thuds from the smoke bombs we chucked into the building. The rat-a-tat-tat of automatic weapons started from across the factory, and we all quickly hit the ground and returned fire. The star-shaped flashes of the enemy weapons in the dimly lit smoke provided all the targets we needed to neutralize most of them. We sent more smoke bombs and flash bangs deeper into the factory and crawled forward to keep the pressure on. After a few more rounds from our end, the enemy fire stopped completely, and it seemed as if we were going to have the easy win that I had initially doubted.

"Bravo Company, stay alert. Wait for my signal." The scout reminded us to be vigilant as she skulked forward through the smoke and toward the hallway of offices.

With the moment of reprieve, we all reloaded and prepped for the next phase of the mission.

Leaning in, my squad mate couldn't help himself. "It's a good thing I saved you from that deadly red; otherwise, this might have been a tough mission."

Before I could respond or punch him, chills ran down my spine as a familiar and terrifying sound changed everything—the *dink, dink, dink* of an enemy canister bouncing in our direction.

"Marines, masks on!"

Our auto-masks exploded from our packs, slipped over our heads, and enclosed our faces. The squad mate next to me dove near the rest of the squad as a canister exploded into a puff of thick yellow dust right between them and me. Standing outside the gas, I could only make out the silhouettes of my crew as a dreadful mechanical voice from our headsets alerted us to the seriousness of the situation.

"Warning: Unknown substance detected. Evacuate the area. Unknown substance detected. Evacuate the area."

My stomach dropped as the dangerous fog began to float in my direction. I tried to do everything in my power to keep an eye on the squad. As pockets of the cloud dissipated, I helplessly watched as most of Bravo Company dropped one by one without making so much as a loud gasp over the walkie. They were able-bodied, hard-ass marines one second and likely dead the next.

Paralysis overcame me as my mind rattled through all the different ways to help them. Time slowed to a screeching halt, and silence swooped in as my mind failed to function optimally as it had on almost every mission up until then. Slowly blinking and hopelessly lost in thought, the deadly smog crept ever so close to my face. Inches from a likely awful death, I had to make a call.

What good will it be for me to die too?

My decision was made, and fortunately, my instincts kicked in. I snapped out of it just before taking in my first breath of yellow death. Assuming a hunched position, I aimed my weapon toward the hallway and headed in the direction of the scout. Entering the hallway, I dropped to a knee and began to crawl. It was all too quiet, but I knew what was waiting for me ahead. Rounding the corner into one room, I rolled onto my back to surprise one of the enemy standing above me. We made the briefest of eye contact, and I was a little shocked that I didn't detect even the slightest hint of fear or even doubt but only intense hatred.

Squeezing my trigger harder than ever, my bullets sawed him nearly in half from bottom to top and his innards spewed down in a heaping mess all over me. I put both feet up to stop his halves from falling on top of me. Nevertheless, blood poured all over my mask, covering the eye lens and breathing vent. Panicking when my next breath was denied, my instincts to rip the mask off didn't kick in immediately, and oddly enough, time stood still as the strangest voice popped into my head.

I can't breathe! I'm sorry, Sarah.

Shaken to the core, I snapped out of my stupor to violently tear the mask from my face and have it slide back into my pack. But in looking for a breath of life, I was instead met by a rain of death from my victim. His blood and guts, still drizzling, went right into my mouth as I shoved his mangled body to the side with my legs. Overcome by the nauseating, irony taste, I gagged and coughed hard trying to spit out as much as possible. In the end, it seemed like a reasonable trade, my life for a mouth full of enemy entrails, but I definitely wasn't the bloodthirsty invader he thought I was.

Popping to my feet, I wiped off as many solid pieces as I could and quickly scanned the room. When I deemed it clear, I turned back to the hallway with my weapon pointed. I dropped back down to a crawl, then found the next three rooms to be empty as I made my way toward the last room on the right.

Again, I tried to surprise the hostile I detected by rolling onto my back, but she got the jump on me and kicked the rifle from my hands. Without thinking, I swept her legs and hopped up while grabbing the 9mm at my side. Her back to the ground, she again kicked the gun out of my hand, then rolled a powerful fist toward my crotch, narrowly missing a blow that would have put me down for the count. Before I could gather myself, she thrust me over her so she could hop to her feet behind me. The familiar *shink* of a dagger being pulled triggered me to pull my knife out as I turned to engage her.

Coming at each other at full force, our blades collided with a metal ting, but my larger frame and momentum got the best of her as she staggered back. She lunged toward me again with knife pointed. I dodged her attack, grabbed her arm with my free hand, and flung her toward a wooden desk that she promptly slid under. After rolling to the ground to grab my 9mm, I popped onto the desk and repeatedly shot straight down through the wood, hoping to neutralize her.

Pop! Pop! Pop! Pop! Pop!

But she had slid from under the desk, toward the door, seemingly unscathed. While my shells were still tinking off the table and floor, I aimed in her direction, but she turned down the hallway before I could get off a clean shot. I was distracted for the briefest second by the subtle light coming through the large window on the far side of the office.

Pop!

The single gunshot from behind me made my life flash before my eyes, and I was instantly filled with regret. Time again slowed to a snail's pace, and I could hear my heart pounding out of my chest. A single frigid bead of sweat dripped from my brow and into my eye, but I never so much as flinched as I looked on at the light coming from the window. Before the horrors of death could fully overtake me, the scout radioed in the building status.

"Bravo Company, entry and hallway are clear. Checking in: Sierra Hotel. Over."

Exhaling out the terror that had seized me, I was brought back to reality. The shot was Sierra taking care of the hostile.

I was perfectly fine. "Checking in: Coyote Royale. Over."

The silence that followed my reply brought a coldness over me.

"HQ, vitals for Bravo Company, over."

Sierra inquired from the end of the hallway, but her voice led me to believe she was getting closer to my office.

"Bravo Company, two strong, six weak. I repeat: Two strong. Six weak. Over."

"HQ, we need a medical evac with decontam at zero six four five. Over."

"Roger medical evac with decontam, Bravo Company. Medical evac with decontam en route. Over and out."

Sierra made her way back to me in the office, and I waved her over to the edge of the room near the window.

"Is that your blood or…?"

"No, I'm good."

"Whew."

Looking out the window, we saw the factory floor in a dim light, but could still see all of the expected industrial machinery and equipment.

Something else caught Sierra's eye, and she pointed. "Light down below."

Surprisingly easy to overlook, there appeared to be a makeshift large room near the center of the factory floor that had white light seeping from the bottom of its walls. It had to be the large energy presence detected by the aerial scans, and that was where we'd find the drugs, munitions, or both.

She gave the signal for us to move forward.

Rifles ready, we headed down to the factory floor to investigate. Backs together, we cautiously entered the main production area while eying the catwalks above. I began leading us toward the glowing room when Sierra redirected us.

"Let's secure the perimeter before going any farther."

Rightfully so, she always kept safety at the fore of every mission. Almost silently, we circled the large space, eyes pointed through our sights, looking for even the slightest hint of movement. Stealthily maneuvering around fully stocked shelves and a scattered fleet of old forklifts, I couldn't ignore that death might be lurking around every corner. When we finally covered the entire area and detected no enemy activity, we both spontaneously sighed in relief.

"Factory floor is clear. Let's investigate the room."

Just after she gave the order, something about the two large wooden crates on the far side of the factory caught my eye. I normally wouldn't have thought twice about them, but they were labeled "Canned Goods" in the local language. While I couldn't speak or even read much of their language, we had sent dozens of crates of rations just like them to the surrounding cities and towns, so I knew the writing. But they were definitely out of place in the factory. One of the ways the enemy developed a stronghold in the area was to feed some of the locals better than we did. So why did the extremists have low-quality food crates in their illegal factory?

I pointed to the crates and motioned to Sierra to head in that direction with me. We lightly stepped toward them, and with one hand pointing my weapon, the other obtained the utility stick from my belt and fashioned it into a pry bar. Throwing my rifle over my shoulder, I reached up with both hands to position the pry bar under the top board of the crate, pushed hard to wedge it in, and with an oomph, pulled down with my body weight.

Crack!

The crate popped open, and the wooden wall in front of us buckled, then slowly started to fall. I chucked the utility stick aside, its metal clanks echoing loudly as it skipped across the concrete floor. I immediately grabbed my weapon, shuffled back, and aimed at anything that might be inside.

The wall hit the floor, and we both pointed our rifles for a moment longer. Another sigh came from both of us as nothing of danger presented itself—only pallets of canned beans, vegetables, pastas, and meats.

"And all we get are those disgusting MREs."

Sierra breathily snickered and then gave me the signal for all clear. She motioned me back to the glowing room, but something still didn't add up. Why would the enemy steal the locals' shitty rations? I was turning to follow Sierra when I caught something else out of my peripheral. The bottom pallet was missing, and in its place, the floor of the crate appeared to be about eight inches higher than it should have been.

"Hold on."

Sierra turned to see me fling my rifle back over my shoulder again and scoop the pry bar from the ground. I went to work on the false floor, finding the seam of the two pieces and pressing down hard. The floorboard popped up. Dropping the utility stick again, I grabbed the board and walked the four feet back to pull it out.

The scout walked past me to discover the real contents of the crates. "These look like what they chucked past me in the hallway."

Reading the side of the canisters, I couldn't disagree. "RPS-X2. You're damn right it is. We need to get one of these to the lab. Maybe it can help the squad if it's not already too late."

Sierra obtained a hazmat bag from her pack and steadily handled one canister from the crate without incident. "That should do. We'll have the cleanup crew handle the rest."

"So, if the munitions were in the crates, I wonder what's in there." My curiosity was palpable as I turned back to the room with light.

"Let's go."

The unmistakable, low hum of a generator could be felt as we closed in on the room. Sierra headed for the door, and of course, it was locked. She molded another bit of explosives from her pack and placed it on the door. We slipped around the corner for safety, and she completed another countdown

Bang!

The door rattled as it flung open. With weapon ready, I flew around the corner first, looking to engage anyone dumb enough to confront us.

"Wait!"

Sierra's yell stopped me dead in my tracks right in front of the doorway. Focusing hard, I was again face to face with a cloud of fog, and felt like my time had come. But luckily, the mist was white, not yellow, so I was certain it wasn't the same stuff that had dropped the rest of our squad. My hypothesis was confirmed as some of the mist began to wisp up toward the ceiling of the factory.

"Thanks. It's just water vapor."

With pockets of visibility through the fog, I could see that the room was clear of hostiles, and gave the signal to Sierra. I stepped in first. It was almost too cold to feel good after the intense heat we'd endured the entire mission. Harsh chills covered my body. As the rest of the frigid haze began to recede, the strange nature of the room revealed itself. Much smaller than it appeared from the outside, there were columns of handles, three deep, lining three of the inner walls. It made the room feel like a grouping of giant filing cabinets.

Signaling that I would investigate, I approached the far wall, pointing my gun with one hand and extending the other. Grabbing the handle in the center of the grid, I gave it a hard tug. But it didn't budge. Leaning back, I was only straining myself.

"Give me a minute," the scout said.

Peering over my shoulder, I saw that Sierra had found a control panel on the wall by the door. She put it through the paces, typing away, eliciting clicks, beeps, and buzzes. All of it returned the red and yellow lights of failure over and over. She continued working frantically until she realized that she wasn't going to be cracking the code.

"Dammit!"

"We can just let the cleanup—"

Pop! Pop! Pop!

She'd drawn her gun and let the computer console have it.

Beep!

With a jolt, the hum from the generator slowly subsided as the room's lighting changed from a crisp fluorescent to a dull yellow. The temperature in the room rose quickly. Sierra waved to me to try the handle again. Before turning back, I caught a glimpse of the silly smirk on her face through her gas mask. She was obviously entertained by her accomplishment.

Getting back in position, I firmly gripped the handle and pulled with a steady force. The handle gave way to what seemed to be a large drawer, and as its wheels produced a deep grinding sound against the rails, I stepped back slowly to make room for it. Sierra appeared by my side as we discovered the black cover that obscured the contents of the drawer.

With our eyes locked inside, I reached down and grabbed the cover. I gave Sierra one last glance and a wink, and with a forceful swipe, I pulled the cover away. Our collective gasp will forever haunt me, and in that horrible moment, I couldn't control myself.

"What the hell is this! A morgue?"

CHAPTER 1

THE END IS NIGH

WHAT THE HELL IS THIS! A morgue? Vicious goosebumps running up my neck forced the morbid thought into my brain.

The frowning woman across the room must have agreed with me. Her arms were tightly crossed as if she was hugging herself warm. And if seeing my breath wasn't bad enough, the interior decorator of the waiting room clearly had some kind of mental disorder. The fairly large room had no windows, so it felt claustrophobic. The walls were a drab off-white, and the bright, obscure hanging art stuck out more like bloody thumbs than sprinkled décor. The boring chairs and end tables evenly lining the perimeter would normally have appealed to my desire for symmetry and open space, except the center of the room was filled with an obnoxiously massive statue of Atlas holding up the world. I thought it was neat the first time I saw it, but every time after, it was just annoying. There had to be a better place for the thing. Worse yet was the carpet that could easily be described as "puke green." Finally, to keep things sufficiently random, there was a sizable aquarium full of marine life built into the inner wall. While the tank seemed totally out of place, it was the most interesting thing around. It was next to the aquarium where I always sat, facing the main entrance.

The train of thought that always followed my being in the schizophrenically designed, frigid waiting room provided a much-needed distraction from the seriousness of my visits. In that sense, I had often debated whether the crude style choices were intentional, as if we were part of some odd social experiment and eventually, a man would jump out and point to the cameras. But deliberate or not, nothing could have fully taken my mind off what was to come next for me on this particular visit.

Over the last year, my life had been turned upside down while preparing for a revolutionary change. A core aspect of who I'd always been was about to be altered. Or corrected. And while they had said I put forth even more effort than the average person, I truly doubted it was sufficient. It seemed foolish not to doubt any amount of preparation. I was basically going to be born again, made completely new. How could only twelve months of preparation "to get you ready" be enough? I remember reviewing the preparation log and being genuinely shocked that it was actually only one hundred and twenty hours. Terrified didn't even begin to describe the feelings steadily growing in the pit of my stomach during this eleventh hour. So, in an effort to calm my nerves, I thought back over everything I had done.

They had started with mandatory tutorials and simulations. It seemed like I spent countless hours in virtual reality, completing various tasks related to the procedure and life afterward. Unfortunately, much of my time was spent on menial tasks that nearly bored me to death.

Standing up.

Walking through doors.

Jumping up and down.

There was one particular virtual session that really struck a chord with me: taking the dog to the park. Maybe it was the fact that personally-owned canines had been illegal for many years since the passage of the Canine Fever Act, or perhaps that public green space hadn't been around for years either. No matter, I couldn't have been more content than when I had my hand tightly gripped around the leash, strolling with pride down the walkway. The simulations only lasted for an hour at a time, but the looks on the faces of the virtual people, or veeps as we called them, stayed with me.

Cutting-edge technology made the veep AI among the most advanced in the world. With respect, they would look directly into my eyes and smile, followed by an exaggerated but nonetheless sincere wave that felt like a grade school crush acknowledging my existence. After the warm greeting, the veep's eyes would trail down my body, and it was always at that point I would get really self-conscious. In that sense, the training was effective because it helped me cope with what was coming. I had to actively remind myself that the veeps weren't weighing my value as a human being in that moment. They were simply looking at my dog.

"What a beautiful pooch!" they would say.

"Thank you!" I would happily respond.

And with a polite nod, their eyes would again travel all the way up to catch my gaze.

Never getting enough of it, I had probably gone through that scene twenty times and asked for it at least ten times more. I would get so engrossed within the simulators that I ignored the environmental countdown to relax my mind for reconsciousness, and they would have to forcefully pull me out. At one point, the main VR operator threatened to bar me from the machine. It would have meant that I couldn't complete my required hours or the procedure. She didn't understand that the hardest part was leaving a place where I felt like a complete person to come back to the cold, unfair, real world.

Harder yet, I had to work with a slew of "recommended specialists" to overcome my issues. That was a grueling six months of mental gymnastics, and I most certainly should have won a medal for getting through it. They smugly called it "proactive psychotherapy" and treated me more like a client or patient than a fellow human being with the full spectrum of emotions. Admittedly, they did their best to empathize and even sympathize to some degree. Yet they doled out tough question after tough question.

"Why do you believe getting a new host will improve your quality of life?"

I cackled out loud because of the nervous itch that instantly seized my body.

"How will you handle life's problems in your new host?"

"You know you won't be able to use your body as an excuse in your new host?"

"Eventually, you'll be just like everyone else. How will you handle that?"

By the end, I wasn't laughing. Being brought to my mental knees, I wasn't so sure I was going to make it. So much pain, insecurity, anger, and trauma erupted to the surface in those sessions. Despite countless tears, something inside kept me going.

The aquarium next to me came to life in an instant. It was feeding time, and a godlike hand appeared just above the water line. Tiny flakes fluttered down through the water, inciting the fish into a feeding frenzy. There was a small catfish, a few exotic types, and then I noticed something near the bottom far corner, something I had never seen before. A tiny gray fish was struggling to get around. I was no marine biologist, but it appeared that his fins were malformed. They seemed woefully too small compared to his body, and he was straining to get to the food—working, puffing, flapping those fins, flapping, struggling, flapping. Meanwhile, a large goldfish was zipping around, scooping up flake after flake as it went by. Were the doctors playing a joke on me? Were they toying with their clients?

God dammit!

Shaking my head, I looked down at my shriveled legs and winced. I couldn't help but let loose an audible groan, catching the attention of a couple sitting near me. But I didn't care. The life that I had been given really wasn't fair compared to some. The super well-offs didn't have to worry about the luck of the genetic draw. They got to choose their babies' traits from the beginning and watch them grow in life tubes. The advertisements claimed that they kept the babies in the ideal conditions for the entire gestational period. Their perfect little babies grew in their perfect little tubes. It was bullshit.

With damn near all my life savings, the best I could afford was to divorce my body. Ugh. I had always hated that description. It sounded colder than the waiting room felt. For whatever reason, I liked the technical term better: *mind migration.*

News of the first successful procedure had broken just a few days after my twelfth birthday. I became obsessed with the idea of getting legs that worked, making a promise to myself that I would save as many credits as possible to one day afford a mind migration. It was a promise that had consumed me for the last decade. But it hadn't become clear exactly what I'd be getting myself into until I actually signed up.

On top of the normal preparation, I had to deal with something that was apparently unique to me. One of my biggest hurdles was wrapping my head around the idea of life without my auto-chair, or Auto as I called him. He had been with me since junior high. In fact, I'd gotten him just a couple weeks prior to hearing about mind migration, and all these years later, he still ran on all cylinders. People in my condition didn't grow much, so there was no reason to buy another one as I got older. And even if I'd had the credits for a newer model, Auto had never failed me. "If it ain't really broke, don't fix it," I always said.

Still, I had always told myself that our relationship would be temporary, knowing I was planning on a mind migration. As odd as it was, though, I had grown extraordinarily attached to Auto, thinking of him much more like a friend or brother than an inanimate object. He didn't even have any AI to help me personify him, and that didn't matter. He was an extension of my being. He was part of me.

After the procedure, there would no longer be a need to keep Auto around. Strange didn't come close to describing how that made me feel, knowing I'd have to say goodbye to him in an hour or so. Even though they worked with others in auto-chairs, the so-called experts didn't seem to have any experience with the kind of bond Auto and I had built. When I asked if I could keep him afterward, they made it clear that our relationship would hold back my progress. They said that, while it would make the whole process that much more difficult, it was "for my benefit."

As I was about to head straight for the most depressing thoughts, I was again interrupted. The auto-doors to my right whooshed open with a gust of dank, muggy air. It was almost refreshing compared to the deep freeze that I had been in for the last thirty minutes or so. I almost didn't notice the commotion until the familiar hum of another auto-chair broke my concentration. I slowly peered over to see my favorite fellow auto-driver. Helen was preparing for the exact procedure as me, and I both envied and pitied that the hardest parts were yet to come for her.

"Helen!"

Startled, she turned toward me. "Oh hey, Ryan!" She zoomed over to me. "Isn't today the big day?"

Nodding emphatically, I almost couldn't contain myself. "Yeah! Can you believe it? The year has gone by in a flash. You don't have much time left either, do you?"

"A couple weeks. I didn't think it could get any more intense, but last week was rough."

While I wanted to tell her it was going to be okay, Helen and I were close enough that I could be honest. "Hang in there. The good news is that when your day comes, there's nothing else left to do but let it happen. The bad news is that it's still scary as hell."

"That's what I heard. Hey, when we're finally on our feet and all this craziness is finally behind us, we should get together and celebrate."

"First round's on me." After the words fell out of my mouth, I realized that the conversation had me smiling for the first time all day.

"Deal! I've gotta get to my last personal-identity session, but it was nice seeing you. Oh, and Ry?" She rolled closer to me.

"Yeah?"

"Stay strong. I know you've heard the horror stories about afterward, but I really want to see you get through it."

Her genuine concern took the edge off of my nerves for the first time that day, and it was enough that I had to joke with her. "Well, someone's gotta give you hope!"

"Hope? I thought we already established that anything you can do I can do better." She loved to zing me.

"Looks like we're going to have a race once we get our legs."

"If you want to recreate the tortoise and the hare, I'm game. Good luck, Ryan!"

"Good luck, Helen! Bye!"

As Helen rolled away, I could feel the silly grin on my face get bigger. I had been so focused on the preparation that it had been a month or more since I thought about how amazing it would be in my new body, or host as they called them. I really hoped my host would meet most of my specifications. They had made it very clear that with the package I'd bought, they couldn't guarantee the perfect host but would try to get it as close as possible. The warning was on every form that I had filled out. Regardless, I was very particular about what I wanted. No shorter than six one, darker hair, green eyes. I had always wanted green eyes. It was my favorite color. I also really wanted a more athletic build where I could truly experience the breadth of human mobility—run, jump, tackle!

Hell, I would have been happy to simply walk down the sidewalk instead of having to ride. No offense to Auto, but it had been my biggest dream ever since I could remember, and to be mere minutes from the start of the process was incredible. Unfortunately, as excited as I wanted to be, my undeniable fear would only allow me to muster muted enthusiasm.

"Ryan D. Carter, the technicians are ready to see you in room eight-thirteen," chimed a monotonous voice from the intercom. "Ryan D. Carter to room eight-thirteen."

Goosebumps formed down my partially functional spine as the voice rang through the waiting room. *They called me! They've finally called me for my mind migration!*

Without thinking, I shifted Auto from stationary to mobile on the code pad. Springing to life, Auto's motor emitted that familiar low hum that was always calming to me. It reminded me that while I couldn't walk, I could still move. But in that moment, I needed a little more self-motivation.

"I can do this. I can do this," I whispered under my breath, then I was off.

Leaving the waiting room and entering the building's enormous foyer was always like entering a different world. Auto rolled off the vomit-like carpet and onto a classy, slate tile floor. Foliage netted the walls, giving the building more of an indoor botanical garden feel than that of a medical facility. Peering up as I always did at the twenty-meter high, domed ceiling, I admired the replica of the Sistine chapel transposed there, adding a bit of ancient class. After peering up at the painting, my eyes instantly locked onto the colossal fountain shooting water in interesting patterns at the center of the foyer. Then I moved past the check-in desk where I waved at Patty.

"Good luck, Ryan! You're going to do great!"

"Thanks, Patty!"

Turning down the hallway toward the elevators, a nurse who was obviously preoccupied suddenly entered me into a game of chicken. I made the instant decision to lose by slamming on Auto's stop button to prevent a collision.

He proceeded to exaggeratedly step out of my path as if to make it a point of how my sheer presence was an inconvenience to him. "Oh, excuse me, sir. I didn't see you coming."

His words were nice, but based on the look on his face, he must have been eating a lemon. *For crying out loud, I don't bite!* As much as I wanted to scream it, I let the thought fade.

For better or worse, I was used to that kind of treatment. While some people were just trying to be nice, it almost seemed as if they thought that

I was a hazard. Granted, the factory recall of Auto's model, which had been the most popular auto-chair in history, probably didn't help. I didn't see what the big deal was. It was true that due to a battery flare up issue, his assembly line mates were responsible for hundreds of fires and maimings, and at least twenty official deaths. But I never felt in the slightest danger. Not even a little. Auto had always been good to me. There was no telling when my luck would run out, though, so it was probably a good decision to have the procedure. But that didn't make it any easier to give him up.

I continued down the hallway to the bank of elevators and picked a winner. Virtually interfacing with the control panel from my code pad, I entered the direction I was headed.

Up.

Maybe it was my nerves, but the elevator took much longer than usual to get to my floor. I became aware that I was sweating profusely despite the consistently frigid temperatures in the building. Then the doors took unnecessarily long to open. It was finally becoming a reality, and I was freaking out subconsciously. After an eternity, the elevator opened and I zoomed in, keyed the eighth floor into my code pad, and hit the enter button. The resulting ascension quickly confirmed that this was, in fact, the slowest elevator that had ever existed.

If that wasn't bad enough, a dry, monotonous pop instrumental from the 2010s assaulted my ears from the speaker system. I'd always questioned how anyone could listen to that music, but I guess I had to be alive during that time to really get it. To my joy, I had successfully distracted myself all the way up to the fourth floor when the elevator dings brought me back to reality. With each floor, I was getting that much closer to my new host and, based on my anxiety levels, that much closer to cardiac arrest.

Ding.

My new life.

Ding.

My new beginning.

Ding.

As the elevators slowed nearing the eighth floor, the queasy feeling in my gut evolved into a full-blown ache. I took a deep breath and held back my lunch the best I could.

Ding.

I awkwardly eyed the doors as they took their time opening. Then a crease of light shown through, and I winced a little as the elevator opened on the brightest hallway. I was frozen in time for that moment, staring dead ahead at a sign that I was all too familiar with.

The top line read, "800 - 812 Mind Migration Prep" with an arrow pointing to the left. The bottom line read, "813 Mind Migration Procedures," and pointed to the right. I had gone left so many times that even the thought of going right felt foreign to me. Almost wrong. It took a couple of deep breaths for me to gather myself.

Inching out of the elevator, I slowly rolled unnecessarily close to the sign. I peered up and then toward my final destination to the right. The hallway seemed to go on forever. Looking back toward the opposite corridor, I had an odd sense of pride for having survived the gauntlet of emotional torment in that direction. If nothing else, it hardened me to the next steps in the process, and then I couldn't help but think that had been the plan all along.

Spinning back around to the right, I engaged Auto for nearly the last time. The gentle buzz of my motor echoed against the bare white walls, and my nerves began to calm just a bit. There were windows into the physical therapy areas I passed along the way, and curiosity got the best of me. I noticed a woman walking between two balance beams, definitely uncomfortable in her gait and leaning heavily on her arms. Anguish was all too apparent on her face just before she fell out of my sight. Technicians swooped in to aid her, and as they lifted her, I could see she was crying hysterically. It might have been my imagination, but her lips seemed to read, "Get me out of this body!" I couldn't help but wonder if that was soon to be my fate. As exhausted as I was from all of the work and worry, I knew that mind migration was the start of a completely new journey with many unknowns.

Am I ready for this? Can I handle this?

While I didn't think it possible, even more doubt bubbled into my mind. For as long as I could remember, I had thought of myself as weak or, more accurately, fragile. The feeling was mostly fueled by the way I had been treated by others my whole life, but after so long, it seemed like my self-image reflected what the world had given me. It took a hard head shake to remind myself that I had earned the right to migrate minds. I had worked harder for it than for anything else in my life, and I was going to see it through no matter what, dammit!

Without warning, Auto stopped.

"Huh?"

It was sufficiently awkward that the emergency brake turned on without reason or warning, and had I not known better, I'd have thought Auto was trying to preserve his existence and, with it, our friendship. Or maybe he was trying to stop me from making a huge mistake.

But I did know better. It was just a program glitch with his model. While it had happened a bunch of times over the last year or so, the timing was so perfectly bittersweet that I couldn't help but to talk to him out loud since we'd soon part ways.

"Come on, buddy. Let's get one last ride in."

I took off my brake and reengaged my old friend. Doors to a new life slid open before me, and just as I rolled through, a realization popped into my head.

This is the last time I will enter a room in this body.

CHAPTER 2

ONE LAST GOODBYE

"I'M HERE FOR MY MIND migration."

The man in scrubs behind the desk was more than intently focused on the data he was processing. Without looking up, he grumbled. "Ryan D. Carter?"

"That's me."

Still focusing on typing, he droned on. "Please face the identification reader, place your right thumb into the print scanner, and look into the face-recognition camera. Then clearly state your full name and sixteen-character vocal passcode. Finally, type the same passcode into the code pad or linked device."

As the gatekeeper for a life-changing procedure, he couldn't have been anymore lifeless.

I turned to the large device and peered up. "Uh…that's going to be a problem."

His rhythmic work came screeching to a halt with obvious annoyance. When he looked over at me, I could spot the exact moment familiar shock came over his face.

"Oh." He double tapped a button on his desk, and the identification reader lowered to my level.

I zoomed into position, and with blips and beeps, the machine came to life. I placed my thumb into the device, looked directly into the camera, and clearly stated the information it needed. "Ryan D. Carter, T6951A0561V0NI0B."

I was rewarded with a green light and a hologram of Atlas the Ant.

"Greetings, Ryan! Thanks again for your investment in Atlas Digenetics with your purchase of a standard mind migration and host package. You've come a long way to get to this point, and the next phase of your journey begins with your acceptance of the terms and conditions that were laid out in your migration contract. To review the terms and conditions, please say 'Review' or tap the Review button on the hologram below. Otherwise, simply say 'I accept' or you can press the Accept button."

"I accept."

"Congratulations! You're all set for your procedure. Please check with the data specialist behind the desk for your next instructions. So long, and happy migrating!"

After all of the waivers I'd signed, that had to be the thousandth time I was reminded of the terms and conditions. Mind migrations were dangerous procedures and Atlas Digenetics, also known as ADG, would be in no way liable should I be dissatisfied for any reason with any aspect or the entirety of my mind migration, including death. All procedures were final, and there would be no grounds to sue. Attempting to bring suit against ADG would result in an immediate countersuit for breach of contract. As all of those lovely memories faded, so too did the hologram of Atlas the Ant.

I turned to the medical worker typing away, who apparently had better things to do. "Ahem."

"Oh, right. You can take a…uh, you can move your seat into the waiting area over there, and a migration specialist will be right with you."

"Thanks!" I figured I would be the polite one while I headed to yet another waiting area.

Having never been to the actual migration area of the floor, I was as curious as ever. Peering around the desk, I could see that the lab was divided into three areas: staging surrounded by privacy glass, processing with life tubes, and the physical therapy area. Workers in scrubs walked about with holo-charts, looking busy with whatever it was they did. I could faintly hear a discussion likely related to the woman I'd watched fall. So much for medical privacy. Regardless, I was relieved that the tone of the discussion seemed optimistic.

After surveying the space, my thoughts raced like those of a child in line for a mega roller coaster. The entire process started to play itself out in my mind from start to finish, something I was purposefully suppressing while I'd waited downstairs. But having it drilled into my brain the last several months, I knew it like the back of my hand.

First, they would need to replicate my brain's central processors, or CPs—the way in which my brain handled information, thoughts, and memories. It was one of the trickiest parts of the procedure because a lot of that "programming" was biologically wired to the physical brain. Once they acquired the "blueprint" of my CPs, they would upload it to the host's brain, and then using tiny medical machines, physically alter the host brain to be as close a match as possible. Too much deviation between our brains, they cautioned me, would result in a botched migration.

With the CPs in place, they then had to copy and compress all of my thoughts and memories into self-extracting packets of data called *thought bytes*. ADG prided itself on being able to obtain thought bytes down to the last microsecond prior to the actual transfer of data. I often joked that they might make a mistake, and then third grade would be stripped from my memory, but that was me just trying to cope with the seriousness of the procedure. After successfully copying all my thought bytes, they would place the packets into the recreated CPs in the host, and if everything went smoothly, they would be processed exactly how they were when first created in my mind. It all sounded so simple until you remembered the potential issues that could occur, which I couldn't bring myself to think about so close to the actual procedure.

The last step was proprietary and not disclosed with much detail. Many speculated that it was at that point they took the soul in your biological body and placed it into the host. While ADG used a "soul" analogy in their therapy, they vehemently denied any knowledge of a human soul. They did, however, make it clear that your original brain would be wiped clean of your mind so that there weren't duplicates of you in existence. Regardless, the whole process didn't sit well with many religious groups, especially that mystery behind the last step. Yet ADG was staunch in hiding behind their patents and troves of lawyers, and the process saved and improved enough lives to appease just as many, if not more than those concerned.

Replaying the whole procedure and all its potential points of failure had only managed to increase my fear. Even after all the hands-on work I'd done for the last year, I had no control over the actual process itself. I had to literally put my life in the hands of strangers—highly trained strangers, but strangers nonetheless—and hope that their processes kept me safe along the way. It was really tough to accept that, though I'd become fairly skilled at ignoring the fear just enough to keep the process moving forward all this time. I kept telling myself that most procedures went off without a hitch and the most likely outcome was that all of my dreams would come true. I would be in a new body with functional legs and could start a new life. Of course, I would still have to get through the weeks of post-migration rehabilitation, but while they would be very tough days, I would be driving most of that work.

My thoughts were interrupted by a technician who wandered over to me.

"Hi, Ryan. I'm Sophia, and I'll be your migration specialist. I have a few questions and items to review with you prior to getting started with the migration process. So you know, this conversation will be recorded for quality assurance and training purposes."

"Okay."

She tapped the ADG logo on her lab coat. "This is Sophia Elias interviewing Ryan D. Carter, pre-migration. Are you feeling emotionally and physically well today, Ryan?"

"Well, I'm nervous. Really nervous. But otherwise, I feel fine."

"It's completely normal to be worried before a mind migration. You're going to be living in a new body for the rest of your life. Your very existence is going to be enhanced, and that will take some getting used to. But you've done all the training. And you may have heard that we've successfully completed over two thousand mind migrations this year already. I worked on over one-hundred-fifty of them myself. So you're in good hands. Has your medical status changed since your physical last week?"

I shrugged. "No."

"Are you on any nonmedicinal drugs?"

"No."

"Since your test migration, have you had any unusual nightmares, night terrors, hallucinations, or any obscure visions, thoughts, or memories?"

"Uh…" The question froze me dead in my tracks, like coming across something on a high school test that I didn't expect.

My nerves and fears had gotten exponentially worse over the last month since the test migration when my actual mind had virtually occupied several host brains for a brief period. It didn't help that the test results weren't disclosed to migrators. Since ADG couldn't guarantee just how closely they could match your host and specifications, it just felt like there was a big unknown looming over the whole procedure. But nightmares? Obscure thoughts or memories? I did have an awful dream about being a soldier the other night, but I chalked that up to all the war documentaries I had been watching. Otherwise, nothing came to mind, so I figured all of my nervousness was related to getting closer to the finish line.

"Ryan?"

Yeah, that had to be—

"Ryan?"

Snapping out of it, I sensed the annoyance in her tone. "Sorry, what was the question?"

"Any unusual nightmares, night terrors, hallucinations, or any obscure thoughts or memories since your test migration?"

"No. Nothing like that comes to mind."

Her face indicated that she didn't believe me. "Are you sure? You seemed a little taken when I asked that."

"Uh, I've had my fair share of nightmares after the therapy and maybe a few weird dreams since the test migration. But no. Nothing that seemed all that out of the ordinary."

"Okay, great. You've chosen our standard migration and host package. Your host was obtained from a physically fit fetus that received mind inhibitors since conception. It was artificially matured to roughly twenty-two years of age as requested. The final result is a host of six feet and two inches tall, tan skin, black hair, green eyes, and an athletic build. We'll be scanning your facial features and biocopying them over the face of the host. Per statute MC-3881, your host will have your fingerprints transposed over his and your genetic markers will overwrite his as well. Does all of this sound accurate?"

"Yes. I remember that from the paperwork."

"Lastly, please confirm that this is your first attempted and only mind migration as per regulation 5981EF. Subsequent migrations attempts can cause psychosis, dementia, and/or death."

Originally, people thought a person could live forever by migrating their mind each time their current body wore out, but it turned out that the human mind could only handle one migration. After that, it was like making a copy of a copy—the integrity of the mind became warped, making a second migration extremely dangerous.

"Yes, I confirm that this is my first attempted and only mind migration."

In my peripheral, I noticed another migration tech operating an automated mover to put a processing tube into place. She made it stand vertically and the viewing glass was facing outward toward me. Once I could see it—see him—time stood still. I didn't know if it was shock or happiness. But it—he—had to be mine. I was looking at my new body. Like looking into a strange mirror at my mind's soon-to-be host. Gone would be the shriveled legs, underdeveloped core, and scrawny upper body. In their place would be muscular legs, exceptional abs, and a chiseled chest. As much as I could have hoped for, he was exactly to my specifications. And in several hours, I would be him and he would be me. Even in those final minutes, it was still hard to believe it was real.

"Pretty amazing, huh, Ryan?"

"Huh?"

She leaned in. "I've been doing this for a couple years, and that look on your face is the look that so many people get. It's why I do what I do."

Sophia was caring, even if she was a little prideful.

"Well, thanks."

"The last item I must discuss with you is the summary of our disclaimer. Once the procedure begins, there's a roughly six percent chance that it will need to be stopped or reversed based on many factors. There's also a roughly one percent chance that you won't make it through the procedure as stated in your contract and liability waiver. Otherwise, the process will be seen through until the end, and you will then begin your recovery. Do you have any questions before we get started?"

I couldn't hold back my disbelief. "Is it as good as advertised? Am I going to be reborn?"

"Mr. Carter, the good news is that you will be getting a new lease on life with new abilities like walking and running. The difficult news, and I cannot stress this enough, you will have quite the painful journey once in recovery. The post-migration phase is difficult in general, and is especially hard for a small minority of our migrators. Fortunately, we'll be with you every *step* of the way, pun intended." She smiled widely at me as her dart of humor pierced a hole in my anxiety.

"Ha ha! Thanks! I needed that laugh. But I do have one last request."

"Yes?"

"Can you give me a couple minutes alone? I need to say goodbye to Auto…err, my auto-chair. As strange as it sounds, I'm going to miss him."

"Not strange at all. Take all the time you need. Head around the privacy glass when you're finished." Sophia tapped the ADG logo on her lab coat again to stop the recording, then walked back toward the staging area.

I sighed as depression began to flood my senses again. My shoulders slumped, and I tried to think about the things I had discussed in therapy. In the end, I just had to speak from the heart.

"Auto, I'm not sure where to begin. You and I have been through a lot together. I've always kept you repaired and up-to-date on the latest firmware. You've always gotten me where I needed to go."

My whole face ached from the sadness.

"When genetics failed me, you were there. When everyone in my life let me down, you kept me going. The change we're about to go through isn't about you. You've always been great. It's about me moving on with my life. I need to truly stretch my legs. I want to use a toilet! But I will always miss our rides down the sidewalk, and I'll never forget your calming motor. It's what kept me balanced for so many years. Let's take one last ride together to the staging area, and then I will say my final goodbye as your rider. It has been my honor and pleasure."

I gathered myself and headed over to the staging area.

Sophia was standing in an elevated glass bubble with the label Control Station printed across the front. Over the intercom, she professed instructions to begin the process.

"Okay, Ryan. You can remove your clothes, and I'll have technicians assist you with getting onto the table."

Meticulously, I took off each piece of clothing. At first, I fooled myself into thinking I was being detail-oriented, but it quickly became apparent that I was really just stalling. Once undressed, I timorously entered the Lift and Release commands into Auto. I could feel my body trembling as he flattened out like a bed, raised me up, and retracted his safety straps. Mentally, I had to prepare myself to get onto the table.

"Well, I guess this is it. Thanks for everything, Auto. I'll never forget you."

The technicians wandered over, but I waved them off. "No. I can do this myself."

I had pulled myself off of Auto thousands of times over the last decade, but getting onto that table would be the last. I didn't care how awkward it was; no one was going to rob me of the experience. I placed my hands firmly down and pulled my body and useless lower half over. The process was as clumsy as it always was, but I did the best I could. Once on the frigid table, I stretched out as much as I could. Despite how cold I should have felt, I was as figuratively naked as I was literally, so my heart was pumping a thousand beats a minute. The stress had even caused a slight delirium that made focusing on the remaining tasks at hand that much more difficult.

One of the technicians typed commands into Auto, and I had the strongest urge to scream for her to leave him alone. For a moment, he didn't move, making it seem like he was ignoring her to stay with me. But true to his programming, he slowly began to roll away from me, farther than he had ever been in the last ten years. The farther he got, the more it hurt. Eventually, he disappeared for good, and that was it.

I sighed. "Thanks again, Auto."

All the fear for what lay ahead had gotten the best of me, and in bidding farewell to Auto, I could only muster a single tear down my right cheek before Sophia chimed in over the intercom.

"You're going to be secured to the table now, Ryan. Let me know when they're tight."

Gray straps shot out from the side of the table and snuggly secured my head, chest, abdomen, arms, and legs.

"That's good."

"Thanks, Ryan. Next, a medical disk is going to appear above you. It's going to complete a full body scan that will make your body temperature rise a little. Just breathe and relax."

A couple of electronic beeps behind me commanded lights in the ceiling to reveal the aforementioned medical disk. It dislodged itself slowly and assumed a rhythmic hover directly above me. Dull tones chimed as the disk scanned me from head to toe and back again. The warmth was actually a little soothing and took the edge off my vulnerable state.

"The disk is going to attach itself to your head now, Ryan. Again, just relax."

With mechanical clicks, the disk transformed into the shape of a helmet and moved into position above my head. The warm air it produced blew my hair about, but it was otherwise pleasant. Steadily, the disk slipped onto my head, and we became one.

"You're going to feel a slight pinch at the base of your skull."

"Ah!" The pinch was a little more than slight, but there was no use in arguing semantics at that point.

The disk-turned-helmet began to buzz.

"Next, Ryan, IVs will be going into the veins in your arms. Please do not move while this is happening. Once successfully in, the IVs will dispense powerful anesthetics and muscle relaxers to calm you, quickly followed by sedation."

Medical tubing snaked out of the helmet and down my arms. Like fangs, the needles appeared from the ends of the tubing and, in a single motion, pierced my forearms and perfectly entered my veins with calculated precision and almost no pain. The effects of the drugs quickly made all my nervousness and discomfort melt away. It was a good thing that I was strapped to the table because I was so high by that point that I felt like I might float away.

"Next, we're going to get you upright for transfer to a processing tube."

The table began to tilt vertically. The steeper the angle, the more I became aware of a sense of sheer horror growing from deep within my medicinal haze. It was a much different and more palpable fear than I had experienced leading up to the migration. Something wasn't right. No, none of it was right, and as I was being rolled toward the migration station next to my host, the feeling completely overtook me. All I could think to do was yell for them to stop, to bring back Auto, and to get me out of there so I could get back to my normal life!

Stop! Stop! Something's not right!

I couldn't get the words out of my mind and through my mouth. Like a roller coaster creeping to its first big drop, there was no turning back. The drugs had already taken over and the chamber door to my migration tube swung open in front of me. All I could do was wonder what kind of hell

35

was awaiting me during and after the procedure. They rolled me into place and spun me around so that I was facing outward.

"Okay, Ryan. You're going to be fully sedated and the mind migration will commence. We'll see you on the other side!"

As the door to my new life closed in on me, a terrifying voice popped into my head.

It's a deadly…procedure to migrate your mind.

CHAPTER 3

CAREFUL WHAT YOU WISH FOR

"**I**T'S A DEADLY SERIOUS PROCEDURE to migrate your mind."

The words of one of my counselors echoed in my head. He'd been nicknamed "the Drill Sergeant," and the more you listened to his aggressive Southern drawl, the more the name seemed to fit.

"It would be the biggest mistake of your life if you took the procedure lightly. Just think about it for a second. We're going to use a bunch of fancy computer technology to suck the living soul right out of your failure of a body. We're then going to process it like cheese into an easily consumable format. Then we take that living soul that has only ever known one body in its entire existence and dump it into a soulless vessel, a brand-spanking-new host that has never had so much as a simple thought, much less all of your screwed-up memories. And believe it or not, that's the easy part."

Over our few sessions, I had come to appreciate his brutal honesty, even if it made me tremble.

"After a day or two, you'll wake up in your new host. Except you aren't awake. And you're not sleeping either. Dipping in and out of the crevices of the host's brain, your mind will be like a child after moving into a new house, looking in all of the rooms, trying to find the best place for his things. The only problem is that the house was just finished being built, and it's possible that not all of the rooms are safe yet. Once your mind comes to that realization, the pleasantness of the situation immediately divulges into pure chaos."

Other migrators and I joked that he was trying to get us to quit the migration program so that ADG could keep our down payments, but again, for whatever reason, I respected his approach.

"For forty-eight to seventy-two hours, your reality—your entire existence—will be reduced to a sprawling collage of pseudo consciousness. The mind that you have counted on your whole life to get you through each day will betray you as it reaches the depths of its new home. It'll be like a Jackson Pollock painting of obscure thoughts and memories, and it won't stop there."

I was almost too horrified to continue the thought, but couldn't stop it.

"At some point, you will become aware of the pain—the deepest, harshest pain that you've ever experienced. I've heard it described as third-degree burns over your entire body followed by a bath in razor blades and salt water. For most, this pain starts without so much as a warning and instantly squelches any peaceful thoughts."

It was at that point he had let loose a little chuckle, making all who were listening even more uneasy.

"What on earth would cause such visceral suffering? Well, it's because of a little thing called your new host's central nervous system. You see, once it becomes aware of you, it does what it was programmed to do for hundreds of thousands of years. To it, you're the most aggressive invading pathogen it has ever experienced. If moving into a new host wasn't hard enough, even before you can put your things down and get settled, you're being mauled by your own defenses. Your host doesn't like you. It hates you so much that it's even willing to hit the self-destruct button and attack itself, you, over and over and over and over again."

As the thought came to its terrifying conclusion, the fear from the session returned a hundredfold.

"You'll have to fight like hell during every moment of consciousness, and it won't be easy. It's like a prizefight where you're a featherweight pitted against dozens of heavy weights. With each blow they strike, your mind will want to comfort you by going into shock. This is where you have to resist the urge to give up. It will be the longest, most difficult time of your life because the unfortunate truth is that the pain won't dull until your mind settles, and your mind won't settle until the pain dulls. We call this the catch-22 period. Of the few migrators we lose, this is where we lose most of them."

Shaking myself from the memory, all my thoughts came to an abrupt halt. It was like coming out of a fluttering dream, and I suddenly couldn't remember anything I had just been thinking. In fact, the harder I tried to remember what was happening, the less that came to mind. Then my attention quickly shifted to the faintest voice coming from somewhere in the distance. It could have been the tiniest whisper from across a room, so I had to focus with everything I had to make it out. Just when I thought I could hear it clearly, a white noise began to fill the background. The static grew louder until it almost hurt. All the while, the voice kept talking even though I couldn't make out any of the words. It reminded me of the old radio my uncle used to communicate off the grid, with all the hissing and popping between what must have been words.

"Ry...ake...dee...brea...I'm   go...coun...backwa...te...wit...numb...mov...yo...ha..."

I wasn't even sure if the voice was talking to me.

"Te..."

An explosion of colors and lights sprayed across the ceiling of my mind. It was the most intense fireworks display imaginable, and for a moment, it completely distracted me from all the other stimulation around me.

"Ni..."

The volume of the static shifted from loud to quiet, and the brightness of the colors and lights tapered off. A burst of energy invigorated my mind, and I concentrated hard to gain some perspective on what was happening.

"Eigh..."

I could feel—and hear—deep breathing. It reminded me of my favorite scuba-diving simulator. But something was behind the breathing that I was struggling to make out. The more I thought about it, the more it sounded like a bass drum beating to a steady rhythm.

Thump, thump, thump, thump, thump, thump.

"Seve...you...doin...gre...Ry...ke....it up."

Smoke! I could smell thick, suffocating smoke from an old-time cigarette, and the aroma of butane from a lighter. My grandpa was the only one I knew with the bad habit. He would take deep puffs and exhale a cloud. He tried to blow it away from me, but it always saturated the room. I knew I shouldn't breathe it in, but part of me liked the smell because it reminded me of him.

"Si…"

Mint! I could taste and feel unmistakable cold from peppermint. It was like I was eating a whole tube of toothpaste, but so minty that it almost burned my mouth and throat.

"Fiv…"

A number! I heard a number from the voice! I wasn't sure what number it was, but I knew I'd heard it and it was a number.

"Four."

Another number! In vein, I tried responding. *Hey! I'm here! Why are you saying numbers?*

"Three."

Hello! Can you help me? I think I'm lost, or maybe something is wrong. What do the numbers mean?

"Two."

Thinking as hard as I could, it hit me. *I had a procedure!* But for the life of me, I couldn't remember exactly what it was. *My legs! It has to be related to my legs. All the procedures I've ever had were for my legs. Or spine. Oh no! Did I go through with the spine transplant? Ugh. Those never go well. I would be so pissed if I spent all those credits and was still paralyzed. But at least I would still have Auto.*

"One."

The walls of my mind began to quake. Returning, the white noise blared louder than ever and the colors and lights flashed with even more intensity. The drumbeat rumbled harder and louder as if there were many hearts beating inside my head. Mind-wrenching anxiety ensued, anticipating that something purely evil was about to happen. Then I came to the realization that the space my thoughts occupied was getting smaller by the second. Claustrophobia set in quickly followed by immediate suffocation.

I can't…I can't…I can't… Feeling consciousness slip away, it took everything I had to finish the thought. *I can't…breathe!*

The deafening sounds, blinding colors and lights, and lack of air were all unbearable to the point that I would have welcomed reprieve in any form. Just when I was coming to peace with the idea that my time was up, my mind began to spiral down like an unplugged drain and all my thoughts swirled away. In their place, a mind-jolting migraine set in, and in disbelief that I could feel any more pain, a god-awful agony consumed my entire existence. As my essence slipped into the abyss, my life flashed before my eyes in an instant. Then silence. Numbness. Darkness. Emptiness. Nothingness. But somehow, I still had consciousness.

Taking account of my surroundings, it seemed as if I was suspended in infinity. I couldn't help but wonder if I had just experienced death. But if this were heaven or hell, there wasn't much to the place. As bad as the experience was, I had always imagined dying would be much worse. Then I thought I was probably just awaiting my actual fate, and therefore, I was floating in purgatory until a supreme being decided what to do with me.

Unexpectedly, a fuzzy image projected itself in front of me. At first, I couldn't make heads or tails of it. Straining to focusing, I could eventually see three figures: a woman and two children. After a moment, they became crystal clear, and I instantly felt very strongly for them. I was willing to do anything for them because I loved them deeply. The only strange thing was that I had no idea who they were. Instead, hollowness accompanied their picture, and I was deathly afraid for their lives.

I'm sorry.

The words forced their way into my thoughts followed by an intense confusion. Then the pain returned, only this time it felt much more external compared to the mental anguish I had just experienced. Doing my best to pinpoint the source of the pain, I was shocked to realize it was coming from what had to be my face. An undeniable urge to open my eyes followed, and as excruciating as it was, I gave it as much effort as I could.

Ugh! Ahhhh!

Fighting through the agony, I miraculously opened my eyes to more pain as the brightest light accosted my pupils. Squinting hard, my view was anything but clear. Remembering that I had a procedure, I anticipated waking in a hospital room surrounded by machinery and medical staff. But something about the light and cold temperature gave me a sinking feeling that I was no longer at ADG.

I struggled to focus, and it became apparent that I was, in fact, lying face down on a very hard surface. I felt burning from my face again, and was certain I had gotten a bad scrape. My ears then perked up to another strange and quiet voice. Listening for numbers, I was surprised not to hear any, but instead a simple question.

"Are you okay, man?"

Am I okay? Okay from what? The procedure?

Then the next undeniable urge hit me.

Get up! With all my might, I rose up from the ground to an erect position. *I stood up! On my feet! With my legs!*

It was then I remembered exactly what I had been through. *Mind migration. They put me into a new body!* Looking down, I confirmed it was everything I could have hoped for. I could even feel the slightest pain in what had to be my left ankle, but I didn't care. My spine was healthy and aligned! They'd told me mind migrations were good, but damn! It was amazing!

My stomach dropped. Something wasn't right. Blinking rapidly, I tried my damnedest to take in my surroundings.

"You okay, man?" A bearded man in outdated, pretentious clothing said. "Hey, you okay, man?"

I couldn't help but back away, stumbling a bit with the worst sinking feeling as I turned to look around. There was a large condemned warehouse behind us and somehow knew I had to get away from that place as fast as possible.

Run!

As if possessed, my lower half responded to the fear, and I instantly darted down the sidewalk. Hell, I was sprinting like I had always dreamed! Even through my confusion, I could feel each and every one of my core muscles expand and contract as I stretched farther and farther with each stride. The wind blowing my hair back only added to the experience.

Trying to get some reference as to where I was, I panned my gaze. There were old apartment buildings lining the street and old-fashioned cars parked along both sides of the road. I hadn't experienced anything like it in the simulations before the migration, so sure as hell wasn't prepared. After blazing through seven or eight blocks, my lungs ached badly, but I couldn't stop myself.

I tried to gather my thoughts to make sense of the situation while still running at top speed. I was scared. I had to get away from something or someone? But what or who? The warehouse? Who was inside? Nothing came to mind, and that scared the hell out of me.

Gasping for air after running for a couple hundred meters, it became impossible to maintain the pace and hope to get away from anyone. My already fearful state had escalated to pure terror, so when an alleyway presented itself to my left, I was compelled to take it. Tires screeched as a car entered the alley behind me, engine revving as it completed its turn. I couldn't bring myself to look back nor could I keep my thoughts focused on where I was going.

What the hell is going on?!

The worst part was that it seemed familiar but completely new all at the same time. Regardless, that car had to be what—*who*—I was running from, and I couldn't let them get me. On my right, a machine shop was closing its garage door, and I needed to be on the other side of it before that happened. As I slid into the building, the skidding tires from my pursuers became muffled by the closing door. Taking the briefest second, I looked for an exit. Spotting a door across the room, I darted in that direction, passing two grizzled machinists on the way.

One of the men pushed me as I tried to get by. "Who the hell are you, buddy!"

Stumbling into a hallway on the other side of the door, I regained my balance and took a left toward what had to be the front of the building. Entering what looked like the front office, I saw two massive picture windows divided by a heavy steel door that led to the street. Dashing for the door handle, I simultaneously grabbed it and read the sign next to the door jamb: "This door is locked. Use the side exit."

"Shit!"

I could hear pounding on the garage door in the back and knew I didn't have much time. Doubling back to the side exit wasn't an option, so I had no choice but to leave through the front of the building. Scrambling to find something to open the door, I compulsively reached around to the back of my waistband expecting to find a weapon, but nothing was there.

One of the machinists entered the room with a scowl on his face, and while I couldn't focus long enough to make out his exact words, I was pretty sure a lot of them were expletives. I eyed the picture windows, instantly assessing that they were too thick to break. Looking back past the machinist, my eyes lit up with excitement when I saw a large hammer on one of the desks. As I dashed toward the desk, the machinist held his ground. Instinctively, I lowered my shoulder and made solid contact into his chest. He stumbled back onto and over the table, giving me the moment

I needed to grab the hammer. Darting back to the door, I came down on the handle with all my might.

Clank!

But it only bent slightly.

"Dammit!"

Panting hard, I gave it another strike.

Clank!

The second hit nearly did it—the handle was holding on by a thread.

I could hear the garage door opening in back, then immediate chatter about my location.

The machinist I'd just knocked over had recovered, and gave me a hard shot right to the kidney as he cursed at me. "You bastard! I'm going to—"

Through the pain, my instincts took over. Whirling around, I bludgeoned him in the temple with the hammer. His hot blood spattered onto my sleeve and face, followed by his lifeless body slumping to the floor.

What in the hell did I just do? God damn, I was some kind of monster. Looking down, I noticed more not-so-fresh blood on the front of my coat, but I didn't have time to care. I just needed to escape.

I slammed the hammer down on the handle again. *Clank!* The door flung open, and I spilled onto the sidewalk of a fairly busy street. An opening in traffic allowed me to cross the street to another alleyway. Once clear from witnesses, I pulled off my coat and used a clean spot to wipe off my face, then tossed the coat in a dumpster as I ran down the alley. At the other end, I turned right on another busy street to head back toward the original street where I had woken up.

I found a nook between two nearby buildings where I was able to hide away and catch my breath. In spite of the chill outside, sweat poured down my forehead and soaked through my shirt. As I huddled down, I had the undeniable urge to pull an old netphone from my pocket. I found the contact, Plan B, and I dialed it up. An automated voice played, but I didn't even need to press the phone to my ear. I dialed the passcode, 9230, and with a ding, it confirmed my entry. The automated voice played again, and I dialed the next passcode, 800— Before I could key in the last number, the phone buzzed, scaring the living shit out of me and causing me to drop it. Looking at the caller ID, chills ran down my spine.

INCOMING CALL FROM THE PADRE.

I was never very religious, but something told me that my life depended on ditching the phone so it couldn't be used to trace my location. I tapped the answer button, set the phone down, and ran like hell.

Once back to the main street, I cautiously walked a couple of blocks, watching the street signs until it made sense for me to make right onto Pulaski. I reached into my pants pocket to find a set of keys. Ahead was a giant, old-fashioned black car, and I inserted the key into the lock, turning it with some force. Lifting the door handle also took a little extra oomph, but then the massive door creaked open. In one motion, I plopped into the driver's seat, pulled the door closed, and started the engine. Gathering myself before putting the behemoth into gear, I remembered that I usually kept a weapon in the glove compartment and leaned over to check, but it was empty. I focused on the road in front of me while catching my breath and attempting to make sense of things. I didn't know where to go, only that I had to drive. And the last thing I wanted was to draw attention to myself, so I shifted into drive, checked my side mirror for an opening in traffic, and cautiously put my foot on the other pedal.

After driving a few blocks, I cracked the window to let the cool breeze dry the sweat off my face and, to a lesser extent, my shirt. The smell of fall in the air was distinctive, calming. I impulsively reached into my shirt pocket and discovered a crushed, moist pack of menthol cigarettes and an old Zippo lighter. While I despised smoking, it was soothing to think about the first drag. I peered into the pack while keeping an eye on the road, and to my joy, there was one left.

Must be my lucky day. Hearty laughter followed the thought, providing a much-needed break in the tension.

I shook the pack to pop out the lone cancer stick and simultaneously flicked open the lighter and flamed it up. Puffing hard, I was afforded the smallest bit of relief as I scratched the addictive itch that had subconsciously overcome me during my getaway. The exhale was almost as rewarding; out went the deadly smoke along with a lot of fear.

Rolling to a stoplight, I had finally settled into my seat for the briefest moment when rage replaced the tranquility in the car.

"The whole damn job was a set up!"

No details came to mind about the job or how I was set up, but my ire grew nonetheless. My renewed frenzy was short-lived as a glance at the review mirror confirmed a car pulling up behind me.

It was a squad car—a son-of-a-bitch squad car with two cops in it.

"Well, shit."

Face forward, I averted my eyes toward the mirror again to look more closely without tipping them off. I let loose a small sigh of relief when I saw the passenger cop laughing while the wide-smiling driver went on and on about something apparently hilarious. Then their conversion stopped abruptly and their jovial faces turned stoic as they stared intensely toward the center of the car's dash, likely at their radio.

Fear rushed over me with even more force. Sweat broke out over my whole body as I watched both cops slowly peer up from their radio. They were looking dead at me, and it took everything I had not to make eye contact with them while still trying to catch their next move. Then the ache of my hands became apparent from the death grip I had on the steering wheel, but I didn't let up even a little. Puffing hard on my menthol, I was ready to hit the gas at a moment's notice.

The light turned green and the cops turned on their siren. Then time stood still, and the all-too-familiar feeling that my legs were paralyzed washed over me. As much as I wanted to jam on the gas, something deep inside said not to. Slowly rolling through the intersection, I finally peered back to the mirror, then exhaled hard. They were gone! They had pulled a U-turn, and the siren was getting quieter as they sped off the other way.

"Phew!"

I anxiously puffed the last bit of the cigarette as I came to the next stoplight. Again, my fear transformed into anger as I realized that I had too many damn questions and couldn't, for the life of me, remember any answers. Who the hell was I? Who was after me? Why did they set me up? Where did the original blood on my coat come from? Why was getting away more important than the life of a machinist? Dammit all if he wasn't just an innocent bystander. I wondered if he would survive the blow, and to my disgust, that might have been the only question to which I knew the answer.

The light turned green, and I gingerly put my foot on the gas just as something caught my attention in the rearview. *Holy shit!*

Crash!

A car rear-ended me into the intersection, and I veered left to avoid hitting a dump truck. Speeding up as fast as the giant, now-damaged car would allow, I cranked the wheel to take the first right turn I saw, and flashed a glance back at the mirror. The car that hit me looked just like mine, and was coming after me. Its front end was damaged, but it was not having any trouble keeping up. I didn't recognize either of the men in the driver or passenger seats, but it didn't matter. I needed to get away.

"Dammit!"

The cherry from my menthol had fallen off because of the crash and burned a whole into my pant leg. Madly patting it out, I was also trying to keep an eye on the road and the rearview when they slammed into me again.

"Son of a bitch!"

Swerving into the next lane, I was able to put twenty or so feet between me and the other car, but they remained close in pursuit. I needed to turn off the main road to lose them, so I hit the gas and barreled through the next couple of greens. Squealing the tires, I swung the car to make a quick right turn, the rear of the car fishtailing around the corner and barely missing a parked car. I headed down a small side road narrowed by all the cars parked on each side. Shortly after, I made a left turn down a one-way road and zoomed down to another main street. Another lucky green, and I was turning right onto another busy road. Finally, eyeing the mirror again, it seemed like I had lost them. As the excitement of getting away filled me, I turned completely around to be sure they were gone. Exhaling hard, a smirk stretched across my face as I thought I might actually get away until I turned back to watch the road in front and reality set in.

Shit! A parked car!

I slammed on the brakes, but too late.

Crash!

Waking up on a stretcher, I realized I must have blacked out. My head and neck hurt, but I otherwise felt okay. Paramedics were wheeling me along the side of the road, and when I tried to sit up, I discovered that my hands and feet were handcuffed to the stretcher's rails. But I had no desire to fight them, so I just laid back and accepted my fate.

As I was being lifted into the ambulance, I caught my first good glimpse of the parked car. It was totaled so bad that it was difficult to tell whether it was green or gray. A cold feeling washed over me as I peered down to the pool of blood coming from the wreckage.

"Who was in the car? Are they okay? What happened?!"

Before a paramedic could respond, another paramedic near the car I had smashed began screaming. I could only make out pieces of what he was saying as the doors to my ambulance closed, but it was enough to force a mortifying thought into my head.

"What the hell have I done?"

CHAPTER 4
LAWS WERE MEANT TO BE BROKEN

WHAT THE HELL HAVE I done?

Damn! A night terror was bad enough, but waking up to pure blackness made it that much worse. My head was pounding, and while that had become normal, the agony was especially bad at that moment. I was still unable open my eyes or talk, but fortunately, my spatial recognition and hearing had kicked in. Even better, I had recently discovered my arms and was able to move them slightly.

That kind of progress meant I could actually communicate with the recovery staff. They would ask me yes/no questions, and if I understood them, I could respond. My left arm provided positive responses and my right arm negative. While they hadn't told me exactly how long it had been since the procedure, I was starting to get into the routine of the nursing aides tending to me on a regular basis—the occasional sponge bath, stretching, changing the bedpan, and checking on my IVs. Each day, I could feel more aspects of the things happening around me. But progress was not without its cost as the nausea I had felt for the last few days soon evolved into awful hunger pangs from not eating solids. Still, I remembered from the prep classes that this meant my digestive tract was up and running. More importantly, it meant my brain was functioning properly.

"Good morning!" a jubilant voice shouted as someone walked through the doorway to my left.

It was familiar, but it wasn't the orderly's. It must have been a nurse or doctor.

"Hi, Ryan. It's Dr. Little. Are you feeling better today?"

I made my left arm twitch.

"Do you still have a headache?"

Left arm twitched.

"Has the nausea subsided?"

Left arm twitched.

"You're hungry, right?"

Left arm twitched.

"Are you able to open your eyes yet?"

I shook my right arm.

"Let me have a look." Snapping on what had to be latex gloves, the doctor opened one of my eyes and clicked on what had to be a flashlight, then did the same to the other eye.

To my dismay, I still couldn't see any of it.

"Good. Your pupils are responding just fine. Combine that with the fact that your numbers are trending upward and all of the tests are coming back normal, and this is all good news, Ryan."

Her words really comforted me through the pain and uncertainty.

"Next up, Ryan, we will begin running a new series of tests that will let us know how you're taking to your host's eyes as well as provide you with some exercises to shorten your vision's recovery time. Now, I know you have a lot of questions, and you will want to be able to communicate in an open-ended fashion, but let me reassure you that your speech and typing skills will come in due time. We mostly want to focus on getting your eyesight back. After that, we will look to get you talking and, shortly thereafter, on your feet!"

On my feet? On my feet! It almost sounded like a joke to me, but then I remembered I did in fact have functioning feet and a working spine, and it was only a matter of time before I would be—

My mind wandered the length of my spine, past my pelvis, and down my legs. I discovered what had to be my feet!

Holy hell! My feet!

Then I quickly channeled all my energy into trying to take it farther.

My toes!

I could wiggle them, and wiggle them I did! They were amazing. I started to do the mental equivalent of crying. I had no idea if the tears were running down my face, but it was the most cathartic bawling I had done in a long time.

People had never understood just how hard it was to be a paraplegic from birth. I did my best to get by, and was applauded for it by literally everyone. But it was difficult for people who could walk to truly understand how society was created with the image of a biped in mind. Even with all of the awareness and technology, there always seemed to be something holding people like me back. Too often I had to abandon my hopes of going into a building or joining my friends on the subway because there was no ramp or the elevator was out of commission. Worse yet, the nightly news always ran pieces about people with disabilities overcoming their circumstances to accomplish their goals. They paraded around the winners of the Special Olympics and did human interest pieces on quadriplegics who'd graduated with honors from prestigious universities. They made such a big deal about war veterans returning home with missing limbs, yet starting successful businesses. Truth was, those pieces always seemed more like indictments of the general population than true praise of my brethren with disabilities. They were basically saying, "If this disabled person can do it, what's your excuse, you lazy bastard?" I never appreciated being indirectly pitted against the fully abled.

Dr. Little must have been pressing buttons next to me when she noticed my feet.

"Wow, Ryan. You've found your toes. Let me know if you can feel this."

The softest pinprick confirmed that I was, indeed, wiggling my toes. I twitched my left arm.

"I'll check that off the list as ahead of schedule. While I don't want to get your hopes up, you should be walking on schedule or maybe even a little quicker. Bet your friends won't do anything nearly as impressive as taking their very first steps any time soon."

Dr. Little was technically correct, though Helen's migration would be a close second. She had been able to walk as a toddler, all the way up until age four when she had a tragic accident in a swimming pool. She mentioned that her walking experiences were like fleeting memories and she still had ghost pains in her legs, though they had no nerve function. To avoid any issues from ghost pains, she approached her mind migration as if she had never walked in the first place, and I thought that was smart.

"Also, Ryan, I wanted to let you know that your mother called. We let her know you should be ready for visitors in the next few days, but for now, we want you to focus on recovery."

Just the mere mention of Mom improved my mood exponentially. Mom had always been there for me. She always told me the story about getting the ultrasound and seeing that my spine was malformed inside of her. The doctors broke the news to her, and she was initially devastated. Then they told her that my chances of survival were about 20%, and she knew in an instant that 20% was all the reassurance she needed. She knew, getting that little bit of hope, that everything would be fine—fine in the sense that I would be born even if I would be disabled. She gave everything she had to taking care of me from that day on and never seemed to flinch in the face of adversity. It was that kind of love that had always kept me going. And while Mom was apprehensive about the mind migration because of the dangers associated with it, she still gave me her blessing in the end.

"Okay, Ryan. I will be placing a button near your left arm. If you need anything in the coming days, just press it. This includes when you feel like you're able to open your eyes. You'll want to give that button a good press because the nursing staff and possibly a doctor will need to be here to assist. I'll come if I'm available. Now let's give it a test press to make sure the button works."

Gently lifting my left arm, she placed a small, rubbery object under my hand.

"Go ahead, Ryan. Give that button a push."

I rattled my left arm as hard as I could, and was rewarded with a loud, dull tone throughout my room.

"Great, Ryan! I'm anticipating that in the next day or so, you will get your vision back. It will probably be blurry at first, but again, make sure to hit that button so we can help out. For today, Sheila will be here in a little bit to give you something to manage the headache and let you get some rest. I'll be back in a couple of days to check up on you. In the meantime, the nursing aides will continue to take care of you and monitor your progress."

The doctor's footsteps were unusually loud as she left the room and closed the door behind her. I was surprisingly relieved for her to leave because it gave me a chance to take everything in.

It appeared that I had gotten through the hell of the migration and come out alive. All the sleepless nights, lost appetites, and grief-induced nausea leading up to the procedure seemed like they were all for naught. Sure, things had been rough since I gained consciousness, but it seemed like the preparation had been sufficient. Hell, it might have been overkill with all the scary stories that circulated throughout the mind migrators in the program with me. Since the exact origin of the mind migration procedure had never been fully disclosed to the public, we were left to reconcile the truth from rumors and urban myths.

Oceanus Laboratories, also known as OL, was a former competitor of ADG. They had been working with the government and military on rehabilitating veterans who'd returned from war with physical trauma. As the depressing story goes, it all started with a very young but gifted soldier who had steadily risen through the ranks of infantry and was being considered for an officer's role. In his last battle, he took a piece of shrapnel to the neck, leaving the once exceptionally intelligent and highly skilled soldier a delirious and spasming mess. The doctors had done their best to put him back together, and as they'd run more tests, they realized that his mind was relatively intact. It had only been his physical body and nervous system that betrayed him after the injuries. In one of his brief moments of clarity, he'd spoken the words that would later become famous for initiating the whole mind migration program.

"Doc, all I need is for my mind to be put into a working body, and I'll be good as new."

Coincidentally, the soldier had been talking to Dr. Rex Martin, a world-renowned neurosurgeon. He was intimately familiar with the difficulties of brain surgery and transplants, and coincidentally being a PhD in data migration, had begun to conjure up an alternative. It involved downloading a person's mind to a temporary storage location, processing it, and then uploading it to the brain of another body. Sounding great on paper, the doctor had been intimately aware of the obvious and numerous ethical and moral issues with a procedure of that sort. Having studied Isaac Asimov, creator of the Laws of Robotics, Dr. Martin had decided it necessary to create a framework of principles to mitigate the possible human rights violations that could come from such a procedure.

THE LAWS OF MIND MIGRATION

One: Migration must be safe for the migrator and the host.

Two: Migrators, or those with power of attorney over potential migrators, must be of sound mind to consciously consent to the procedure.

Three: Hosts must never have established minds (i.e., organic thoughts or memories) but should otherwise be fully functional specimens.

Four: Migrators must be physically, mentally, and emotionally supported before, during, and after the process if at all possible.

Five: Migrators' original minds, and all copies thereof, must be fully deleted from their biological brains and computer storage devices once the success of their migration has been confirmed.

The theory had been that the minds of physically disabled veterans could be migrated into able-bodied, able-brained hosts, and they could live normal lives after serving their country. But even with the laws established, the process hadn't sat well with veterans' rights groups. They'd vehemently rejected the procedure, stating it was like performing medical experiments on individuals who had already sacrificed enough. As a result, no one in Congress had supported legislation legalizing it at first. No one had wanted to risk losing veteran, active-duty, and military-family votes.

That had only slowed down the industry's lobbyists. They leaned heavily on a congressman who had been in a wheelchair, and eventually were able to sneak the Alternative Physical Rehabilitation provision into a much larger bill that had supposedly been meant to improve the lives of people with disabilities. Once word came in of its passing, protests had broken out all over the country and at least one hundred lawsuits were filed. In the end, the language in the provision had been altered to specifically exclude active duty and veterans. In their place, the disabled public became fair game. Shortly after, OL ran an advertisement targeting people with major physical disabilities.

"Be the first to complete our revolutionary new process that could vastly improve the quality of life for people like you. OL means a new lease...on life."

They'd done a lottery system where eventually they whittled down the millions of applicants to a single candidate. While the facts of the case were sealed in court documents, the story goes that there was a woman named Amanda Robinson who had been born without arms. Growing up, she had done all right for herself, considering. She had gotten a decent education, eventually landed a good job, and finally, started a lovely family. It had seemed like she had it all. But Amanda had dreamed of so much more. While some had painted her as greedy, I understood her desires. She wanted to feel the world with hands. She wanted to hug her children and husband. More than anything, she had wanted to feel normal.

On top of all the personal reasons, OL had assured Amanda the process had proven safe in laboratory trials. They had trained hundreds of mice to solve a variety of puzzles involving a running wheel, a maze, a red button, and a box covering a hunk of cheese. Once migrated, the mice in their new hosts solved the puzzles exactly as they were trained before the procedure. After years of studies, they had finally gotten their success rate above 99%. With those assurances, Amanda willingly agreed to be the first human participant. Part of the requirement of doing so, as rumor had it, was that she had been required to become an official employee of OL and would have to travel the world advocating for the procedure. And they'd even told Amanda she could seek out lucrative endorsements. It had been a pretty sweet deal on paper. But like the majority of pioneers throughout history, it hadn't ended so well for Amanda.

Depending on who was telling the story, there were usually two or three reasons why Amanda's migration had failed. Many said there had been faulty cryogenic hardware used to slow down her heart rate. Others professed that there had been a computer glitch that scrambled Amanda's brain. Still others claimed Amanda's host had been an actual person with existing thoughts and memories. A few had even said it was all of the above. Whatever the issue, Amanda's original body had been in jeopardy of dying right before the migration. They'd had to rush the process in an attempt to save her life, but unfortunately, preparing for the procedure had put her life in danger in the first place. Even though she survived the migration, she was a shell of her former self after the fact.

I was always unsure if it was dramatic storytelling or truth, but ironically, the part of Amanda's mind that accessed the primary motor cortex had been lost in the migration. That meant not only were her new arms useless, but she was also unable to walk. To make matters worse, her ability to communicate had been greatly diminished. I still remember the saddest way it was described to me. The previously bright twinkle in her eye had fizzled, and her will to live and love had not accompanied her to her host. Needless to say, her family was devastated. Once national lawyers got wind of the situation, it wasn't long before the Robinson family filed a gross negligence suit.

In spite of all the waivers and insurance for the process, OL still went bankrupt from the bad publicity and suit. With OL found liable, the first part of the settlement had included paying all the Robinsons' legal expenses, but as usual, there was a hefty lump sum for damages as well. Some say it totaled over a billion credits, or *dollars*, as they used back then. Next, OL was court ordered to create a trust fund to pay for Amanda's care indefinitely and pay her husband and children ten times their yearly income for fifty years.

But the money hadn't been able to replace what the family had lost. While Amanda's husband had been a patient man, having lived with a woman without arms for much of his life, he quickly succumbed to depression after tragically losing any semblance of his wife. The constant paparazzi attention hadn't helped. It was only six short months after the industry-shaking court ruling that he had reached his limit and committed suicide. The children and Amanda, more or less a vegetable, went into state custody, and the trusts were locked until the children turned twenty-one. That had been the end of OL and Amanda's story; it obviously hadn't been the end of the mind migration procedure.

The last part of the settlement had contained a provision forcing Oceanus Laboratories to sell their research to the highest bidder to help pay for their legal expenses, the damages, and the trust. Enter Atlas Digenetics. For years, they had been on OL's coattails with a mind migration procedure. The fully detailed failures from OL proved invaluable in moving the science of the process forward, and it only took ADG two more years of trials to determine exactly what had gone wrong with Amanda's migration. They decided that cryo-freezing was too risky to be part of the procedure and determined sedatives to be safer. They also developed better ways to monitor and manage vital signs for the duration of the procedure. Soon after, the first successful mind migration hit the news.

Cameron Walsh, a man crippled from a motorcycle accident, had thrown caution to the wind and agreed to be the subject of the next official procedure. He was in his twenties and had no close family whatsoever, making it obvious that he was well vetted. As corporate advertising goes, the mind migration had gone off without a hitch.

All new mind migrators were required to watch a series of holo-logs that featured Cameron before he completed his migration. He walked viewers through the process step by step at a high level. It was honestly pretty helpful because it was clear that he was no actor, and he was allowed to speak somewhat freely. At some points, he was honest about the fears he had and how the process had been created to acknowledge those fears and address them accordingly. He even went so far as to say that some fear was normal and expected even after all of their helpful measures. Cutting to Cameron after the procedure, the holo-logs presented him as a completely new person ready to take on a brand-new life. While holo-logs were dated, they helped to show just how far the process had come over the last decade.

As tragic as it was, Cameron had become every bit the celebrity that Amanda should have been. His original body was cleaned up and became part of the Smithsonian's display on mind migrations. Once a year, he returned to ADG's main office—the one I was in—for interviews and a major speech. Cameron's next visit was scheduled for a few weeks after my release, so I had my counselors guarantee me two front-row seats. I had been open to Helen about being a shameless Cameron Walsh fanboy, and while she'd cracked a couple of jokes at my expense, she had seemed relatively interested in seeing him speak too, so my plan was to ask her to join me since she'd be out by then as well.

A bang across the room brought me back from memory lane, and I could hear the door to my room open. That could have only meant one thing. Rob, the orderly, was making his rounds.

"Hey, Ryan! How you doing today?"

I shook my left arm.

"Good to hear, buddy. I am just going to freshen things up. Was the doctor tough on you today?"

My right hand moved.

"Just let me know, and I'll have a talk with her."

Detecting a hint of sexism, I still appreciated his attempt at rapport.

That said, I was more impressed at how well he'd mastered his craft. His attention to detail while working expeditiously was quite astounding. As he rattled through his duties, I heard another presence enter the room. It had to be Nurse Sheila because of the number of beeps that occurred rapid-fire to my left. I assumed she was checking my numbers and about to give me the good stuff.

"Hi, Ryan. It's Sheila. Everything is looking good. I just gave you something for your headache, so that should subside pretty quickly. You'll also feel a bit tired, but just relax, and you'll be able to get some good rest."

As I began to shake my left arm to acknowledge her, the woozy feeling had already set in. Yet something didn't feel right. The familiar fear I had been experiencing throughout recovery returned with an increased intensity. I wondered if the drugs they were giving me had anything to do with my anxiety, but before I could think that through, she interrupted me.

"Okay, Ryan. We're all done here for now. We'll see you later."

Hearing them leave, I no longer had any distractions from the horror that was growing from within. Somehow, the darkness in my mind got even darker and a strange feeling of being lost overwhelmed me.

Where am I?

CHAPTER 5

DON'T MIND MY DRIVING

HERE AM I?

Awaking disoriented, I was instantly met with more darkness. My headache was not nearly as painful as it had been the last few times, which was a relief. I could distinctly remember the procedure and some of the progress I had been making with the recovery staff. Yet there were dreams or other memories and thoughts I had that seemed a bit off.

There was a feeling that I couldn't quite shake, nor could I easily describe. It was almost like walking into a room and completely forgetting the reason I had gone in there. That was a pretty common occurrence that everyone could relate to. I was such an introspective kid that I was always fascinated with those moments as I could almost pinpoint the exact second when my mind failed me. Right when the feeling of losing it would set in, I stopped everything. I wanted to take account of where I was and what I was doing. Then, like most people, I retraced my steps—or in my case, Auto's tracks—and thought my way back to the reason I had entered the room. If I couldn't remember after all of that, I just chalked it up to not being that important anyway. But I was always a little disappointed when that happened because most times I knew I had a good reason for entering the room. Occasionally, though, there was that eureka moment where I fully recalled the reason and carried out my original plan. To me, this was like scratching a mental itch, and it was so relieving even for the most mundane tasks.

The more I thought about it, though, the more that feeling didn't really describe what I was going through. With all the odd dreams I'd been having, it was sort of the opposite. It was more like walking into a room with a specific purpose, and that purpose was clear as day in my mind. I knew exactly how I needed to carry it out and could almost see my future self doing it to perfection, too. But once in the room, I got the overwhelming sense that I shouldn't be there, that even though I knew precisely why I was there, I didn't belong. I was hoping for some kind of eureka moment to help me overcome that feeling, but up until that point, I was still just feeling out of place. Part of the problem was that I couldn't pull away any specifics from the dreams—only vague imagery and the feelings that accompanied. I was beginning to think there was some unknown force keeping me from fully grasping what was happening.

My thoughts came screeching to a halt as I was overcome by another urge to open my eyes. Even though I was more than a little apprehensive after the last time, I was powerless to ignore the impulse. With another herculean effort, I was finally able to open my eyes to a blurry view. Just like before, bright light made it difficult to see, but my sight was quickly orienting. Upon reaching for it, the button under my left hand was nowhere to be found.

"Where am I?"

Straining to see, a hazy but familiar circular object appeared in front of me. I couldn't quite make out what it was at first, but one possibility was a valve wheel. Then I wasn't certain. With a little more effort, I settled on the fact that it was a steering wheel to a car!

But that only lead to more confusion because if a steering wheel to a car was in front of me, it could only mean one thing. *But I don't know how to drive!* That would be ludicrous since all I had ever done was test drive an auto-chair-compatible car once after my sixteenth birthday, and that had been far too intense for me. No, the only four wheels I was comfortable with were on Auto.

Looking again, I traced my arms all the way down to my hands, and sure enough, I was gripping the steering wheel of the car. *The accident! Wait, what accident?* Shocking me out of my stupor, the blaring sound of a car horn forced my eyes to the road. *Chaos!*

Cars were changing lanes, turning, and parking! Clusters of pedestrians were crossing the street! Vendors were yelling on and on about their foods and wares! Fighting to catch my breath, I came to a bizarre conclusion. I actually wasn't out of breath, and to my surprise, I knew exactly how to drive. With a closer observation of the road, it was quite calm, and I felt right at home in the driver's seat.

The car had to be vintage or more like ancient compared to modern automobiles. Estimating its size, I seriously wondered how it was street legal being larger than most of the delivery trucks on the road. Some might sarcastically call it a "boat," but even though I knew next to nothing about old cars, I was somehow certain of the make. It was a classic black Cadillac.

From the backseat, a deep voice bellowed about a business partner needing to get his act together or there would be consequences. The voice commanded attention from another softer voice that acknowledged and complied.

I cautiously peered into the rearview to see who I was chauffeuring. A colossal specimen of a man was taking up a seat and a half. He was burly, and by the looks of him, he could handle himself just fine in a fight. His jet-black hair was slicked back, but there were little speckles of salty gray here and there. His broad chin and the perfectly trimmed goatee circling his mouth provided a hint of nobility, but the subtle crow's feet around his eyes gave away that he was probably older than the rest of his features let on. Both his black trench coat and gray suit were expensive and recently pressed.

I inhaled deeply as a bit of dread accompanied the observation. Who was he, and where was I taking him? The scent of a nice but intense cologne filled the car, and at first, I thought it was mine, but then I had a realization.

The Padre.

It was his cologne, and I didn't fear him. I respected him because he took care of me.

In the back seat, the Padre was holding the oldest netphone I'd ever seen, talking to a low-resolution hologram. The fuzzy little man of light was pleading with him for another chance at something.

"Please, Sir Padre. We made a mistake, but we really need this relationship to keep the business moving. What do you need to make this right?"

His reply was very calm. "Your backers owe me. You'll tell them to settle that debt. You have twenty-four hours."

"Twenty-four hours! That's impossible—"

Again, the Padre's response was measured. "Twenty-four hours, Mr. Kline. Another mistake, and our business ties won't be the only thing that will be severed."

"Yes, sir. Thank you, sir."

Without as much as a goodbye, the Padre tapped two buttons on his netphone, and the backseat went dark. It was an odd conversation to overhear, that was for sure, but I knew not to pry into his business. Instead, I leaned back and slightly turned my head.

"Thirty minutes from the site, boss."

The Padre groaned instead of responding, then cracked his window open slightly. Reaching into his suit coat, he retrieved a nice-looking Cuban, his cutter, and a lighter. He snipped off one end of the cigar, placed it into his mouth, and flamed up the other end with intermittent puffs. The fragrant cologne was replaced with a spicy smoke, and part of me liked it. Another part of me wanted to hold my breath.

"We expecting any trouble tonight, boss?"

I checked for his response in the mirror and caught the tail end of the cloud exiting his mouth. Taking the cigar between the fingers of his right hand, his impressively bulky sterling silver ring shined through the smoke as it always did. It was the skull of a dog, and it had ruby eyes.

"Don't we always?" There was not even a hint of sarcasm in his tone.

"Good point."

Focusing back on the road, I didn't really recognize the city we were in, but oddly enough, seemed to know exactly where I was going. We were making our way through a nicer part of town judging by the older but still luxurious condo complexes lining several of the streets. Seemingly omnipresent skyscrapers loomed over us for several miles, and the large intersections we passed were overflowing with business types crossing the streets and huddling on the corners. Based on the position of the sun, they were on their way home from work. Finally, the leaves on the various trees caught my attention. They were beginning to turn color, so it was definitely autumn.

The niceness of the area evaporated as we entered what some might describe as a ghetto. Boarded-up buildings and condemned homes were the backdrop of aimless wanderers floating along the streets and open lots.

On the other side of the neighborhood, I could see a plume of thick black smoke ahead. Soon we passed a car burning out of control in a vacant lot. Driving past, I was fairly certain I could see the flaming skeletal remains of the driver, and a cold feeling washed over me for just a second before I shook it off. The sun melted behind the smoggy horizon in front of us as we drove through the city limits. A chill developed in the air as the day's warmth gave way to dusk, and again, I felt compelled to lean back and ask another question.

"What do we know about the buyers?"

"Russian. Traveled a long way for the product. Expect quality."

"What's their ETA?"

"Thirty minutes after us. Though they sent a scout."

"He armed?"

With a hiss, he put his cigar out in the ashtray and blew out a pocket of smoke. "No. *She* isn't."

"Sounds pretty routine."

"Just stay sharp. There could always be an incident like the Korean job, and we don't want to be caught flat-footed."

"Did you ever find out what happened with them?"

"Those sons of bitches were tweaking when they came to make the deal. That's the last time we'll be working with them."

"Sounds good, boss."

The "bad" neighborhood vibe shifted to something even more depressing as we approached an old industrial strip. Like the entire area had been abandoned for a decade or more, the soot-covered factories and plants were shells of their former greatness. An area that had once produced quality products for the world and jobs for the locals had been reduced to a blight on the region. Many of the buildings had become gloomy squatter villages, apparent by the countless trash can fires dotting the scenery. Seeing dense gray smog piping from a few rooftops, it was encouraging to know that a few factories and plants were still in operation. Yet the air quickly thickened with a metallically sulfur smell, and a bit of nausea accompanied.

Taken with the grungy scenery, my thoughts were only interrupted when the ride suddenly lost its smoothness to potholes littering the road. Focusing back on my driving, I did my best to avoid the craters, but the car's loose suspension was the true savior, making the ride relatively smooth regardless. In that sense, it lived up to the nickname of "boat" as it felt like we were simply sailing choppy water. Just a few blocks farther and the top of a massive steel mill complex became visible in the distance, and I knew it was there that the exchange would happen.

"Any special reason why we went with this site instead of one of the usuals, boss?"

"They purchased our top-end product and requested a little more anonymity than usual. It used to be the only place we dealt back in the day, but it hasn't been necessary for a while. Either way, don't worry. It will be fine."

If the road wasn't bad enough, we were headed for the oldest, rustiest drawbridge I had ever seen. At first, I thought it was designed with interwoven steel to make a waffle pattern. But getting closer, I realized it was just rusted out holes in the structure. Gulping hard as we got closer, my mind told me we should find another way, but my foot thought differently as it pressed firmly on the gas to speed up about ten miles an hour faster. The second we were on the rotting, reddish-orange structure, the iron let loose the deepest moan, which continued every second we drove. It was impossible not to think about it giving way and us falling to our deaths. The thought made me want to peer over the edge, but a part of me felt that I didn't need to. Somehow I knew the remains of a once grand river were just thirty feet below. Countless cargo ships and smaller freighters had traveled thousands of miles, in some cases, to and from the steel mill, bringing raw materials in and taking quality steel out. It was painful to think that it had been reduced to a festering wound on the earth, weeping toxic sludge and low-grade radiation, the result of callous, negligent industry spewing tons of pollution into the air and local water systems. Rumor had it that the desperate locals were still able to kick up the occasional fish from the muck. The joke was that the fish had three or more eyes and felt like tinfoil in your mouth. I didn't know who I felt sorrier for, the people or the fish, but one thing was for sure: it was a terrible place to live.

Leaving the bridge, the moans died down as did my anxiety, and I leaned back to provide another update. "Five minutes out, boss."

Without a word, the Padre reached for the briefcase on the seat next to him and punched in a combination. The case popped open, and I peered into the mirror to see the assembly beginning. Each step was done with such precision that it was impressive to watch. With the leather and wood grip in one hand, he clicked it together with the silver frame in the other. Next, he connected the long-scoped barrel to the frame with a metal clink. The cylinder, full of cartridges, was put into the holder, and with an upward slap, it rattled into place. I noticed the dog skull insignia had also been forged onto the side of the piece, and I was a little jealous of his style. Finally, the Padre pulled open his coat, and the weapon disappeared.

Ahead was a corroded archway over the road, its age-worn lettering difficult to read.

PURITAN STEEL CO. - WHERE HARD WORK AND INGENUITY BUILD THE FUTURE!

Just before the sign, the mangiest mutt I had ever seen caught my attention. It was on the side of the road viciously tearing up the remains of a dead something or other. Briefly seeing it pull chunks from the carcass, I wondered if the victim was another dog or perhaps an unlucky drifter. Shaking off the morbid thought, I drove under the archway and turned the car onto the mill's campus. The main building stretched at least four or five football fields in length, and at the end, I was again presented with a sign that I could barely make out.

"Employee Parking."

Driving next to the wreckage that was once the mill's main building deepened the depression the industrial strip had brought on, but I was happy that I got to take it all in before we entered. I gently pulled the car into the parking lot and immediately noticed the rotting frames of abandoned cars sprinkled throughout, filling roughly half the spaces. I parked the car near the building, turned off the headlights, and took the key out of the ignition. Sinking into my seat, I was trying to mentally prepare for the deal. Most times, they went off without a hitch, but occasionally, there were issues. The Korean job was a prime example, and just thinking about it stressed me out. So I stopped.

Rolling down the window, I reached into my shirt pocket to retrieve a menthol and my Zippo. With a snap, the cancer stick was lit and my nerves calmed just a bit. I was certain my addiction was just as much to the burn of the lighter's fuel as it was to the nicotine. Still, that first deep, endless drag was heavenly. It always took off even the sharpest of edges from the day. I was certain that I was breathing shallow all day long in between smokes but that first puff reminded me to take things slow, to take it all in stride, and to relax. It was a shame that it was deadly poison that would eventually kill me.

Interrupting my thought, I could hear the Padre dial up our eyes on the area. In between my drags, I heard him go over some of the standard logistics that made the job seem even more routine. We would enter the building in just a few minutes and make our way to the drop point. A table with a lantern on it had already been set up to facilitate the transaction. We would be waiting there with product in hand for about thirty minutes when the buyers arrive. We always insisted on verifying the amount of money brought by the buyers before ever showing any of the product. Once that was confirmed, we would allow them to preview the product. As long as both parties were satisfied, the buyers leave with the product, and we would wait for another thirty minutes to leave with the cash.

Knowing we would be going in soon, I wrestled open the glove compartment and felt around for my 9mm. Locating the grip, I pulled it out, and in one motion, dropped out the magazine and checked the chamber, then the action. Confirming its loyalty, I reloaded the piece while surveying the area for anything interesting. It was as boring as it was desolate. Finally, I ensured the safety was enabled, leaned forward in my seat, and crammed the piece into the back of my waistband.

Maintaining weapons had come easy to me since my military service days. In fact, I wouldn't have landed the gig with the Padre had it not been for all the things I'd done for my country. But as a vet, it was pathetic that I couldn't find decent employment through normal means, and that fact alone was one of the biggest stresses of my life.

Tossing and turning whenever I tried to sleep, I couldn't help but constantly think about my squad. Even during moments of prolonged silence, images of my buddies flashed through my mind, and I relived them being shot, blown up, or gassed. I had been dwelling a lot on those who had died, the countless men and women who'd made the ultimate sacrifice, but lately more so on the ones who had survived. They—*we*—were never the same, though some of us were worse than others. Some needed daily assistance to deal with life after losing limbs or suffering brain damage. Others needed endless mental therapy to cope with what we had done or what had been done to us. Still, some of us needed all of it to lead some semblance of a normal life. The whole line of thinking never sat well with me because it was a damn shame that service people weren't better taken care of in the godforsaken country they defended. Worse yet, politicians never missed an opportunity to pay lip service to vets and active duty right before they sold them down the river.

The Padre's netphone buzzed bringing me back to the task at hand, and the rearview mirror lit up from the bright hologram.

"It's time."

Putting on my game face, I was like a Little Leaguer before a tournament—nervous, excited, serious. Knowing the Padre had my back always gave me a sense of invincibility too. He'd been doing jobs for a long time, and he hadn't had many major issues.

I took one last puff on the menthol, swiped it from my lips, and flicked it hard out of the window. Slowly exhaling the deadly smoke through my nostrils, I pulled the cross from under my shirt collar, lowered my head, and closed my eyes.

True to his nickname, the Padre led a prayer as he had done before every single job. "Lord, please provide us with your protection as we attempt to complete the job that has been put in front of us. Please provide us with buyers who are of sound mind and soul and ready to make a deal. Please ensure, should something happen, that our resolve is quick and our aim is steady. We ask this in the Lord's name. Amen."

"Amen." In one motion, I opened the door and stepped out into the dank air.

Spilling out of the car with the empty weapon case in hand, the Padre walked around and popped the trunk open. He placed the empty case in and pulled out a bulkier aluminum briefcase that had to contain the product. With his breath visible in the air, he slammed the trunk and approached me.

"You good?"

"Unless you know something I don't, I'm good."

"They should know you're carrying when they approach us. Just don't draw unless we're obviously headed down that road."

"I got it, boss."

"And one last thing."

"Yeah, boss?"

"You've handled yourself well since I brought you in, and good help is hard to find. If tonight goes well, we need to talk about an even better gig for you. As much as I like you on the road, you might have better talents that we can take advantage of. Think of it like a promotion."

"Thanks, boss! You've always been good to me and mine."

We walked toward the building, and I pulled out the oversized copper key that would let us in. Pushing it into the rusted deadbolt with too much effort, I strained to turn it to the left with one hand. Grabbing the door handle with my other hand, I leaned back to let my weight do the work of opening the heavy steel door. The door screeched against the concrete ground something awful, and the echo must have traveled for miles. I held the door so the Padre could enter first.

"Thank you, Charlie."

Entering the building to follow him, the door was already squealing shut behind me as intense confusion overtook me.

Who the hell is Charlie?

CHAPTER 6
SEEING IS BELIEVING

WHO THE HELL IS CHARLIE?

My eyes shot open and I frantically moved my arms, inadvertently hitting the button under my left hand, which turned out to be a good accident. A nurse quickly appeared—a nurse that I could see!

For crying out loud, I can see! I thanked all that was holy, and even those who weren't, that my host's eyes were working, and hell, my vision was pretty damn clear too!

Without thinking, I said, "Hey!" *I can talk! What a glorious day!*

"Ryan, are you okay?"

I responded as fast as I could, and it came out as a mumble at first. "Yes…I mean, no. I'm…better than okay. I can see! And I can talk!"

Her smile was so refreshing compared to the darkness and odd dreams that were my reality that last several days. Or weeks. Or whatever it was.

"It's Sheila, right?"

Still grinning wide, she went to work typing away at the machine next to my bed and confirmed my guess. "Yes! Wow, your hearing progressed great as well."

"It's all I had, so I leaned on it."

Her smile faded ever so slightly. "Your numbers are a little elevated, but that's normal considering you just gained your eyesight and speech back at the same time. Usually, it's a day or two after the vision that you can talk again, so consider yourself fortunate."

"Sometimes it's better to be lucky than good!" I sounded drunk, but at least I could talk.

"I'll let Dr. Little know about your progress. She'll be here in a bit to run some tests and make sure you're progressing safely. In the meantime, you've got a visitor. I'll let her know you're ready for her." Sheila tapped a couple more buttons and then promptly left the room.

With only the slightest bit of sunlight coming through the windows, I could tell it was dusk. To compensate, a postmodern lamp in the corner provided dim lighting, which seemed intentional since I was sensitive to light. Other than the usual medical equipment, a paint-by-numbers portrait was the only thing on the salmon-colored walls. There were two chairs and a walker in the corner, and a window where birds had sung to me the last several days, quickly becoming something I looked forward to when I was conscious.

I had been in countless hospital beds in my time, and they were all fairly similar. Many nights were spent feeling at the mercy of doctors and nurses to keep me alive and healthy. It was really bad when I was younger because Mom could only stay so many nights before it really messed with her sleep. She would have to leave me occasionally, and while I was used to loneliness in general, it was especially bad when I was away from home for long periods. Luckily, the slight loneliness I was feeling in that bed was completely different. I was in a new body!

Peering down to take myself in, I was like a marionette with countless tubes and cords going in and out of me. My hospital gown covered me pretty far down, and that was when I noticed the best thing of all. *My legs. My legs!* For the first time in my life, I saw my legs as muscular and full of life. For the first time, I saw feet suitable for walking. Tears welled up in my eyes because after twenty-two years without walking; needing help from Auto, Mom, and others; and the resulting anguish and depression, it all rushed back to me in an instant. It was almost too much to bear, so I forced myself to taper off those feelings before I passed out. Because of the strange dreams I had been having, the last thing I wanted was to be unconscious any more than I had to. Then I recalled something else exciting.

I had a visitor! It had to be Mom, for sure! I might as well have been a little kid in that moment—I definitely wanted my mom. Despite how well the procedure had gone, I was still scared as hell. I needed her, and I knew, like the good mother she was, that she needed me too.

It was at that moment I saw her in the doorway, and we made eye contact. My excited and anxious demeanor was immediately replaced with a soothed and comforted one as it usually was in her presence. But the more I looked at her, the more it was obvious that something was off. The way she was looking at me was more than alarming, and it took me a moment to figure out what it was.

My mother's loving gaze was completely absent from her face. Instead, there was a look of uncertainty and mistrust, something that I had never really seen from her. A bit of shock came over me at the realization that while I was looking at my mom, the woman who gave everything to give me the best life possible, she was looking at a stranger's body with my face superimposed. Having been apprehensive about the whole procedure in the first place, she was going to have a very difficult time throughout my recovery. But it was something that her and I were going to have to accept.

"Ryan. Is that you?"

She was unusually timid.

"Yes, Mom, it's me."

I tried my damnedest to control my warped voice. Tilting her head to get a better view, she slowly moved toward me, grabbed one of the chairs in the corner, and pulled it next to my bed without breaking her stare at me. Gently sitting down, Mom leaned in quite close to my face. I couldn't help but feel like an art exhibit or animal at a zoo as she examined me with the utmost concentration. Her intense stare into my newly-functioning eyes was reminiscent of the way people used to stare at my legs, and that was a bit jarring coming from Mom.

"Sorry. It is you, right, Ryan?"

"It's me, Mom."

Still looking skeptical, she said, "Okay, do you remember the conversion we had before you had your procedure?"

Blinking a few times, I searched my mind. Just like the dreams I'd been having, most of my memories were fleeting. "Somewhat."

With a tremble in her voice, she proceeded. "Okay. Humor me a little. What did we talk about?"

Straining my new brain to remember the details, I knew that she had been worried for my safety. "I know you didn't want me to do it. You thought it was dangerous."

"Yes, go on."

I was really happy to see Mom, but also beginning to realize why they put off visitors for some time after the migration. I shifted in the bed to buy myself more time. The answer was on the tip of my tongue, but it was difficult to dig that deeply into my newly migrated mind so soon.

"I'm sorry, Mom. But it's tough for me to remember some things right now. I just can't do it."

Her eyebrow went up, and she got right in my face. "What did you just say?"

Confused, I tried to explain. "I can't quite remember the details of our discussion."

"No! The other thing!" she insisted.

"What?" I was more than befuddled by that point.

Her eyes lit up, and a smile stretched as far across her face as it could. "You said, 'I just can't do it!'"

"Yes. Sorry, Mom. I just can't do it right now."

"Oh my God, Ryan! My baby, it's you!" Overly thrilled, she splayed her arms and hugged me awkwardly.

Attempting to reciprocate, I flopped my arms around her. But I was still perplexed. "I don't understand."

She pulled back a little and again looked deeply into my eyes.

"'I just can't do it' was your way of telling me you had a problem because of your legs!"

"Oh. Yeah." Shrugging my shoulders, it all sounded familiar, but nothing specific came to mind.

"Oh, come on! Don't you remember?"

I tried again to reach to the depths of my mind, but all I could muster were vague recollections.

Her expression slightly broke, reflecting the dampening in her spirits. She sighed and gathered herself. "Ryan." She looked away for a brief moment and then back. "As you know, you struggled when you were young. You couldn't crawl as a toddler, let alone walk, so you made do by dragging yourself on the ground with your arms. When you were old enough, I told you, 'Do it like they do in the army, Sergeant Ryan Carter!' You would pull yourself all around the house, saying that you are an army man fighting the enemy. Occasionally, you would get stuck or something would block your path. It might have been the stairs or your baby gate, but I would always

72

find you in the oddest places because of your quests to save the house from danger."

She took a deep breath.

"But once you could talk, you made your way around the house. And when you would come to a barrier of some kind, you'd say, 'I just can't do it, Mommy. I just can't do it.' And I would come to the rescue and hold you. Then we would have the same conversation every time. I would tell you, 'You can do everything you need to do, sweetie, and Mommy will take care of the rest.' I told you that hundreds of times. Each time you discovered that the world, as aware and advanced as it was, was made for those of us who could stand upright. And each time you came to that realization, you would tell me, 'I just can't do it, Mommy. I just can't do it.' But I had taken a vow when you were born that I would be your liaison through this world, and I would take care of you as long as you needed it. I always reminded myself of that promise and tried to hold as close to it as possible."

I expected a flood of deep, loving memories to come back to me, but could only recall bits and pieces. None of it was clear enough to assign emotions. It almost seemed like I remembered my childhood in the third person. It was like watching myself as a toddler come to obstacles that I couldn't overcome, and calling for Mom. I could see her picking me up and holding me from a distance. I did remember her talking to me, but what was being said hadn't quite come back to me yet. Still, I knew I should have felt something for those memories, so I did my best to conjure up the emotions artificially. Unfortunately, that was when my head began to pound, and I groaned.

"Oh no, are you all right?"

"I'm sorry. Headaches have been common since I've regained consciousness. It's not your fault." I tried to comfort her even though that particular headache was likely caused by all the brain activity her presence was causing.

"No, Ryan. Don't apologize. It is my fault. All of this is my fault." She gasped and began to weep. "Had I taken better care of you, of myself... you would still be in the body I gave you. You wouldn't have had to save all your credits. You wouldn't be in this hospital, in this strange body. You wouldn't have had to risk your life to get a set of working legs. No. I failed you as a mother even before you came into this world, and I spent the last twenty-two years trying to make up for it. But the one thing that could make it better—this mind migration—I told you it was a bad idea. It scared me thinking that I could lose you."

She grabbed a tissue from the nightstand and wiped her face before continuing.

"But the procedure was the one thing that you wanted more than anything. I could see it in you the moment you heard about it. At no point in the last ten years have you said, 'I just can't do it.' Not once. You went for it even though I didn't think it was a good idea. It just goes to show you. What the hell do my concerns matter anyway? I'm the reason you're here. I'm the reason you suffered your whole life. I'm so sorry, Ryan. If you are really in there, Ryan, I'm so, so sorry!"

With a great moan, she sobbed harder than ever.

It was awkward struggling to keep up with her words and emotions, which was a shame because I knew something important was happening. I didn't know if it was the drugs or if I was truly experiencing limitations of my new, freshly migrated mind. The doctors said it would take some time. I knew it made the sadness of the situation that much worse, but I couldn't quite comprehend or express those feelings in that moment.

"Oh, Mom." I moved my hand to hold hers, but my mobility was still lacking.

Not noticing, she took a deep breath and pulled herself together. With bloodshot eyes, she made direct eye contact again, and there it was. It was the look that had eased my troubles throughout my life, the comforting glance that had always made everything better.

"Ryan, I really hope this turns out well for you. I just wish I could have done more for you."

As limited as my mind was in that moment, I still knew exactly how to respond.

"Mom, please believe me when I say that you've done more than enough for me. As hard as life was, I'm happy with who I am and the opportunities I have had because of the sacrifices you've made. When I get on my feet, I know things will be better for both of us."

She sobbed some more as Dr. Little entered the room, instantly awkward.

"Oh, I'm so sorry. I can come back later."

Mom motioned the doctor in. "No, it's okay. I'm leaving anyway. Ryan, I'll call you in a few days."

"Before you go, I just want to say thanks."

She inhaled deeply. "You're welcome, sweetie." She got up and headed for the exit as Dr. Little stepped out of the way.

"Oh, and Mom?"

"Yes, dear?"

"I love you."

"I love you too, sweetie." I tried to wave, but could only lift my arm about six inches off the bed.

Smiling, Dr. Little tried to comfort me. "The first visit after the procedure is always tough."

"Yeah. I was feeling a little detached from my thoughts and memories. That's normal, right?"

"Absolutely. Give yourself a break. Your mind and body go through a lot of changes in the first few hours and days after gaining your sight and speech back. That being the case, we need to run some tests."

"Okay."

I heard the familiar beeps while she typed into the computer console.

"A health disk is going to do the work for these scans, so just lie back and relax."

Like before, a hatch in the ceiling opened and a tiny floating saucer with flickering red lights appeared. It hummed down to about three inches from my face, drifted down to my toes, and back up again.

"Ryan, the disk is going to affix itself to your head and give you a slight poke in the base of your skull. Just breathe through it."

Sure enough, the disk changed into a helmet and fastened itself to me. Then it stabbed me, but the sensation was more startling than painful that time. Looking at the screens, Dr. Little pressed several buttons and a projection appeared at the foot of my bed. It had a colorful illustration of a human brain and a column of numbers on the right side.

"There it is—your new brain."

I really didn't know what to say, so I just tried to take it all in.

"You see the areas that are green, Ryan?"

"Yes."

"Those are the areas of your host's brain that your migrated mind has reached so far. As you can see, it's shaped toward the occipital and temporal lobes in the back and sides of the brain. This is not uncommon, but normally, we see more of a circular shape from the center of the brain out. The good news is that you have your vision and speech back. The bad news is that it could be up to a week before you get the majority of your motor skills back. That's when we can start physical therapy."

"Compared to my whole life, a week doesn't sound so bad."

"It really isn't, but we have so many migrators who get anxious and annoyed with the process that they actually slow things down. We want you upright and using your new host just as badly as you do, but you have to learn to crawl before you can learn to walk. Now, do you see the numbers to the right?"

"Yes."

"The top number, forty-eight percent, is the percentage that your mind has progressed, and the twelve percent in the middle indicates the next likely jump in percentage."

"What's the bottom number?"

"Oh, I wouldn't worry about that number. It's the percentage of resistance that your mind is experiencing as it expands into your new brain. A normal range is between forty and sixty-five percent. Yours is a little elevated at fifty-six percent, but again, it's in the normal range."

I partly remembered discussing those numbers in preparation for the migration. Even after all of the projections they run, there was still a possibility that the host's brain would reject your mind, causing many issues from simply slowing down the process to dementia and even death.

Dr. Little pressed the same buttons as before, and the projection faded away. Another button push, and I could feel the medical disk dislodge itself from my head, which was much less noticeable than when it attached. It glided up, flattened out, and disappeared into the ceiling.

"You will begin post-migration psychotherapy with the counselors in a day or so. I am going to give you something to help you rest."

She pushed one last button, and the fast-acting sedative hit as fast as usual. My eyes began to close as Dr. Little pulled the door behind her to leave.

It reeks like death in here.

CHAPTER 7
SOME THINGS YOU CAN'T UNSEE

"IT REEKS LIKE DEATH IN here."

The putrid stench assailed us immediately upon entering the forsaken steel mill. While I had become accustomed to it over the years, it never failed to grab my attention and make entering the building feel like a mistake. We trekked through a long, narrow hallway barely lit by LEDs lining the floor, compliments of the site setup crew. Cobwebs littered the ceiling and walls, and the chill from outside had followed us, making our breaths visible. As we walked, the intricate tags of the local street gangs came to life in vibrant blues and greens. They'd apparently used bioluminescent paint that reacted to the faintest hint of heat and moisture in the air, two things the Padre and I produced in ample quantities. Part of me wanted to smack the shit out of anyone who defaced property. But another part of me had always thought of the really talented ones as street artists whose obvious gifts were wasted on vandalism. Too bad there weren't enough good jobs or companies savvy enough to hire them, or we might have figured out a solution to the gang problem in the area.

After walking for a couple minutes, we approached a dark opening. The Padre pulled out his netphone and shined it all around to orient us. We were near a solid cement stairwell. There was a nasty wreckage of steel and plastic to the right of the stairs. Collapsed and sunken into the foundation, the elevator car must have fallen from the top level. Scorch marks and scattered debris gave away that there had been an explosion, and the ample amount of melted steel confessed that the resulting fire was extremely hot. The skeletal remains of a human hand could be seen just in front of the rubble, and I couldn't help but imagine what they had experienced right before it all ended for them.

It was probably a squatter who thought that an elevator that high up was the safest place to stay. Loading up all their belongings, they may have been taking stock of that day's haul when the ground beneath them failed. Or maybe they were sleeping when the cables gave way, and their gut dropping and the sound of grinding metal woke them up right before impact.

Boom!

Shaking the thought from my head, I stepped onto the first stair and peered up as the Padre aimed a light from his phone up the stairwell. I caught a glimpse of the hike ahead, and while the building appeared massive on the outside, it seemed like Mount Everest at the bottom of the steps. The Padre tapped off his phone and moved the large briefcase into his right hand to hold the railing with his left.

"Know why they designed the mill like this, Charlie?"

"To keep the employees in shape?" I couldn't help but jest.

"The plans for these buildings were created by some of the most advanced architects in the country. They wanted it to be the most efficient mill campus in the country, using the best designs in the world."

"This doesn't seem efficient at all."

Winded from the ascent, the Padre took a deep breath. "Well, workers in these buildings were unionized thugs. That meant they could work together against the company's—and their own—interests. One of the slimiest things those malcontents would do was stop operations at the plants. Like spoiled brats, they'd hurt the whole company and their brethren until their demands were met. They would hold the whole company hostage until their stupid demands were heard. Luckily, the steel mill owners here had the forethought to design a building that made it difficult for workers to get to the mill operations area. Should a shutdown or sit-in be organized, it was much easier to cut off reinforcements and supplies from getting to the lazy troublemakers on the inside. If it were me, I would have let 'em sit in and then starved them to death."

As much as the Padre liked his stories, something didn't add up about that one.

"If this place was designed so well to protect itself from workers, why'd it fail all those years ago?"

Catching his breath again, he said, "Well, other companies outsourced to China and eastern Europe. At that time, they didn't have to pay taxes on those factories and the labor was dirt cheap. For years, they were making record profits, and it looked like they would finally break workers here into taking much less. But the damn standard of living was so high here, it didn't work. They closed up shop and moved all their operations overseas."

If the smell of death was bad when we came in, it was steadily getting much worse the higher we climbed. Then a trail of coagulated blood led us up the next several sets of stairs.

"Didn't China fall to a workers' uprising a few years ago?"

"Impressive, Charlie. Most people have no idea what's going on in their own neighborhood, much less the world. Yes, those bastards threw their country into anarchy. To this day, half the country starves while the other half starts wars with the surrounding countries. And they have the nerve to talk about corruption."

"Before I was discharged, there was some talk that we might send troops in. As much as I wanted to help, we still had our hands full in the Middle East."

"No troops. We should just bomb them all back to the Stone Age."

The Padre was never shy about his political leanings.

As we approached the last set of steps, we had to carefully avoid the obviously human entrails that punctuated the trail of blood, and upon getting to the last few stairs, I could finally see the rotting corpse that had produced all of the mess. He must have dragged himself up the stairs as a last-ditch effort to survive, though that clearly hadn't worked. To that end, time had not been kind to the poor sap; the bloat of death had set in long ago. The Padre was so gassed that we had to stop in the thick of the stink. To stop from gagging, I turned away to look at the main production area of the mill.

It was magnificent! The moon shown through the windows and holes in the roof, illuminating nearly a dozen enormous rusted buckets hanging from the high ceilings. Farther down, the casting area had a series of giant funnels that were used to gather the steel for processing. Below was a conveyor system that must have moved hundreds of thousands of steel beams, rods, and sheets through the plant. The moonlight also revealed the thick layer of glaze that had caked up on the remaining windows. It was as amazing as it was depressing to think that this place used to produce the finest metals for the world over.

"Our exchange will happen over there." The Padre pointed to a lantern about two hundred feet from our present location, then led the way toward it.

The clicks of our four heels mimicked the gait of a horse strolling through the gigantic building, and as the smell of rotting flesh faded, it was replaced by the stink of mildew like a basement after flooding.

A sudden explosion of movement in the darkness scared the hell out of me. "Shit! Shit! Shit!" Trying desperately to focus, I ripped the 9mm from my waistband and pointed it into the distance, ready to unload. When my eyes finally adjusted, embarrassment quickly set in. It was ghastly pigeons that had fluttered off a ledge and nearly given me a heart attack. To make matters worse, the Padre was completely unfazed. I tried to shake it off while I put my 9mm back into my pants, but it seemed like the night was destined to be strange.

As we neared the lantern, a table became visible underneath it.

The Padre grunted as he lifted the large case and plopped it next to the light. "Look alert. They'll be here soon."

We both pulled out our weapons and performed the standard diagnostics, which killed the deafening silence of the place and was somewhat calming. I put mine in the front of my waistband so the buyers would see it upon arrival, and the Padre made his disappear back into his coat. After another twenty minutes, the stairwell came alive with new sounds. My fists tightened as the noise grew in intensity. Our buyers had arrived. As usual, the Padre stood placidly motionless.

For security reasons, the conversation to complete the transaction was random. To begin, a proper greeting would transpire with our guests, followed by them asking to purchase a random luxury item. More than formalities, the buyers were given several keywords that had to be included in their responses. Too much deviation or error in these keywords would be—well, it wouldn't be good. After a successful greeting and inquiry, the buyers would place a briefcase next to ours, near the light. That was when we would take turns confirming we all brought what we'd agreed to.

I couldn't remember just how many of these jobs I had worked, but they all went basically as planned except for one. A couple of Korean buyers had brought less money than agreed. They'd kept looking around and had been asking weird questions, so naturally, I thought they were the feds, though the Padre later confirmed they were actually just high. The Padre had also known they were trying to short us the second he opened their case. He'd slammed it shut and reached to grab our product. One of the buyers had grabbed the Padre's arm, shouting something in Korean. By the time they'd looked up at me, they were gazing down the barrel of my 9mm. I'd hesitated for just a moment, and one of them knocked the gun from my hand. It had discharged into the wall while the other drop-kicked the Padre in the chest, staggering him. I had been able to clock the one closest to me in the jaw, but he'd recovered quickly and swept my legs out from under me. They'd both run off, one of them shooting at us so we would stay down for cover. After gathering ourselves, we had been able to focus enough to fire several shots in their direction, but we hadn't been able to stop them. Fortunately, about 20% of the payment had fallen from their briefcase on the way out, and they'd never laid a hand on the product. While it could have been worse, that job had taught me that our line of work was dangerous and nothing was guaranteed, no matter how routine it felt.

The sounds from the stairs were at their loudest when two silhouettes appeared on the landing of the stairs. They paused in the stink just like the Padre and me, and after thirty seconds, walked toward the light. Basically asking to be noticed, their white suits quickly became apparent in the shadowy mill. The one on the right had the payment in his left hand, and he moved it to the right as they made their way to the table. Both men were of average height and build. Both had scruffy half beards and messily combed-back hair. They would have looked pretty damn classy if they were going to a nightclub, but it just seemed odd for a job. Still, their expressionless faces brought me little comfort.

"Good evening, gentlemen," said the man on the left.

It was difficult for me to understand his thick Russian accent, but the Padre didn't seem to have a problem.

The Padre nodded. "Good evening to you, sirs."

"We are in the market for a late-model American car. Do you happen to know where we can find a black 2006 Dodge Charger with a five-point-seven-liter Hemi V8? We are willing to pay top dollar for it if it has been properly restored and has low mileage on the current engine."

Taking a deep breath, the Padre offered a consolation as he always did.

"Please forgive me, but I only have a red 2010 Chevy Camaro with a six-point-two-liter GM LS3 V8. The mileage is twenty thousand. Luckily, it will blow the Charger you want out of the water. Would you like to take it for a test drive?"

"Yes, I would. Is the car available here and now to test drive?"

"It is. Do you have a valid ID and something of value for us to keep as a show of good faith?"

"Most certainly."

Laying their briefcase flat on the table next to ours, each buyer extended his right thumb to the front of the case. After several clicks, a loud beep echoed through the mill and the case popped open slightly. They lifted the top and looked over the contents briefly, then turned it around to us. The refreshing smell of money filled the air.

The Padre did a quick visual scan of the currency, and in my peripheral, I could see crisp one-hundred-dollar bills wrapped to delineate stacks of what had to be at least ten thousand. From the top stacks alone, there had to be ten, but I wasn't sure if there was another set underneath. It also wasn't my business to know. In all the jobs that I had been on, I never knew the product or the dollar amount being exchanged. All I knew was that the job paid better than any other I could get, and that was enough for me.

The Padre slowly reached into his front right pants pocket and pulled out his netphone. He tapped it a couple of times and then held it over the cash. With three beeps, the phone lit up a very bright green. The Padre confirmed the information on the screen, tapped it twice, and gently dropped his phone back into his pocket. Closing the cash case, he moved it to the side.

"Much appreciated for having sufficient collateral. Allow me to provide you the keys to the vehicle so that you can test drive it. I promise you will be pleased."

The Padre placed his thumb on the front of our case. A beep followed, but instead of a click, there was a burst of air like the discharge from a compressor, something I had never really noticed in the past. Then, as customary, the Padre turned the case around. On the earlier jobs, my curiosity had led me to try to catch a glimpse of the product before it was turned, but the Padre had it down to such precise movements that the visual escaped me every time.

Once around, the case provided a bright-white light that illuminated our buyers. Pulling our case closer to them, their wide eyes looked over the product intently. As their eyes raced back and forth like they were reading news clippings, grins slowly stretched across their faces, and for whatever reason, it gave me a cold feeling on the inside. Then my train of thought was interrupted by something odd. The briefcase made a popping noise, released more air, and the light faded with a squeal.

"What the hell!"

Even through the Russian accent, I could feel his anger. Without thinking, my hand moved to my waistband.

The buyers' eyes followed.

The Padre looked stunned for a brief moment, then snapped back into character and extended his hand to my chest while still facing the buyers. "My sincerest apologies, sirs. Please let me take a look at the vehicle to ensure it is functioning correctly."

The buyers forcefully spun the case back at us, and the Padre went to work frantically. The top of the briefcase was slightly closed, hiding the product while the Padre felt around and pressed several buttons in sort of a combination pattern. He appeared to be turning a dial and flipping several switches as well. Our buyers began to roll their eyes as he worked for about a minute, and for the first time since I had known him, the Padre looked somewhat nervous.

"And I will just finish installing this spark plug…and there we have it!"

The burst of an intense light stung as it hit me, and I squinted hard. My eyes adjusted quickly, and just as the Padre was turning the case back around, I caught my first glimpse of the product.

The product? The product!

Trying not to draw attention to myself, I blinked hard a couple times because I couldn't believe what I had just seen. When I'd first taken the gig with the Padre, I'd assumed we were drug dealers, high-end drug dealers to high-end buyers. But I couldn't have been more wrong, and that explained everything: why we did deals in such secrecy, why I was paid so well, why we had such a specialized briefcase. My shock was still fresh when the exchange resumed.

"I assure you that the vehicle was not damaged in any way during the previous incident. Feel free to test drive it again to be sure."

The Padre's composed demeanor returned as the buyers' eyes widened again when they resumed inspecting the product. A sinking feeling grew inside me as I began to realize the type of people we were doing business with. They were men who would go to great lengths to buy our product.

"We will confirm the quality of the vehicle with our mechanics. Given the temporary malfunction, if the vehicle is not as good as advertised, be assured that we will expect a full refund as well a fee for our troubles."

Surprisingly, the slight annoyance in the buyer's voice made his broken English easier to understand.

"You can expect nothing less from us, sirs. It has been a pleasure doing business with you. Please feel free to drive the vehicle off the lot."

The buyers closed the briefcase, lifted it from the table, and stormed off.

My eyes followed the case as I was still reeling from what I had seen inside.

"You okay?" The Padre had more than curiosity in his voice.

I knew if I acted strange, things could get bad really quick. "Yeah, we just never had a case break down like that. It had me worried for a second there, but I was impressed that you were able to fix it so quickly and save the deal."

"Sometimes I feel like I have to do everything to keep things running. That's why it has been nice having someone like you to rely on. It's the reason for the promotion we talked about."

"I appreciate the opportunity, boss." It sounded like the Padre was holding the promotion over my head rather than looking out for my well-being, but I showed no signs of questioning his sincerity.

While I was mostly sincere, I had already begun to mistrust working for the Padre. I was doubting the promotion even more, but another part of me thought the money was just too good to pass up.

After the proper thirty-minute wait, the Padre firmly gripped the money case by the handle and pointed toward the exit. Approaching the stairs, I glanced back at the body on the landing, less disturbed by it than before. We headed down the stairs. At the bottom, I eyed the elevator remains as we entered the long hallway toward the exit where we followed the LEDs out. I opened the groaning metal door one more time for the Padre and followed closely behind. As the door screamed to a close behind us, anger and despair overcame me.

I didn't sign up for this shit!

CHAPTER 8

IT'S ALL PART OF THE PROCESS

"**I** DIDN'T SIGN UP FOR THIS shit!"

Tony, the therapist, nodded as Gerald shared his feelings with the group.

"I can still smell my flesh burning. I can feel my skin bubbling. It's as if it was literally burned into my memory. And everyone keeps saying they're glad I'm alive and breathing." Gerald took a deep breath. "Big deal! I'm not so sure I would have made the same decision if I was given a choice. Divorcing my body can do a lot of things, but in my case, the thoughts… the nightmares…the hell that I live every day, really make it hard to be grateful for this body."

In therapy leading up to a migration, some counselors likened the time immediately after the procedure to being burned alive, when your new immune system kicks in and takes its ire out on you. Poor Gerald experienced both the real thing and a mind migration. He had been working on a construction site when the new building caught fire and immediately consumed him. The way he told it, he would have certainly died had his wife not approved the last-minute, emergency migration. As amazing as it was that he was alive, the fact that he'd kept his sanity through it all was the most impressive thing.

"After what seemed like an hour of burning, I basically died. I was gone. I was sure of it. But then suddenly, I had a flicker of consciousness—a flicker that forced me to relive each and every agonizing, gut-wrenching second over and over. I told myself that I was just burning for my sins, for everything I had ever done wrong. Every last goddamned awful thing I had ever done was running through my head. Things I did as a kid, things

I had done as an adult. I repented hard, but clearly, I was the scum of the earth for the torture that was being thrust upon me. It wasn't until I heard the doctor's voice that I realized I wasn't dead. He was counting, and as the numbers got lower, so too did my suffering. Part of me was relieved that I wasn't actually in hell, but another part was disappointed. I was so tired of hurting and begging for mercy. I'm still exhausted every day. It may have only been a week to get here, but it felt like an eternity."

The group nervously shuffled a bit as the gravity of Gerald's words sunk in.

Tony broke the momentary silence. "Gerald, your experience is not uncommon for such a rushed procedure. Everyone else in the room had six months to a year to prepare. Believe it or not, I am pleasantly surprised at how far along you are. With our help, you should be able move past the grief of your situation and be happy again one day. It just takes time."

We were gathered in a large corner space in the recovery lounge. There were ceiling-to-floor windows on three sides of the room, and the natural light was easier on the eyes than halogens. Still, it made the room warmer than I would have liked. The cafeteria wasn't far away, and the scent of beef stew made my stomach rumble because I was one of those odd people who had always loved cafeteria food.

"Does anyone have any words of encouragement for Gerald to take away?" Tony peered around the semicircle of auto and manual chairs.

"I do."

"Thanks, Jaime. Go ahead."

"I wasn't burned alive, but pain has been a normal part of my life for the better part of two years. My doctors discovered a disorder in me, where my body incorrectly synthesized proteins, leading to the development of cancer in many of my internal organs. I was given six months to a year to live, and I made the decision then to migrate out of my faulty body and into one that functioned correctly. The countless hours of chemo and radiation therapy made it difficult to complete the psychotherapy. Well, three weeks ago, I learned that the cancer had spread to my liver, lungs, and bones. I still had two months of prep work to go, but didn't have time. While I can't remember what happened leading up to the procedure, I will never forget the pain of the cancer sweeping over my insides like wildfire. That pain is fresh in my mind even to this very moment. So, I appreciate that you are here and that you're willing to share your experience. Stay strong and let me know if you ever want to talk."

Gerald sat back in his chair, and his eyes fluttered. He seemed surprised that anyone could relate even a little to the excruciating pain he was still experiencing.

"Thanks, Jaime," said Tony. "Who's next?"

A lanky redhead in an auto-chair next to me chimed in. "My story's a little different, but I was also rushed. Society has come a long way in accepting that gender identity is a fairly fluid concept. But my family never saw it that way, and my mother would go on bigoted rants anytime the topic was brought up. She sent me to a religious school, and as a result, it took me through most of my teens to finally figure out that nearly all of the grief in my life was over the fact that I was born a woman when I've always been a man."

He shifted in his seat, confessing his discomfort at telling the story.

"After turning eighteen, I finally had enough credits and courage to prep for the migration. When my mom found out, she kicked me out of the house. I lived with friends and on the streets while I went through the program. But word quickly spread to my old classmates why I was homeless. They found me in the city one day and beat me to within an inch of my life. The trauma stopped my brain from processing the beating, but I still have phantom pains throughout my new body to remind me of what happened. The silver lining in it all was that my mom made the final call for the procedure to happen because she would rather have me alive in a man's body than not at all. Without a second chance, I would have missed the opportunity to see her progress has a person. We actually talk every week now."

Jim, whose birth name was Jeannette, gave Gerald a half smile and a nod after finishing his story.

"Thanks, Jim. Gerald, we will resume this discussion during our one-on-one. We really appreciate your contributions, and we're all going to keep supporting you the best we can. Ryan, would you like to wrap up today's sessions by sharing your story with the group?"

I was a bit caught off guard, but had known my time was coming eventually. I inhaled deeply and stared at the argyle pattern on the floor.

"Since I couldn't explore the world like other kids, I was always curious.

Even at a young age, I had an unquenchable thirst for knowledge. I read countless books and watched every documentary I could get my hands on. Hell, I even taught myself Morse code just because I was bored. But none of it was enough. I would look out the front window and wonder what the world was like out there, and I knew something had to give, so I quickly changed my focus from simply researching to exploring. I was determined to know everything about historic landmarks and places that I would probably never visit. I wanted to know what it felt like to be near the volcanic ash that had consumed the Big Island. I wondered what it was like to meander through the remnants of the Fallen Tower of Pisa and the Great Wall of China. None of those places were auto-chair accessible and we couldn't have afforded the travel anyway, so I used VR to visit them. The experience was amazing even if it wasn't real, though I guess it didn't help that we could only afford the second-generation VR headset. Most kids thought it was lame back then, but those are some of my fondest memories. Even though I was disabled, I tried to make the best of it."

The smile that had slowly crept onto my face faded quickly.

"Then at age six, everything changed. Out of the blue, my father left us. No goodbye, no note, no nothing. One morning, he was gone. When I asked my mom where he was, she said he was working a job across the country. Weeks went by, and I asked about him more and more. After about a month, I knew he wasn't coming back."

I coughed hard to clear my throat.

"At first, I didn't understand it. My folks never fought that much. They generally seemed to like each other. They met right out of college and had been together ever since. That was when I connected the dots as to the only reason he would leave, the one thing that would drive him to throw it all away."

It still stung to think about that realization all those years ago.

"It was because of me. His only child, his one attempt at procreation, and I was born with a malformed spine. I didn't walk. I didn't run. I didn't play. I was just needy. I needed to be bathed. I needed help using the bathroom. I needed help getting food. His only child wasn't much of a child at all. I was just a lot of work to care for."

It was surprisingly cathartic to say all of that out loud to the group.

"It wasn't long after he left that I began taking to heart what a burden

I was. After talking to my mom about it, she burst into tears and assured me that he left for his own reasons and that it didn't have anything to do with me. It was the only time in my life that I felt like my mom was lying to me. But I knew she was doing it to protect me, so I gave her a break. As difficult as it was for a six-year-old to comprehend, I knew life was going to be even more difficult with just my mom and me, so I decided that I would need to be a lot more self-sufficient. I mastered the manual chair I had been scared of. I learned to operate the stair lift so Mom didn't have to take me downstairs every day. Then for the next six years, I worked as hard as I could physically and mentally to put Mom and me in a good position. I always got top grades in school and even started to clean up around the house as much as I could. Things weren't great, but we managed."

Another cough forced itself out.

"Still, while we made the best of life, I felt like there was something more I needed to be working toward, a bigger goal than just getting by. That's when the two biggest things happened. My mom gave me my one and only auto-chair. And then not so long after, I saw the news about mind migrations. Suddenly, I had purpose. Suddenly, I had direction. With all of the existing medical bills my mom talked about, I knew I would have to save for a long time in order to afford the procedure. But I was more than happy to."

I felt like I was being long-winded, so wanted to wrap it up.

"Anyway, I'm humbled and thankful to finally be in an able body. I am also thankful that for the first time since I was six, and even in a room full of diverse strangers, I feel like I belong. Sure, I'm still working out the weird dreams that came along with the migration, but if that's the worst of it, I know I'll be okay. Thanks, everyone, for listening to me blabber."

As my voice died down, the sound of the air conditioner became apparent.

"Thanks, Ryan. Does the group have any words of encouragement to share?" Tony swiped past a few pages on his handheld holo-pad.

Jim spoke up first. "Hang in there. I was having weird dreams too, but they'll continue with your medication and therapy, and those will settle down."

Jaime encouraged me as well. "Yeah, just keep the goal in focus. You're just trying to get your mind back to one hundred percent, and that's different for everyone."

Tony wrapped things up. "Well, that's it for today. We made a lot of progress, and I want to encourage you all to capture any additional thoughts in your journal apps. As we've told you from day one, a mind migration is an ongoing process and it takes work to move that process along. Remember: we have a scheduled off day tomorrow, but if you need anything, you can just message me from your bedside terminal. Thanks again, everyone."

The newer model auto-chairs that the others had were nearly silent as they came to life. I couldn't bring myself to replace—*betray*—Auto with a newer model, so I'd opted for a manual chair during my rehab. I was about to head back to my room when an ad on the monitor across the room caught my eye.

"Looking to use your new host's hands and brain in a fun and interactive way? R & F Automotive is looking for part-timers and volunteers to restore early-twenty-first-century gas-powered vehicles for the entertainment industry as well as collectors. No experience necessary. Apply today!"

One of the old-timer vehicles they showed was black, and in an instant, I had the feeling that I recognized it. The odd thing was that I had never been interested in any of the technology from that time, so wasn't really familiar with any of them. It was almost like a déjà vu that didn't make any sense. Then vivid flashes of random items shot into my mind. *Steering wheel. Manually driving. Cadillac. Crashing!*

I had no idea what a "Cadillac" was or why I was so moved by the thought of getting into an accident in one of them, but I knew it had to be related to the strange dreams. I wasn't scheduled to meet with Tony for a couple of days, but needed to discuss my dreams with him sooner rather than later, so I approached him as he was putting his holo-pad in his bag.

"Excuse me, Tony?"

"Yes, Ryan?"

"Do you have a few minutes to meet with me? I know our next one-on-one isn't until Friday, but there's something I wanted to discuss."

"Sure, Ryan. Let's head back to my office." Tony pulled the strap to his bag over his head, and we both headed for the hallway. "How's physical therapy coming?"

The steady click of Tony's designer shoes created a comforting rhythm to our pace.

"Good. Everything above the waist is working great. We'll be attempting my first steps in the next couple of days."

"That's great. It's going to get tougher as you get closer to the end, but as long as you keep a positive attitude, you should be fine."

We rounded a corner, and the clicks from his shoes disappeared on the carpeted hallway where all of the offices were located. I wheeled into Tony's office and stationed myself near the discussion couch. Tony placed his bag next to his desk and sat down in the chair across from me.

"Now, what is it you wanted to discuss?"

"Well, in general, I think the migration has gone well. My only real hang-up is the strange dreams I've been having. When I wake up, I can recall a very visceral, very real experience that took place in the dream, but none of the imagery feels familiar to me. It's almost like I'm seeing through the eyes of someone el—"

"Seeing through someone else's eyes?"

"Yes."

He let loose the slightest grimace, making me question the dreams even more. "Is this type of thing common, Tony?"

"Strange dreams are a normal part of the procedure. And when you're awake, you technically *are* seeing through someone else's eyes—your host's. But to feel that way when you dream, and to think of it as real…while it's a bit concerning, it's not entirely unheard of."

Fear grew in me as Tony spoke.

"So what do we do?"

He looked away, like he was instantly lost in thought.

"Tony?"

Shifting in his chair, he turned back and looked me dead in the eyes. "Ryan, what I'm about to tell you—ask of you—it's technically not part of the process. It's also a little unorthodox. But hear me out."

His brief pause had me on the edge of my wheelchair.

"We normally say that it's fine to discuss any aspect of your migration you want: the mental aspect, the physical toll, the emotions, and so on. Hell, we tell you to journal everything that comes to mind because it helps your new brain get used to your way of thinking. And with all of that, I think you have done a great job to this point."

He cleared his throat.

"However, based on your dreams, I think we need to take a different approach through the final stages of your migration. I want to encourage— No, I highly recommend that you do your best to ignore your strange dreams. I know that may be difficult given how real they seem to you, but as we discussed, your mind is trying to reprocess all of your thoughts and memories, and they can get scrambled a bit in the beginning, before your mind has had a chance to properly put things back together. You're experiencing a conglomeration of movies you've seen, books you read, games you've played, etcetera. I've heard of a few cases like yours, and if you're not careful, the dreams can consume you."

"What do you mean?"

"I'm not trying to stop you from expressing yourself. I'm merely saying that we should try a different approach, and it doesn't have to be permanent. We have three sessions remaining. How about we discuss everything except the dreams for the next two, and if you think it's not helping, we can come up with a plan in our last meeting to get you what you need. Does that seem fair?"

"What about my journal? Can I try to write about the dreams there?"

"Again, I suggest that you just let the dreams come and go as they will and don't dwell on them. Journaling about them won't make that possible."

Tony's advice didn't sit well with me since I was never the type to ignore something and hope it went away. His comments really did go against everything I had been told. On top of that, writing and talking about the dreams felt like the right thing to do. The past few nights, I had anxiety trying to fall asleep because I had a feeling the next dream was coming my way. And each morning, I felt disappointment when I tried to jot down details only to realize that I couldn't remember much of them. In that sense, thinking about letting the dreams go actually did bring me some relief. In that sense, maybe Tony was right. Maybe focusing too hard on the dreams was dangerous, and letting them go would bring me peace. Still, I needed to know more about the dreams before I could put them to rest.

"Answer me this. Why do I get the feeling like the dreams are foreign and yet so familiar to me at the same time? I mean, I know my brain is still mush right now, and I've got a ways to go, but the dreams almost seem like old memories…old memories that I am experiencing for the first time, as strange as that sounds. Like someone else's memories came with mine during the migration. From one dream, I can even faintly recall smells."

Tony nodded as I wrapped up, obviously anxious to get in his next words.

"It just seems like your mind is taking longer to fully reprocess than others. Like I said, it's not unheard of, but it can be problematic if we're not careful. That's why I recommend going against the book and letting the dreams pass. I've seen some great results in the few cases I've seen. Full disclosure, I'm completing my proposal to conduct a voluntary study on this exact topic, but I'm not quite ready yet. I need to make sure everything is right before bringing it to the migration board."

"So, there's no way that something weird happened during the migration? They didn't stick someone else's mind in here with me, did they?"

Tony's optimistic expression broke. "Look, you've gone through the process. You know how it works. We migrated your mind into the empty vessel you're currently in. There's been no precedent for migrating multiple minds into one host. That said, as you know, no migration is perfect. How a migrator's mind gets reprocessed in its new host is guesswork at best. Yours just happens to involve some oddities causing your dreams. Fortunately, all other signs are that your migration was an absolute success, and I believe that's what you should be focusing on. Not the one little thing that seems off."

Tony was right. I had always worried too much about everything in life. It was strangely refreshing that a familiar trait of mine came over in the migration, even if it was annoying. So maybe for once in my life, I could just let something go. Maybe for once in my life, I could relax.

"They just seem so real." The statement fell out of my mouth as I tried to let the thoughts go.

A genuine smile came across Tony's face. "What's real, Ryan, is that in a couple of weeks, you're going to literally walk out of this place a completely new person. Now I suggest you go get some rest after the group discussion and what we've talked about here. If you have any other questions, send me a message from your bedside terminal or drop on by."

With a deep breath, I decided that I would try Tony's approach. I was going to try to let the dreams come and go.

"Thanks, Tony. I've been so overwhelmed by the whole process that I've actually thought very little about my legs, and I should be bursting with excitement since I'll be walking soon. I'll try to ignore the dreams and see how it goes." I engaged my wheelchair and approached the door.

"Good luck with everything, Ryan. Oh, and do you mind closing my door on the way out?"

"Sure thing."

As I closed the door, I was startled when a woman's voice popped into my head.

What the hell is wrong with you? He's lying!

CHAPTER 9

IN SICKNESS AND IN HEALTH

"**W**HAT THE HELL IS WRONG with you? He's lying!" Sarah's contempt was palpable.

"You know we can't pay the bills if I don't work. We need this, Sarah."

She stared over her glasses at me.

While I never got into the details about what I did, Sarah knew I worked for the Padre, and his reputation wasn't exactly a secret. She was against the idea from the beginning, so I'd had to tell her I would quit the job when we got back on our feet to get her to even begrudgingly sign off on it.

"Charlie, you shouldn't be working for that guy at all. Now you're talking about a promotion?"

"It pays a hell of a lot better than all the other jobs. Hell, with the promotion, it'll probably pay me as much as my last two jobs combined! And the Padre has never lied to me before."

"You know the bad guys they talk about in the comic books? That's the type of guy the Padre is. This so-called promotion is not an opportunity. It's probably a trap to lure you deeper into his organization. I've asked you this before: What happens when you get yourself killed or go to jail and the money stops rolling in? What then?"

After the last job, it was difficult to argue with Sarah on any kind of moral ground.

"Look, we need the cash from the next few jobs. Then maybe I can talk with the Padre about getting out."

"Do you really think he's just going to let you walk away? After all the money he's thrown at you? Haven't you *seen* things? Haven't you had to *do* things?" She shook her head and waved her hand in my face. "You know what? I don't want to know. The less I know, the better. I just want you to be done, and I think talking to him about is a mistake. You should just stop showing up."

I shrugged. "I hardly know anything about what the Padre does, Sarah. Right now, I'm just a glorified driver and bodyguard. That's it. But to your other point, things will definitely go south quick if I just stop showing up. That's not something you do to the Padre."

Other than seeing the product on the last job, it wasn't that far from the truth. Ditching the Padre without some kind of explanation was not an option.

Sarah glared at me for a moment and then broke into a coughing fit. I reached for her, but she forcibly pulled away. Shoving her hand into her pants pocket, she retrieved her inhaler and forced it into her mouth, squeezed hard, and inhaled deeply. Gasping for air, she took another hit. With deep, wheezing breaths, she finally fell into my arms and cried. I had had experience with her condition before we met, but that didn't make it any easier to see my wife as sick as she was. It made it harder.

"Sarah, I wish I could make this all go away, but you remember what the doctors said at the last checkup. They were hopeful for us. I'm hopeful."

She gathered herself and sat up. "Charlie, right now, my top priority should be keeping me and the kids alive and healthy. Instead, I'm worrying each night what shape you'll be in when you get home. Or if you'll be coming home at all."

"Sarah, you have to—" I jolted back as a flying minidrone buzzed past my ear. I quickly regained focus as it turn back toward me and hovered into position next to Sarah's head. Its tiny lens zoomed in on my face. "Lucy! How many times do I have to tell you not to fly that damn thing near my head!"

Sighing, I walked toward the hallway and stopped at the first door on the left.

Like a giant bumblebee in the summer, the drone followed behind annoyingly close. Its buzz was right in my ear as I tapped on her door.

"Can I come in?"

A faint voice replied, "Are you and Mom getting a divorce?"

"What? No! Lucy, I'm coming in."

I opened the door and stepped in. Every time I entered that room, I hoped to see something new, different, and better. But every time—every goddamned time—it was my baby girl just lying there, bedridden, with machines breathing for her. The drone buzzed past me to its charging pad, and I took the seat next to her bed. I had sat in that seat countless times for countless hours, and when Lucy slept, had quietly cried countless tears. But that time, I didn't say a word for several moments and just watched Lucy as she fiddled with the controller of the drone. Like all kids, she was amazing. But she was my oldest, so there would always be a special place for her in my heart.

"Lucy, I'm sorry you heard us yelling. I'm sorry I yelled at you. Your mother and I are just trying to figure out the best way to keep the house together while I'm working these weird hours. Like we talked about before, sometimes adults get stressed out and we yell, but your mother and I are very happy. We love each other, or else we wouldn't care enough to fight. We love you."

"Promise?"

"I promise."

"Dad, you know, I only fly Drony because I can't get up and see what's going on like I used to."

"I know, sweetie. Just try to keep it away from Daddy's ears because I can get jumpy. Now, how are you feeling today, Princess?"

"Some pain from yesterday's treatment, but nothing I can't handle. I'm strong. I can take it. Right, Dad?"

"You're damn right. Hopefully, the doctors get you better soon so you don't have to be strong so often. Once you get better, we're going to take you camping like we used to do when you were little. How's that sound?"

"That's sounds great, Dad. I can't wait."

I looked at the monitor next to her bed and saw similar numbers as I had the last week or so. They weren't great, but I had seen worse. I tapped the button to administer her medicines, then leaned in and kissed her forehead.

"I will check on you later, honey. Get some rest. I love you."

"Love you too, Daddy."

I got up, walked back to the hallway, and gently pulled the door shut behind me. I went back out to the living room, but Sarah had already gone to bed. Back to the hallway, I walked past Lucy's room and stopped at the last door on the left.

It took everything I had not to completely lose it as I opened that door. There was my little boy, and his monitor wasn't nearly as optimistic as Lucy's. I sat down next to him and felt his face. It was cold, but that was normal. The nurse who visited the other day said Joey was doing okay. I couldn't help but wonder if she was just trying to make us feel better. I wouldn't be surprised if he was just clinging to life, and the machines were doing most of the work. He hadn't woken up in almost two weeks, and it didn't seem like that would change anytime soon. I never felt good after seeing my sick kids, but something about that night really moved me.

I had to agree with Sarah. The job paid great, but I wasn't spending any time with my family in their time of need. They weren't getting any better, so maybe it was time to just rip the Band-Aid off and have a conversation with the Padre. It wouldn't be easy, and he might not like it. But it was probably—no, it was definitely the right thing to do.

I left Joey with a couple of tears running down my face, but otherwise kept my composure. I had cried enough, and it never did any good anyway. I just wished there was something more I could do, but the longer they were ill, the more powerless I felt.

Walking into our room, I found Sarah on our bed doing a breathing treatment. I sat down beside her and rubbed her back. She resisted a little but not enough to signal that I should stop.

She put away the treatment machine as she spoke. "This isn't the first time in our relationship that I have had to wonder each night whether you'd be coming home or not. When you were in Pakistan, not a day passed that I didn't pray you were okay. I just thought that once you got discharged, we were past that. We have kids now. Sick kids! I'm sick! I know these treatments and medicines are expensive, but if we lost you, none of it would matter anymore."

"I think you're right. I've been so preoccupied with bringing in money that I've neglected the kids and you. I have one more job that I already committed to. After tomorrow night, I'm done and we'll live off of our savings until I land something legit."

A scowl seized her face, and she fired back at me. "Fine. But that's another night your ass can sleep on the couch. Every minute I'm close to you is another minute it hurts thinking about losing you. Now I need to get some rest."

Her words stabbed me in the heart, but I knew she was protecting herself. Still, I was pissed things had gotten as far as they had and I couldn't fix them fast enough. Leaving the room, I skulked down the hall, glancing at my kids' doors as I made my way out to the living room. Needing to blow off steam, I headed for the fridge and grabbed a bottle of Beta Queen, my favorite beer. Cracking off the cap, I headed out to the balcony to catch the cool breeze. I plopped down on the old lawn chair and reached into my shirt pocket for the pack of menthols. Shaking the pack until I found a winner, I retrieved it with my mouth. After snapping my Zippo alight and puffing hard on the cigarette, I sloppily slouched into the chair.

"Ahhhhhhhhhhhh!"

In an instant, the exhale made the world livable again.

The subtle buzz of the city crept into my ears, and that was always calming. The white noise from the cars, occasional horn honking, and even the sirens from emergency vehicles had become a normal and expected din that reminded me I was home. As I tried to relax, my mind wandered back to high school and meeting Sarah.

It was beginning of freshman year at Frantz High where Sarah and I had seventh period together, Spanish One. With brains to match her beauty, she was top of the class and the head sophomore cheerleader. It was all the motivation I needed to ditch the school band I had been in all summer and try out for every sport. It always seemed a little creepy in retrospect, but at least I had good intentions, and with my home life, I needed every excuse to get out of the house. Fortunately, I turned out to be quite the athlete. Halfway through the football season, I was promoted to junior varsity, and able to score touchdowns against the bigger, older kids. On a particularly amazing play where I broke three tackles for a score, I ran over to Sarah and gave her the ball. I didn't know who was more embarrassed at the time: her when I did it, or me when I was penalized for delay of game for giving away the game ball.

Regardless, it got her attention in a big way, and she approached me after the game.

"Hey!"

Shocked she had acknowledged my existence, I almost didn't respond. "Uh, yeah?"

"You think you're hot shit, but you're just a little boy with a big head. You ever try a stunt like that again, and I'll have my boyfriend beat your ass."

Somehow I knew she was just trying to save face with her friends more than scold me. Sure enough, the next school day, I was emptying my cafeteria tray when she appeared out of nowhere.

People called me by my last name back then, and Sarah let it ring with ire in her voice. "Reno!"

"What now? Didn't you chew me out enough last night?"

She pointed at my chest but never broke eye contact with me. "You got some nerve, embarrassing me in front of the whole school like that."

Without hesitation, I told her the truth. "I just wanted you to know how I felt about you since the first time I laid eyes on you."

She wasn't amused, as was apparent by her eye roll. "Is that some kind of cheap pickup line that you use on all the girls?"

"No, just you. I mean. It's not cheap. It's the truth." Then the dumbest grin stretched across her face.

"Well, then, if you're so into me, kiss me in that corner over there."

Taken by her forwardness, something didn't add up. "Won't your boyfriend mind?"

I didn't think it was possible, but her grin got even dumber. "You didn't let the defense stop you last night, so why would you let a boyfriend who may or may not exist get in the way?"

Anyone could have figured out how that turned out. We both got suspended for making out in the hallway and they moved us to separate Spanish classes. To my dismay, we never did have another class together. Regardless, from that day on, we were inseparable. High school went by in a flash, and she was ready to graduate. We had a great plan that she would choose a college where I could get a scholarship to play ball. She went to a state school, so I thought my grades wouldn't be such a big deal. And that was when the simpler times ended.

I fell behind in many classes, in spite of all the hard work I put in. I couldn't figure out why since I was otherwise a fairly smart person. It wasn't until the middle of senior year, when one of the guidance counselors suggested on a whim that I take a random test, and I discovered that I had a mild form of dyslexia. But the other thing I didn't anticipate was just how depressed I would get my senior year without Sarah. And jealous. I was certain she would find some college dude who was better than me, even though she assured me she never would. I still tried to work my tail off so I could get into her school, and was hopeful all the way up to my final report card.

GPA of 1.9.

It was enough to graduate, but exactly .6 points off from being eligible for even the university's remediation program for athletes. It was exactly .1 point from being eligible to play for a junior college. *Crushed* didn't even begin to describe how I felt the first time I looked at the paper. That was quickly followed by anger. But shortly after, I realized I had to make a decision that would be the best for me and Sarah, and so I did. I waited until the summer when we were together to break the news to her about my grades. She had the same emotional wave as I did, miserably disappointed at first and then pissed off at me for not trying hard enough. She even told me that I had screwed up everything. But she quickly apologized and said we would figure it out. Then I told her how I had figured it out for us, and she wasn't very happy.

"The marines? Are you crazy?"

"Sarah, I've been doing some soul-searching. Clearly, books aren't for me, and there's no way I'm staying at home even a month after graduation. The marines will keep me in shape, and I'll learn a lot of skills. After four years, I can come home and land a decent job. Lots of places hire veterans. And then we can be together."

"So that's it? It's going to be all roses and sunshine in the marines? Charlie, you can get yourself killed! There were people all over my campus protesting our involvement in the India/Pakistan conflict, and yet troops keep getting sent over."

"Those kids are just scared of fighting for something bigger than themselves."

Her patented scowl conveyed her disagreement even before she responded, "I don't know who you're quoting, Charlie, but those young adults are fighting for peace. That's pretty big."

I couldn't help but feel inadequate. "Look, I know you have all this knowledge and experience since you've been to college for a year, but it didn't work out for me. That doesn't mean it can't work out for us. This is the best I got."

"I really wish you would have talked to me before enlisting, but I guess it's too late now. If there's anything I've learned in the last year of being apart, it's that I know I want to be with you. Forever. But I need you to promise me one thing."

"Yes?"

"Don't let the marines—don't let *war* change you. I fell in love with that big-headed, little boy who was brave enough to break the rules to bring me a football. I need that same kid to bring himself back home to me in one piece when he's done serving."

"I'm counting on it. I promise."

That summer, we were inseparable, possibly to a fault. Then she drove me to the bus stop where I'd be picked up for boot camp.

As we lined up next to all of the other couples who were saying goodbye to each other, she leaned in. "Charlie, you know I love you, right?"

"Uh, yes."

"And you love me, too, right?"

"Of course!"

"Good. You're going to be a father."

Her words hit me like a right hook from a heavyweight, and in that moment, I wanted to ditch the marines altogether to take care of her.

"Holy shit! I mean, uh, really? Oh. Oh wow! But I'm leaving, and I won't be able to…"

She shook her head and then nodded. "I knew once the test came back positive what it meant for us, for me. I can handle it."

"What are you going to do about school?"

"I'm looking at Johnson College. My credits should transfer, and they've got a decent chemistry program."

"You're coming home? Dammit! One of the main reasons I enlisted was to make something of myself while you were away, and now it's my fault you won't get to graduate from a university!"

"Don't worry, Charlie. I got this. It's why I waited until now to tell you. You just focus on deploying and coming back alive to help me raise our daughter. By the way, I like the name Lucille. What do you think?"

Overwhelmed, I just nodded and took Sarah in my arms, and I held her so close and so tight. Tears flowed from both of us while in the distance, I heard the rumble of the bus.

"Ten-hut! All recruits, line up for roll call!"

With one last hug and kiss, I said goodbye to Sarah and our little peanut and headed for the bus line. Even after all my preparation, dread was growing deep within me. It wasn't until I was already on the bus and it pulled off that I realized I wasn't scared of boot camp, deploying, or war. The thing that terrified me the most was becoming a father, and as awful as it sounded in my head, part of me never wanted to come home to see what kind of failure I would be.

My reminiscing on the balcony was suddenly interrupted by the buzz of my netphone. Reading the message, a cold feeling overcame me at what it said.

THE JOB'S BEEN MOVED UP TO TONIGHT. PREP THE CAR AND PICK UP THE PACKAGE AT LOCATION X.

"Shit!"

I put my smoke out on the ledge, chugged the beer and tossed it in the bin, then dashed inside. I grabbed my coat off the dining room chair and my keys and wallet from the kitchen counter. I thought I would have at least another day to figure out how I was going to break it to the Padre that I needed to quit, but it looked like I was going to have to wing it when I saw him. The whole thing didn't sit well with me. The invincibility I felt running jobs with him in the past was quickly fading, and in its place was a growing fear of what might happen.

"You really think he's just going to let you walk away?" Sarah's words echoed in my head as I walked through the front door.

The door closed behind me, and I made a vow to myself.

"No matter what, I'm going to walk!"

CHAPTER 10
ONE STEP FORWARD

"**N**O MATTER WHAT, I'M GOING to walk!"

I had said those words to my mom hundreds of times when I was younger and never understood just how upset it made her.

She had scowled and given me a somewhat canned response each time. "Honey, you were just born with different abilities. You're fine the way you are."

But then the tears had followed. As strong as she had been, she'd cried. Not in front of me, but I'd known she had been doing it—in the kitchen, in the bathroom, in the basement. Somehow that hadn't stopped me from saying it for a couple more years.

At school, the other kids played kickball, tag, and soccer. While I had gotten good in a wheelchair, I hadn't been able to compete with their speed and agility. The only other kids in wheelchairs were mentally challenged on top of being unable to walk. I had felt for them, but it was difficult for me to cope, not really fitting in with any of the groups at school.

And so I'd kept telling my mom that someday I would walk. And she'd kept crying.

Things got really bad once Dad left, and then, I'd known I had to stop saying that. I'd known I couldn't keep telling her something that wasn't in the cards. I couldn't keep telling her something for which she felt responsible, and keep making her cry. She'd had enough on her plate, taking care of me. That was why her reaction had been so shocking when, years later, I told her that I was saving for a mind migration.

"Mom, I'm going to get legs. I'm going to walk."

"Oh, honey, you know we've talked about this before."

"No, Mom, did you see the news? They successfully migrated a person's mind into another person's body. He was in a motorcycle accident and couldn't walk like me. After the operation, he can walk in his new body. His name is Cameron Walsh."

"Ryan, those types of procedures cost a lot of credits, and I'm sure they're very dangerous."

"Mom, it's very dangerous not being able to walk. Look how hard you have had to work just keep it all together for us. If I got a new body with legs, I could finally take care of myself. I could even take care of you!"

"That's sweet, but I don't want you going and getting your hopes up."

"Mom, remember when you said I could do everything I needed to? Remember?"

"Yes."

"Well, I need to do this. Even if I have to save up for my whole life, I need to do this for me, and I need to do this for you. I want to walk, and I'm pretty sure this is the only real way. I promise you that, one day, I'll be in a body that can walk."

Ten years later, I was keeping that promise.

"That's it, Ryan. Carefully lift yourself out of the chair using the two balance beams."

The day had finally come where I could attempt the first steps of my life. I was more than a nervous wreck, but considering how well I was functioning otherwise, I was somehow also fairly confident. The legs and feet were the last to function even for normal migrators because your new brain had enough trouble reprocessing memories and thoughts and keeping vital organs functioning. Sending messages all the way down to your legs and feet wasn't as high a priority, so it just took time. On top of that, the area of my original brain that would have been responsible for walking had never needed to develop, so my mind migrated with a stunted ability to tap into that part of my new brain.

I had gone through the battery of exercises to strengthen the connections between my brain and my lower half. But engaging everything to take actual steps was another task in and of itself. I remembered the woman who had fallen when I was zooming through the hallway on my way to the migration. Being in that same position, I realized that the hardest part was mentally putting forth the effort. The ground was padded, and to some extent, they didn't mind you falling if it helped you on your path to walking again.

I gripped the balance beams hard, and with as much strength as I could muster from my core, quads, and hips, I thrusted into the erect position. I shook a bit, and my weight was heavy on my arms, but then my joints and bones settled into the gravity pulling me down, and the result was clear.

"I'm doing it! I'm standing!"

"Good job, Ryan! Now, focus! Lead with your hands and take a step."

With both arms, I reached out as far as I could on the beam and leaned slightly to the left to force my bodyweight from both feet to just the left. I engaged my abs and hips again, but to simply lift my right foot off of the ground—first the heel, then the ball of my foot, and then the toes. Once it was free from the ground, time slowed down. I could feel every inch of movement. I could feel my toe pointing up to allow my heel to plant solidly on the floor, and I was about to make contact with the floor and complete my very first step. Suddenly, a tingling sensation shot from my toe to my brain, and it surprised me enough to make me lose my balance.

"Ryan, hold onto the beams!"

But it was too late. I was falling.

Thud!

"Ow!"

The technicians swooped in and helped me back up to the support beams. I repeated the process five or six times with each attempt ending up on the floor one way or another. Every time, the shock came from my toe and ended up in my brain.

"Your mind is struggling to process the steps," a voice expounded from across the room.

"What?"

"If you had developed the ability to walk even at an early age and then lost that ability, you wouldn't notice that feeling when you're about to press your foot against the ground." Dr. Little clarified.

"So what does it mean? How can someone like me learn to walk?"

"You'll need to get used to it, Ryan. A foreign mind is sending new signals to the feet of your host. The body doesn't exactly know how to process these, and certainly isn't efficient with the information. Some of it fizzles as it makes its way to your M1. Sorry, your primary motor cortex. Also, some of the information even gets scrambled."

She looked around for a moment.

"Picture the path from your brain to your toe as a two-lane highway. After all of the prep work you've done, your mind is good at telling your brain to send signals to your toes. Those seem to be just fine. But it's the return trip where the highway is under construction. The only way to smooth out the path is to keep sending signals over it. So, if you can fight through the sensation, you can force the connections to be made more effectively and consistently each and every time. Give it another few tries, but instead of being apprehensive to the tingling feeling, anticipate it and embrace it. Force your body, brain, and mind to get on the same page."

"I can do that."

I grabbed the beams tightly again. Taking a deep breath, I closed my eyes to filter out all distractions. I picked my right leg up and moved it through the air. Planting my heel on the ground, I could feel the limpness shoot through my body all the way to my brain.

"I can feel the sensation."

"Come on, Ryan, you can get through it," a tech encouraged me.

The numbness was getting stronger, but I was able to place more weight on my foot as I rolled to the ball of it.

"That's it, Ryan. You're almost there! And...and...and..."

Toes...planted!

"I took the step. I took my very first step ever! Oh my god! I did it!" I laughed hysterically as tears began to run down my face.

"Okay, Ryan. You're doing great. Try to take the next step."

"I can do that!"

Transferring all my weight to my right foot, I lifted my left leg slowly. I went to place my left heel onto the padded floor and could feel the moment of initial impact like before. But something was a bit off. When I tried to move weight onto that ankle, a new sensation filled my mind. It reminded me of one of my dreams where that ankle had been injured. It felt painful for just a second, and then at that moment, both my legs became possessed.

"Ryan?"

I fully planted my left foot.

Then my right.

Then my left.

Then my right.

Dr. Little was astounded. "Oh my god, Ryan. What has gotten into you?"

"I have no idea, but this is amazing!"

"But be careful as you come to the end of the balance—"

I walked past the end of the beams and onto the recovery room floor. I was still walking! The technicians were speechless while they tried to keep up with me.

Left!

Right!

Left!

Right!

Then another urge took hold of me. "I've always wanted to jump."

"Ryan, no!"

But again, Dr. Little was too late. I began jumping like a fool.

Up!

Down!

Up!

Down!

"Ronnie and Suzie, can you please help Ryan back to the balance beams before he hurts himself?"

The technicians came toward me, but I decided it was time for my first game of tag.

"You can't catch me!"

They were definitely not ready for the moves I was putting on them. "What's a matter? Too slow?"

"Dammit, Ryan, you're going to hurt yourself. Now stop it!"

Just as the fun was reaching a pinnacle, a voice popped into my head. *Who the hell is Ryan?*

Instantly, my legs weakened and gave out. Luckily, I was able to catch myself on the padded floor without much incident. Ronnie and Suzie were close to follow, and they helped me back to my wheelchair.

"That's enough for today, Ryan. Let's get you back to your room to rest."

The technicians wheeled me through the hallway, and Dr. Little followed.

Still excited, I tried to explain what happened. "It was the strangest thing. At first, I couldn't walk without falling. Then I could do anything I wanted with my legs—walk, jump, run. Then my legs felt like Jell-O again. Have you ever seen anything like that before?"

Dr. Little was quick to respond. "No. Nothing to that extent. We've had quick learners, but you walked without the slightest limp or stutter in your step. You jumped on day one. You were dodging physically fit techs. I'll need to look at the mind migration historical journals, but that seems like a first to me."

"What could cause something like that? What would make me special?" I was seriously at a loss.

"My hypothesis is that you experienced a rapid neural expansion. Your stunted mind must have figured out a way to harness your now functional M1. It sent a flood of information that your brain processed like autopilot."

"Okay." I only sort of followed her logic.

"To that end, the M1 did its best to process the information as it came through. It did an exceptional job for thirty seconds or so, but then it appears that the information being sent across your brain was interrupted or stopped."

"Okay, so what does that mean?"

"Think of your primary motor cortex as a fire. In fully functional adults, it burns bigger and hotter the more activity they do, playing basketball or going for a jog. The fire roars because a lot of information is being processed through it. Move the left leg here. Move the right arm there. Twist your torso. All of it happening in milliseconds. When they stop those activities, the fire dies down and resumes a normal burn."

It was starting to make sense, so I nodded for her to continue.

"Well, your M1 had only handled things from your waist up your whole life. It certainly didn't have to manage strenuous activities. However, the exercising you attempted today acted as a catalyst. Like lighter fluid squirted onto a camp fire, it burned bright and hot for several seconds, but once the fuel—or in this case, the information—ceased, you reverted back to your post-migration state of just learning to walk. You collapsed."

"What would cause the information surge? Why did it stop?"

"My guess is that your will to walk is strong, and the pre-migration work you did helped to store up your mind's best guess at walking. Turns out your mind's best guess at walking was spot on. That said, you clearly need more time for a more consistent experience. We'll continue with the sessions to eventually sync everything up for the long run."

Once in my room, I asked to try standing up and sitting on my bed. The technicians helped me just a little, but I was able to do the rest.

"See, I'm getting the hang of this."

Ronnie and Suzie snickered as they left the room.

"Wow, what a day. My very first steps. My very first jumps! And tag!" But then I was reminded of the voice that preceded my collapse. *Who the hell is Ryan?*

Whose voice was that? More importantly, why was I hearing voices at all? It was never mentioned as part of the process, and the voices seemed to start right after I spoke with Tony and agreed to ignore the dreams.

Dreams.

And now voices.

I had successfully ignored the dreams for days, but I felt like it was finally time to look at my journal app to see if any of it made sense.

JOURNAL ENTRY #1

The first bits of consciousness that I can recall post-migration are a compilation of emotions and imagery that seemed foreign to me. If it was a dream, it felt awfully real.

There was a blinding light. I awoke to being outside. I had to run. I felt like I had done something bad, but was pretty sure really bad people were after me. Then I was manually driving. Driving fast. Then I was in an ambulance. Did I get into an accident? That would make sense since I didn't know how to manually drive.

JOURNAL ENTRY #2

I had another weird dream.

I was working. I was manually driving again. The air smelled gross. Was I smoking? A large abandoned building. Maybe a factory? When I went inside, it smelled gross. Something bad might happen in there.

JOURNAL ENTRY #3

I was in the scary building. I was with someone who I both trusted and feared. A giant man. Who was he? We were meeting some other men. A transaction? An exchange? Of what? Maybe I don't want to know, but I felt like I already did. It scared me.

I never wrote another entry because Tony said I should give it a rest. But after rereading what I had wrote, a named popped into my head. *Charlie.*

Why did I suddenly think of that name? Who was he? Was he the man in my dream? I felt like Tony was holding something back, and my mind began to wander. I thought about what could have happened to me during my migration. Maybe they got the wires crossed when they migrated my mind! Maybe they *did* migrate someone else's mind along with mine! Who knows what the hell it could be? I had to go to Tony and ask him point-blank what he knew about my situation.

I awkwardly lifted myself from the bed and down into my wheelchair and rolled myself as fast as I could around corners and past others in the hallways. I finally made it to Tony's office and stormed in while he was with another patient.

"What do you know about my dreams?! What do you know about Charlie?!"

"Ryan, calm down. We're not scheduled to meet for a couple days. I'll need you to come back then."

"No, dammit. We need to talk right now!"

"Kate, I'm sorry. Could you please excuse us? Maybe we can pick this up at lunchtime. I will let you know."

"Sure, Tony." Kate wheeled around me and gave me the stink eye on her way out.

I slammed the door behind her.

"Now, Ryan, what are you going on about?"

"I'm still having strange dreams, and they're getting worse. I'm seeing through the eyes of someone else. Living his life. And today, in physical therapy, I took my first steps. Hell, I walked a lot of steps, and I jumped, and even ran around the technicians. But then a voice popped in my head, and it said, 'Who the hell is Ryan?' Now, what the hell do you make of *that*? Is someone else in my brain with me?!"

Tony sighed. "Ryan. Listen to yourself."

"What, dammit?"

"You're questioning your identity. You're asking about someone named Charlie. Voices, Ryan?"

"What are you getting at?"

"Look, I think it's great that you had a productive—very productive—session of PT. And you should be happy about that. Instead, you're in here yelling and getting emotional. You're being blinded by the anomalies of your migration rather than the successes. This is exactly what we talked about before!"

"Anomalies? These are more than just anomalies. Hell, they seem like more than just dreams, too. And they're affecting me even when I try to ignore them. Now, if you have any idea what's going on, you need to tell me!"

"Okay, Ryan. Just calm down." Tony looked around, then lowered his voice. "There was something that I didn't mention before. I thought you were already scared enough, and I didn't want to make that worse."

"Just tell me already!"

"Have you heard about the first failed mind migration with a human?"

"Yes, everyone has heard the stories. Amanda Robinson, right?"

"Yes, but I'm sure a lot of what you heard was embellished from years of passing the story on. People made up a lot of things, like there was trouble during the freezing process or that there was a computer glitch."

"Yeah, something like that."

"Well, I worked with the people on that project. In fact, there were no issues during the migration. By all accounts, it was a success. Her mind was fully transferred into a new, fully functional brain. She even seemed to make it out of what we now call the 'catch-22 period' and was able to speak about it afterward. It wasn't long after that, that she complained of having bad dreams…terrible dreams. Then she complained of voices. Voices that made her question her identity. Just like you, she thought there was another mind in her brain taking over."

"Well, what was it?"

"The theory was that her mind wasn't sufficiently prepped to handle the rigors of migration. Back then, there wasn't nearly as much pre- and post-migration therapy like we have had for the last ten years. Like the support we've been giving you." Tony inhaled and looked out the window. "Eventually, Amanda was consumed by the idea that she was a different person. She began calling herself 'Jessica.' Jessica had no idea who Amanda was or what a mind migration was."

The more Tony talked, the more my anger turned into fear.

"The theory was never proven, but it seems pretty sound. Even minds in their native brains can experience multiple personality disorders, or worse, schizophrenia. Eventually, Amanda's host brain had a meltdown and she never recovered. She developed full-blown dementia and remained in a vegetative state for the rest of her life."

"Tony, am I going crazy? Am I going to be like Amanda?"

"I highly doubt it. I've had a few migrators cross my path with similar symptoms. You seem keenly aware of the fact that the dreams are a danger to your overall recovery. That's a great sign. But I can't stress this to you enough, Ryan, you just need to give your mind time to reprocess everything. You need to give the dreams, thoughts, and memories a chance to be filed away where they belong. Otherwise..." He flinched and looked away.

"Otherwise, what?"

He turned back to me. "They could become canon to your mind, Ryan. A sort of pseudo reality for you. And if that happens, it could be a really bad thing. So, we really need to refocus your mind sooner rather than later. Remember to stay positive!"

While it wasn't the answer I was looking for, it made sense to me. Almost instantaneously, I began to feel some relief.

"Okay, Tony. You're saying I should stay the course? I should just let the dreams come and go?"

"Yes, please. And I'm also going to increase your medication by twenty percent. I think that will help you relax some more."

"Thanks. And, Tony?"

"Yes?"

"Sorry for barging into your office."

"You know what, Ryan? Don't even worry about it. That's why we're here. That said, you may want to apologize to Kate for interrupting her session."

"Will do. Thanks." I closed Tony's door behind me.

Just as my eyes adjusted to the bright light of the hallway, the voice from before responded in my head.

I don't care what he says. I want this to be over.

CHAPTER 11
TOO WEAK NOTICE

"I DON'T CARE WHAT HE SAYS. I want this to be over."

I was deep in thought as I removed the license plate from the big black Cadillac. For obvious reasons, every job was completed using a different car and every car had to be prepped to make sure it couldn't be traced back to anyone important. The Padre preferred that we handle the prepping ourselves, instead of the vendor, just to make sure nothing was missed. He also preferred big, old, black Cadillacs because they reminded him of the good ol' days.

I finished swapping out the license plate, then filed down the VINs. Next, I installed the untraceable net connector as well as a police monitor and a decoy switch on the vehicle's stock GPS. When the car was running, it would relay coordinates from an identical car across town. That car wasn't doing anything particularly interesting to the gang in blue. Finally, I put my trusty 9mm into the glove compartment and slammed it shut.

Starting the car, I performed the standard diagnostics on the mechanics and electronics of the car, including what I had installed. Moonlighting as a grease monkey in the marines had come in handy in a lot of ways, but it was especially useful when doing quick assessments on older cars. I popped the hood, and after a quick visual inspection, I was satisfied. I made my way back to the driver's seat to double-check the gauges and switches, and revved the engine hard a few times. Listening carefully for any signs of distress, everything seemed kosher to me, so I cut the engine.

I, on the other hand, was beginning to get anxious. Even if the job went off without a hitch, talking to the Padre about quitting made that particular night different. My nerves forced me to wrestle the pack of menthols from my shirt pocket. I blew into the opening for a better view.

Two left.

I thought I had better make them count since it was going to be a long and unpredictable night. The addictive itch made sure sweat was running down my brow, but I would live. I sent a message over the net to my contact, confirming the transportation was ready, and quietly waited for a reply.

As the minutes ticked by, I began thinking about what I would say to the Padre. I could have made something up about my health, and said I wasn't fit to do the job anymore. Then I thought I could tell him I wanted to go back into the military, so I needed to distance myself from our line of work. I was never a great liar, though, so I didn't feel great about either of those approaches.

The more I thought about it, the more I felt telling the truth was my only option. At least mostly the truth. I would tell him that things were bad at home and I needed to take care of my family. I was certain that would be enough for him to let me go. What I hoped he didn't care about was that I had seen the product—the highest-end product we offered. It was bound to happen given my proximity to it on jobs, so I couldn't imagine the Padre would care all that much. It made quitting that much more important to me, but it also made the fallout of quitting that much more of an unknown.

In thinking about the outcome of the night, I started to go down a really dark path when my netphone buzzed with the go-ahead signal. I started the car and put it in drive, clicked open the garage door, and slowly wheeled onto the main road while rolling the windows down. I loved the cool, muggy night since it gave me the slightest bit of relief from the stress of the job. The smell of the city quickly filled my nose, and I figured that it was as good a time as any to have one of the two smokes. I crammed my hand into my shirt pocket and grabbed one. Then, in one motion, I placed it in my mouth, lit it, and puffed hard several times.

"Ahhhhhhhhhhhh!" The sound escaped my mouth as I blew smoke out of the window, and so did quite a bit of fear.

The city was unusually dead that night, and I hoped that it would stay that way until the job was done. After about twenty minutes of driving, I pulled into an alleyway, pulled off to the side, and placed the car in park. Turning off the headlights, I pulled out my netphone and sent a message to my contact. Then I popped the trunk. After a brief moment, three dark figures appeared from the shadows and darted behind the car. The car rocked up and down as the thud of something heavy hit the trunk. The rocking continued after they slammed the trunk shut with a thud, and as fast as they had appeared, the figures were gone. I waited the standard five minutes and sent another message to my contact. Then I waited some more.

The Padre was a measured man, so I imagined he wouldn't put up much of a fight to me being done. He might even give me the old speech about my potential and say he's sad to see me go. Maybe he'd send me off with some hush money.

Ha! Who am I kidding?

He was probably going to be pissed and might even throw fit. And if that happened, I didn't have many options. I had a strong feeling that, to the Padre, the only thing worse than quitting would be cowardly backing out of quitting after the fact. He wouldn't respect me ever again, so there would be no turning back once I initiated the conversation.

Another message buzzed on my netphone with two sets of coordinates. The alley lit up as I turned on my lights, and I made my way back to the main street. The burning smell from my menthol filter reminded me to flick it out the window. I had about a thirty-minute drive to figure out how to bring up the topic to the Padre.

Should I do it before the job? Will that put him in a bad mood up front? Should I wait until after? Will he feel like I lied to him the whole night?

There was no easy answer to the question, so like I had done many times in my life, I would rely on my gut in the moment.

As I crossed the neighborhood line into the Padre's westside turf, I remembered that it was known for two things: the Padre's crew and feral dogs. At night, you couldn't drive a few blocks without seeing the glowing eyes of a grungy mutt or two trotting through a parkway or attacking someone dumb enough to walk the streets after sunset. Rumor had it that a rival gang dumped dozens of mistreated strays into the area to make it unsafe and, ultimately, make the Padre move. But a more likely explanation was that the dogs were attracted to all of the food scraps people were tossing out after public garbage pickup was discontinued in the area five years before. Either way, the Padre benefited from it. Since the neighborhood was such a mess, the police didn't bother patrolling it. In fact, in many ways, the feral dogs added to the Padre's mystique. No one had ever seen or heard of the dogs attacking the Padre. Instead, rumor was that the dogs were loyal to the Padre and he had trained them to attack on his command. I had even heard that he made bodies disappear by chopping them into small pieces and feeding them to the dogs, making them bloodthirsty. Occasionally, I would see a dog on the street with a large bone in its mouth, and it always made me wonder.

I turned onto Spruce Street and pulled up to the Padre's apartment building-turned-ghetto mansion. Then I tapped the message button on my netphone.

READY WHEN YOU ARE.

But something was stopping me from tapping the Send button after typing the message. My hand was paralyzed. I felt like I was sitting at a crossroad and clicking Send meant going in a direction. I wanted badly to be done, but actually making it happen did more than scare me. It was terrifying. I always felt invincible when running jobs with him, and that would all change the instant I asked to be done. In my head, I quickly ran through the permutations of how to quit without actually confronting him as Sarah had suggested. I could reach out to some old marine contacts who would be discrete in helping me and my family relocate. But the kids were far too sick to travel under regular circumstances, much less trying to secretly move.

No.

There was only one way forward. I tapped Send hard, then sighed. I actually felt a bit of relief as I sank into my seat and waited. I pulled the pack of smokes from my pocket and stared menacingly at my last menthol.

"Better save it for later."

The front door to the Padre's headquarters swung open, the doorway completely filled with his colossal silhouette. He lumbered his way to the back seat with briefcase in hand, opened the door, and plopped down. The shocks of the car cried under the stress of the Padre's mass, and the right side noticeably sank. Looking in the mirror, I watched him light up his

Cuban and blow smoke into the front seat, and I caught another glimpse of his dog skull ring. Then he grunted in discontent. He seemed stressed.

"Hey, boss! How are you?"

"Fine, Charlie. Are we on target?"

"Yes, sir. The net code is A5J3W1H6."

I engaged the transmission and began heading toward the exchange point. It was about a twenty-five-minute drive, so I thought it would be a good time to broach the topic of quitting.

"Hey, Padre."

Peering into the rearview, he was fiddling with his netphone, and I wasn't sure if he'd heard me. I gave him a few seconds but still no response.

"Hey, Pa—"

"What!"

He seemed unusually irritated, so I figured I had better ease into the discussion with some small talk.

"Is everything all right? The job got moved up with short notice."

"You know what? Everything is *not* all right, Charlie. I try to be a reasonable man. I try to be fair, considering. But I guess in this line of work, you can't expect honesty. You can't expect loyalty. You can't expect for a damn job to be scheduled and for that damn job to *stay* on schedule. It would be one thing if there were security concerns. But this is just a case of cold feet turning everyone's lives upside down. Well, we'll do this job, and then we'll be reining in our business partners to make sure this doesn't happen again!"

I was a bit taken aback by the tone in his voice. His anger seemed more reactive than usual, and while I knew he was stressed, it seemed like he was trying to hide something else. Either way, I wasn't going to pry.

"Oh. Got it, boss. Sounds like a good plan."

"Sorry, Charlie. There's a lot riding on this, and others don't seem to be taking it so seriously. It's not like buying a new shirt where a dozen stores have what you need. Our products take months and sometimes years to acquire!"

He went on as I momentarily forgot about quitting and remembered the product I saw during the Russian job. Slightly disgusted, I knew I had to bring up the topic of quitting.

"And to top it all off, this damn neighborhood is going to shit faster than I can keep it together. If I had my way, I'd run every one of the poor slobs out of this place."

"Sorry to hear all that, boss."

"No, Charlie. I'm sorry. How are you?"

"Not so good, boss. It's my family."

"Oh no. What's the matter?"

"Everyone's sick…well, everyone but me. Both kids are on machines. Little Joey hasn't woken up in a couple of weeks. Lucy is with it but still struggling. And then there's Sarah. She's just not getting any better, and she's having trouble maintaining the house while I'm out on jobs. So they really need me to be home with them. I feel really bad about it, but I won't be able to do any more jobs after tonight. I'm really sorry."

"Charlie." The Padre sighed.

I wasn't sure if his sigh meant he was disappointed or just processing the moment.

"I need to know that you'll see things through for this job. You can do that, right?"

"Of course, boss! I'm good for this one. Just moving on—"

"I told you I had plans for you. The promotion."

"I really appreciate it, but you've already done so much. I just need to be with my family in case things get…" I couldn't finish the sentence as I was choking up at the thought of losing any of them.

"Okay, Charlie. Just focus on the road and the job."

It had gone about as smoothly as I could have hoped, and it was that moment, for the first time in as long as I could remember, that I felt an overwhelming sense of relief. I had always known I was in a bad line of work, but was always able to rationalize it by saying it was for my family. Still, it constantly bothered me—a lot. After seeing the product, I couldn't rationalize it any longer. Any argument for Sarah that I had to keep the job seemed hollow. I needed to be a husband and a father, and I couldn't do that if I was running around putting my life in danger.

The light of a hologram filled the backseat. The Padre skipped his usual cordial greeting and began digging in about the need to prep the product and how timing was important. To my surprise, the other voice didn't sound timid or apologetic like it always had. Instead, the Padre got scolded, and it was more than a little jarring.

"The buyer came through late, and they had reservations. You'll do as your told, and you'll be a good little delivery boy about it."

"Yes, sir." The Padre's tone completely changed as he conceded to the voice.

If that wasn't odd enough, the next thing the hologram said was also strange.

"Now, are you able to follow through with the other item we discussed for this job?"

The Padre hesitated for a moment, unusual for his netphone discussions that normally droned on and on, especially when he was mad. The momentary silence was palpable, and I was certain I could feel the Padre's eyes fixed on me for whatever reason. But I didn't budge, and I sure as hell didn't look in the mirror. I would be damned if I gave him the slightest hint that I had heard anything about anything.

"Don't worry about that, sir. It will be handled," the Padre assured the figure of light.

But the more I learned about the job, the more it bothered me. First, there was a time change, and apparently, the Padre was ordered to make that happen. And then, there was something on top of the normal exchange? What could it be? The Padre seemed more frustrated than worried, but I couldn't help having a bad feeling about the night.

The light in back faded suddenly, and quiet resumed. Trying to fight the awkwardness, I stuck to the routine of the jobs. "What do we know about the buyers?" I asked.

"Brazilian. More of our top-shelf stuff. The partners screwed this one up and got someone who doubts our ability to come through. Well, we'll show them, and then they can kiss my ass."

"What's their ETA?"

"Thirty minutes after us."

"A scout?"

"Not this time."

It really seemed like the job was thrown together in the eleventh hour. It was sloppy, and for my last job, I didn't like it at all.

"Got it, boss. We're going back to the old Halas warehouse for this job? Anything change since the last time?"

"Yes, I will be entering first through the north door instead of the south so that I can get set up and complete the transaction quicker. You'll be parking around the block and entering through the south."

"Isn't the north door on the street?"

"It'll be fine, Charlie. Just get us there on time."

"No problem, boss. We're fifteen minutes out."

I took the on-ramp to the expressway and changed into the middle lane. The road was empty at that hour, but we'd need to take a different way back since we'd likely get caught in rush hour traffic. I drove for some time, and then exited onto the main street nearest our destination. After a couple of turns, I could see the warehouse in the distance.

"Five minutes out, boss."

It was really more like three minutes, but I decided to take a few indirect roads so we could slowly roll up to the front of the building. It would help to ensure there wasn't any trouble waiting for us. Meanwhile, the Padre put out his cigar, obtained the parts from his briefcase, and assembled his weapon.

The part of the city we were in had changed a lot over the years. Once it was an extension of the industries with warehouses and machine shops aplenty. Now it was sandwiched in with overpriced apartment buildings and yuppie shops and bistros. It probably wouldn't be long before gentrification rid the whole area of any blue-collar jobs and the buildings that housed them.

I slowly pulled up to the front doors and left the engine running. The Padre opened his door and began to rock himself out of the vehicle. Then I had a sudden realization.

"No prayer tonight, boss?"

He paused for just a moment and looked over at me. "Since we were short on time, I said the prayer at home. Sorry, Charlie."

He seemed caught off guard by the question even though he had said a prayer on literally every other job we had ever done. It was more proof that it was an odd night. The Padre spilled out onto the street, and the car's suspension sighed in relief once he was finally out. He walked to the trunk and swapped briefcases, then appeared near my window.

"Drive around to Pulaski and park the car on the street."

The Padre turned toward the building and disappeared through the doors. I headed for Pulaski and found the first available spot. I looked around for passersby, spotting a bum about forty yards away as well as a bike rider crossing the street a block ahead. Nothing to worry about. I retrieved my 9mm from the glove compartment and decided to skip cleaning it since I was more visible than usual. I secured the gun in the back of my waistband and popped out of the car.

Shoving the car keys into my pocket, I made my way through the alley toward the warehouse. A machine shop I had never seen before seemed oddly familiar, just looking at the garage door. As I approached the street in front of the warehouse, I was overcome with déjà vu. Sure, I had been to the warehouse a few times before, but there was something new about this feeling. The slightest hint of fear snuck into my thoughts as if I had experienced something awful there before. The strange thing was, I hadn't. The few jobs we had done there went as smooth as could be, so I shook off the feeling and kept walking. With one eye on the warehouse, I crossed the street into the next alley leading to the south entrance of the building. As the sun peeked over the horizon, the scene was quiet and the building was innocent and calm. Rounding the corner, I instantly jumped onto the concrete stairs and grabbed the metal door handle to enter.

It will be all over after this.

The thought popped into my head accompanied by more relief that it was my last job. I entered the dark warehouse and closed the door behind me.

Life as I know it will be over after this.

CHAPTER 12
WHAT DOESN'T THE FUTURE HOLD?

L IFE AS I KNOW IT *will be over after this.*
I mused as I exhibited the most picture-perfect posture while brushing my teeth at a standard sink. My feet were firmly planted on the floor as I brushed in and out and all around. I even rocked back and forth and side to side to fully grasp how it felt to shift my weight from leg to leg. Walking was becoming like second nature to me and the whole migration process was coming to an end, and I couldn't help but think that it was bittersweet. The last ten years of my life had been defined by one singular goal.

Walk.

It had consumed my thoughts and kept me focused. It made me work hard and push myself past perceived limits of a paraplegic. It made me fight through the adversity of being disabled and isolated, to some extent. And it was basically over. I had achieved success in the one thing that meant the most my entire life, and as odd as it was, I was actually at a bit of a loss. I remembered reading in history class that, years ago, people used to stop working at age sixty-five. They called it "retirement." But when those people stopped working, they lost their purpose in life, their drive to live, and they tended not to live too long after. Luckily, retirement had been illegal for a couple decades to protect people from themselves. Still, that was the only word that came to mind when I thought about how I felt in that moment: *retired.* I had retired from trying to walk and was moving on to simply being a walker. It reminded me of a question from the premigration counselors.

"How will you handle life's problems in your new host?"

I scoffed at the question before because it seemed silly. "All I need is a fresh set of legs, and I could take on the world," had been my reply.

And for the most part, that was true. But what I couldn't fully grasp back then was that a functional body came with having a completely different mindset. It would open up countless possibilities for me, which was a good dilemma but a dilemma nonetheless. How would I use the extra time, energy, and abilities afforded to me by being physically fit? How would I tap into my new physical potential? They were good questions, and I didn't know exactly how to answer them.

I spit the tooth gel into the sink and rinsed out my mouth. Approaching the urinal, I was still amazed at using the restroom while standing. My host's endowment was quite impressive as well. Shaking off the drips, I stepped over to the shower and turned on the water as hot as my hand could take. Quickly jumping in, I got to work meticulously washing every inch of my new body down to my wiggly toes. It seemed like my torso and legs went on forever and bending to wash everything felt so satisfying.

Pulling the curtain back, I was presented with a room barely visible through the steam. Drying myself with a large, soft towel was also a fulfilling experience. Next, I solidly planted one foot onto the bath mat followed by the other. I was figuratively and literally grounded as I went back to the sink and wiped the fogginess from the mirror. I had to keep looking at myself because everything was finally becoming real, and in spite of the questions about what lay next for me, there was still a deep contentment setting in. They sure had done a good job of biocopying my original face onto my host, and it made me feel like me. With a silly grin, I tamed my thick, messy black hair using the ADG-issued blue comb.

I was delighted when I saw my clothing arranged on the bed. Instead of a colostomy bag, I slid on snug underwear that settled very comfortably. As deliberately as I could, I inserted my legs into my black slacks one at a time, tickled to see each foot pop out at the bottom. I slowly buttoned up my white shirt, all the while reveling again in the length of my upper torso. I slipped on my black jacket, fixed the collar, and zipped it halfway to complete my look. My paperwork had been processed, and I had been medically cleared to go home. I felt ready to take on the world. But before

I did that, I needed to visit a friend who I had heard was recovering nicely and would be ready to walk soon.

I left my recovery room for the last time and headed down the hall to another. I tapped on the door, and there she was.

"Well, aren't you a sight for sore eyes?" Helen's sarcastic side had migrated just fine.

"You're not looking so bad yourself. How do you feel?"

I sat in the chair next to her bed.

"Like hell. But I'll live. More importantly, look at you. Walking and stuff. Is it as good as advertised?"

"The thin air up here makes me a little dizzy, but otherwise, it's pretty awesome. It was really hard getting to this point, but definitely worth it. I'm excited for you to get upright and moving soon too."

"Ha. After the catch-22, I'll take what I can get."

"Yeah, that was rough, but I know you'll be fine. You're pretty tough."

Helen and I met on the job at NeoTech Enterprises. NTE was a multinational conglomerate that claimed to specialize in everything, whatever that meant. The main office was known for employing disabled adults like Helen and me, which was the reason I'd applied in the first place. But I always thought that the large tax credit they received for hiring us made their advertising a little disingenuous. Their motto: "To stay ahead of the competition, you have to do things differently. That's why we take pride in our differently abled workforce." Even though I was happy to have found work, part of me was still resentful of them.

Helen and I were in the same department, data processing, where they put most of 'us.' It was a mindless job, but it definitely paid better than most. We worked there for about a year before we actually met, and that was a day I would never forget. I had rolled into the elevator, and there she had been.

"Morning. Which floor?"

By the flatness of her voice, it had been clear that she hadn't drunk much of the coffee she was holding.

"Fourteen. Thanks."

"No problem. That's where I'm going." She typed the number into her auto-chair.

"Yeah, I thought I had seen you around." I tended to notice others in auto-chairs.

"Sure."

She hadn't seemed interested in discussion, but on that morning, I had been.

"So, you like it here?"

"Well, it's a job."

"I know, right." On that, we'd agreed.

An awkward silence had set in after my last comment, but that had been partly due to me realizing I was really attracted to her. Sure, she had been easy on the eyes, but she just had an air about her. I always had a thing for confidence, possibly because I lacked it.

As we neared our floor, I had wanted to say something witty for her to remember me by. "So, have you seen the new beverage in the café? I'm thinking about *chai-ing* it."

And while the comment had been definitely memorable, it had been quite lacking in the witty department.

She'd squinted at me, then let me have it. "Oh, I get it. You think that because we're both in auto-chairs, we probably have something in common and can tell each other lame jokes like we go way back."

As the redness of embarrassment set in, I had known I couldn't leave it at that. "Okay. I deserve that for telling such a bad pun, but I did notice your taste in auto-chairs matches mine, so we're not that different, you and me."

With a ding, the elevator door had opened.

"Nice save. Maybe I'll see you in the café later, and we can *chai* that new drink together. See ya."

She had gone left and I'd slowly rolled right, but from that point on, I'd felt like we had a connection. I had been able to appreciate the fact that she'd been guarded in response to my small talk. It meant that she had standards, and the fact that she'd ended it on a good note made me feel like I had a chance.

Over the course of the next several months, we'd hung out casually off and on and even run in some of the same circles of friends from work. There had been a bit of flirting here and there, but neither of us had been able or willing to put forth the effort to ask the other person out. Though, at one point, I mentioned that I had been saving for a mind migration and found out we had even more in common.

"Get out of here! I've been saving for one too! My folks started a fund for me after I finished recovering from the pool accident. No idea where they got the credits after all of my surgeries, but it was a nice chunk of change, and they gave me the account when I turned eighteen. They said I could use it for whatever. School was paid for by scholarships, so I figured walking would be the next most important thing. That's when I began researching divorcing my body."

"Ugh. Don't you hate calling it that?"

"Eh, 'mind migration' sounds all formal and stuff. The way I see it is that I had a bit of bad luck with this body, so I want to separate from it like a divorce. And I'm hoping for a host that would match the age and growth simulation of this body so I can look and feel like I was supposed to."

Helen interrupted my trip down memory lane. "Ryan? Did we lose you?"

Shaking my head, I replied, "Sorry, just thinking about how far we've come."

A genuine smile stretched across her face. "Pretty crazy, huh? And to think, we might not be friends if you hadn't made that bad joke in the elevator a couple years ago."

"At least it was good for something."

"I guess."

"Hey, Helen, I wanted to ask you something. I'm not trying to freak you out or anything, but since you've been conscious, have you been experiencing any weird dreams? Anything that seems real but obviously isn't?"

She scrunched her face a bit as she searched her migrated mind for a response to my question. "I haven't had anything like that in the last few days. Right after the procedure, I knew this brain was mush, and there were some strange things then: colors, lights, sounds. And I guess there were a few odd dreams in there, but all of it seemed like what I had discussed with the counselors."

"So, nothing that seemed real or maybe unfamiliar?"

"Unfamiliar? That's weird. No, nothing like that. Why, what's up?"

It would have been nice to have a friend who could relate to my dreams, but I didn't want to stress her out any more than the procedure already did.

"Oh, nothing, I was just having some oddities that the doctors said were fine, but just wanted to see how you were doing."

Helen's expression broke into one of concern. "You sure, Ryan? I'm surprised you aren't running circles around me. Are those 'oddities' bumming you out?"

"You know, it's not a big deal. We can talk more about it when you get…when you walk out of this place."

Dr. Little entered the room. "Ah, Ryan, I didn't know you knew Helen."

"Yup. We go back a couple years."

"Seems like forever." Helen's dry quips always stung just a little, but she had toughened me up over the course of our friendship.

"Well, great. You two should share notes about your post-migration phases. It's always nice to have a friend who can relate."

Even if Helen couldn't relate to my dreams, Dr. Little made a good point.

"Vitals are looking good, Helen. Did you want to review your brain chart, or did you want to wait for Ryan to leave?"

I immediately felt like a burden.

"He's fine. Let's take a look."

As the shaft in the ceiling opened up, I was relieved that the health disk wasn't coming for me. Then we all turned our attention to Helen's chart.

"See that nearly perfect circle?"

"Yes."

"Your host's brain is taking quite nicely to your mind. We'll play it safe, but as long as things keep progressing, I'd say you're looking at a shorter rehab than most. If you don't have any questions, I'll let you two get back to flirting."

"Oh, we're not—" Helen and I said in unison while blushing.

We all busted into laughter as Dr. Little left the room.

Alone again, I turned back to Helen. "I'm really happy for you, Helen. I thought I worked hard for my migration, but you really took it the extra kilometer, and it's paying off. Thanks for being an inspiration even to another migrator."

"That's sweet, Ry. You can thank me in drinks when I get out of here. Fair?"

"Two Toms' Tavern it is, then. I'll let you get some rest, but if you need anything or just want to talk, hit me up on my netphone."

"Oh, Ry. Don't worry about me. Go explore the world with your new legs. Maybe go for a jog or something. I'll see you later."

"I will. Thanks! Bye!"

I couldn't help but grin like an idiot as I walked out of her room. She was an amazing person, and I really valued our friendship, which was another reason we had never taken it to the next level. But it seemed like anything was possible moving forward since we would both be walking. Either way, it was time to leave ADG, and I couldn't have been happier.

Strolling through the migration recovery area toward the exit, I saw the other poor souls who were struggling to walk post-migration. Then I waved at Mr. Personality at the front desk, who barely noticed me while he frantically typed. The motion-sensing doors detected me, and I went back down the hallway that had borne witness to my final ride with Auto. I had thought about him every time I sat in a manual wheelchair, but to my surprise, I didn't really miss him. There was none of the separation anxiety I was certain I would have. I must have been realizing, at that moment, that all good things had to come to an end, and at least, Auto and my story had a happy ending. Well, for me, at least.

Looking farther down the hallway, I could see the many rooms that I'd wheeled into in preparation for my transition. Ironically, that side of the building looked foreign to me since the migration. No longer needing to virtually interface, I manually pressed the down arrow with my thumb as hard as I could when I reached the elevator. The wait for the world's slowest elevator was actually calming that time around, and I just let my mind wander for the few moments it took.

With a ding, the doors opened. I stepped inside and was greeted by the familiar dry, old pop instrumental. Another ding, and I was walking through the hallway. With a steady gait, I strolled through the foyer, my heels clicking against the slate floor. Everything from the fountain to the vines on the walls seemed to have a new glow as if I was seeing them for the first time, and technically I was, with my new eyes. Chills ran down my fully functional spine as I peered up to see God's finger transferring life into Adam. The reference finally made sense to me.

I meandered past the unnecessarily cold waiting room where future migrators were waiting anxiously for their procedures. There was Atlas holding the weight of the world on his shoulders. In contrast, I felt like a weight had been lifted off my shoulders, and I could finally feel comfortable in my own skin. The aquarium in the wall was calm, but I was still able to quickly spot the disabled fish from afar. Part of me instantly identified with him while another part of me had already begun moving on to the mindset of a fully abled person, the goldfish.

The inner exit doors acknowledged my presence, and I felt like a rock star with each step I took through the vestibule. I was fully aware that, waiting for me on the other side, was the busy city I had navigated for years in an auto-chair. To that end, I tried to prepare myself to be underwhelmed. Still, I knew it would be different, and that feeling was confirmed as the outside doors opened the world to me.

My eyes adjusted as I tried to take it all in. The sun was bright, the sky was blue, and the air was crisp. Two steps onto the pavement, I stopped suddenly, almost against my will, and my mind and body were stunned by my surroundings. The cool breeze. The smell of the city. The zipping cars. The chirping birds. The intimidating buildings. The hustling masses.

The realization was instant. While I was familiar with everything, everything was not familiar with me. Meaning I was just another walker, and as awful as that might have sounded to some, it was glorious to me. All I had ever wanted was to fit in.

A kind fellow did his part to really cement the feeling. "Hey, buddy, get outta my way!"

For all of the unsaid things people did while I sat in Auto, no one ever really uttered words like that. It was assumed that I would be in the way, but standing like everyone else meant it was assumed that I would walk like everyone else. I quickly and quietly reveled in the moment, then let it fade so I could move on.

Making my way to the bullet-bus stop that last saw me a paraplegic, I waited in a standing position for the very first time in my life. There was only one bullet-bus that was auto-chair-accommodating, so I always had to tack on an extra thirty minutes or so to my travels just to wait for it.

The bullet-bus rapidly approached, and I prepared myself for its stairs. From one hundred twenty kilometers an hour, it came to a complete stop in an instant, and the doors flung open. I jumped on and put my thumb in the fare acceptor, and it chimed with approval as it always had. It appeared that they'd successfully migrated my fingerprints. Looking back in the bus, I would be standing up against strangers for the start of my trip, but having never really experienced that before, I looked forward to it in a weird but non-creepy way.

The bus took off with a burst of speed, and I struggled a bit to keep my balance. I gently bumped into the people behind me, but they didn't seem to care. Otherwise, the ride was smooth. Eventually, seats opened up, but I passed every single one up to stay standing while holding onto the handrail above. The half-hour trip went by in the blink of an eye, and before I knew it, I was getting out at the bus stop near my childhood home—the home where I'd spent my entire life, but a home where I had never taken as much as a single step.

I walked the few blocks to my street, turned, and saw it sitting there: the house with the ramp that school kids made fun of. Moving forward, it would be the house that no longer needed a ramp. Instead, it would be the house with stairs that got twice the traffic!

Stopping in the front yard, I slowly peered up to the picture window I'd spent so many years looking through. I always wondered what it would be like to just walk down the street. Like a lot of the dreams I had, I would finally be able to actualize them. That was when the awe from being in a new body quickly waned, and I realized how much work was ahead of me. In fact, I had new life goals, new purpose, and of course, new challenges for the first time since…ever.

First, I had to have a difficult conversation with Mom. While it was a requirement to have assisted living for one month after a mind migration, that was as long as I wanted to stay at home. Mom had given me several thousand credits to celebrate the procedure, which was enough to get an apartment. Mom had taken care of me long enough, and I knew she would move on to the next phase in her life faster if I was out of the house.

Next, I had to go back to ADG to see the Cameron Walsh speech. They'd performed my mind migration, the single greatest thing that had ever happened to me, and part of me would forever be grateful that such a procedure existed. But I having been gone for less than an hour, I quickly realized another part of me never wanted to go back—ever. Going back meant reliving the journey I had just completed, every painful moment, every doubtful second. It was something I would have to deal with eventually because I had to complete the final session with Tony. But the speech would be the week before that, and I was hoping Helen would accompany me for moral support.

Lastly, Tony's advice to ignore my dreams had turned out to be good, if only in the short term. It allowed me to focus enough to finish my rehab and go home. But the dreams were still happening. I wanted to do some digging on my own to see if I could make sense of them. Who was Charlie? Why did I have first-person accounts of him that seemed so real? What had happened to him? I thought I might try the old family shrink to see if I could get a different perspective and possibly a new direction.

But at that moment, I just had one goal. I needed to *walk* into my house for the first time. Each step was one closer to the next phase of my life. Each stair was helping me move on from my disabilities. As I approached the top, I reached for the door, and it was like the final effort needed to turn the last page in a major chapter of my life. I opened the door, and the scent of home sweet home hit me in the face, causing my eyes to well up. And while still thinking about putting the past behind me, a voice popped into my head.

Let's get this over with.

CHAPTER 13
WHEN YOUR HEART IS NOT IN IT

L ET'S GET THIS OVER WITH, I thought as I stepped around metal crates in the long hallways barely lit by the LEDs in the floor. It seemed fitting that my last job would be at the warehouse. The other jobs we'd done there had reminded me of my last major mission while I was enlisted—one I would never forget.

We had been deployed to the city of Quetta. Having completed a few missions early on, it had been a couple months since we'd seen any action. Then we finally intercepted communications that an enemy sect was using a "warehouse-like building" to store arms and other paraphernalia. The problem had been that there were around fifteen warehouses matching the description within the city limits, and none of the aerial scans narrowed the possibilities.

I was part of a reconnaissance team sent to investigate one of the buildings. Our intelligence stated that the warehouse we were assigned had been vacant since troops hit the ground some eighteen months earlier. There for information not a firefight, we had specific orders, should we encounter the enemy, not to in anyway engage unless we had no choice.

We rendezvoused on a weeknight after curfew so the locals would be off the street. The air had been dry, but it was exceptionally hot. Combined with fifty pounds of gear, it hadn't taken long for me to work up a good lather, and judging by the dark spots on the fatigues of my squad mates, they hadn't been exactly comfortable either. We were perched on top of an empty apartment complex across the street from the warehouse, surveilling through the roof windows.

Of our eight-person team, I was one of two chosen to enter the building for a more detailed sweep. I had finished the AIT stealth lessons with top honors, so it just made sense. I was partnered with Corporal Sierra Hotel, who was the only deployed marine that scored higher in stealth than me. So, while I outranked her, it only felt right that she gave the orders on our missions. Together, we were the best infiltrators the marines had, on paper. And while we'd had some success on previous missions, I never took anything for granted on foreign soil. No matter how quick, quiet, and covered we were, I always assumed there were eyes on us. The stress had made those types of jobs that much harder.

Sierra and I made our way down from the roof using the fire escape and quickly slid to the edge of the building. She gently peered around all corners to ensure no one was guarding the building or walking by and gave me the signal to contact the crew on the apartment roof for more clearance.

"Bravo Company, this is Coyote Royal. Are we clear for departure? Over."

"Coyote Royal, you have clear skies, and you're next in line. Safe travels. Over and out."

We darted across the street and took cover in a shadowy inlet of the warehouse. Another check for signs of life down both ways of the street came up negative, so we made our way around the building to the loading docks. I placed a small ground scanning devices in front of each dock to analyze the driveways and determine if any vehicles had recently pulled up to the building. If we had gotten a hit, we would have kept that in mind while searching the building. We waited the few moments it took for the scan to complete.

"Beep!" was heard over all of our headsets.

"Coyote Royal, we have confirmation of turbulence. Please proceed with caution."

We located the side entrance, and I drew my weapon. Sierra obtained the oil gun from her bag and applied it to the hinges and latch assembly. Almost silently, we opened the heavy door and slipped into the pitch-black building. We gently closed the door behind us and then lowered our night-vision goggles. Proceeding through the green rooms and hallways, our steps were silent and our breathing controlled.

After searching a few offices containing nothing of interest, we came to the main storage room and took a knee in a dark corner. Peering around, we determined that worn boxes on shelves, a few stacks of pallets here and there, and a rusty forklift near the loading dock were what had returned the positive results from the scan outside. I hit the button on my wrist unit to scan the room for large concentrations of metal—arms or ammunition. Sweat dripped down my forehead and off my nose while we waited the ten seconds for that result.

"Buzz!"

Other than the forklift and some random equipment, the scan turned up nothing.

I hit the button again to search for plastics because some groups had begun manufacturing weapons that could circumvent our metal scans. They weren't typically as powerful as their metal counterparts, but the enemy was willing to do anything to move their agenda forward.

"Buzz!"

Again, nothing significant.

Thinking that the mission had been all for naught, I turned off my wrist unit but inadvertently changed it to scan for heartbeats instead. That setting had been next to useless for the last several months since the enemy was fitting their armies with pacemakers that would block or scramble the scan.

"Beep!"

A positive result. For heartbeats.

What the—

"Coyote Royal, we're acknowledging your new flight path. Please proceed with caution."

My partner and I looked at the results on my wrist unit, and both nearly fell over. Shuffling to keep our balance, slight noises echoed through the old building.

Thirty-six heartbeats detected.

It had to be a misread. In disbelief, I turned the unit off and on again. To not alarm Bravo Company, I turned off the results transmitter and rescanned the area for heartbeats.

"Beep!"

Still, thirty-six heartbeats detected. We were in a completely empty and silent warehouse where there were apparently thirty-six people.

I caught Sierra's eye to express my disbelief, and she shrugged in response. My partner made the signal to move out of the corner to investigate. With backs together, we gently walked around each set of shelves and peered around every box. With each passing moment and no signs of a life, I began thinking my wrist unit must have been faulty. I made the signal for wrapping up the mission and returning to the team.

As we walked across the perimeter of the room toward the exit, we took a path that was obstructed by a stack of pallets. Sneaking closely around them, I felt the floor give ever so slightly with the faintest hollow noise under my last two steps. I stopped. Sierra had walked ahead until she noticed I wasn't following, then turned to me. I pointed down, and she doubled back to examine the ground. There was a ninety-degree cut in the ground leading under the pallets, so we came to the conclusion we should move the pallets. Pulling them aside, a three-by-three rectangle revealed itself on the floor. On one side, a much smaller rectangle was visible. I flung my rifle over my back and knelt down. Touching the small rectangle in the floor, I was able to remove the cover piece without much effort. Within the small hole, I found a handle to what had to be a door.

Looking at Sierra, I considered that we had specific orders not to engage the enemy. But we also needed to determine if there were any weapons stored there with the scans coming back odd, so we had to make a judgment call.

I gave a thumbs-up to her, and she returned it. We had to get that door open and see what was below. Sierra readied her rifle and aimed it downward. On the count of three, I gripped the door handle, pulled up as hard as I could, and then let it go while simultaneously swinging my weapon into my hands.

But we were only presented with green darkness. Not a soul was down there. Only a ladder leading down about six feet. Peering in, we saw three walls and a tunnel opening.

With cover from Sierra, I slid down the ladder first and immediately took aim down the tunnel. She quickly followed, and we oriented ourselves to maximize our shot zone. We crept down the tunnel to a metal door about thirty feet into the tunnel. While the door itself appeared to be heavy duty, there wasn't any obvious locking mechanism. As we closed in, I furnished the listening cone from my gear and gently placed it up to the door. Like the morgue room we'd discovered in the factory, we had been again presented with a low hum from what must have been a generator.

I pointed at the hinges and latch assembly on the door, and she quickly oiled them up. I readied a smoke bomb from my pack and gripped the door handle with my other hand. Sierra aimed at the door as I yanked it open with all my might. The brightest light blinded us through our night-vision goggles, but I was able to pull the pin on the bomb and throw it in before anyone could approach us.

Sierra and I flipped up our goggles and dove into the room, aiming our weapons in various directions through the smoke. Fingers perched on our triggers, we were ready to engage at a moment's notice. But once our commotion subsided, the ambiance of the room returned and it became obvious that the room had no hostiles in it. To be sure, we waited the few seconds it took for our eyes to adjust to the light and for the smoke to dissipate. Then we saw everything, and I was forever changed.

I shook my head because it was too painful to finish the memory and I needed to focus on the job at hand to fulfill my duties to the Padre.

I continued following the floor LEDs to the largest room in the building where the Padre stood near a table in the far corner. I made my way toward him, noticing the warehouse had gone to hell since our last job there. The lantern on the table cast odd shadows over evidence that squatters had vandalized everything left of the warehouse. You almost wondered if the yuppies taking over the neighborhood welcomed the buildings becoming dilapidated and condemned so they could justify the "redevelopment" that destroyed any remanence of industry. They would undoubtedly replace the building with more overpriced espresso shops where people with too much time and money congregated to agree with each other too much on too many things. Pretension aside, those places never made much sense to me since my go-to morning drink was simply coffee with cream and sugar.

"How's the car, Charlie?"

"We're good, boss. Do you need me to wear my piece up front?"

"No. That won't be necessary."

We waited in silence for the next twenty minutes until the sounds of someone entering through the rear entrance could be heard. There had to be a few people because the rumbling of several footsteps didn't stop for a couple of moments. They weren't very subtle, that was for sure.

With my eyes focused on the door they would come through, I was slightly taken aback when two large, dark figures entered followed by a smaller one. As they got closer, I could make out the silhouettes of two shockingly enormous men. The other figure was holding something. Once in the light, I could see two bodyguards wearing military-grade vests and jackets while the man behind them was well groomed in a nice black suit and holding a briefcase.

"Good evening, gentlemen." His Portuguese accent was distinct, but his English was just fine.

"Good evening to you, sirs."

"I am in the market for a restored Cessna 172. Do you happen to know where I can find one? I am willing to pay top dollar for it if it has been properly restored and is accompanied by a capable pilot."

The Padre inhaled deeply, then went through the motions. "Please forgive me, but I only have a restored Cessna 182. I do have a capable pilot. Would you like to see the aircraft to ensure it is to your liking?"

"Yes, I would. Is the aircraft available here and now to see?"

"It is. Do you have a valid ID and something of value for us to keep as a show of good faith?"

"Most certainly." The man placed his briefcase onto the table, retrieved a netphone from his inner coat pocket, swiped it a couple of times, and tapped it twice. The case clicked open and the man turned it around to us.

The Padre skipped his customary visual scan and went right for his netphone. Scanning quickly, he seemed pleased with the results, and he placed the phone back into his pocket, closed the case, and moved it to the floor next to him.

"Much appreciated for having sufficient collateral. Allow me to provide you a preview of the aircraft so that you can properly assess it. I promise that you will be pleased."

The Padre placed the product case gently on the table and opened it. I used to be neutral to the sound of the case opening, but it now filled me with despair. As usual, the case was turned toward the buyers before I had a chance to glance at the product, but I was fairly certain I knew what it was. The smaller man driving the transaction moved closer to the table to get a better look at the contents. Like every other buyer, his eyes darted back and forth almost like he was reading something, and like clockwork, a grin crept across his face. The man had a pleasant look about him, but his smile seemed more maniacal than anything.

"This aircraft is more than satisfactory. I will have the mechanics at my hanger do the final diagnostic on it, but I do not have any concerns right now."

"Thank you, sir. And in terms of a pilot, please pardon our inability to find a qualified one within the time frame we were given. Therefore, I would like to provide my assistant to you as a show of good faith while we locate an appropriate pilot for you."

I had been holding a sharp gaze on the buyers until the Padre finished that last sentence. Awestruck, I turned to the Padre, back to the buyers, and then back to the Padre.

"Please excuse me while I give my assistant some final instructions."

The Padre gestured me back a few feet and leaned in to whisper with a look of certainty on his face. "You quit when I say you quit. You're going to provide protection to our clients for a few days while we sort out the last parts of the deal. Do a good job, and maybe we'll talk about you being done when you get back. Maybe."

I was welling up with equal parts anger and fear as the Padre spoke. There was no way in hell I was going with any of our clients, and sure as hell not on the night I was trying to quit. For him to set me up without even so much as a discussion meant I could never trust him again. At that moment, it became quite clear what I needed to do even if it was going to be one of the craziest things I had ever done in my life.

With the utmost confidence, I whispered back, "No."

The Padre squinted at me, seeming legitimately confused. Then he scowled. "Excuse me?" Anger seeped through his teeth.

"I'm not going with them."

Clearly frustrated, the Padre dug into me. "I'll pardon your momentary lapse in judgment as stress-related, but it's for your own good that you go with the buyers. Show me up on this job, and you're not going to like what comes next."

What comes next? What the hell did that mean? Are my worst fears were coming true? My family had suffered enough through no fault of my own, and it seemed like I was putting a target on their back if I didn't keep working for the Padre. But something inside of me said that if I didn't end it that night, it never would end, so I stayed firm.

"No."

His intense stare into my soul broke as he moved back up to the table with a customer-service grin on his face. "Gentlemen, my apologies, but please excuse us while we finalize some details. Please take the product with you and wait by the door in the rear. I'll be sending my assistant with you shortly."

Obviously annoyed, the neatly dressed man shot back, "Sir, I will remind you that we are on a strict time schedule and only have a few minutes to spare. Please send your assistant to us quickly so that we may get back on the road to our next engagement."

One of the massive men in front slammed the bulky briefcase closed and effortlessly lifted it from the table. They wandered back to the hallway, and then it was just the Padre and me. I turned back to the Padre, but instead found myself looking down the long metal barrel of his hand cannon.

Click!

The chilling sound of the hammer lifting up shook me to my core.

"When you signed on for this job, I told you that you'd have to do things that you might not like. You agreed to those terms. Now, I know you saw the product on the other job, and all of a sudden, you want out. Did you think we were saints? That's not how the world works. I didn't want to tell you this, but I know your family has spotted lung. I know they don't have much time. If you want to see them for as long as they have, you'll do as you're told. Oh, and just so you know, one man's disease is another man's fortune. Where do you think we get our products from?"

My rage boiled over. "No!"

In a single motion, I knocked the gun from the Padre's hand and decked him in the eye with everything I had. As a mountain of a man, he barely moved from the hit but was clearly dazed. I pulled my 9mm from my waistband, but even in his stunned state, he was able to knock it from my hand and push me away. I gathered myself enough to kick him in the gut, staggering him, and then I took the opportunity to get another hard hit to the same eye. Blood spurted onto my coat, and he toppled over. It was time to run like hell. With the back exit blocked by the client, I needed to leave out the front door, so bolted the forty feet in that direction.

"You get your ass back here or you're dead! You and your family are dead! You hear me, Charlie!"

The warehouse was filled with his echoes as I grabbed the door handle. Opening the rusty door, the morning's sun flooded the building, and I looked back momentarily to see the Padre pulling out his netphone, likely to call for backup. Not watching my step, I landed in a massive hole in the concrete stairs, fell two feet, rolled my left ankle hard, and then, face planted onto the sidewalk. Struggling to stay conscious, I could hear the door shutting behind me, and as it did, images of Sarah and the kids popped into my head. In that moment, I could only muster one thought.

I'm sorry.

CHAPTER 14
ONE LAST CRY FOR HELP

"I'M SORRY. I KNOW THIS isn't easy for you, but I think it's the only way we're both going to be able to move on." I truly believed it.

Mom looked up at me, her eyes welling with tears. "Honey, what if something happens? What if you need me?"

I shook my head. "Mom, I'm looking at apartments just in the city limits. It's a thirty-minute drive on the speedway, or if I need to get out this way, I can take the bullet and be here in about the same time."

"I know, but the last twenty-two years of my life were spent taking care of you. It's really all I know at this point."

"And that's precisely why I think it would be best if we make a clean break. It'll be jarring at first, but we will live and learn. You should travel. Or you could even go on a date!"

Her red eyes opened wide, and she sighed. "Oh, Ryan. Everything's just changing so quickly. I was scared half to death when I heard someone entering the shower this morning, and then I realized it was you. Maybe I should talk to someone about it."

"You can always talk to me. But you're right. Sometimes talking to professionals is helpful."

I put the starfruit juice in the refrigerator and the bread in the pantry, finishing up with the groceries I'd just carried in the house for her, another first.

"It will be okay, Mom. You have always deserved a life beyond just taking care of me, and it's time for you to have it. Let me know if you need anything else, Mom."

I had about a half hour before Helen was meeting me to go to the Cameron Walsh speech, so I decided to go to my room for a bit. Walking toward the stairs, I paused at the lift that had taken Auto and me up and down so many times. I had done that just about every time I found myself needing to take the stairs since coming home. It really highlighted how I had a whole new perspective and feeling of genuine control of where and when I moved. That was becoming the norm for me, and to my delight, it was getting more and more difficult to remember finer details of just how disabled I had been. Still, the many memories would be with me forever.

The worst was when I had forgotten to fully charge Auto. Getting stranded anywhere was no fun, but it was especially bad in the city. There had to have been hundreds of people passing me, all staring as they'd walked the three feet of pavement around me. Worse yet had been the kind souls who thought I was homeless and had put physical credits in my lap. It probably made me a bad person, but I'd never stopped them to give the credits back. Regardless, my mom had been used to dropping everything to come to my rescue. More than anything, I was glad those days were over. On the contrary, I could come to the aid of others if they got stranded.

Focusing back on the stairs, I deliberately took each step with care, feeling every inch of contact between my feet and the wood. Making sure to plant my heels hard, I used my powerful hips and quads to propel me up and forward. I had no use for the railing since I wanted to do it all with my legs. At the top of the stairs, I walked down the hallway to my bedroom on the right and headed for my desk. Placing my netphone down, I pressed two buttons to bring up the holograms of the apartment advertisements I had flagged. I flipped through them, trying to decide the best one for me.

There was one unit that stuck out above all the rest. It was a large space—three bedrooms—and it even had a balcony. The building was older, but to me that meant it had more personality and a sort of nostalgia by proxy. I was compelled to apply for the place in that moment and sent a message to the building manager.

After I hit submit, I swiped through my netphone and stumbled upon the journal app I hadn't opened since recovery. The dreams hadn't stopped, but I felt like I was doing a good job of ignoring them per Tony's advice.

But part of me was curious about what I would find if I searched for works of fiction that had a character named Charlie. If I found anything even remotely similar to my dreams, I would be able to put them to rest. And so, I did some quick searches: books, movies, plays, video games.

The whole process reminded me of when I had first gotten Auto, and to celebrate my new automated mobility, my mother had put together a scavenger hunt. She gave me a map of the neighborhood with clues on it, and I had to figure out what and where the items were. It was the most fun I had ever had as a child, and I'd really appreciated my mom for taking the time to put it all together. After two days of looking, I'd begun to see the logic in the items she'd chosen and the places where she'd hidden them. I had been looking in an area for an extended period of time, and then realized that I was looking for the wrong thing in the wrong place. That was the feeling I was having about the search for Charlie. I was pretty sure I was looking in the wrong place, and that feeling was validated by the lack of meaningful results. Then my research was interrupted in the most pleasant way.

"Hey there, tall, dark, and handsome!"

Ready to joke back, I turned around but found myself speechless.

Helen, in all her glory, was *standing* in my doorway. My mind was as paralyzed as my legs had been my entire life. I had made it a point in my life never to objectify people or reduce them to their parts like so many people had done to me and my shriveled legs while I sat in Auto, but this woman's long legs, creamy skin, and light brunette hair came together into one hell of an attractive person. Her tight jeans, white blouse, and leather jacket all emphasized her curvy figure, and in my stupor, all I could do was mutter.

"Holy cow."

Quick as always, she rebutted. "Now, Ryan. It's not nice to call a woman a cow."

"No, it's just...that...you're...you...you're standing. Walking. And you're here. In my house. We always talked about hanging out more, but it's nice that we're finally able to do it. With legs! Holy shit!" I thought it was a nice save.

"Right. Well, it's nice to see you too."

I motioned for her to enter my room. "Yes! Come in. Have a seat. If you want. I don't sit much these days. But you can if you like."

"I'm good with standing."

"So how were the last parts of your procedure? Did you fall off the balance beams like me? I did at least a dozen times."

She scowled. "Yes, it was rough, but I got through it. Like I thought, it wasn't nearly as hard as the dark times right after migrating."

"Agreed."

"How's life been at home?"

"Good! Mom's adjusting slowly, but she'll come around. I haven't really let loose by running or sprinting yet, but it's definitely on my to-do list."

Helen glanced at the hologram on the desk and moved next to me for a closer look. I could almost feel her beauty emanating from her, and she had the most intoxicating fragrance on.

Pointing to my search result, she said, "So, what's this?"

"Oh, this. It's nothing."

"It doesn't look like nothing."

I figured I could share my situation with her since she had completed her migration. "If you remember I had asked you about having strange dreams or memories that didn't seem like your own? Well, I am still having those, and I was just trying to do some research to make sense of them."

She nodded. "Oh. Smart. Find anything interesting?"

"Nothing yet, but I'll keep looking. I made it one of my new life goals. Had to do something to fill the emptiness left by getting legs, as strange as that sounds."

"Not strange at all. I had the same feeling when I was leaving ADG. So, I decided I want to complete a triathlon! I'm sure the running and biking will be fine, but the real hurdle for me is getting back into the water for the first time since the accident."

"Wow. That's awesome. You've got me beat. The only other thing I have planned is to get an apartment."

"Yeah, I feel like I have handled the whole procedure pretty well. All that hard work really did pay off. That said, I know the speech is important to you and all, but I have to admit that I'm not really looking forward to going back to ADG tonight. Part of me just wants to—"

"Move on?" I couldn't help but interrupt.

Then we turned to face other, meeting only inches from each other's face, and I looked deeply into her gorgeous brown eyes as she batted them.

"Yeah. You too, Ry?"

As taken as I was by her, I didn't miss a beat. "Definitely. But another part of me sees it as the horse that I need to get back on. You know, to fully move on."

"Yeah, I guess you're right. Man, it sure is nice having someone who can relate during recovery. I'm not sure if I could have gotten through it so well without thinking about you the whole time." She smiled.

My whole body tingled. "Yeah, I thought...still think about you a lot. Knowing how tough everything was, I was worried about you. Every step I thought, 'How will Helen handle this?' Then I would remember how much of a badass you are and that always made me feel better. And seeing you standing next to me now...is just..." I noticed that she was hanging on my every word, staring intently at my mouth, my lips.

"You were saying?" She leaned in.

I was nervous, but slowly moved toward her. I had never kissed a girl, let alone an amazing woman like Helen, and so all I could do was draw from books I had read and movies I had seen. She closed her eyes and puckered up, and I followed suit. The glorious meeting of our two sets of lips was about to happen, and it would be the most glorious thing to happen since getting legs.

"Ryan, honey, the next bullet-train to the city is leaving in ten minutes!"

Thanks, Mom.

Helen quickly pulled back and gathered herself. "Yeah, we better get going, Ry."

Disappointed, I muttered, "Oh, sure."

I tapped off my netphone, shoved it into my pocket, and we were off. We spent the entire walk to the bus stop avoiding what had nearly happened in my room, though, other than the first time in the elevator with her, I had never felt very awkward around Helen—at least, no more awkward than usual. This time was no different. The bullet arrived and we boarded, then chose to stand the whole time to take advantage of our new bodies. In no time, the bus came to its abrupt halt, and we exited toward the ADG facilities.

"It looks different," Helen said.

"Yeah, it kind of does. I think we held the place in such high regard for so long because it held the key to us walking. Now it doesn't have anything else to offer us but the painful memories of the migration."

"I was talking about the new paint job of the west wing, but I get what you're saying."

Classic Helen and Ryan. Me overanalyzing and her cracking dry, silly jokes.

"Oh, yeah. That too."

We strolled by the Garden of Gods and Titans, passing small crowds of other speech-goers as we made our way down to Hawkins Hall. Helen and I furnished our tickets at the box office, went through the weapon detectors, and headed down the auditorium walkway to the front row. We found our seats and settled in just as the announcer gave the introduction.

"Good evening, ladies and gentlemen. Thank you all for attending tonight's speech by the world-famous Cameron Walsh. As the first human to successfully complete a mind migration, he has a unique perspective into the early days of the procedure. He is also its biggest advocate. Please give a warm welcome and a round of applause for our fine guest!"

The packed hall was roaring as energetic entrance music played over the speakers. A simple light show contrasted by party fog drew our attention to the right side of the stage. I was more than happy to stand up and clap as loudly as I could. Helen wasn't as excited, but playfully joined in. And then, there he was.

For a man of medium stature, he had incredible posture. There was also a genuine essence about him that said, "I'm an important person, but I'm no different than anyone of you." He waved at the right side of the crowd and then the left. Each side responded by making more noise as if on cue. He nodded in acknowledgment, all the while looking slightly embarrassed by the attention. If it was an act, he deserved an award. Finally, he settled into the center of the stage.

"Thank you. Thank you all."

The crowd died down, and we all took our seats.

"Greetings, and again, thanks for making this speech a possibility. Your continued interest in mind migrations is what makes the procedure possible—a procedure that is getting better and better each day!"

Intermittent cheering and applause followed, and he waited for a break to continue.

"Today marks the tenth anniversary of when I learned that gas-powered motorcycles are dangerous."

Guilty laughter rolled throughout the room.

"Today also marks the tenth anniversary of when the fine folks at Atlas Digenetics started the process to save my life."

Whistling and more applause followed, but Cameron put his hand up.

"They were attempting something that, to that point, was only science fiction. Their competitors had tried and failed. The public was in an uproar at how inhumane the process was. 'Let him die in peace,' they said. 'Let his soul rest!' And in the face of all that adversity, they persevered. Instead of letting a life go, the fine folks at ADG chose a different path. They tried to save a life in the only way they knew how. I will forever be grateful for the gamble they took on me all those years ago. It has allowed me to live a fully productive life after a horrendous accident nearly took it all away."

He paused for effect, clearly well-practiced at making these speeches.

"I know many of you have had accidents in your lives. Many of you have even made mistakes that you regret. Hell, maybe you even had your fair share of bad luck. If you're like me, and I bet many of you are, you firmly believe in second chances. You want another crack at the thing called *life*. Especially when it didn't pan out for you the first time. That's one of the big reasons why my number one goal since getting my second chance is to spread the word. That word is *miracle*, and it's the only way I know how to describe the live-saving procedure known as *mind migration*."

Applause filled the room again, and this time Cameron let it go on for a moment. It eventually died down, and he spoke in segments to emphasize his words.

"To that end, I travel the globe, celebrating that miracle and letting others in the scientific community know the facts:

"Mind migrations are safe.

"Mind migrations are necessary.

"Mind migrations are the next best thing to the miracle of life itself."

More explosive applause.

"For these reasons, we must all do our part to protect God's original miracles by preserving them through the use of mind migrations. And yet, understandably so, there are still doubters."

He turned to my direction, and had I not known any better, I would have thought he was looking dead at me. I was so focused on the speech that I hadn't noticed Helen had reached over to hold my hand.

"Ten years ago, I was a shell of a person on the brink of death. They told me about the procedure, and I was initially skeptical, even with the few choices that I did have. Then they showed me my host—the body that I've called home for the last decade—and there was an instant connection at that moment, one that lives on to this day."

Cameron's words about a connection with his host made my mind swirl like just after my migration. Something strange was happening, and I was helpless to stop it. Thoughts began to overload my brain and chaos ensued as my mind tried to process what was happening to no avail. There was no pain like before, but Hawkins Hall was quickly fading to nothingness. Cameron, the crowd…it was all going away. My hand went limp in Helen's as everything was disappearing in front of me, and then, silence.

I blinked.

It was all gone. I was in a vast black abyss.

I blinked again to be sure, and instead of being in Hawkins Hall, saw only endless space that was entirely black except for me. Strangely enough, I was sitting in Auto.

"Hello?" My voice echoed hard in the expanse.

As I had done thousands of times, I engaged Auto to spin me around in a circle. I was hoping someone—anyone—was there to help me figure out what was happening. But there was no one. I spun back around, and suddenly, I saw something. Something in the distance. It was a blurry white figure.

"Hello!"

The echo was so loud that it nearly hurt my ears.

Startling me, a raspy whisper hissed back, "Ryan."

"Yes?"

"Ryan."

"Yes? Who are you?"

The voice wheezed back at me, "You have to save me."

"What? Who are you? Save you from what?"

It was difficult to speak with the echoing making each word that followed harder to hear and say.

"Save me, Ryan."

"Save you from what!"

"Ryan, you have to save me!"

"I don't know who you are, and I can't help you if you don't explain yourself."

"Ryan."

"Yes?"

A painful silence filled the void.

"Save me from myself!"

The echo was so loud that blood poured from my ears and eyes, and I was certain that was the end for me. The deafening voice was about to put me out of my misery when a familiar voice broke through the insanity.

"Ryan! Ryan! Are you okay?"

I opened my eyes to Helen, frantically shaking me in my seat at Cameron Walsh's speech. Rapidly fluttering my eyes to make sure it was real, I gathered myself and sat up. Suddenly I knew exactly what I had to do.

I looked Helen dead in the eye. "I have to get out of here right now!" I popped up and darted in front of her, toward the exit.

"Are you okay? What happened, Ryan?"

I tried to respond, but Cameron had said something that got the crowd excited again, which drowned out my words. I didn't have time to say it again. Instead, I bolted for the doors before Helen could even get out of the front row. While racing up the aisle, I could hear the speech coming to an end.

"Thank you all again. And remember…"

As I pushed open the doors to the lobby, I caught Cameron's final words.

"…never give up hope."

CHAPTER 15

HOPE'S FUNERAL

"**N**EVER GIVE UP HOPE."

That was what I always told myself. But it was a funny thing, hope. It could keep you focused even during the worst of times. It could move mountains. It could change the course of history. It could keep you chasing a dream that was unattainable. Hope was amazing, but as strong as it was, its absence was just as powerful.

When I went to third grade at a new school, I had hope. A lot of it. My third-grade teacher, Mrs. Whittaker, asked me what I wanted to be when I grew up. Had she asked me that question even six months before, I wouldn't have had a good answer. But then, I had taken a liking to one particular career.

As certain as a ten-year-old could be, I responded, "Firefighter."

Firefighters not only got to wear cool equipment and train to be big and strong, but they got to help people—people who were in need, people who were desperate. A job with decent pay and benefits, a job with respect from most people was the most a kid with a rough home life could ask for. While the hours would be tough, I could get used to it.

As I got older and learned more, I realized that it didn't matter what I wanted out of a career. Teachers only asked questions like that to keep you dreaming. Even counselors with the best of intentions were only there to distract me from the real social problems that became obvious when, at fifteen, I visited a local fire station. I asked the fire chief what it would take to become a firefighter. Even then, I expected the work-hard speech, saying that anything was possible. But I must have caught the chief on a particularly honest day.

"Son, is your dad or mom a firefighter?"

"No."

"Do you have an uncle or other close relative who's a firefighter?"

"I don't know any other relatives."

"Look, you don't just become a firefighter these days. You really have to know someone. Someone's gotta know you."

I was crushed to say the least. I looked up and down in the hiring manual on the net, but nowhere did it say you had to be a family member of a current firefighter to apply. As depression set in, something completely different dawned on me, and I actually learned a valuable lesson from the experience.

Everything was political.

Turned out that the corrupt city government had implemented an under-the-table nepotistic hiring policy that ensured only good ol' boys and their sons and daughters got to fight fires in the city. Ever since it became national law to privatize police and fire, they got away with pretty much anything they wanted.

In that sense, they had a lot in common with the Padre: operate with impunity. I was sure he'd killed my family. Last I spoke with them was the night before I was arrested, and when I tried to implement Plan B, I never got confirmation that it went through. I tried dialing our apartment with my weekly call for two months, but it went right to voicemail. Hearing Sarah's recorded voice hurt more and more each time. Then, a week ago, someone finally answered.

"Hello."

The man's voice shocked me, but I was just relieved to be talking to someone.

"Hello! I need to speak to Sarah. Are my kids all right?"

"Who is this? If you're talking about the family who lived here before, they disappeared. Don't bother calling here again." Click.

"Shit!"

The Padre's goons were likely all around me, and it was only a matter of time before I'd take a shiv to the gut. It had been a year since I was railroaded in court, and I hadn't even been sentenced yet. Hell, I hadn't heard from my public defender in ten months, which was why I was shocked when a private lawyer showed up the other week. Before he would likely dangle hope in my face, I figured I'd have a little fun.

"I was found guilty."

"Uh, hi, Mr. R—"

"The name's Charlie. I was found guilty. Case closed."

"Okay, Charlie, do you mind if we talk about the details around it?"

"Yes, I do mind."

"You were convicted of five felonies: driving a car with the VIN removed, redirecting your vehicle's GPS coordinates, reckless manual driving, two counts of injuring another as a result of reckless manual driving, and vehicular homicide. Each of those could be fifteen to twenty-five years behind bars by the time you get to sentencing. The prosecution also wants to add criminal conspiracy, given the nature of your vehicle. Add to that the dozen misdemeanors and a couple pages of citations, and you'd be lucky to get life. They may even request the death penalty."

"Guilty."

"I specifically asked to meet in the visitors' trailer for a reason. I'm not a normal lawyer, you see. I'm actually part of a legal task force that is trying to nail down who we believe to be your employer. Mr. Ernesto Guerrero. You probably know him as the Padre."

"Guilty, I said!"

"Hear me out, Charlie. In exchange for your cooperation, we would be able to get the prosecution to set your sentence down to time served. But we need concrete information that would lead us to the Padre's whereabouts and the activities in which he is involved. You could be a free man in a couple years after the case against Mr. Guerrero has concluded."

A free man? What the hell did he know? I would never be free again. You didn't mess with the Padre and live to brag about it, and neither did anyone you loved. Regardless, I was once again in a similar position as the one Mrs. Whittaker put me in, in third grade, and a thought summarizing that feeling popped into my head.

What do you want to be when you grow up? Alone and dead in prison? Or alone and dead on the streets?

Since the man in the suit was the first person to speak with me in weeks, I decided to play his game and see what he had to offer.

"What about my family?"

"Yes, I was afraid you would ask about them. They disappeared around the time of your arrest, and in spite of our efforts to contact them, they seem to be off the grid."

"You mean dead!"

"No, Charlie, we don't have any leads, but the local police also haven't found any…bodies either. Do you have any idea where they might be?"

"Ah, what the hell."

"I beg your pardon, Charlie?"

"I'll do it."

"Do what?"

"I'll tell you everything I know."

His face lit up. "That's great news, Charlie! I guarantee you won't regret this. Now, we'll want to get you transferred downstate where the Padre won't have such easy access to you."

"Don't worry about a transfer. I just want to tell my story."

"All right, when do you think you could provide your official deposition on the matter?"

"How about right now?"

Shock came across his face as he scrambled to grab his briefcase and fumbled around in it to get his netphone to record me. I told him everything. Every last damn detail that I had ever known about the Padre. The jobs we did. The locations. Rough amounts of money exchanged. The product I had seen on the one job. I was like a faucet of truth spewing every last ounce until the well went dry.

"This will be very helpful in the case against the Padre."

"I hope so."

"And that's why you must die."

Before he could grab the gun in his briefcase, I was able to punch him in the neck to stun him, and then I slammed his head onto the table to knock him out cold. I'd known what the meeting had been all along. I had known he was asking about my family to give me a false sense of hope. I had known the transfer was a way to separate me from the rest of the pack and execute me out in a field somewhere. I had known he worked for the Padre like so many around me likely did. But it had been worth it to get a rise out of him, and it had been probably the last bit of payback I would get to the man who had put the finishing touches on ruining my life.

After thirty minutes, the guards discovered me lying face down on the trailer floor next to the unconscious lawyer. They still roughed me up a bit, but I had gotten plenty worse beatings in my life. They took me to solitary, and I just laid there. For a whole week, I laid there thinking about life, thinking about what could have been. My mind was still busy replaying all of my memories for the thousandth time when they finally came to take me back to a holding cell. It didn't help anything. When put into a no-win situation like I was, you may try to rationalize it by choosing the lesser of the two evils. But when the stakes are high, making those decisions changes you.

It was like what we had discovered in the cellar of that warehouse in Pakistan. Despite the screwed-up things we had already seen during that tour, Sierra and I had had no clue what to expect, and we certainly hadn't been ready for the truth. After the smoke had settled, we'd seen the hearts of thirty-six people had been removed from their chests and delicately placed in suspension within medical tubes. Machines were gently pumping life into the hearts, keeping them beating at a stable rate. As I had walked down that gauntlet, I was able to hear the rhythmic beats of the hearts like the steady pounding of a base drum. That was when I'd noticed a note on the wall across the room. Approaching with some hesitation, I'd read it.

"Invader scum. These are the hearts from your brainwashed foot soldiers. There are thirty-six of them—the daily average of cluster bombs you dropped on us for your murderous war. This is only a fraction of the lives taken compared to how many we have lost and will continue to lose. As you continue to break our hearts, we will continue to take yours."

I had instantly wanted to mow down as many of the enemy as I could find. I had been seething with ire, to the point that I was shaking. What the hell did you do after reading a note like that? What the hell were you supposed to do when you find a place like that? How was I supposed to deal with it? None of my training had prepared me for anything remotely close to that. The enemy had been trying to get to us, and it had been working.

Then nausea had overcome me as it became clear where we were. So deep in morbid thought, I hadn't notice that Sierra had come up next to me and just finished reading the note.

She had connected the dots almost instantly. "The morgue."

"What?"

"The thirty-six bodies that got sent home for burial. The Y-incisions." Sierra grimaced and walked back through the room.

In that moment, something had dawned on me. As much as I hated the enemy, and as much as they said they'd wanted us to leave, they hadn't been stupid. They had known that by killing our men and women and taking their hearts, soldiers would snap, the war would intensify, and the whole climate of the country would sink into even more bitter turmoil. We would drop more bombs, and they would take more hearts. So, it had become clear to me at that moment that they hadn't been looking to stop the war but had a stake in making it worse. In fact, the people most affected, the nonaffiliated locals, had been caught between the enemy and us, and they hadn't cared whose bullet killed their loved ones. They'd hated us all. Then I'd remembered Sarah telling me about the protesters back home who had been asking for peace. As livid as I was, I had known what had to be done.

"Corporal, we're shutting this down, and we're telling HQ that we didn't find any arms at this location."

Sierra had been rightfully skeptical. "Come again, Sergeant?"

"We're shutting it down. We're not letting the enemy keep our wounds open any longer. They're not going to win this time."

"Uh, sir, yes, sir."

I had gone right up to the generator, pressed two buttons, and pulled out a cable. The hum of the room began to die down and the ventilators slowly came to a halt. In an instant, the silence became deafening and the previously fluttering hearts hunched down, finally able to rest.

"Sir, what do we do with them now?"

"Can you line the door with C4 on our way out? So the next person to set foot in here will trip it?"

"Yes, but I don't understand."

"If we say this place should be taken off the munitions map, we'll never come back. But the enemy might."

Our conversation had been interrupted by Bravo Company. "Coyote Royal, no communication in fifteen minutes. Do you copy, over?"

"Bravo Company, this is Coyote Royal, over."

"Team Trinity has landed successfully. I repeat, Trinity has landed. Do you copy?"

"Copy that, Bravo Company. What are our orders now? Over."

"Is your flight close to landing? Over."

Sierra had looked at me with one eyebrow up.

"That's a negative, Bravo Company. The destination is not in sight. I repeat, the destination is not in sight. Over."

"Then let's all rendezvous with team Trinity to celebrate their successful trip. Over and out."

Sierra and I completed the trap and got our asses out of the city and back to base. That night, I drank as much hooch as I could get my hands on. Being severely dehydrated in a desert climate hadn't boded well for PT the morning after, and I'd thrown up more that morning than any other time in my life. Maybe combined.

Going to the med bay for fluids, the nurse had joked with me. "Did you get stung by one of those deadly reds?"

Oddly enough, the memory of that time felt more reminiscent than traumatic. Maybe the years after my service had finally allowed me to get over everything that happened. Maybe it allowed me to accept the decisions I made.

Kids would do that to you. Lucy had been my life when I'd gotten home. Then Joey had been my life too. I'd made a promise to myself when debriefing from my last tour that I wouldn't let my baggage hold back Sarah and our family. I had to be there for them. I had to show them love. All of the things I'd never gotten as a kid, I wanted to give them. It was the least I could do, considering the sacrifices Sarah had made while I was deployed.

But I'd realized early on that I couldn't try to be the dad that I'd always wanted. No. That would have set the kids *and* me up for failure. If that wasn't what they'd needed or even wanted, they would resent me, and I would reset them. They hadn't been me, and they'd needed a father who would be attentive to their needs. There weren't any shortcuts or easy routes to parenting. You had to know when to talk to your kids. More importantly, you had to know when to shut the hell up and listen. While kids couldn't know as much as adults, they sure were perceptive, and it was with all that information that you had to figure out how to be the best parent you could be.

That was what had made everything so much worse. I had been a shitty dad. When I was around, I had been preoccupied with the next job coming up. When I hadn't been around, I had been breaking the law doing those jobs. And because of me, they were gone. They hadn't even gotten a fighting chance because of the screw-up-of-a-father I turned out to be. So, not only was I not the parent that they'd needed or even wanted, but I had been worse. As bad as I'd had it as a kid, at least I was given opportunities. I had taken that away from them when I'd agreed to work for the Padre, and it hurt me deep down in my soul. It was the kind of pain that really made one feel isolated. I'd felt as lonely as each one of those thirty-six hearts that we had found that night. Those hearts had no hope left, and neither did I. Just like them, it was finally time that I put myself to rest.

Every night at 9:55 PM, the intercom rang with commands to get into our beds for lockdown and roll call. Once in our beds, straps locked us in, and the automated outer doors to the holding cells opened up. Roll call was completed by guards who walked past each cell and scanned the inmates before the doors eventually closed and we were unlocked from our beds. The building was really old, so they must have added the automation after the doors were installed. Early on, I'd noticed a box taking up half the ceiling that had to house the chain mechanism for opening and closing the door to my cell. The room engineers hadn't been completely dumb, so you couldn't reach it with your hands or really tamper with it in any meaningful way. Additionally, the doors wouldn't open if you weren't locked in your bed, and you wouldn't be unlocked from your bed until the door closed. But there was an opening on top of the box that I thought would make my plot possible.

For several weeks, I stole sheets from the laundry room. Each night, I'd put another one on my bed until they reached thirty feet in length when all tied together. Then I paid a guy my last pack of menthols to get me a piece of metal that was hook shaped. It didn't have to be fancy, but I definitely needed it to be small and able to grab onto the chain of my door. With that, I finally had all the pieces I needed.

During the day, I ran the sheet around my bed, along the wall, over the door, and left the hook hanging just out of sight until the last minute prior to lockdown/roll call. I had to get the hook just right so that the chain grabbed it as the door was closing, not opening; otherwise, the roll call guard would notice. There wouldn't be much room for error, but I didn't have anything else to lose, so it was worth a shot.

With the little time I had left, I knew I needed to write a letter to the person I'd hurt the most even though I was dreading it. My palms were sweating as I grabbed the pen and paper, but I was steady as I wrote. Finishing the letter brought a little bit of peace to me, though short-lived. Moments after I set down the pen, sirens blared over the intercom and the lights flickered in the hallways. With my senses instantly flooded, it took all my willpower to focus on the task at hand. My time had come.

Darting to the far corner of the room, I stood up on the toilet and grabbed the hook. Holding it tightly in one hand, I gathered the slack of the sheets in my other hand. In one motion, I heaved the hook toward the slot in the box.

Clank!

"Dammit!" I missed.

I reeled the sheet back in and gripped the hook again as I heard the guard doors opening down the hall. The savage growling of the K9 units added to the intensity of the moment as I gave the hook another chuck. It rattled through, and I was certain I had failed again. But in trying to pull back the sheet, it was stuck. It was done! I hit it exactly the way I had planned.

I immediately dove into bed, fitted the tight sheets around my lower neck, and then, pulled the covers up to my chin to hide the evidence. Everything was in place, and if it was going to happen, it would be in just a few moments.

The cell door began to open with a repeated clank, clank, clank. I could feel the hooks moving in unison with the chain, and as I had planned, it stayed perfectly in place. Once the door was fully open, two guards appeared in front and scanned my open cell. One of the guards aimed his flashlight right into my eyes, but I didn't flinch at all as I stared directly at the ceiling. He paused for what seemed like an entire minute as his rabid dog lost its mind in my direction, and I was sure they were onto me. I began to mentally prepare for another beating and more time in solitary.

"Dammit, George, get over here! Another idiot is frothing at the mouth. We need to cut out the damn light show because these bastards are sensitive!"

Thank God for Bob's seizures.

A comforting feeling washed over me in those final moments. No longer did I need to worry about everything under the sun. No more did I have to feel sad about never becoming a firefighter. I no longer had to carry the burden of the thirty-six hearts. I didn't have to be in pieces over losing my family. I didn't have to feel like a failure as a father anymore. I was going to do something good as my final act. Something good for me. Something good for the world.

The intercom screamed that lockdown/roll call was over, and the lights and sirens died down. I had roughly thirty seconds until the end, and just like when I was lying face down on the concrete, Sarah and the kids flashed into my mind. *They were so precious. They deserved so much better than a person like me in their lives. Maybe, in another life, I would return to be a better person. Ah, what the hell did I know?*

The mechanism for the door kicked on, and I could see the bottom of the hook sitting on top of the box. The door began to close, and I panicked when the chain failed to immediately grab the hook, but a second later, I could feel the tension around my neck getting stronger and stronger. Tighter and tighter until the life was being squeezed out of me through my neck. As the door shut completely, the lack of air finally got to me as I half-heartedly tried to fight against it. It wasn't long before numbness overtook my body, and flashes from my past appeared, becoming my very last thoughts.

"I love you, Sarah. I love you, Lucy. I love you, Joey."

Ugh!

"No! I can't breathe!"

CHAPTER 16
DOUBT TRUTH TO BE A LIAR

"NO! I CAN'T BREATHE!"
Jumping out of bed, I was drenched in sweat and my heart was pounding out of my chest. I was trying desperately to catch my breath and remember what the hell had happened in the nightmare I'd just come out of. Scrambling to grab my netphone, I opened the journal and began frantically typing.

> I was locked away in a jail. A hook and a chain. I couldn't breathe but why?

At that point, I could basically feel the details leaving me. Like a tiny puddle when the sun comes out, all of the specifics quickly evaporated from my mind. It was frustrating as hell because I felt like something very important had happened. In an attempt to keep it together, I thought about all of the dreams I had been having. They were all very similar in that I would wake up to fear and anxiety followed by the worst feelings: sadness, depression, despair, hopelessness.

But something different was brewing this morning as the terror from dreaming of suffocation subsided. For the first time since the migration, I felt a sense of total relief. Deep down in my core, I felt like everything had been resolved, and while it didn't make any sense to me, it still felt like major progress.

My thoughts were interrupted by the buzz of my netphone, and I was thankful it was Helen.

"Morning!"

"Oh my God, Ryan! Are you okay?" Her voice was trembling.

The euphoria from my breakthrough muted my reply. "I'm actually doing fine. I'm really sorry that I left you the way I did last night."

"You had me so damn worried going home. Not cool!"

"Sorry! I had a strange episode during the speech. I felt like I had to get out of there. I just went home and passed out in my bed."

"So, you're not completely freaking out anymore?"

"No, I actually think what happened might have been a good thing. I'll be talking with my family counselor later today, and I'll bounce it off of him. But in general, I think I'm good."

"Well, damn. I'm glad to hear that, Ryan. Just keep me posted and let me know if you need anything."

"Thanks! I definitely will."

"Now that I know you didn't jump off a bridge, I can start my day. We're still on for drinks Friday night, right?"

"Wouldn't miss it for the world!"

"Great. I'll see you then!"

"Bye!"

I felt bad for worrying her, but it felt good to know she cared. She really helped round out my support system, and to that end, I was glad to be seeing Dr. Dean later that day. He was familiar. For years, he had known my family, and had been very good at helping me get through issues. Most importantly, he was removed from the mind migration process, so I was thinking that kind of outside perspective would be helpful.

Jumping into the shower, my morning routine was complete in the blink of an eye; I was fully dressed. Interestingly, I was excited that mundane activities were finally becoming mundane and I could focus on more important things with my new abilities. Heading downstairs, I pulled up the news hologram on my phone while I ate a large bowl of oat bran, and while shoveling the first big spoonful into my mouth, some very important news appeared.

NO LONGER A COLD WAR: FPR INVADES HAWAII, DECLARES WAR ON OUR NATION.

After twenty years of jockeying for position in parts of the Middle East and Asia, tensions came to a head today in the

South Pacific. The Free People's Republic mechanical forces used advanced stealth technology to land on the west beach of Kauai just after 4:30 AM local time. They began firing on Fort Kamehameha shortly after, resulting in twenty military casualties, two civilian casualties, and significant property damage before the invading forces could be disabled. President Joy Rogers is meeting with congressional leaders and foreign allies to prepare for the impending war.

War was a normal part of life for me. I was just two years old when our military was forced to pull out of the Great India/Pakistan War, or GIP with a soft *g* as it was referred to by the antiwar folks. They'd say, "We got gipped (gypped) by the war," completely unaware of how offensive the phrase actually was to many other groups, though they were right in that the war was unjust. Pakistan had been harboring extremists who'd sought to destabilize India in hopes of spreading to that country. Not only had our involvement in the conflict failed to reduce the number of those extremists, but some also argued that we'd only increased the group's numbers due to locals uniting against a common, foreign enemy. International pressure had made it impossible to maintain a presence in the area, and troops as well as the then newly deployed mechanized marines were quickly brought home. Surprisingly, the conflict had still turned out favorably for India and Pakistan. Within a couple of years, the two governments were able to isolate the extremists and nullify their influence.

Only a few years later conflicts began with the former nation of China where the Free People's Republic (FPR) originated. For years, that country had been in a state of chaos as the majority of the population rebelled against China's government and military. Again, we'd sent in forces to assist in maintaining global order, but it wasn't long before the surrounding countries, including parts of India and Pakistan, began to help the rebels. It had taken less than a decade for the loosely affiliated countries to combine into a super nation.

After "losing" GIP and with pockets of fighting with FPR, our country had experienced tough times. Some economist said we had been technically in a recession for the last fifteen years or so. But it really mimicked what the history books described as a depression. There was mass unemployment, home foreclosures, civil unrest, and increased police forces. Luckily for me, Mom had been employed by Grant Machinery for the last thirty years. Originally, they'd provided pneumatics and hydraulics for commercial and industrial use. Once GIP started, the government quickly contracted the company to supply the military and municipalities. Mom maintained the distribution systems that had made sure all deliveries were accurate and timely. She had gotten plenty of overtime during the war and after, so while things were tight, we always seemed to have enough to get by.

Still, Mom had been conflicted with the position she'd held for so long. On the one hand, she had been able to provide for us to live a decent life. On the other, she'd felt like she was aiding in the efforts of questionable conflicts. She told me stories about how she'd had to sneak into the back of her office building because protesters blocked the main entrance and parking lots. While protesting had been illegal for the last ten years or so, there was still the occasional group that gathered in front of the building before being chased off or arrested by the police. Mom hadn't blamed them for being passionate, but it hadn't made going to work for her any easier.

While I was unhappy about a new war, it was relieving to think about something bigger than my mind migration even for just a few minutes. It reminded me that no matter how bad I thought I had it, others had it far worse.

Wrapping up my breakfast, I walked into the living room to ask Mom her opinion on the international situation. Sitting in her favorite relaxer chair, she had a hologram pulled up on her netphone of what looked like different balls of yarn.

"Did you see the news?"

She swiped the hologram off. "I did."

"How will that play out at work?"

She shrugged. "I'm sure it'll be like it's always been."

I sat down on the love seat across from her. "You know, you don't need to take care of me anymore. Maybe…maybe you could find another job."

"Oh, sweetie. I've thought about it. But trying to switch jobs in this economy isn't smart. I guess I'm just hoping that I can keep the job until I reach the maximum age limit, then I'll just live off my savings."

"Don't worry, Mom. I'll take care of you when you can't work anymore. I promise."

"I appreciate that, honey, but I hope you won't have to. I really want you to move on with your life even though it'll be difficult for me to adjust."

"Mom! Moving on doesn't mean I won't be in your life. It just means I won't be living with you. But I'll call you just about every night to check in."

"It's not the same, but I'll take what I can get."

"All right. Well, I'm heading to Dr. Dean's."

"Tell him I said hello. Love you, sweetie!"

"Love you."

I got up and threw on my shoes and jacket before bursting out of the front door and down the stairs. I had a pep in my step as I boarded the bullet and arrived in the city in the blink of an eye. It was a decent walk to Dr. Dean's office, but I was happy to stroll with the crowds and take in the scenery that I had always taken for granted.

In the lobby of Dr. Dean's building, I decided to skip the elevator and take the stairs to the third floor. Entering the office, I nodded at the doctor's longtime assistant and said, "Hello!"

He tilted his head in curiosity for a moment. "Ryan Carter, is that you?"

"Yes, sir, it is."

"You did one of those brain transfer things, right?"

I didn't feel like correcting him. "Yes, sir."

"That's amazing. Good for you. I just need you to put your right thumb in the scanner over here to verify your identity."

"No problem."

Beep!

"Great! The doctor is waiting for you, so you can head right in."

"Thanks!" I stepped across the small waiting area and opened the door, finding him daydreaming out the window. "Hello, Dr. Dean!"

Startled a bit, he turned and his eyes lit up. He walked in my direction with his hand extended "Ryan! Look at you! What a big change!"

I gripped his hand firmly and gave it the best shake I could. With all of the intimate details he knew about me, standing eye-to-eye with him for the first time was a bit jarring, but his sincerity kept the mood light.

"How's your mom?"

"She's doing well, considering. She says hi."

"You know I told her to schedule an appointment to talk through her feelings about your procedure, but I haven't heard anything yet. Let her know that I'm available."

"I will. Thanks!"

He motioned me toward his office couch. "Please lay down and get comfortable."

I took off my jacket and hung it on the wall hook by the door, then stretched out on the couch, realizing that for as many times as I had been there, this was my first time without Auto. Even though I could have had him flatten out, Auto was not nearly as comfortable as the couch. With a sigh, it was easy to relax.

"So, I'm guessing by the looks of it, the migration went well?"

I caught him up on everything leading up to my first dream. He had always been a great listener, like every counselor should be, but he also provided great perspective as well.

"That's great to hear, Ryan. You know, I'm no expert, but I've always been fascinated with mind migrations. *'Dubito, ergo cogito, ergo sum.'*"

"What's that?"

"*'Dubito, ergo cogito, ergo sum'* is the quote on which I based my dissertation. A lot of armchair philosophers shorten it, but I tend to think that waters it down, and to some extent, removes a crucial part of it. 'I doubt, therefore I think, therefore I am.' The 'doubt' is very important. You mentioned that during the catch-22 phase, you truly questioned whether you were alive or not. The very fact that you could doubt it meant that you existed the whole time."

Of all the counseling I had gotten at ADG, no one had summed it up that succinctly.

"Wow. That's a great way of looking at it."

"Yes. Pretty neat stuff."

"Dr. Dean, there is something else I wanted to talk to you about."

"Yes, of course. We have time."

"Apparently, it's normal for people who complete a mind migration to have dreams and visions and hear voices. It has something to do with your mind being reprocessed in the new brain, and it usually has to do with media that you've consumed in your life—like books, movies, video games, and so on. They say it can last for a couple of weeks after the migration. Well, I'm still having dreams and visions and hearing voices."

"Okay."

"And if they were obscure and random, I actually wouldn't be nearly as worried. But mine seem related to one another. They seem real."

"What do you mean by related?"

"Well, in the dreams, I see through the eyes of a person, a man. I'm pretty sure his name is Charlie. And as Charlie, I do things…things I've never done in real life. Most of the details escape me when I wake up, but I have been able to piece together a few things in my journal. In one dream, I'm running from someone. In another, I'm manually driving an old car. Then there's a dream about a family where everyone is sick, and yet another dream about betrayal."

"Hm. I could see how these experiences reflect aspects of your real life. You always wanted to run. I'm sure you've at least subconsciously wanted to manually drive. It's a lot of fun. You could consider your paralysis a form of sickness, and you may have subconscious feelings that someone has betrayed you. Perhaps you feel this way about your mother. It's a stretch, but maybe Charlie is an incarnation of your subconscious, and your mind created him as a defense mechanism."

"The thought had crossed my mind, but the voices make me think otherwise."

"And what has happened with those?"

"They question things. Who is Charlie? Who is Ryan? It's gotten to the point where I am actually researching characters named Charlie in the media I've consumed."

"Oh?"

"Yes, but I haven't found anything that adds up. So that has led me to my next guess."

"Which is?"

"Maybe Charlie was a real person."

"How would that be possible?"

"Maybe they screwed up my procedure. Maybe they migrated another person's mind into my host's brain. I don't know. But up until last night, it really bothered me."

"Up until last night?"

"I was at the Cameron Walsh speech and blacked out in my seat."

"And you're okay?"

"Yes, that's what's strange. I woke up at the theater, and I had the worst feeling. The words 'save me, Ryan' came to mind. I panicked, got home as fast as I could, and locked myself in my room. Then I laid on my bed to try to calm down, and fell asleep."

"And you said you feel better today?"

"Yes! I had another dream last night, though. In this one, I think I was in some kind of jail, and I had the feeling that everything would be over soon. I can't really remember anything else. Just exceptionally good today."

"So, if this Charlie person were real, what do you make of the dream?"

"I don't know for sure, but I was thinking that Charlie got what he deserved. And that's what I needed to...experience for it to be over. This is the best I've felt since before the procedure, so I'm not too sure *what* to make of it."

"Well, that's great, Ryan. Our time is up for now, but it seems like you're handling everything really well. I'd say keep trusting your gut as you go forward. You're a strong person, and I know you'll keep making great progress."

"Thanks!"

I popped up, grabbed my coat off the wall hook, and headed out of the building. Dr. Dean was as helpful as I thought he would be, and if my good mood couldn't get any better, I actually had another reason to be in the city on that day. Barb, the building manager for the apartment I applied for, had left a message agreeing to show it to me. I messaged her to make sure she was ready, and with a little time to kill, decided to skip fast transit and walk the five kilometers to the building. After forty-five minutes, I pressed the button for Barb to let me in.

Buzz!

I swung open the outer door and darted up the stairs to the inner door.

"Hello there. You're here to look at 75A, right?"

"Yes, I'm Ryan. Hello."

She motioned me to follow her down the hallway, and we made our way to the elevator which might as well have been from the movies as it had no virtual interface. Hell, you had to manually open two sets of doors. There was no way I could have lived there comfortably when I was with Auto. After the elevator ride, she led me down a long hallway, and we stopped in front of a dark wooden door. I was pleased that they had updated it with an automated, wireless lock. Barb retrieved the netphone from her pocket and tapped two buttons.

Click. Click.

Beep.

The door creaked open slowly, and a gentle puff of stale air infiltrated my nose. We were met by a dark, empty kitchen as we walked in, and with my eyes forward, I could see the pastel green curtains covering what had to be the sliding balcony door. The curtains filtered the sunlight producing an uninviting tint, and it soon became obvious that the apartment in no way lived up to the vibrant photos I saw on the net. But surprisingly, instead of disappointment, anxiety began to grow.

"Like the ad says, the rent is twenty-five hundred, and we need two months up front. The security deposit is a thousand. Any questions?"

"No. Thanks, Barb."

"Just message me when you're done so I can lock it up."

She left after a couple clicks of the door, and an intense silence seized the room. My anxiety heightened as I took a couple more steps into the living room. Then I stopped to take it all in. To the right, I saw the hallway leading to the bedrooms and bathroom, but my nerves were most intense as I eyed back at the curtains—the balcony. Something deep within me was beckoning me to check it out. The only way I could describe it was that it felt like I was going to get back something I had lost. But my anxiety was quickly turning to fear.

My feet were heavy, but I muscled through the apprehension to reach the other side of the room. Upon moving the curtains aside, the bright sunlight made me squint as I firmly grabbed the handle. It felt oddly familiar as I flipped the lock with my free hand and the clammy air outside rushed onto my face accompanied by the din of the city. My nerves calmed ever so slightly as I took my first step outside, then another. Completely on the balcony, the buildings across the street seemed to go on forever in both directions, but I wanted to see just how high seven stories was so I stepped to the edge. High enough, it turned out. Then I eyed the fire escape. It was weird wrapping my head around the fact that stairs could possibly save my life someday. I was used to them being a barrier.

Satisfied with the balcony, I was about to go back inside when I realized something. The conflicted feelings I'd had when entering the apartment had melted away. It would be a new home, but more importantly, it was the first step toward a new life. And from a financial perspective, I was getting twice the place for the same price as other, smaller apartments. As elation grew in me, my musings were interrupted by a hard wind that blew right into my eyes.

"Ow!" Closing my eyes for just a moment, shock immediately overcame me when I opened them back up. "What the hell!"

Nighttime!

Blinking repeatedly to make sure I wasn't crazy, I looked all around me. The streetlights were on, and I couldn't remember if they had always looked that vintage. Taking a deep breath as I attempted to rationalize my situation, my nose was attacked by the disgusting smoke from what had to be an old-fashioned cigarette. Glancing down, I assumed I would find that a neighbor above had flicked their butt onto my balcony. But that wasn't the case at all.

The cigarette was in my hand!

Then that hand began to creep up from my side and toward my mouth, and though I fought it like hell, it was only a second before I placed the cigarette between my lips against my own will and inhaled hard.

"Ahhhhhhhhhhhh!"

Suddenly, everything was okay. All the anxiety from the day waned completely in that instant, and an undeniable peace replaced it. Satisfied with the view of the city at night, I looked back at the apartment. The lights were on behind the curtains. Instinctively, I took one more hard puff and put the cigarette out on the ledge. Blowing the remaining smoke out, I pulled open the sliding door and took my first step in. Before my eyes could adjust to the light of the room, I heard a noise in the direction of the hallway.

"Hee-hee hee-hee hee-hee."

Fluttering my eyes to gain focus, I saw where the noise was coming from.

"Hee-hee hee-hee hee-hee."

A little girl in a pink shirt and overall jeans was laughing at me. Not knowing who she was, I wanted to ask if she was lost. But instead, the strangest words left my mouth.

"Hi, sweetheart!"

The cutest smile stretched across her face. "Daddy! Let's play hide-and-go-seek." Then she disappeared down the hall.

I, too, had to smile wide as I marched through the living room to follow her. Entering the hallway, it was only a couple steps until I arrived at the first door on the left, and knocked.

"It's Daddy. I know you're in there. Here I come!"

"Hee-hee hee-hee hee-hee."

Opening the door, I was met with pure sadness, and my stomach dropped as I took it all in. The little girl was standing in the middle of the room with her eyes closed. She was deadly pale and had countless medical tubes running from her to some machines by her bed.

"Lucy—"

She opened her pitch-black eyes and let loose a demonic growl. "You're not my dad! Where's my dad?"

CHAPTER 17

THANKS, BUT NO THANKS

"YOU'RE NOT MY DAD! WHERE'S my dad?" I questioned the strange man who had entered Mr. Fredrick's office.

As my social worker, Mr. Fredrick stepped in to explain. "Now, Charlie, we talked about this. Mr. Reno and his wife are going to be taking care of you from now on. They're good people, and I'm sure you'll feel right at home with them soon enough. You just need to give them a chance."

Mr. Reno grinned through his bushy auburn beard as he sat in the chair next to me. "Yeah, Son. We're really excited that you'll be joining our family. We don't have much, but we already have a room made up for you. I hope you like baseball."

I never knew that there was such a thing as an involuntary stink eye until that moment. I couldn't control myself. He gave me bad vibes and was nothing like my dad.

"No. I like football."

His grin faded slightly. "Oh, that's okay. We'll find something we both like."

He began talking with the social worker about the terms of my custody, and I kind of zoned out since I didn't really understand. Mr. Reno had a very average build underneath his black trench coat and wore his hair neatly parted to the side. His red-and-green flannel and tan slacks were nice even if they had some obvious wear to them. The scent of his cologne was tolerable, but judging by the cloud that followed him into the room, I was guessing he used half the bottle that morning. He was chewing gum with his front teeth and snuck in words between chews and breaths, and it was the most annoying thing even for my ten-year-old self.

"Well, Charlie, I know your time with us has been difficult, but leave here knowing that we tried to do our best by you. You have my number if you need anything from me. Otherwise, we've already packed your things into Mr. Reno's car. I wish you the best in life."

If I had a choice in the matter, I would have stayed with Mr. Fredrick at the Gates Home for Boys, or just "Gates" as we called it. Some of the other guys there were rough around the edges, but I didn't mind. It toughened me up. Most importantly, I had finally felt stable since arriving around a year and a half before meeting Mr. Reno. But part of me knew that I couldn't stay there forever, and it was probably best that I went to a regular school and made regular friends. Still, I needed to know something before I left.

"What happens if they find my parents?"

Mr. Fredrick sighed. "Charlie…it is best that you focus on your new life with the Renos. You'll be notified if any word comes of your folks."

Mr. Reno stood up and shook Mr. Fredrick's hand, then motioned for me to follow him out the door.

I threw on my winter coat and hurried along. "Bye, Mr. Fredrick."

"Goodbye, Charlie."

We walked silently through the old halls of Gates, and I tried to take in the building one last time. I wondered if I'd be back soon like Tommy. His last two sets of parents hadn't worked out, and he was back after two months each time. It was something you learned to get used to being without your real parents. Sometimes grownups came into your life. Sometimes they left. Getting used to it didn't make it any easier, though. It made it feel like everything in life was temporary, and while that was true on the largest of scales, it was tough to deal with as a kid.

Approaching the front office, Mr. Reno gave some paperwork and his ID to Mrs. Simpson. She then pressed a couple buttons on the computer in front of her, and with a buzz and a click, the exit door across the way opened. One of the security guards came through and escorted us toward the parking lot. Cold air blasted us as we went through the doors. Snow had fallen a few days prior, so the trees and ground had a pleasant frosted look to them. The streets and parking lot had been recently plowed, so they were clear, but many of the cars in the lot still had a bit of snow on them. Not

Mr. Reno's. He had an old—really old—station wagon with blue paint and delightfully wretched wood paneling. It was in good shape, considering, and having known him for all of thirty minutes, the car made sense.

He ushered me into the passenger seat. The car's tan leather interior was very neat, hinting that it was recently detailed. There were bits of pine in the air from the older-looking Christmas tree hanging from the rearview. Then Mr. Reno assumed the driver's seat, and all traces of pine disappeared. They were killed dead by his now intolerable cologne permeating the entirety of the close quarters. I would have outwardly gagged, but remembered Tommy telling me that it was best not to show too much emotion to new parents too soon. He said it tended to freak them out. So, despite my lack of oxygen, I persevered.

Mr. Reno started the engine, and talk radio gently filled the car. Startling himself, he quickly turned it off. "Sorry about that, Charlie."

I was a bit disappointed because we didn't get to listen to any radio at Gates, but nodded in acknowledgement as he drove us out of the parking lot. I immediately began to enjoy the ride. We weren't allowed to go more than one hundred yards from Gates, so anything was better than the same old, same old. Still, after thirty minutes, the silence became awkwardly apparent to me.

"What school will I go to?"

"Orchard Elementary. We'll be passing it on our way home." His words were accompanied by the tiniest of smiles under his beard, undoubtedly happy that I wanted to talk.

"Is it any good?"

"It's fine. We will get you settled in the next couple of days, and then enroll you."

"You don't like football?"

"It's not that. Just been a lot more into baseball since my favorite team finally won it all—a while ago by now, I guess. But if you like football, that's okay."

"Where's your wife?"

The smile he had during the last two questions disappeared. "You'll meet her soon enough."

We merged onto the expressway, and the white noise that followed let the conversation naturally conclude. After driving for a little while, we finally exited to a town that could have been described as humble. It definitely wasn't run down, but it sure wasn't the rich city I imagined and hoped for. We drove through a quaint downtown area, then into a neighborhood.

"There it is." Mr. Reno extended his arm in front of my face, pointing to the school I would attend.

"Not bad."

The building seemed recently renovated, which was reassuring, but it was also a fairly large school, which made me a little nervous. We turned down a small street and pulled into the driveway of a house that had to be a hundred years old but well cared for. Upon thinking that, I was instantly daydreaming about whether he had taken me through a time machine back forty or fifty years. Since that would have been before my parents were born, I imagined I could fix things for all of us, and my future self wouldn't be in the position that I was in, and life would be great. But then, my ten-year-old brain began to hurt trying to work out all of the paradoxes associated with time travel, and thankfully, Mr. Reno interjected.

"What do you think?"

"Oh. It looks nice."

I prepared to open my car door when he stopped me.

"Charlie, there is one thing I want to talk to you about before we go in."

I settled back into my seat and looked over to him.

"You seem like a bright boy. You're going to find as you get older, you'll have to work for everything you want. I wanted a son, and so I put in the time, effort, and money to get you. Background check. Paperwork. And it was a lot of money. But I know it will be worth it. I know you're going to work hard for me, and I'll make sure you're taken care of."

"Okay."

"So, we're going to get you a list of chores to start doing after we get your things in the house. I think it's best you keep busy at all times, so at the top of your list will be shoveling the walkway leading to the garage."

Peering out of the car and around the house, I saw that all of the sidewalks were spotless except for the one he mentioned, like he had saved it just to give me a chore. But wanting to make a good first impression, I simply said, "Sure. I can do that."

Unknown to me at the time, that conversion would define our relationship for the next several years. There was always a roof over my head and food in belly, but he worked me like a dog. Just like that walkway, he would leave random chores for me—chores that he could have easily completed himself while doing other things around the house. But Mr. Reno consumed his own life with work, so it must have seemed logical to him to consume mine as well.

One time in eighth grade, I tried to put my studies over my chores. "Do I have to wash the car today? I have a science test tomorrow, and I need to study."

As calm as he always was, Mr. Reno replied, "Yes, and you're going to reorganize the garage after you're done with the car."

"Again? I did that last week. It's organized! I promise!"

"Do you really want to have 'the talk' again, Charlie? You need to understand that work makes you stronger than any test ever could."

Worst of all, I had trouble reading the assignments, and didn't understand why at the time. I knew the letters and words, but sometimes couldn't quite recognize them. Still, I was fairly certain that I would have gotten by just fine had I been allowed to focus on my studies. It was then that my resentment for Mr. Reno began to grow.

But the summer after eighth grade changed everything. After shoveling the walk on my very first day at the Reno residence, Mr. Reno introduced me to his wife. Mrs. Reno seemed nice enough, but she had a nasty cough. Later, she would tell me it was something she had caught while working in the city for many years. As a result of her sickness, she couldn't do much around the house, and things only got worse from there. My guess was that the medical bills had started piling up right around the time Mr. Reno took me from Gates. Those first few years, he worked overtime just about every night, and I had to do everything else around the house. I took care of Mrs. Reno as good as any kid could, and while my life was technically better than it was at Gates, I couldn't help but feel like I had been sold into slavery. I even tried calling Mr. Fredrick a couple of times, but he always asked the same question.

"Are you being abused or neglected?"

"I don't know. Not really. But something isn't right. I feel like he's working me too hard."

"You said the same things about us, Charlie. And his wife is sick, so give him a break. Now, please, only use this number if you are in real trouble."

So, I kept working for Mr. Reno, and Mrs. Reno kept getting sicker. It wasn't until Mrs. Reno was clinging to life that Mr. Reno finally showed me a bit of his human side.

"Don't worry about washing the linens this afternoon."

It was clear that the anguish in his voice originated from deep within him. It was rare that he ever took anything off my plate, and as twisted as it was, it made me a little happy that his wife was dying. Regardless, he had trained me to always ask to do more if any of my chores were ever in question.

"I'm happy to do it for you. I can even organize the basement when I'm done."

"That won't be necessary, Charlie. You just relax."

Mrs. Reno passed away a week later, and we had a quiet service for her where only a few relatives and friends showed up. Her coffin could probably have been described as *bargain*. But shortly after she was in the ground, Mr. Reno revealed to me just how much he cared about her and about me. In turn, he also showed me just how flawed a man he was.

"When Martha got sick, the doctors told us that it would eventually kill her. A few months later, when she took a turn for the worse, she told me her dying wish. It was to have a little boy around to help out with the house. She said it would be good for me to have someone like you around before she passed, but I think she mostly meant after." Mr. Reno choked up a bit. "You probably hate me after all I've put you through. After all you've been through in life." He cleared his throat. "Just know that love will make you do strange things. The way we...I treated you the last five years was all I could do to cope. I'm sorry, Charlie."

After that, the chores stopped coming. All the work I did to make the house immaculate was suddenly for nothing and it slowly withered to mediocrity and sometimes worse. I did as much as I could to keep it together while preparing for high school.

Mr. Reno didn't do much at all other than go to work. When he came home, he immediately headed for his study without as much as a greeting. He'd sit there for hours, reading books and quietly moping. There were a few nights where the moping wasn't so quiet, and I was certain I heard him sobbing from across the hall. Seeing him become so fractured after losing the one he loved was difficult. But as the orphan he had exploited for years, I had no pity for him, even when I tried. I almost wanted to take joy in his suffering, but something inside me said that wasn't right either.

High school classes started that fall, and I welcomed the distraction from my depressing home life. The guidance counselor thought it might be good for me to get involved in some kind of extracurricular activity, so I took up drums with the school band. Even though I couldn't read a lick of drum music, I was serviceable playing by ear. But shortly after, I met Sarah and joined the football team. As much as I hated him for it, all the work Mr. Reno had made me do had kept me in good shape, and I'd turned out to be quite the athlete. Even more surprising, Mr. Reno came to a couple games, and when my talent became obvious to him, he even complimented me.

"That sport could actually take you places, Son."

It wasn't long after that I introduced Mr. Reno to Sarah. Not that it mattered, but he seemed to think very highly of her. He said she seemed to have a good head on her shoulders and that she might even be wife material if we stayed together through college. When she left for school and I got depressed, Mr. Reno had some interesting words of encouragement for me.

"Charlie, the emptiness you feel since she's been gone, the void that no one else can fill? Just be glad that you will see her again. Don't take it for granted. Do whatever it takes."

His words could have been mistaken for romantic if I hadn't experienced firsthand the insanity that he considered love. And despite how far he had come since the passing of Mrs. Reno, there was still a deep-seated rage within me for all the years of forced labor. It finally came to head upon receiving my final report card right before graduation. After one look, it was obvious what it meant for Sarah and me, and I nearly lost it at school. Begrudgingly, I was able to harness that immediate ire into a catalyst to be unleashed later.

Entering his study that afternoon, I held the damn paper right into his dumb bearded face. "Look at this! You see this, old man? Do you see this? It's bullshit!"

Falling back in his chair, he tried to gather himself to read the report.

Just when he was almost able, I threw it at him. "You said if I worked hard enough, everything else would take care of itself. You said I'd learn more from chores and school wasn't important."

The paper fell onto his lap, and he finally got a look at it. "Oh. Charlie. I'm...I'm—"

"Let me guess. You're sorry?! You're always sorry these days! Well, 'sorry' doesn't get me into school. 'Sorry' doesn't give me my childhood back. 'Sorry' won't bring back your demented wife!"

He began to nod as his expression shifted from shocked to morose. "You're right, Charlie. You're right. I was a horrible husband and a terrible father."

"No. You don't get to call yourself that—'father.' You couldn't have your own kids, and you sure as hell were anything but a father to me."

His tears kept flowing, and so did all of the anguish that had been bottled up in me for so long.

"I've made up my mind. I'm enlisting in the marines. I'll train. I'll see the world. I'll serve this damn country. Then I'll be with the woman I love, and I'll never speak with you again. I won't visit. I won't write. And some day, should I ever have kids, they will *never* know the name Mr. Reno and the bullshit he put me through! I'm changing my name back to..."

At that moment, the strangest thing happened. Before I could finish my sentence, the lights went out and complete darkness overtook my ability to see anything. The sunlight that was literally just coming through the windows in the study was gone. That wasn't how I remembered it, and it sure as hell didn't make any sense.

"Mr. Reno?"

But I knew he wasn't there. It felt like nothing was there except emptiness. *Am I hallucinating in solitary again? Maybe they never let me out after beating up that bastard lawyer.*

But that couldn't be the case because I specifically recalled getting out. Those damn guards roughed me up on the way back to my regular cell.

Maybe this is hell.

It would only be fitting that I would end up burning for all my sins. And after everything I put Sarah and the kids through, death seemed easier to deal with than living with so much regret. But there wasn't any fire or brimstone around me either. Still, one thing was for sure; my grip on reality was slipping, so I needed to figure out where the hell I was and what the hell was happening.

"Hello, *-ello, -ello, -lo?*" The echo was almost painfully loud.

Flick!

Like the opening of an old-fashioned play, a spotlight shined directly onto me.

I spun around looking for a frame of reference, but as far as I could see, nothing else was lit and the blackness went on forever. Spinning around again, I kept looking for anything or anyone in the void. It got to the point where I would forget where I had begun as it was infinitely dark in all directions.

Flick!

Another spotlight? But where?

Light was still only on me, so I turned around again, and something appeared in the distance. In spite of the sniper training I'd had, I squinted hard with both eyes to try to make out the target. It was blurry, but I was fairly certain it was a figure of some kind. I tried walking toward the figure, but the ground beneath me felt like sand. No matter how many steps I took, the figure was still the same distance away.

"Hey, *hey, -ey, -y!*"

My ears felt like they were going to bleed. Shouting was not going to work, but I was determined to make contact. That was when I remembered another piece of training from the service that just might help me out. Not sure why it dawned on me, I figured I would give it a shot. Lifting my right hand in the air, I placed my middle finger hard against my thumb, and with all of my might, I pressed down.

Snap!

The echo was loud, but bearable. Most importantly, the figure moved seemingly in acknowledgement of the sound.

Snap!

The figure moved again. *It has to be hearing me!*

Snapping four times, then two times, I said hi in Morse code. It must have worked as I could see the figure raise what had to be his hand.

Snap! Snap! Snap! Snap! Pause. Snap! Snap!

It said hi back!

"Friend or foe?" I snapped.

"Friend."

Before I could say anymore, the figure began moving again, but bizarrely enough, the never-ending space made it difficult to know if the figure was coming toward me or actually getting larger in size. Squinting hard, the figure was finally getting clear enough to see.

It was a boy! Or young man. But something was odd about him. His bottom half was much wider than I would have expected for such a small person, and it didn't appear like his legs were moving at all as he approached.

A wheelchair? If it was, it didn't look like any wheelchair I had ever seen. Still, knowing that the person ahead of me was disabled actually calmed my nerves a bit. He continued to zoom in, and his appearance was anything but scary as it became clearer.

But who is he?

When he was about twenty feet from me, he stopped.

It was definitely some kind of weird futuristic wheelchair that he was in.

Neither of us moved for a moment, and I decided to break the tension. I waved with my right hand, and to my shock, he simultaneously waved his. Then both of our hands went down at exactly the same time. In disbelief, I leaned my head in to get a better look, and he mimicked the motion identically. I waved my left hand. Him too. I turned around and peered over my shoulder. He spun around and looked back as well.

We faced each other again, and I snapped, "Name?"

Below us, the longest crease of light appeared much brighter than the spotlights on him and me. Looking up, we saw what looked to be a tear in the void, letting the light in, and it was getting wider. As it opened up, the loudest suction noise began to pierce my ears, making it difficult to think, and like a vacuum, a strong pressure began pulling us upward. Somehow I knew that we didn't have much time, but all I could think to do was snap again.

"Name?"

Light was consuming the entire space, and it wouldn't be long before we'd be swept up into it, so I snapped it a third time.

He finally replied, "Ryan Carter. Name?"

I was barely able to get out my name just before our time was up. "Charlie Rios."

CHAPTER 18

A SLIP OF THE TONGUE

"CHARLIE RIOS." THE NAME FELL out of my mouth as I walked through the main doors at NTE.

"I'm sorry, sir, but who are you talking to?" Another employee at the company looked at me like I was crazy.

Part of me didn't blame her. I had no idea where that name came from or why I had said it. Shaking it off, I turned my attention back to the business at hand. Since the leave for my mind migration was coming to an end, I had scheduled a late morning appointment with HR to have my job reinstated.

It was surreal walking into the building for the first time ever without Auto. The foyer that had always seemed to go on for kilometers when I rolled through, took just a few long strides for me to complete. Entering the hallway toward the bank of elevators, I pressed the UP button. To my pleasant surprise, the elevator Helen and I had first met in was the one to open first. With a ding, I hopped in, pressed the button for floor number forty-two, and settled into the middle since it was just me. But as the doors began to close, I heard clicking heels racing toward me and a middle-aged, good-looking businesswoman appeared. Instinctively, I put my hand between the doors. Sliding in past me, she gathered herself in the back corner. To my delight, her perfume was nice and subtle, and the ride up wouldn't be so bad.

"Thanks!" She had an odd exuberance in her voice.

"No problem. Which floor?"

"Fifty-six. Thanks again."

After pressing her button, I stepped back to the other corner to allow her maximum room, and could feel her eyes following me back to the spot. Trying to limit the awkwardness, I offered some small talk since I was a pro at it.

"You must work with the big accounts on that floor."

She busted into the hardest laughter, nearly scaring me. I had always thought of myself as a funny person, but she was giving me a little too much credit.

"Yes. I work with the...big accounts. But, tell me. What do you do?" Unblinking, she leaned in closer than I would have liked, and it almost seemed like she was looking through me or talking to someone behind me.

Leaning back slightly, I quickly offered a response. "Me? I'm in data processing."

Her ogling demeanor subsided as a perplexed look took over. "But you don't look—"

"Disabled? Well, I'm not. Anymore. I had a mind migration, and I'm just getting back to work."

"Oh, you're one of those." She snootily turned around in an attempt to end the conversation.

I couldn't let it die so easily after that. "Is there something wrong with that?"

Hesitant, she turned back around. "Well, how do I even know if you have a soul or not?"

Her ignorance aside, she was being just plain rude.

"How do I know if you have one? Or if anyone has one? And who the hell cares?"

Her face turned just short of angry.

"Look, you might not be the religious type. No problem. I was just making small talk anyway."

The elevator chimed, and the doors revealed my floor.

As I stepped out, there was no way in hell I was going to let the conversation end like that. "Small talk is about things like coffee and the game last night, not about whether someone's a legitimate person. I'm glad you kept talking because after the little bit of flirting you did, I almost liked you."

Even if the last part was a lie, it was worth seeing her jaw drop to the ground. The doors began to shut, and I turned down the hallway and walked away. Truth be told, I was kind of glad that she reminded me of the bigotry a certain percentage of the population had for us migrators. Much of it came from the religious groups that were opposed to the procedure from the beginning. Others simply lumped us in with all the other minorities as causing the "moral bankruptcy of society."

To ADG's credit, they did mention migration prejudice as something to be aware of. But they did so in such a clumsy way that it wouldn't have stuck out to most people even if they were unfamiliar.

"You realize that others will look at you differently after your mind migration? Some may dislike you simply because you're not in your original body," was all they'd said on the subject.

Having researched the phenomenon, I was trading one form of obvious oppression, my disability, for another not-so-obvious one. It was worth it to be able to walk, but it still stung to experience it firsthand.

It had already been an interesting morning, and I hadn't even made it to my destination. Fortunately, I was quickly approaching the glass wall and doors of the HR offices at the end of the hallway. I took a deep breath and entered.

The department assistant immediately greeted me. "Hello, sir! How may NTE help you today?"

"Hi. My name is Ryan Carter. I am here to be reinstated for work after a medically related leave of absence."

"No problem, Ryan. Please place your thumb in the ID reader, and I will have the next available personnel representative assist you. Your wait time is approximately five minutes. You may have a seat."

I was fairly certain that she had gone to Cyborg University and was a monotonous communications major. Still, I verified my identity for her and waited the five minutes.

"Ryan Carter. Please report to room four-two-two-one."

Entering the office, I saw it had the best view of the city.

"Hi, Ryan. I'm Emily Turner, the personnel rep who will help you out today. I understand that you're scheduled to be reinstated next week."

"That's correct."

"We're glad to have you back. I hope everything went well medically."

"Yes. Thank you."

"We reviewed your employment while you were away. Upper management needs me to bring something to your attention."

My heart sank since upper management had never even acknowledged my existence, much less had a need to "review something with me."

"Okay."

"Well, we completed an audit on your employment record, and I must say that you have been outstanding since day one. Before your leave, you never missed a day of work and your processing had a ninety-nine-point-nine-seven-five percent perfection rate. That puts you third best in company history. With all of that, we'd like to offer you a promotion."

Stunned, I could only muster a nod as a response.

"We'd like you to be our newest lead generator."

And there it was. Lead generations was the black hole of all departments. Years ago, NTE figured out that automated lead generation, which had been the standard for decades, was no longer as effective as a person reaching out to potential customers. Completely commission-driven, with very hard work, some luck, and possibly an inside track, a decent living could be made through cold hologramming and ad placement. Rumors would periodically surface of lead generators who made thousands of leads in a month, leading to five-figure paychecks. But most employees in the department struggled to stay afloat, and it was no secret that they had the highest turnover in the company. So, why me, Mr. Top Data Processor? My guess was that the company was scheduled to lose the tax break they had received from my disability once I returned and wanted me to start earning my keep.

"If it's all the same, I would prefer to stay in data processing for the time being. Maybe when I get my feet under me again, I would be open to the transfer."

"I'm sorry, Ryan, but the offer only stands for this meeting. We are looking to consolidate our quarterly rosters, and it would be another year or longer before you would be considered again. It really is a good move for someone like you."

"Someone like me," she'd said so smugly. Maybe she really believed that she was doing me a favor. As disgusted as I was, it was probably a good move in the short run. Otherwise, they'd probably find a frivolous reason to get rid of me altogether. So, I figured I would take the job to keep an income while I got settled into the new apartment. Hell, there was even a possibility that I would actually be good at it. But if not, I would quickly start looking for something different.

"Fine."

"Thank you, Ryan. I'm sure you'll do just as well in your new role. Please put your thumb in the ID reader to confirm your position switch, and we'll handle the rest of the data work on our end. You will have a trainer meet with you for two hours, and based on the schedule for next week, it looks like we'll need you to come in tomorrow afternoon for that training. Lastly, I need you to report to your data-processing workstation to wrap up any remaining and incoming data-processing requests. Feel free to head up there after this meeting. Any questions?"

Can you and the company kiss my ass? But I couldn't bring myself to say it. "No questions."

I pushed my thumb into the ID reader like a good little lemming.

"Again, we appreciate you accepting your new position, and we look forward to your continued success."

After wrapping up the blackmail that had just taken place, I headed for my old cubicle on the fourteenth floor. It was modest, with tan paneling and white tabletops. No chairs, of course. Only company approved flair could be posted inside, and I had never felt like getting approval for anything special, so I'd just hung up my data-processing awards. To the company's credit, all desks on the fourteenth floor were auto-adjusting, so that made it easy to raise up so I could stand while completing the last bits of work that I had.

Pressing my thumb into the ID reader, my desk transformed into a data-processing workstation. A virtual keyboard appeared a couple inches above the desk, and widescreen holograms displayed the information in a semicircle around me. There were a few items waiting for me to process, and I quickly handled those.

Ready to ID out, I reached my thumb toward the ID reader, but instead, my eyes were drawn back to the holograms, and I inexplicably froze. An inner force was stopping me from leaving, and without thinking, I navigated my workstation to the data-search function. Feeling like my body was on autopilot, my hands began typing.

CHARLES RIOS

Enter.

6,471 RESULTS FOUND.

With complete disregard for time and having no idea what I was looking for, I began diving into article after article involving anyone with the name Charlie Rios. There were birth announcements, obituaries, and general news items. One of the Charlies even invented a reusable chewing gum. You just had to wash it with soap and water and put it in the refrigerator to restore the flavor.

Yuck.

After what had to be an hour or so, a light bulb finally went off, and my searching stopped. A news blurb without a date or location reported that a man named Charlie Rios was a suspect in custody for an accident involving his car and another, and was sent to the hospital. There weren't any other details even after I filtered for related stories. Nothing else of relevance was returned, but that didn't matter. I found out what I needed to know from the search.

He is real! Charlie is real.

Somehow, I could see what Charlie did, what Charlie saw in my dreams. Just when I thought my searching was over, the autopilot kicked in again, and I began to type more letters.

SPOTTED LUNG.

Enter.

4,198,210,245 RESULTS.

I had heard of the disease before, but never knew much about it. Skimming through a few sources from the results, I discovered that, at its height, spotted lung had affected about 20% of the city's population. It had been a super virus that mutated to feed off air pollution which, decades ago, was aplenty. The bug had settled in people's lungs, and as they'd breathed in the dirty air, it forced the host's lungs to absorb the pollution much more deeply into the tissue than it otherwise normally would. It had especially affected children, the elderly, and people with compromised immune systems, but occasionally, healthy adults caught the virus as well. Originally, the disease had an 80% mortality rate, and people around the globe feared it was the end of humanity. But treatments had advanced pretty quickly, and for the last several years after the discovery of a cure and subsequent vaccine, only 5% of infections had been fatal.

The disease had been strange in that it forced pollution to be concentrated in the lungs, but it had preferred its host to be in otherwise good health. Nearly all of the other major organs—heart, brain, kidneys, and occasionally the liver—were usually unscathed, or close to it. A good thing for those who'd survived, but it also created a morbid opportunity for a local crime syndicate with a high-ranking member in the city coroner's office. They had waited for the infected to die and, prior to the body being sent to the morgue, had harvested any remaining healthy organs to sell on the black market. The scandal had broken nearly twenty years ago, and the crime syndicate was dismantled with its leadership going to prison. But nowhere could I find the names of those leaders, which seriously bothered me for an unknown reason.

"Excuse me, Ryan Carter. You have reached your data-search limit, and you have no remaining pending data. Please ID out and leave for the day."

It was no surprise that the department supervisor was as pedantic as ever. It didn't matter. I had found what I didn't even realize I was looking for. The next thing I wanted to do was speak with someone at ADG, maybe Tony, to get some perspective on what I was experiencing, and the proof I'd found that Charlie was real.

"Yes, sir. I will see myself out."

IDing out and exiting the building as fast as possible, I was excited to be joining Helen for dinner that night. It might have been a little early for food, but it was definitely the right time to start drinking.

Two Toms' Tavern was a local jewel in that it had excellent food and beverages without the long waits that some places had. It wasn't a very auto-chair-friendly place, but I had persevered a few times before getting my legs because it was that good.

Rob the Bartender was wiping the place down when I entered, and as usual, he was the breath of fresh air I needed after interacting with boring, rude people all day. To my surprise, he instantly recognized me.

"Ryan! Dude!"

"How's it going, Rob?"

"Can't complain! How's being erect?"

Yes! I had waited ever since the migration for someone to make that joke, and it was even better when I finally heard it.

"Ha ha. It's great. Can I get a half-liter of Bobby Brüce, please?"

My favorite ale had hints of caramel, but the exceptionally smooth malt finish made drinking it somewhat dangerous. I'd be a couple in before I realized just how buzzed I was.

"Coming right up, my walking friend."

It was only me and a few other day drinkers there, but I knew it would pick up a little as the night went on. I grabbed a table in back to give Helen and me a little more privacy since it was a night to celebrate our completed journeys and those ahead of us. It was no secret that the drinks and talk would be flowing all night.

Two beers in, and the main door to the pub flew open, and there she was. In all her migrated, gorgeous glory, Helen entered. The setting sun behind her emphasized her natural glow. Time stood still, and I almost didn't notice her looking around for me.

"Helen!" I waved exaggeratedly in an attempt to embarrass her.

She nodded in acknowledgement and gave a playful scowl.

As she headed to the table, I stood and opened my arms, and she slipped into them as perfectly as I had always imagined. We held each other tightly for an extra second.

"How's it going, Ry? Anymore weird blackouts?"

Tipping my glass, I gave my best witty response. "Nah, but let me get four or five more of these in me, and we'll see how my new liver holds up."

Rob interrupted with his awful cowboy impersonation. "Howdy, ma'am, what can I get ya to drink?"

"McHenry Stout, please."

"You got it."

Before we could dig into our first conversation, some drunkard in a leather jacket played an awful, decades-old rock song on the music box, so we had to yell at each other to talk.

"How many are you in?" Helen shouted across the table.

"This is my third. You'll need to drink fast to catch up."

"That's never been a problem for me, and now I have the body to do it right."

"And what a body it is."

She grinned. "Did you go back to NTE yet?"

"Yes, today. You'll probably definitely guess what they're doing to me."

"What? Are they firing you? No. Worse I bet. Are they sending you to lead—"

"Generations. You got it."

"Those bastards! I knew they were awful, but damn, did they work fast. I bet I'm next."

"Yeah, they didn't give me much of a choice, so I said screw it and took the job."

"Ugh. Looks like my job hunt just started."

We continued talking and drinking until last call at 10 PM. Topics ranged from quitting NTE and starting a small business, to how our families were handling our migrations, to dropping everything and just traveling the world. We were fairly drunk as Rob came over and politely told us to leave. Then I realized the big news that I had forgotten to share with Helen.

"I got a place!"

"What?"

"An apartment! I have to show you. Let's jump on the next bullet."

The city was dead at that early hour, and the bullet was empty. We stumbled through the hallways of my building but managed to stay quiet enough so that none of my neighbors yelled. As I reached for my phone to unlock the door, Helen grabbed me with all her might and threw me up against the door. She pressed her whole body against mine, grinding into me in the best way possible. Eye to eye and breathing heavily, she pushed her luscious lips against my quivering ones.

Amazing!

We stood there for what felt like a minute before I reached one hand up to caress her neck. Not wanting to spoil the moment but also not wanting my neighbors to see, I grabbed my netphone with my free hand and pressed the unlock command.

Click. Click.

Beep.

The door flung open, causing us to spill into the dark kitchen. We stumbled to the only piece of furniture that I had, an old couch, and plopped down in the middle. She reached for the zipper to my coat and began the frantic fight to rip off my clothes. I began the same struggle with hers, and coats and shirts and pants flew across the room.

"Clumsy" didn't begin to describe the scene, but it wasn't because of nerves. Both of us actually seemed quite comfortable, probably because of the trust we had developed over the friendship. Instead, the awkwardness of our movements was most likely because we were in newer bodies that were heavily influenced by liters of strong beer. Regardless, we were releasing all the painfully obvious sexual tension that had built up since we'd first met and for basically our entire lives being numb from the waist down.

We continued kissing as she moved to straddle me. In underwear only, we made out intensely for several minutes, just enjoying each other for the first time. Eventually, we got to the point when things would either progress or stop, so one of us had to say something.

Helen pulled her face back ever so slightly to lead the way. "So, I've never gone all the way. You?"

I hesitated, afraid to give away my amateur status.

"Ryan?"

I looked down, embarrassed. "This is my first time…even kissing."

She pulled away a little more to look me in the eyes. "Hey, not bad for a rookie? Do you want to do more?"

"Do you?"

A silly grin came over her face, and she leaned in. "Yes! Let's figure it out together."

She took off her remaining clothes, and the sheer sight of her made me tingle. Then I revealed myself to her, and she smiled in acknowledgement. The moment I had always fantasized about was finally coming true, and with the best person I could have ever imagined.

She straddled me again, resting nervous hands on my chest.

I gave in to the urge to explore her naked body with my hands. Turned out that they got a hell of a ride going over all of her breathtaking curves— her thighs, the small of her back, and all the way up to her shoulders. My hands finally settled upon her perfectly sized breasts and began massaging each one intermittently.

"That feels great!"

Still awkward but trying to take in the moment, I became aware of her right hand as it started the descent down my body. First, on my chiseled chest, then sneaking down to my exceptional abs, and even farther until she began playfully bumping into my host's large endowment. Without hesitation, she began teasing it.

"Oh wow." The words fell from my mouth as her hand worked wonders.

Things progressed quickly from there as we moved to recline lengthwise on the couch for the best access to each other. Being on top, I continued the hand play, but this time moving down her body to find the pleasure zones I had learned about years ago in anatomy class and on the net. While I wasn't completely sure what I was doing, her moans made it seem like I should keep going. Meanwhile, she continued working me with her hand, which felt amazing. Then she again moved things along.

"I guess we should just try doing it."

"Okay. So, I should just..."

"Yeah."

I got into position, and she helped to guide me in. We both made the gentle noises of pleasure as I ever so slowly slid deeper. It was heaven! She then reached down and began stimulating herself while I instinctively started a methodical thrust. It was as beautiful and hot as two drunk, newly mind-migrated people having sex could be. And then I realized I wasn't going to last much longer.

Luckily, she felt the same way, and let me know. "I think...I think I'm going to finish!"

Her body began to tighten up from the inside out, and that was all it took for me to be done as well.

I couldn't contain myself. "Yes! Yes! Yes!"

And there it was. She and I were no longer virgins. Panting and spent, I collapsed on top of her. Our sweaty bodies slid against each other, but it felt good since everything was still tingling. After a minute of holding each other, I popped my head up to look back into Helen's eyes, and with the biggest grin, she broke the silence.

"Wow, Ryan."

"Wow, yourself!"

"That was much better than I had imagined."

"Definitely."

I rolled off of her so that we could sit up and look at each other.

"Seriously, Ryan. I've thought about it. We work so well together on every level. I don't want to rush things any more than we already have, but I think I'm falling in love with you."

Taken aback at just how indescribably incredible the night had turned out, I was speechless for just a moment. Then I knew exactly how to respond.

Looking deeply into her eyes, I told her exactly how I felt. "I love you too, Sarah."

Her face went from satisfied to disgusted in an instant. "What the hell did you just say?"

CHAPTER 19

CROSSING THE LINE

"**I** LOVE YOU TOO, SARAH."

I hung up my phone and settled into the seat at the bus station. She would be picking me up in about an hour, and I was nervous as hell. It wasn't just because civilian life was starting for me again. That was the easy part.

In an hour or so, I would meet my daughter for the first time and have to figure out how the hell to be a father. It was something I didn't know the first thing about since all I'd had was a deserter and Mr. Reno. But I had promised myself the day Sarah told me about Lucy to not be anything like them, and I had every intention of living up to that promise, even if the war had changed me.

On top of that, I had to figure out how and when to ask Sarah for her hand in marriage. We had messaged each other a little while I was in Pakistan, but most of the time, the communication block put in place to stop extremists from coordinating had meant that we hadn't been able to communicate with our loved ones with any regularity. So, after four years apart, it only felt right to get to know her in person again. I assumed that she had been faithful to me while I was away, as I had been to her. Having heard all the horror stories from my squad, I'd prepared myself for the worst. No matter what, I was certain I loved her and wanted to be with her. I just needed to know she loved me and wanted to be with me. More than just the words, I needed to see her love.

Then there was the question of work. I needed to find a job fast because the living situation was complicated. She'd ended up finishing her degree at Johnson College. However, the loans she'd taken out had made it tough to make ends meet. Sarah and Lucy had moved in with her folks and lived there up until Sarah had gotten her big break. On a whim, she had applied for a lab assistant position at Chronos Chemicals. They'd loved her résumé and interview so much that they offered her the job. After she did the math for her salary, the rent for a place, the commute, daycare, and other expenses, she would have had exactly fifty dollars left over for all other basic needs. So, Sarah initially declined the position, letting the company know that it hadn't made sense financially. When they'd called her back and offered to pay for rent and daycare, she hadn't been able to refuse. The problem was that the company had only done that because Sarah was technically a single parent. I would only be able to stay with them for a month or so before the extra benefits would stop, and so, I had to look for work immediately.

There were a couple ads for jobs, saying "Veteran's Apply," but I was fairly certain they were temp jobs trying to satisfy a quota. Part of me hated to settle, but anything was better than nothing just to get some cash rolling in.

Deep in thought, my wait at the bus stop flew by, and a message came through from Sarah saying they had arrived. Chills rolled down my spine as it felt like I just got orders for a serious mission that began that very second. I swallowed hard as I walked out to the parking lot.

There she was. There they were. Sarah and my little girl. Then all of the self-doubt that had built up over four years melted away in an instant.

"Charlie!"

"Sarah!"

She hurried over and gave me the biggest hug, letting her feelings be known right away. Lucy mimicked her mother's excitement, trotting to keep up and then bouncing around our legs as we stood tightly in each other's arms for a minute or so. Both of us took turns letting loose muted laughs and cries as we hugged and kissed and touched each other's face.

Lucy's soft voice interjected as she tugged on my tan fatigue pants. "What are you wearing?"

She had difficulty pronouncing *R*'s, and I knew that would need to be worked on eventually, but in that moment, it was the most adorable thing I had ever heard.

Sarah pulled away to introduce Lucy and me for the very first time. "Lucy, this is your daddy. Like we talked about before, he just got back from fighting the bad people across the world, and now he's here to be with us."

Lucy was a bit bashful, and I couldn't blame her.

Instinctively, I knew I needed to get on her level to talk to her, so I dropped to one knee. "Hello, Lucy. I'm really glad to meet you. I know you don't know me, but I want to be the best dad I can be now that I'm here."

"Will you give me candy?"

Sarah laughed.

I smiled. "Well, as long as your mom thinks it's okay, I will definitely be giving you some candy."

"Yay! I like candy."

I had left from that bus station a single man full of uncertainty, and returned a confident man with an amazing family. It was one of the best moments of my life, and I remembered wishing it could have lasted much longer. But soon, the tough times returned. The search for work was much harder than I could have expected. I managed to land one of those jobs that targeted veterans returning from the GIP conflict. Sure enough, they kept me on for sixty days and paraded around their veteran numbers, then let me go just before they would have to hire me full time. My next two gigs were exactly the same, and while we were able to squeak by, I was starting to lose faith that I would ever find steady work. Fortunately, the next job I landed, at Spades Manufacturing, was full-time assembly line work that offered decent pay and above-average benefits. It was shift work, but I was used to odd hours in the war. Things were just starting to look up for the three of us when Sarah let me know more good news over breakfast.

"Charlie."

Having just come home from a midnight shift, I almost didn't hear her. Shaking off my daze, I responded, "What? Oh. Yes, dear?"

"Lucy's days as an only child are numbered."

"What!"

"Yup. Number two is on the way."

"Oh."

"I waited until I was eight weeks to be sure."

I was still trying to process what she was saying. While I was too tired to show a lot of emotion, I knew exactly what needed to be done. I had saved enough to buy a modest ring for Sarah, and kept it on me at all times for fear that she would find it. I also didn't want to miss the right opportunity if it presented itself, so I had asked her folks for permission months prior.

Dropping to one knee right there in the kitchen, I presented the ring to her and put myself out there. The shocked look on her face was priceless as I kneeled.

"Sarah, I've loved you since the first day I saw you. I want to spend the rest of my life with you and our family. Will you marry me?"

"Oh my God! Yes! Yes! I love you!"

And, shortly after, we were married by a justice of the peace with Sarah's family and Lucy in attendance at our small ceremony. As exciting as all of it was, being married with two children meant that I needed to bring in as much money as possible. The week after the wedding, I began taking as many double and triple shifts as I could. I would do so for the next couple of years. Working the line was backbreaking to say the least, but that part wasn't the issue. After a while, the long hours and shift work caught up to me. Sleep was hard enough to come by with the night terrors and other bad dreams, but trying to do it at random hours with small children around made it nearly impossible to get any good rest. Most days I was a walking corpse mustering up just enough brain power to keep the line moving. I was even less lively at home. It was just after Joey's second birthday that Sarah finally confronted me in a serious way.

"Charlie, are you okay?"

I took an extra second to process the question. "Uh. Yes, honey. I'm fine. Why?"

"We hardly see you anymore. When we do, you're trying to sleep, but I don't think you're even getting much rest. You haven't had color in your face for a while, and I'm worried."

"We need the money, Sarah, and I'll live."

Sarah broke into a coughing fit. She had started having those the last couple of months, and it didn't seem like she wasn't getting better. Lucy and Joey had developed coughs as well, and it reminded me of Mr. Reno's wife, but I tried to think more positively.

After she gathered herself, Sarah made it clear that something had to give. "Charlie, you're killing yourself at this job. Can you try to find something with fewer hours, at least?"

"Sarah, you remember how tough it was for me to get this gig. Who knows how long it will take to find something else."

"I know, Charlie, but we need you around more since we've all been sick. Will you at least try?"

"Okay. I'll start looking next week when I have a day off."

To my credit, I did look. But none of the job postings seemed like they could keep us afloat or had benefits. Then it wasn't long after I began the search that we were called in by our family doctor. Sitting in his office, I'll never forget the cold feeling that came over me as it turned out to be one of the worst days of my life.

"I'm afraid I have some bad news. All of the test results have come back positive for spotted lung."

"Dammit!" I couldn't hold back. My worst fears had come true.

Sarah, not being as familiar, probed to find out more. "What does that mean for me and my children?"

"Well, even a couple years ago, the prognosis would have been pretty grim. However, with recent treatment breakthroughs, we should be able to effectively manage the infection in each of you. Depending on your budget, some of the equipment can be sent home with you so that you don't have to be in and out of the hospital."

"Dammit, Doc. How long do they have?" I had obviously already hit the anger phase of grief.

"Again, it's tough to say these days. Hopefully, we can manage the disease long enough for them to fight it off or for us to come up with even better treatments. While I can't say for sure what will happen, the future is looking brighter than ever for those with SL."

Looking at the cost of the equipment, Sarah and I would have had to empty our savings account and still rack up massive debt to get all of the best machines and devices to treat her and the kids. If we were just barely getting by before, we would be hanging on by a thread after that. To add to it, Sarah had always said that I couldn't keep working the line forever, but I couldn't give it up without some other way of bringing in money. It was then that my fortune turned for the better, or so I had thought. I got a call from an old service buddy that changed everything.

"Sam! How the hell are you?"

"I'm great, Charlie. Civilian life treating you well?"

"Oh, you know. Each day is a struggle, but we keep on keeping on."

"I hear that. You working?"

"Yeah. I'm on the line at Spades. You?"

"Actually, I landed a sweet gig in the city. The pay is incredible, and I work only four to five nights a week for only a few hours at a time."

"What do you do?"

"Stocker. Sort of. I get a message saying to be at a location at a certain time. I show up, and there are packages, sometimes two or three at a time. Then I get another few messages to move the packages to parked cars in the area. After another hour or so, I'm done and get to go home. They wire the money, taxes paid, directly into my account, and I enjoy the rest of my night."

"What's the catch?"

"I really haven't found one yet. I mean, I guess I don't know exactly what I'm moving, but part of me doesn't care. All of the other work I was doing before was killing me, and the pay was garbage compared to this. Say, you wouldn't happen to be interested in a related job, would you?"

"Moving packages? I don't know."

"No. I was told that there's a position open for delivery and security, and thinking about it now, it seems right up your alley."

"Delivery and security of what?"

"Again, I don't know any details, but I bet you'd get even better pay than me when they find out all of the skills you have."

"Is there a number for me to call or someone to talk to about applying?"

"No. It's not like that. Tell you what. I'll let my contact know you're... *interesting*, and if they want you, they'll set something up. At least, that's what they did with me."

"Sounds good. Thanks, Sam!"

"No problem. Take care of yourself, Charlie."

To my surprise, it was only a couple days before I received a phone call.

"I'm looking for Charlie."

"This is him."

"We'd like to interview you for our delivery-and-security position. Can you meet tonight at ten PM?"

As odd as it was to have an interview at that time, I didn't want to pass up the opportunity. I had a sick day coming to me at Spades, so I figured it was worth a shot.

"Sure. Do you want a copy of my résumé? Where should I meet you?"

"Don't worry about the résumé. Will you be driving a car?"

"Yes."

"Then we'll send you two sets of coordinates. One will be where to park and the other will lead you to where we'll meet. Be prompt."

Sure enough, at 9 PM, I received two messages. I grabbed my coat near the kitchen. Not knowing what would come of it, I didn't mention any of it to Sarah.

"Honey, I'm heading out a little early tonight. I'll see you in the morning. Love you!"

In between coughs, she responded, "I love you too!"

Arriving before the appointed time, I parked the car in the first location and walked to the second. It turned out to be the vacant building of a restaurant that had long been closed. There was an old sign on the front door.

FOR DELIVERIES, GO AROUND TO THE BACK.

Assuming that meant me, I headed to the back and found a fresher-looking note nailed to the rear door.

ONE OF THE CARS PARKED IN THE ALLEY IS NOT LIKE THE OTHERS. FIND THE RIGHT ONE TO PROCEED. YOU HAVE 5 MINUTES.

Panic instantly set in as I turned around to see if anyone was watching. But it was dark, so I couldn't tell. I thought about walking away at that moment because of how strange it was, but after a couple years of mindless work on the line, the critical thinker in me came alive pretty quickly. I saw the row of cars down the alley and headed over.

Each one was vintage. They were all massive and black. At a quick glance, they all appeared identical. They were Cadillacs from back in the day. I ran around each car, noticing that even the license plates were the same. Running out of time, I realized that the alley light was sufficient to see everything but the tires, so I pulled out my phone and enabled the flashlight. It was a waste of time looking at the tires for the first three cars as they were all the same. It seemed like that was the case when I got to the fourth, but the driver's side rear tire was a different brand. Looking closer, I found something sitting on top of the tire. It was another note.

A MAGNETIC BOX CONTAINING THE KEY IS OVER THE PASSENGER SIDE FRONT TIRE. DRIVE THE CAR TO THE PLACE WHERE THE SUN NEVER SHINES BUT THE PEOPLE NEVER SLEEP. YOU HAVE 20 MINUTES.

"The sun never shines? But the people never sleep? Think, Charlie. Think!"

I was confused, but wherever the place was, it couldn't be far since they must have allotted time for me to figure it out and get there in twenty minutes. I hadn't spent much time in the area, but I always took a mental photo of areas I traveled, something that had stuck with me from my service days. Scanning the local streets in my memory, there was only one place that made sense.

The Nighttime Motel! It had a reputation for two things: drugs and prostitutes. That had to be it.

Too excited to think clearly about the situation, I grabbed the key, jumped into the car, and adjusted all of the settings. The car immediately showed its age with the shifter being on the side of the steering wheel. But it either had been driven very little or had been restored to near factory condition because the engine roared like it was new and the odometer read one hundred miles. I believed it.

The drive to Nighttime was only about ten minutes, but that was enough for the neighborhoods to blur from working class into the bad part of town. I tried to prepare myself mentally if anything should go down, but really had no idea what to expect. Pulling into the parking lot of the motel, I gazed around. Still no one was in sight. Looking at the entire complex, it must have gone out of business given that there wasn't a single light on, including the front desk's. Eyeing the doors to the rooms, I could see even in the dark that the numbers had been etched off of all but one.

B13.

I parked the car in the darkest corner, shoved the key into my pocket, and headed for the room. Going up the stairs, I saw two shadowy figures appear at the end of the second-floor balcony ahead, and behind me, another two figures at the foot of the stairs. Bracing myself for a fight, I leaped up the last few steps and put my back against the wall. Two silhouettes remained at attention at the bottom of the stairs and the other two approached my position.

One of the silhouettes spoke with the slightest Hispanic accent. "We've been expecting you, Charlie."

I sighed. "What is this?"

"It's your interview. Now the boys are going to make sure you're not armed or wired, and then you'll come with us."

With arms up, I allowed the rough frisking. I wasn't scared, but also wasn't impressed. Was all of the over-the-top production really necessary? Regardless, I had come this far, and figured I might as well see it through.

We entered B13. The man who had talked outside clicked a button on a lantern atop the table in the middle of the room, which provided just enough light so I could see their faces. They were fairly young, maybe a little older than me, but definitely looked tough.

"Sit down."

I squatted on the chair next to the table, my patience for the situation quickly waning. "Seriously, guys, a simple what's-your-biggest-flaw type of interview would have been fine."

"Shut up," The other goon said.

Pissed off at being shushed, I figured I would hold my tongue to see what would come next.

From the darkest corner of the room, a deep voice bellowed, "You'll be asked three questions. Answer each one correctly to receive the next one. Miss one and my associates will see you out."

The voice really commanded my attention, and in turn, the annoyance that had been building in me since arriving melted instantly into seriousness.

"Yes, sir."

To my surprise, the lantern doubled as a projector, and it lit up the far side of the room with a line of text.

> WHAT'S WRONG WITH THE FOLLOWING LINE? THIS
> SENTENSE CONTAINS TWO MISTAKES.

Not a word question!

While I had basically overcome my dyslexia, the anxiety of thinking that it might kick in usually proved worse than anything. Focusing hard on the question, it became obvious that the misspelling was a mistake, but what was the other one? Was it a riddle or trick? My mind swirled. As crazy as the situation was, it reminded me of my days in the service. My adrenaline instantly kicked in, and I was in problem-solving mode like my life depended on it. My family's lives did.

"Your answer? Now," insisted the deep voice from the corner.

For some reason, the added stress of the situation made me think very clearly for the split second I had before replying, and I was fairly certain I knew the answer. "The word *sentence* is misspelled. The word *two* should be *one*, and drop the 's' from 'mistakes.'"

Without any acknowledgement, the projector blinked, and an odd image with three people appeared. On the left was a large, muscly man in camo with a shotgun on his shoulder and a dumb smirk on his face. In the middle stood an average-built man with a leather jacket, hands behind his back, and a look of conviction. Finally, an attractive woman in a red dress stood on the right. She had the deepest frown on her face, and her hand was reaching into her clutch.

"Which of these people do you trust the least? Why?"

It had to be one of those character tests where any answer I would give would say something about me. I knew I had to answer honestly, but also that they were looking for something in particular. But what?

"Your answer? Now."

Out of time, I worked the problem out loud.

"So, the first guy might be big, but he doesn't take his job seriously. It's a joke to him. There are at least four different ways to take him out. While I don't trust him, he's not the worst offender here. Now, I know better than to ever underestimate an unhappy woman, but she seems more cliché than dangerous. The person I trust the least is the guy in the middle. He looks like he has nothing to lose, and once his mind is made up, he's capable of anything."

Again, no indication of right or wrong. Just another blink of the projector, and as fate would have it, it was more text.

"Which of these is the most important aspect of a delivery-and-security job? Why?"

The money.

The product.

The people.

I immediately gravitated toward "people" because it was the most important to me, but that wasn't what the question was asking. Then I thought that since I would be delivery and security, the product might be the most important. But thinking a little harder about what he was looking for, I was fairly certain I knew the answer.

"Your answer?"

"Money. It's why we're all here. Without it, the product and the people don't matter."

The projector clicked off, and I waited in silence for what seemed like an eternity.

"Congratulations. The job is yours." From the shadows, the voice extended his hand, which might as well have been the paw of a grizzly.

That was when I first saw the dog skull ring with ruby eyes. Getting up from the chair, I reached out in an attempt to get the perfect mesh between the webs of our hands, and did my best to match his grip without straining too much. His hand was hot but dry, and it turned out to be the best handshake that I had ever been part of. He stepped forward from the shadows and into the light, and his titanic frame matched his voice in that it commanded the attention of the room. His gaze into my eyes was direct and unflinching, and I offered the same back to him.

"Please join us in prayer to bless your hiring."

Somewhat bewildered, I simply complied and put my head down.

"Lord, please provide guidance to Charlie as he steps into his new role with us, and allow him to be successful. Should he turn out to be a snitch, cop, fed, or otherwise fail at his job, please grant us the power and permission to smite him on your behalf. We ask this in the Lord's name. Amen."

The rest of us said quietly in unison, "Amen."

"And with that blessing, you are now mine, Charlie. Your first job will be tomorrow night, and it'll come with ten thousand."

"Ten thousand?"

"Yes. Taxes are handled up front, and in the end, we'll deposit ten thousand directly into an account of your choosing. Turn out to be good, and we'll just keep sending more your way. Do you have a piece or do we need to provide one?"

"Will a nine-millimeter do?"

Putting his hand into his coat, he retrieved the largest handgun I had ever seen outside the military, and its insignia matched his silver ring.

"This is my weapon of choice, but I suppose a nine-millimeter will do. Now, gentlemen, can you please provide Charlie with his new netphone and show him back to the car?"

As we walked down to the parking lot, I was equal parts excited and nervous by the whole situation. Still, there was one thing that I was dying to know. "I didn't even catch his name."

Both guys laughed at me, and they should have proceeded to tell me his name. I remembered specifically that they made a joke questioning my credibility, and then they told me his name. But something strange happened instead. Both guys froze in place like statues and stopped talking. Hell, they stopped moving altogether. Not even breathing. Then I noticed that nothing was moving, and there was no sound from the surrounding area. All of time and space was standing still until I glanced across the street and saw movement. I quickly realized it was my friend in the wheelchair from before, Ryan, who was watching me. At that moment, I remembered my boss's name and knew without a doubt that I needed to tell Ryan.

"His name is the Padre."

CHAPTER 20

RUNNING FROM THE TRUTH

"**H**IS NAME IS THE PADRE."

The phrase came from my mouth as I opened my eyes. Like the dream from a couple nights ago, I awoke quite peacefully, but the tranquility faded quickly as I was brought back to reality. Without blankets, my living room was rather frigid. Having never had more than a few drinks at a time, my guess was that I was experiencing my first hangover. My head was pounding something fierce. It felt like a living hell. Sinking behind the cushions, the couch tried its best to eat me whole, but I was able to squirm out and sit up against one of the arms. I rubbed my eyes and shuffled a bit more to settle back into the coach, then the nausea set in. I caught the faintest scent of Helen's perfume on the couch and was instantly reminded of the night before.

"Shit!"

Popping up from the couch, I located my pants, clumsily put them on, and retrieved my netphone. I frantically tapped to call Helen while I paced around my apartment.

"Come on! Answer!"

A hologram of her appeared, but it was her away message.

"Hi. You've reached Helen's holomail. Leave a message."

"Dammit!"

I tried calling again, and again I got the damn holomail. Gathering my thoughts, I got a glass of water from the kitchen and headed for the bathroom to get cleaned up. As I was brushing my teeth, I began to think about what happened.

Why the hell would I call her Sarah? The only Sarah I had ever known was in eighth grade, and while she was nice, I never even so much as liked her, let alone loved her. There weren't even any celebrities named Sarah who interested me in the slightest.

After rinsing my mouth out, it dawned on me. I could feel a force within telling me that I did know a Sarah—a Sarah who I was really close to and, in fact, did love. Considering it some more, I remembered thinking her name a few times since the migration. That could only mean one thing.

Charlie!

I was certain that the words were coming from Charlie. He must have been with a Sarah, and when I was with Helen, it must have triggered something. Still, while the prospect of having Charlie in my mind somewhere should have terrified me, it no longer did. Though, like before, I couldn't recall specifics, thinking of Charlie and the dreams and visions that accompanied him brought me a sliver of comfort. Still, the issues with my migration were starting to affect others, and I needed to get some perspective to deal with them. I could only think of one person to contact who might be able to help me.

"ADG. How may I direct your call?"

"Tony Smith's netphone."

"One moment, please."

With a click, he answered, "This is Tony."

"Hi, Tony. It's Ryan, Ryan Carter."

"Ryan! How are you?"

"I'm okay. I was just wondering if you had any time to talk with me about…the issue I'm having with the mind migration."

"Yes, I think I have some time next week after hours. Can I pencil you in for Thursday?"

There was no way that it could wait until Thursday, and so I thought of the only way I could persuade Tony to meet sooner. "It's actually a big deal. Something's happening to me, and I have proof. I know you're looking for something to bring to the migration board, and maybe my case is just that. Can you meet today?"

"Can we discuss on the phone?"

"I would rather talk in person."

Tony sighed. "Okay, Ryan. I can get to my office at three PM. Can you meet me there?"

"Yes! Thank you!"

While I was still bummed about Helen, I was excited that Tony found time for me, and the timing couldn't have been better. I quickly showered, got dressed, and took the bullet to NTE for my two-hour training session. On my way to the elevators, a rich, creamy aroma redirected me to the café. I thought something hot and tasty might take the edge off my splitting headache, and had gotten there early enough. Jumping in line, I could see over the counter for the first time and had full view of the old-fashioned machinery that coffee technicians operated to produce the frothiest, most delicious concoctions ever. People from all over the city came to NTE to get their morning fix since the coffee bots found everywhere else couldn't come close to the handcrafted quality.

Martin, my favorite barista, was working the credit register, so I knew I would get my favorite drink exactly how I liked it. Like everyone else in my life, I knew he would get a kick out of my mind migration, so I prepared for that whole conversation. With a fool's grin stretched across my face, I moved to the front of the line and looked him dead in the eye as he greeted me.

"Welcome to Fresho Espresso. What's your fuel of choice?" To my surprise, his expression didn't budge as he spewed the corporate spiel without the slightest hint that he had served me hundreds of drinks in the past.

I thought the biocopy of my face was perfect, so I figured Martin was just used to looking down at me in Auto. Then one of my pre-migration counseling sessions popped into my head.

"Eventually, you'll be just like everyone else. How will you handle that?"

Apparently not very well since it brought my train of thought to a screeching halt. I could feel my smirk rapidly melting away while I had completely forgotten my standard order. In a stupor, I stood there silently, trying desperately to gather my thoughts while the line behind me continued to grow, adding even more anxiety to the situation.

"Sir?"

"Sorry! Let me get a coffee with cream and sugar."

"Hot Joe! Tan and sweet!" Martin shouted before I even realized what I had done.

A coffee! With cream and sugar? That wasn't the caramel latte I had ordered countless times before. I couldn't even fathom what the hell had just happened before he moved the transaction along.

"Please provide your thumb, sir."

Following his instructions, I paid for my painfully average beverage and made my way down to the pickup station. Thinking about it more, it wasn't an ordinary screw-up with the coffee. It also wasn't simply part of the migration process. When I asked for the regular coffee, I was certain it was what I wanted rather than the "fancy" drinks I used to love. That was the moment I started to see a pattern of mental lapses and confusion and was again certain of its origins.

Charlie.

It was too bad I couldn't talk with Tony in that moment, but instead had to prepare for the most boring dead-end job ever. So, with the mediocre java in hand, I made my way to the thirteenth floor. Arrows directed me through several narrow hallways and around a few corners to the New Hire area of lead generations. I approached the receptionist's desk.

Without looking up from the hologram of a man in front of her, she exaggeratedly extended her hand with only her index finger pointed up to let me know how much of an inconvenience I was, and for a moment, I was reminded of my days in Auto.

When the receptionist finally made eye contact with me, she quickly clicked off her hologram and batted her eyelashes at me. "Oh, hello."

"Hi. I'm Ryan Carter."

"Hello, Ryan. The pleasure is mine."

"Okay. I'm here for training."

"Oh. Right. Training. Let me see." She did a quick search for my name on the holo-screen, and a name appeared. "You'll be training with Mike. His office is on the other side of the department, so you can head over there, and you could also head over to my place later, if you aren't busy."

"Uh. Thanks, but I've got plans. I'll go see Mike now."

ADG never prepared me for the occasional sexual harassment, but I shook it off and headed toward the double doors of the lead generations department. Having never had clearance to the area, I didn't know what to expect, but as soon as I touched the handle, a buzz and click let me know that the doors had unlocked. I pulled on one handle, and as the door opened, my ears were assaulted by the sound of hundreds of monotonous voices droning on and on about becoming a lead for NTE. My eyes were accosted by the intense light of hundreds of holograms filling the space between the floor and ceiling. Waking up that morning, I had been certain that my headache couldn't get any worse, but the hell in front of me proved me a fool. As I headed over to the office labeled for Mike, I overheard one of the lead generators give their canned speech.

"Do you consent to us sending your contact information to a sales representative who will provide you with a demo of our latest products?"

"Do you consent to us providing your contact information to third parties so that they may contact you with special offers?"

"Do you consent to us keeping you on the list as a potential customer in the future?"

As awful as it was, it wasn't half as bad as when I finally met with Mike, or Mr. Personality as he turned out to be. The "training" he provided wasn't nearly two hours long. As dry and boring as they came, he definitely stuck to teaching me the role and did nothing to sell me on why I should like the position. It was one thing to act like a robot processing data, but it was another to do so while talking to real people. The whole experience made it clear to me that I wouldn't be very successful in the department, so would need to look for a different job pretty quickly. With a lot of time left before meeting with Tony, I decided to head to my old cubicle to grab the data-processing awards and double-check if any process items had come in. When I got there, the awards had already been removed and my thumb check resulted in access denied.

I was about to leave, but an urge made me try to ID in again, and again, it failed. A burning desire to perform a data search began to grow from within me just like before. Consumed by the thought, I headed downstairs to see if the netbar had any open workstations. I had spent many hours in the netbar because the large window in the front of the room actually let sunlight in, something we never got on the upper floors.

An overwhelming sense of frustration came over me when I saw that all workstations in the netbar were being used. I paced around for just a moment, then saw someone gathering his things to leave. After he IDed out, I pushed my thumb in and was presented with a message.

YOUR ACCOUNT DOES NOT NEED ACCESS TO THE
NETBAR. PLEASE CONTACT AN ADMINISTRATOR IF YOU
THINK YOU HAVE RECEIVED THIS MESSAGE IN ERROR.

Dammit!

I had an undeniable desire to perform a search, and the limited search functionality available on my netphone would not suffice. Peering around, I saw a woman in the netbar who was about to ID out and headed over to intervene. Before she got her thumb into the reader, I walked by and "tripped" over her bag.

"Oh, I'm so sorry!"

We both scrambled to pick up her things and put them back in the bag. At the same time, I scooted myself in front of her holo-screen. We stood up together as she flung her bag over her shoulder, and we looked into each other eyes.

Her initially frustrated face softened instantly. "You know what? Don't even worry about it."

"No, no. That was rude of me. Let me repay you. How about dinner tomorrow night?"

She blinked hard, then gave me a wide-eyed smile confessing that she was definitely interested. "Oh. Well, sure."

Diane gave me her contact info, I apologized again, and when she went to look at the holo-screen behind me, I nonchalantly blocked her view.

"Oh, don't worry, I'll be using the workstation, and I can't wait to get to know you better over dinner."

She grinned and headed out the door.

The workstation was mine, and I could complete all of my data searches. For a moment, my mind went blank as to what I needed to search. Then my hands went on autopilot like they did before and they began to type.

THE PADRE

Enter.

1,500,981 RESULTS FOUND.

Again, without thinking, I began pouring through article after article, looking for anything that stood out to me. After having gone through everything relevant, I was about to give up when a voice in my mind spoke.

Search for Ernesto Guerrero.

Typing in that name along with "the Padre" came back with only fifty-seven results. The headlines were all dated starting around twenty years ago, and they were interesting to read.

RAGS TO RICHES: ERNESTO GUERRERO, LOCAL BUSINESSMAN, ELECTED ALDERMAN, MARKTOWN.

MARKTOWN ALDERMAN SECURES GARBAGE PICKUP FOR FIRST TIME IN SIX YEARS.

ALDERMAN GUERRERO REDUCING CRIME THROUGH JOBS PROGRAM.

The entries were fascinating, and the guy sounded like a real hero to a neighborhood that had a reputation for turning itself around. But then I read further and discovered the actual fate of the Padre.

LIKE FATHER, NOT LIKE SON. ALDERMAN ERNESTO GUERRERO ARRESTED BY POLICE OFFICER ERNESTO GUERRERO, JR.

ALDERMAN INDICTED FOR ENABLING ORGANIZED CRIME.

FORMER ALDERMAN ERNESTO GUERRERO, AKA THE PADRE, ACCEPTS PLEA; PROBATION ONLY.

BODY OF FORMER ALDERMAN GUERRERO FOUND.

After reading the last title, I couldn't contain myself. "Yes!"

My audible excitement disturbed some people around me, and as I motioned them an apology, my mind swirled to reconcile the fact that the Padre was dead. Part of me was so relieved and excited because I knew it would bring peace to Charlie. Another part of me was in disbelief. The Padre was formidable, and he must have gotten in really deep if someone was able to take him out. I wanted to know more, so I selected the last article to read further. Then I received what I thought was an error message at first, but then I focused on what it said.

ARTICLE NOT FOUND. CEASE AND DESIST SEARCHING.

Weird. Trying to open the article again, another box appeared.

ARTICLE NOT FOUND. IT IS IN YOUR BEST INTEREST TO STOP SEARCHING.

What the hell?

The messages made me more frustrated than scared, and with force, I tapped the article one last time.

LOOK OUT THE WINDOW.

My anger evaporated into sheer terror in an instant, and I slowly peered over my shoulder just in time to see a giant man in a black jumpsuit place his palm against the glass.

Crash!

Bolting from my seat as chaos broke out in the netbar, I headed for the foyer without a second thought. In the front of the building, there were two more men in black entering through the turnstile doors and looking in my direction. There were two more exits I knew of, and I headed for the closest one. As I darted toward the elevators, the building security officer finally noticed me.

"Hey! You can't run in here!"

Proving him wrong, I sprinted for the stairwell and busted open the door. Sliding down on the handrail, I dropped down to the second lower-level before I heard another door open, but it wasn't the ground-level door that I came from. Stopping, I peered down over the hand railing to see who was below me. Two more men in black.

"Shit!"

My expletive resonated throughout the hollow space as I exited the stairwell at LL2. Having never been on that floor, I used my general knowledge of the building's layout to get to the stairs on the other side of the floor. Janitor equipment and supplies crowded the hallways as I weaved around corner after corner. Jogging the maze for a minute, I could see the door to the other stairwell at the end of the hallway, but something inside of me told me to stop. If the men found their way to LL3 before they even knew where I was going, they would surely be in the other stairwell. Sure enough, the door began to open as an unexpectedly familiar ding gave me an idea. I doubled back without being seen by the men entering the floor, and to my relief, discovered a freight elevator just as its doors were opening. Maintenance was rolling out an oversized piece of machinery, and I slipped into the elevator behind them without detection. Desperately scanning the floor options, I noticed the parking garage button, and with all my might,

I pushed it. In all my history with slow elevators, this one took the cake. After an eternity, the doors began to close just as the men in black appeared in the hallway in front of me.

"Hey!"

I threw myself into the corner of the elevator while keeping one eye on the doors. I wasn't sure which god was looking out for me, but they closed just before the men could get a hand in. Still, they knew where I was going, so I imagined I wouldn't be able to escape so easily. I would just have to hightail it the very second the door opened.

Two more floors.

One more floor.

Ding!

Dashing from zero to full speed in a second, I was out of the elevator and past three rows of cars before I heard the echo of the stairwell door opening. I glanced back for just a second, seeing all six of the men coming after me. Passing one last row of cars, I turned out of the garage and onto the street. In my peripheral, I could see the next bullet headed for the stop ahead of me, and I had to be on it or I was dead.

Waving my hand, I got the driver's attention, and she made the instant stop to pick me up. I squeezed between the still-opening doors and pressed my thumb down before she could even ask for fare. Heading for the back of the bus, the seat I chose had a small window for me to make eye contact with the men in black right before we accelerated to one hundred twenty kilometers per hour. Gasping for air, it took me several minutes to calm down before I realized my headache was worse than ever. Looking at the passing streets, I realized my luck had continued in that I was heading toward ADG.

Tapping the button to alert the driver of my stop, I had another two minutes to contemplate the situation. *Who the hell were those men, and what did they want with me?* I had no idea, and the bus came to a complete stop before I could really come up with any kind of theory. Still in running mode, I was out of the bus and into the ADG building in a flash. Tony's office door was already open, so I walked in and shut the door behind me.

"Hi, Ry—"

"I know for sure, unquestionably that someone else is in my brain. Someone who is real. Or at least they were real at one time."

"Okay. Slow down. We talked about this before, right? A man named—"

"Charlie! Yes. He's real. And he's in me. Or my brain. I don't know. But I found some old new articles on him and his old boss. When I looked up his old boss, just before I came here, I got chased out of my place of employment by men in black. What the hell is going on?!"

Tony reached for his holo-pad as he responded, "Wow, Ryan. That's fascinating." He began writing something down on the pad as he continued to talk. "Let's try some silent meditation where you lie on the couch, eyes and mouth closed for twenty minutes." He finished writing.

"Dammit, I don't need any—"

He flashed a hologram of what he wrote.

QUIETLY PLACE YOUR NETPHONE ON THE COUCH AND MEET ME IN THE GARDEN OF GODS AND TITANS IN TWO MINUTES.

"You know what? Silent meditation sounds good."

As odd as his message was, I was open to anything that would help me understand what the hell was going on. Doing as told, I walked into the maze of green, tall shrubbery and waited until Tony appeared. He put his hand on my shoulder and motioned us to walk through the labyrinth.

"Sorry for the dramatics, but it's better that we talk out here with a little more privacy. You never know who could be listening in on the netphones. Fortunately, the network adapter to my holo-pad broke, and I never got around to fixing it."

"Okay." Having never considered being surveilled before, it was something I made mental note of.

"After you reminded me about Amanda Robinson, I got curious and started doing a little digging."

We turned a corner, moving deeper into the maze.

"Digging into what?"

"ADG's records from the beginning."

"How's that relevant to me now?"

"Well, some of the old records that I looked at aren't adding up in terms of dates, new hosts, and services rendered."

Around another corner, there was a long straight away, and I walked a ways before scratching my head. "I don't follow."

"It might be nothing, but the inconsistencies are enough for me to want to keep looking into it, and if some of my hunches are true, then I might have an explanation for your...condition."

"Tony, why are you telling me this? Can't you lose your job?"

We took another turn and entered the open center of the labyrinth. The familiar statue of Atlas was there as well as some marble benches dedicated to various gods and other titans, and we stopped.

Tony sighed. "Job? If this is as big as I think it is, my job might be the least of my concerns. But that's just it. If I'm working for dirty people, that makes me dirty by association, and I didn't sign up for that. I want to know the truth, but more importantly, I feel responsible for you. I feel responsible for all of the migrators that have come through my doors."

"Tony...I don't know how to thank you."

"I'm the one who should be thanking you for pressing the issue. I'm sure this hasn't been easy for you."

He motioned me back to his office, and when I got there, I grabbed my netphone from the couch. "Wow, Tony. I feel a lot better. Thanks for your help."

"No problem, Ryan. I'll see you later."

I took the next bullet to my apartment and used all the energy I had left to get to my couch and collapse onto it. It still smelled like Helen, and sadness budded from my core. I knew that I needed to call her again, but all I could think about was sleeping off the rest of the hangover. Stretching out, I could feel the warmth and fuzziness of sleep setting in when the damnedest thought popped into my head.

I am a giant asshole! Diane is in for a hell of a surprise! The least I can do is let her know that big men dressed in black might be coming for her because I was under her ID, but I can't contact her myself or they might find me too.

I remembered someone who'd bragged about sending anonymous messages in college, swiped my netphone, and a second later, I got an answer.

"Hello?"

"Mom, I need your help!"

CHAPTER 21

THE EYE OF THE BEHOLDER

"**M**om, I need your help!"
My eyes opened after yelling the odd phrase, and all I could see was the off-white, textured ceiling above me. I could see an interesting ceiling fan upon looking farther, and then my eyes were drawn to the strangest poster on the wall.

The Dome 4.

The Dome had just been in theaters last year, followed by talk of making only one sequel, let alone three. Shaking it off, I continued looking around. The space was filled with interesting items—an odd computer desk, the fanciest holo-clock I had ever seen, and right next to the bed in which I laid was the most disturbing thing of all: a state-of-the-art wheelchair with an interesting code pad on the side. Though, the mechanic in me couldn't help but noticed that, as advanced as the wheelchair was, the wiring and battery on the back had to be a disaster waiting to happen. Pulling too hard on the right wires would likely cause an overload and probably worse. The distracting thought was nice, but then the strangeness of the situation hit me tenfold.

Where the hell am I?

Before I could figure it out, my body took over and called out again. "Mom! I need your help!"

"Okay, sweetie! I'll be there in a minute."

More confusion set in when the woman's voice came from the other room. Trying to take it all in, I struggled to sit up to get a better view and immediately wished on everything that was holy that I had just laid there instead. The dread that ensued nearly caused me to black out.

My legs! What in the hell happened to my legs?

It's like they weren't even there. I couldn't feel anything. I couldn't move *anything* below my waist. If that was true, then how the hell did I—

"Hi, sweetie." A tall, middle-aged woman with blonde hair entered the room and came to the right of the bed.

She lifted my shirt and began moving and tugging on something that was connected to me. I finally looked down and was again instantly disappointed that I had. She was swapping out my colostomy bag that apparently had been collecting overnight.

The war! It had to be the war. While I didn't remember it, I must have been blown up, and paralyzed in the process! That had to be it.

"Thanks, Mom." More words came out of my mouth against my will. While a part of me thought that the woman was familiar, another part of me had no idea who the hell she was or why I was calling her Mom.

"Oh, no problem, sweetie. What's on your schedule for today?"

"I'm taking the seven-fifteen bullet to work. Then I'm headed to ADG for my first personal-identity session. I'll be back by six."

"More counseling? Haven't you had enough?"

"Mom. We talked about this. There's a lot of hard work that goes into preparing for the procedure."

"You were crying in your sleep again last night. Are you sure you want to go through with this, Ryan?"

Who the hell is Ryan? What procedure? None of it made any sense, and I was starting to get anxious at the fact that nothing I wanted to say or do was happening.

"Yesterday's session was tough, but it also proved something to me. If I can handle living without legs my whole life, I can handle anything. I know you're scared of the mind migration, but it's something I have to do."

"And you know that no matter what, I'm always going to worry about you."

My mouth curled up, ready to snap off a witty response, but then I just let it go. "Thanks again, Mom," I said to the woman as she wrapped up the work she was doing on me and took away the bag of waste.

"No problem, sweetie. I'll have breakfast ready for you downstairs."

Yawning the sleep out of my lungs, I began dragging my body off the bed and onto the wheelchair, and while it was a bit clumsy, it also felt routine as I tumbled into the seat. Typing into the code pad, safety straps snaked around me and clicked into place. Behind me, I heard a beep, and then noticed one of the lights next to the code pad labeled Charging turn off as the motor kicked on with a low hum.

"Come on, Auto. It's time to take on the world." With my right hand, I reached for the joystick in the center of the code pad and pushed it to the left.

It was strange to use my right hand with such precision, and the wheelchair spun quickly in that direction. I pushed forward on the stick to go around the bed and toward the closet, then grabbed what appeared to be a minimalist office-job uniform. I was amazed by my ability to take off my pajamas and put on the uniform with little difficulty and no assistance.

Fully dressed, I rolled out of the bedroom in the wheelchair and went down the hallway to the bathroom. I wasn't sure if I was more scared or excited to look in the mirror, but I was definitely a little disappointed when I went past it and headed straight to the linen closet to get a washcloth. Then I navigated back to the sink to brush my teeth, and that was when I finally got a look at myself in the mirror.

I know that face! The young guy in the wheelchair!

How in the hell is that even possible? Where is my body?

Somehow, I was *seeing* through his eyes and living through his body. It had to be the most lifelike dream I had ever experienced, and I tried everything to wake myself up, to no avail. My hands wouldn't carry out a slap or pinch and my head refused to shake the reverie away. Since it didn't seem like I had any other options, I decided to just see the dream through.

I—*Ryan* finished brushing his teeth and went to the top of the stairs. Integrating with the wheelchair lift, Ryan and I were slowly lowered down the stairs and around the corner as the meaty smell of cooking bacon filled my—*his* nose. The sizzling sound followed as we were firmly planted on the floor before disengaging from the lift. We headed straight for the kitchen, and by that point my—*his* mouth was watering.

"Your plates on the table."

Zooming over to the space at the kitchen table with no chair in front of it, he grabbed the fork and began digging in. It had to be the best eggs, bacon, and toast I ever had. There was also a carton of starfruit juice, which seemed strange but tasted outstanding. While eating, I overheard what had to be a headline of the news on a television in the other room.

"Economists say that the country is finally recovering after losing GIP. More on that at eight."

All of it must have been a dream because we had definitely not been losing when I'd been discharged a couple of years ago. The tides had really been turning, and had we found the enemy HQ and a few more weapons stockpiles, it would have been over in an instant.

"How are things at work, Mom?"

She came to the table with a plate of food for herself and sat down. "They've been relatively quiet since the protest last week."

"That's good."

Ryan finished off his breakfast, took his dishes to the sink, and headed for his jacket hanging by the front door.

"Love you, Mom. I'll see you tonight."

"Love you, sweetie."

On the way to the coatrack, we passed a small table in the hallway. On it was a virtual reel of pictures, and at first, it was just rolling through Ryan's childhood. Right before we passed it, an intensely familiar photo appeared of Ryan's mom standing in the front yard of a house different from the one we were in. I couldn't put my finger on exactly what was familiar about it, maybe something in the background. Either way, it just seemed like the weird dream was only getting weirder.

Throwing the coat on, we exited the house and made our way down the winding ramp. It was a short ride to the bus stop where there was a large painted rectangle on the pavement indicating where the bus would stop. It was then I noticed that the pavement wasn't concrete or asphalt, but what had to be solar paneling. There was always talks that they would implement the solar panel roads someday, but between the money, politics, and difficulty of construction, they had never gotten around to doing it.

While we waited, Ryan pulled out his netphone. Like nothing I'd ever seen before, its sleek design and compact features seemed futuristic. He tapped a button.

"Show me Mount Kilimanjaro, real time."

The most realistic hologram I had ever seen manifested itself, hovering just above his horizontal netphone. It might as well have put us directly on the base of the mountain because I could see granules of dirt and details of the porous surface of the rocks. Individual blades of grass were fluttering in the wind, and a group of hikers wearing safari shorts, fedoras, and sweat-soaked shirts were making their way up one of the paths. So breathtaking was the imagery that I almost forgot we were half a world away, experiencing the muggy chill of what had to be around early autumn.

A sound in the distance interrupted our exploration of the hologram, and I noticed a strange bus barreling in our direction at what had to be close to seventy miles an hour or more. I was sure it wasn't our bus since it couldn't possibly stop in time for us to board. Then, about fifty feet from us, I marveled at its ability to rapidly slow down and come to a complete stop exactly within the painted rectangle. Busses like that were only rumored in science magazines from what I remembered.

The bus's door for those with disabilities opened and a mechanical lift transformed outward. It clamped onto the wheelchair and pulled us up and into the bus. Once there, Ryan wheeled us up to the front near the driver, pressed his thumb into what appeared to be the fare acceptor, and then moved back into a wheelchair space to settle in for the ride. In an instant, we jerked into motion and the bus merged into a large center lane that didn't have any other traffic. From then on, it was the smoothest ride I had ever experienced on public transit.

Looking more closely at the advertising on the ceiling and walls, I realized it wasn't exactly "public" at all. An ad filled the space over the back window that read: "This hyperbus proudly brought to you by EAP, the transportation enterprise you can trust."

After making a few more stops in the suburbs, the bus began to fill up as we headed for what had to be the city. I realized then that we were on an interstate through the city I lived in, so should see things I recognized. I was instead presented with a different, newer, cleaner version of my memories. There were almost no buildings that looked rundown and not even one homeless person on the streets begging for money. It also wasn't just Ryan who dressed like a minimalist. The pockets of people walking on the sidewalks blended in with each other, making it hard to distinguish where one person ended and another began. The last thing I noted was that every single car on the solar road was completely spotless, making them act like powerful mirrors of the sun. That explained why I constantly had the urge to squint, even though Ryan seemed used to it.

We passed the old Armada Hotel and Suites building where a union of housekeepers had picketed for fifteen years straight over better working conditions and wages, one of the longest active pickets in history. Not only were there no protesters, but the building looked like it had been converted to accommodate business offices and conferences, and I wondered what the outcome of the protest had been. Part of me hoped they'd won. Then I was slightly comforted as we approached the heart of downtown, where much of it was unchanged, though the addition of video boards on every skyscraper was new. Some of the smaller buildings seemed to have been replaced with large greenspaces, each one with a large, animated billboard advertising one company or another. Otherwise, I could easily pick out Carey Tower and the Payton Building.

The bus stopped almost instantly in front of a building that seemed oddly different. A video sign said it was NeoTech Enterprises. I specifically remembered that company being new because of their silly jingle that sounded like something right out of a children's book.

"NeoTech: Our products are newer than new, and they will make you you-er than you."

For whatever reason, it seemed like my subconscious was fond of them because the sign showing tenets of the building only had NTE and some coffee shop. In this dream, they were a massive corporation, when in reality they hadn't even completed their IPO.

Ryan moved us into position, the door opened, and the mechanical arm grabbed and gently placed us onto the sidewalk. We rolled a short way to the door of the building for those with disabilities and entered a large, impressive foyer. Ryan made a beeline for the coffee shop and waited in line.

"Hey, Ryan! How are things?"

"Good, Martin! How are you?"

"Great. Can I get you the usual?"

"Yes, please."

"Sticky icky with froth!" The guy behind the counter shouted.

Ryan pushed his thumb into the payment acceptor, and we moved down the counter to pick up his drink. Then my dream turned into a nightmare as he picked up some fancy coffee drink that was probably too rich and sweet for any self-loving person to enjoy. But apparently, he did. After getting our hot cup of milk and sugar, the elevators were our next destination. On our way in, we ran into another person in a similar wheelchair that Ryan must have known well.

"Helen! How are you?"

"Oh hey, Ry! I'm good. How are you?"

"Just fine. I have my first PID for the migration today. I'm a little nervous. How's your preparation going?"

We boarded the elevator, and she pressed the number fourteen.

"Not bad. Still in general counseling, but we'll be shifting to PID in a couple weeks."

"I hear it only gets harder as we get closer, Helen. The offer still stands if you ever want to talk; just give me a call."

"I might do that. I don't know if it's work or the personal drama that's bugging me, but the sessions have left me drained. It wouldn't hurt to get a different perspective from someone going through it all. Thanks, Ryan!"

"No problem."

The doors dinged open, and Ryan allowed her to wheel out first, then we headed our separate ways.

"See ya, Ry!"

"Bye."

Ryan took us to what had to be his cubicle, parked at the oddly designed desk table, and put his thumb into a device. Startled as the desk converted into an elaborate setup of screenless, hologram-like computer technology, I was reminded it was just a dream when my—*Ryan's* body didn't jump.

"Good morning, Ryan Carter. You have twenty-two thousand data sets to process. Have a productive day."

Ryan began to wave his hands like the conductor of a symphony, and the holograms responded as different screens of seemingly random data appeared, changed colors from red to green, and then rotated to the next screen. Taking intermittent sips of his coffee, he hardly slowed down working with one hand. He was apparently doing an instantaneous visual verification of data before moving it on to an automated check, all of which were coming up green. I could only assume that meant they were being correctly processed. It was a sight to see him work, but a couple hours in, and I wanted to jump off a bridge. It was ten times worse than working the line. I prayed that something would wake me up so I didn't have to sit through all of it, but to my disappointment, I couldn't even zone out.

Then, out of the blue, a piece of relevant data caught my eye. A name field on one screen listed Lucille Rios. That had to be my baby girl making her presence known in my dream. Unfortunately, Ryan was moving so quickly that it went back to being the most boring job I'd ever had to sit through. He finished out his workday, apparently clocked out by putting his thumb back onto the device, and caught the next bus across town to the campus of another company.

Atlas Digenetics.

Upon entering the main building, NTE's foyer was put to shame. There were plants growing on the walls and an intricate water fountain in the center. What must have been a waiting room had a huge statue of the titan Atlas, giving the whole place a neat feel. We headed for an elevator at the far end of the space, and into the keypad on his chair, Ryan tapped the number eight followed by a series of other seemingly random numbers. We got into the elevator, and the ride was much slower than I would have liked, but the old-school instrumental playing on the speakers made it tolerable. The doors opened, and without the slightest pause, we headed left toward a receptionist's desk.

"Hi, Jake. I'm here for my first PID."

"Right! Let me have you thumb in, and the team will be with you in a few minutes."

Ryan obliged Jake's request, then headed over to a small waiting area.

I read over the obnoxiously tall advertisement hologram across the room.

HAVE YOU BEEN DIAGNOSED WITH A FATAL DISEASE?

IS YOUR QUALITY OF LIFE BEING HINDERED BY
THE PHYSICAL STATE OF YOUR BODY?

DO YOU NOT IDENTIFY WITH THE BODY IN WHICH YOU WERE BORN?

WELL, ATLAS DIGENETICS MAY HAVE A SOLUTION FOR YOU!

WITH CUTTING-EDGE TECHNOLOGY AND THE MOST WELL-
TRAINED DOCTORS AND EXPERTS, ADG IS PROUD TO BE THE ONLY
COMPANY IN THE WORLD PROVIDING **MIND MIGRATION**. YOUR

DISEASES AND PAIN WILL STAY WITH YOUR OLD BODY, BUT THE
POSSIBILITIES ARE ALMOST ENDLESS IN YOUR NEW HOST.

THE BODY OF YOUR DREAMS IS AROUND THE CORNER.

ASK ONE OF OUR SPECIALISTS FOR MORE DETAILS.

Then I realized the hologram had to be so tall for all the fine print
after the advertisement to also fit. For a procedure like that, I was certain it
probably said something along the lines of "results may vary, and we're not
liable for anything ever."

Ryan laughed and whispered under his breath, "I'm glad they're good
at what they do."

The more I thought about *mind migrations*, the more a peculiar
fear began to well up in me. Part of me was scared simply based on the
implications of such a procedure. Still, some of the fear seemed much older
as if I had some kind of previous knowledge of a similar procedure that I
couldn't quite pinpoint with everything else going on around me.

"Ryan Carter. Please come to room eight-zero-zero-three."

Shaking off the dread, we wheeled toward the office rooms, then the
room where a tall, bearded man in slacks and a button-up shirt stood
outside.

"Hello, Ryan. I am Dr. Morris. Please move yourself by the couch and
get comfortable."

We rolled into the large room with old-fashioned carpet and vintage
books lining the walls. A professional-looking woman sat near the center of
the room, on the other side of the therapy couch.

Dr. Morris walked in behind us and took a seat next to the woman.
"Ryan, this is my colleague, Dr. Pritchett. She'll be assisting with your
personal-identity session today and possibly moving forward."

Dr. Pritchett extended her hand. "Nice to meet you, Ryan."

Ryan rolled up to her and obliged.

Both doctors took a seat across from the couch while Ryan settled near
it.

Dr. Morris moved things along. "Does your auto-chair have a flat
setting?"

Ryan nodded. "It does."

"Some of our clients feel the sessions are most effective if they lie down." He opened his hands making a flattening out gesture.

Damn. The kid's physically disabled, not mentally.

I could tell Ryan detected the condescension when he responded dryly with, "I'm fine. Thank you."

"Great. Then we'll begin. Like all of the conversations you've had with our specialists, this will be recorded for quality assurance." He cleared his throat and tapped the company badge attached to his shirt pocket. Picking up the holo-pad next to him, he began reading a script. "As your reading material stated, PIDs are meant to help you harden the idea of 'me' into your mind before it has been migrated into a new host. ADG research has shown that a weak definition of self can cause adverse effects on the overall migration process. Adverse effects include being rejected as a candidate for mind migration, delayed migration recovery, quick onset dementia post-migration, or death during the procedure. Do you understand how vitally important these sessions are? And do you have any question before we go any further?"

"I understand, and I do not have any questions. Thank you."

Dr. Morris swiped the holo-pad to the next page and handed it to Dr. Pritchett, and she spoke next. "When I ask you, 'Who is Ryan Carter?' what comes to mind?"

"Well…I picture myself. Myself in Auto. I see me doing the things I like to do, like virtual vacations. I think about my legs and how they hold me back. I think about my mom and how hard she's worked to keep me alive and as healthy as possible."

She typed something into the holo-pad and swiped to the left. "How do you think that definition will change when you're in your new host?"

"All of it will change. No Auto. I can do *real* vacations. My legs will be great. And Mom will finally get a break."

More typing and another swipe. "Okay. Next question: Does the definition of a word or phrase change based on its context? Where it's said or by whom?"

I couldn't help but shrug.

"I guess."

"Can you give me an example?" Dr. Pritchett probed deeper.

Oddly enough, I could *feel* Ryan thinking for just a moment, and then I could hear the words before he said them.

"Oh, I don't know. If I said, 'We have bad blood,' to a friend, it means we have a bad history together. If I say, 'We have bad blood,' at a hospital, it could mean that they can't use the blood for their tests."

"Good, Ryan. Now what about books? If you read the classic *Sports of Royalty* novel set, does it change depending on who reads it or where they read it?"

"No, the books themselves will always be the same pages and words. But, I guess the reader's interpretation of them might change depending on who is reading them and where they are."

"Great, Ryan. The last introductory question I wanted to ask you is—"

Everyone froze in place, and after the momentary shock of it, I remembered that happening in other dreams I'd had. Or maybe they were memories. I couldn't tell at that moment. I wasn't sure if Ryan was frozen as well, but I did feel the urge to stand up. Attempting to do so, I could feel myself pulling apart the connection that Ryan and I had like stretching pizza dough out until it started to tear. Inch by inch, limb by limb, I climbed out of Ryan and into the frozen world. Stretching out to stand tall, I was facing the doctors, and did a quick glance around the office. Finally, I turned around to look at Ryan.

The wheelchair was gone, and Ryan didn't seem disabled at all. He was standing just as tall and as fit as me. It was like looking into a mirror, only there was no mirror. Then terror sunk in as I realized what I was seeing.

He's taken over my body!

CHAPTER 22

DIGGING UP THE PAST

"**H**E'S TAKEN OVER MY BODY!"

Helen glared back as I tried to explain what had happened the other night. "Ryan, pretend that you're me for just a moment, which I know sounds wild since you're telling me that sometimes you're not you anyway. But humor me."

"Okay."

"What's a woman to believe? The man she...likes a lot...is having episodes every time she tries to hold his hand or be intimate with him? Or he's actually just scared of commitment and lied about me being his first?"

She was more hurt than angry, but was plenty angry.

"You *are* my first! You know that I didn't even work...down there, before the procedure."

She rolled her eyes. "Yes, but what about the couple weeks lead time you had on me after the migration? Is that when you slept with Sarah? Is that when you told her you loved her?"

The server awkwardly interrupted our conversation. "Is there anything else I can get you folks?"

We both tried to act normal as we asked for and received refills on our espressos.

"Helen, there is no Sarah. At least not for me. This is what I've been trying to tell you. I think she was Charlie's wife or something. I think that when you and I got together the other night, it triggered something in him, which triggered something in me. I don't know. I don't understand it all yet. That's why I was digging at work. You heard about what happened. I was chased all over NTE by giant men in black!"

Through her teeth, she responded, "I heard that the video footage only shows you hacking into someone else's—a woman's—account at the netbar, and then running around the building like a madman."

"They must have altered it!"

"Who's 'they,' Ryan?"

"I don't know! The henchmen! Or maybe NTE, to justify firing me without getting the cops involved!"

"You're lucky 'they' only terminated you and didn't send the cops to your house."

"Helen! You have to believe me. No one else knows about this."

She looked across the room as she sipped her drink, then cleared her throat. "There's something I never told you, Ryan. Something that is important for you to know. I kept it from you because I wanted to move on from it, but I know now that isn't possible. When we first met, I was still with someone...Brian. We had been together since high school when he asked about my auto-chair, and when I waited for a joke, he was actually quick to relate that he had MS. We hit it off, and spent most of our time together after that. Talked for hours about our future together. College. Marriage. Kids. We were madly in love...or at least that's what I thought. Our senior year was when I noticed something odd. Every month, he'd miss school for days at a time, saying he was getting treatment for his disease. But he wouldn't call or message me during those times, and I never understood it."

She took a sip of her coffee, then continued. "It went on through college, only we didn't go to the same school, so I talked to him less. When I asked him to call me more, he said the treatments made him too tired. I believed him, and stayed faithful to him. But as time went on and his condition worsened, it got difficult for him to keep up a façade. About the time you and I met, I had started to find evidence that Brian was lying about everything. Other women's numbers, receipts for extravagant purchases... drugs, and not his prescriptions, either." She flinched. "It turned out that Brian's parents felt sorry for 'giving him a disease,' even though that was nonsense. They had allowed him to do whatever he wanted. Skip all his treatments, run up the bills on their credit. He was intentionally wearing out his diseased body, and planned to divorce it and start his 'real life' afterward."

"That doesn't sound like a good plan."

"I know. Worst of all, I didn't leave him when I found out. I was used to being his backup plan. I thought being with him was better than being alone. I was wrong. After a drug overdose, he was finally migrated in an emergency procedure. Even after all that, if he had changed his ways post-migration, it wouldn't have been so bad. But his destructive ways only got worse. It's been almost two years since I saw him for what he was and left him. I couldn't handle the lying and cheating, but mostly, I couldn't bear to watch as he slowly killed himself with the help of his family."

"That sounds awful. I'm really sorry, Helen."

"It was—it is. He was the one that really convinced me to migrate. That was one of his last lies. He said that with healthy functioning bodies, we could start our lives together. I had always thought about migrating, but he really pushed the urge into an obsession. I actually looked into migration right after his, but with my first counseling session, I realized that I was doing it for him and he didn't even love me. He couldn't even love himself. I left him, and it took me another year or so to commit to migrating for me and no one else."

"I'm really glad you did."

"So now that you know, what am I supposed to believe? Your paranoia, your episodes, your conspiracies? How do I know I'm not being strung along again?"

My thoughts swirled at Helen questioning my intentions, rather than my sanity. That hurt more. I knew that hurt her me. Part of me wanted to march right into ADG and let my anger erupt in front of all their staff. I paid good credits to get a body that functioned normally, and Charlie wasn't supposed to be part of the package. He was putting me and those around me in danger, and it wasn't fair. Another part of me just wanted to burst into tears. With the exception of Tony and Helen, no one really knew what I was going through. Though in Helen's case, she didn't believe me. I barely believed the whole thing myself in between episodes.

For the first time since migrating, I felt like I had as a kid when I began to understand my disability. The initial feeling of helplessness had been almost as paralyzing as my physical limitations, but even if Mom did a lot for me, I wasn't helpless. I'd worked very hard to do the best I could, and at no point in the last ten years did I say, "I just can't do it." I had no intentions of throwing in the towel just because things had gotten tough. That was when two things became clear to me.

First, if I was going to get through the "Charlie" situation, I would have to work hard and smart to figure it out and keep moving forward.

Second, I needed to surround myself with strong people who believed in me. Tony was a start, but Helen was just as important. In spite of her doubts, she actually knew me better than anyone since migrating.

Looking around the café, I chose my words carefully. "I've never been good at talking to people, let alone women. You remember in the elevator. I tried to woo you with a bad joke, and you were having none of it. But you also didn't completely reject me. Whether you appreciated the effort or actually liked me then, I still don't know, but one thing was for sure. You had no pity for me. You were in an auto-chair too."

I looked her in the eye. "But that's what made me fall for you in an instant. When I gave you less than my best, you challenged me. When I was so used to being coddled, you gave me shit for everything. As odd as it sounds, I immediately respected you for that. That initial respect has only grown steadily into a deep attraction. So, the other night when you said you loved me, I was the happiest man in the world. I almost couldn't believe it. A tough-as-nails woman feels so strongly for me? Nah! But I knew you meant it, which validated all my efforts to be a decent person."

Her expression finally softened a little.

"And as hard as all of this is for you—and I know it is—this is my reality. Every moment, I'm wondering if I'm slipping away. Each morning, I'm coming out of some crazy dream, not *about* Charlie but *as* Charlie. Hell, you've seen it. I'm not even safe from him when I'm awake."

Her stern look returned but not nearly as intense. "So, what are you saying, Ryan? What do you want from me?"

"The last thing I want to do is hurt you. But the more I learn about Charlie, the more it becomes clear. I can't guarantee my own safety, let alone yours. In that sense, you're absolutely right to question me. But in thinking about the last couple of weeks, I've realized something else. We're both at our best when where together."

Helen's face softened even more, cuing me to put myself out there.

"I never knew true love until I met you, Helen. Take a chance on me. Take a chance on us."

She revealed the slightest grin and took a deep breath. We waited in silence for a moment, and when she was ready to speak, she said only one word.

"So."

So? Confused, I pried. "So…what?"

"So, I guess we're going to have to figure this 'Charlie' thing out."

It was the best thing she could have ever said. But the urgency of the situation left me no time to be awestruck if she chose to be with me; there were pressing things I needed to do. Pushing my thumb into the table's ID reader, I motioned for Helen to get up. I gave her the biggest hug, and she reciprocated.

Pulling back, I looked her in the eye again. "Come with me. There's something I need to look into."

We headed for the door, and without a word, we walked to the nearest bullet stop.

After ten minutes, her curiosity finally got the best of her. "Where are we going?"

"There's a part of the city where many of my dreams take place, but many years ago. I was going to walk through the neighborhood on my netphone, but after my run in with those guys, I'm not taking any chances. Going there in person will ensure we don't make too much noise on the net, and I'm hoping it will help me figure out the next steps to learning what happened to the Padre."

"Didn't you say that that Padre character died?"

"Yes, but with everything else that's going on, something's not adding up. Now, it's a rough part of the city, but I think we'll be okay if we keep to ourselves."

Zipping past street by street, we stayed on the bullet longer than I ever had, until we were on the other side of the city. A big sign alerted that we'd be getting off at the next stop.

WELCOME TO MARKTOWN: ON THE CORNER OF PROSPERITY AND OPPORTUNITY.

Jumping off the bus on to the corner of a major intersection, I spun around trying to orient myself.

"I think we have different definitions of 'rough,'" Helen quipped.

We were in the downtown area, but none of it made any sense. Street names were different. Lots of ritzy businesses and restaurants had replaced the modest shops. The apartment buildings and houses were obviously upper class. Even the roads had been recently solarized with the latest panels.

Helen looked at my puzzled expression with concern. "What are you thinking?"

"I don't know. It's not what I expected."

A silly grin came across Helen's face as she pointed at a nice shop across the street.

"Maybe Charlie really wanted me to get a new handbag!"

"Yes. That's definitely it. Anyway, let's walk."

"Oh, boo!"

We headed down Plum Street, and nothing hinted at the former ghetto run by the Padre. Then I remembered the little bit of research I was able to do on him, and I couldn't hold back my thoughts.

"The son of a bitch did it."

"Who did what?"

"Charlie's boss. The Padre. He became alderman of the neighborhood years ago and started to turn it around, economically."

"So, you still think this is the same place?"

"Has to be."

We kept walking until we found ourselves in a residential area, and none of it meant anything to me. I was about to give up hope when I spotted a building that didn't quite fit in with the new look of the area.

"There." I pointed at the two story, tan-brick building with thick windows and ivy covering one side. It was in great shape, considering how old it had to be. The old-time marquee attached to the second floor was partially burned out, but I could still read it.

MARKTOWN COMMUNITY CENTER: AMATEUR ARTIST SHOW. THIRTY CREDIT COVER.

"You recognize it?"

"No, but let's check it out."

A smaller sign near the entrance to the building became visible as we got closer.

NO PERSONAL ELECTRONIC DEVICES (PEDS)
ALLOWED PAST THE FRONT DESK.

Entering through a heavy wooden door, the dirty checkered linoleum floor and green walls provided an authentically quaint feel, and its stale air reminded me of grandma's house. The room was sparsely decorated save for a chalkboard with a list of events hanging behind a mustachioed man behind an impressive antique desk.

The man greeted us with a smile. "Hello, friends."

I followed suit. "Hi. We're interested in the art show."

"That'll be thirty credits from each of you."

He presented a credit acceptor, and we extended our thumbs while smiling through the shock of the ridiculous cover.

"Any PEDs on you?"

"Yes," we said simultaneously, then smiled at each other

He dryly replied. "Cute. We'll keep those up here while you look around." Over the counter, he extended a long stick with a black net at the end of it.

We dropped our netphones in, then headed through the double doors to a large room scattered with paintings, sculptures, and "unique" pieces on the walls and floor. There was even *something* hanging from the ceiling, but I wasn't interested enough to look for long. Filling half the room, a crowd of people wearing anti-trendy-but-still-trendy clothes were standing around having low, monotonous conversations and nodding a lot.

"Neat." Excited, Helen headed across the room to one of the more *interesting* works.

I was still trying to take the place in and meandering around until I noticed a man float over to Helen and begin talking to her. I figured I'd join them to see what it was all about.

"…just put it together from long pieces of scrap metal and plastic I found in the alleyways in the city. A little bit of hot glue, and *voila*."

His method would have actually been fascinating if it wasn't obvious that he was trying to put forth as little effort as possible to be considered an artist. The whole thing looked like a failed junior high science project disguised as minimalistic. It still wouldn't have been so bad, except he started laying it on pretty thick.

"I really helped 3D 4R art rise to its current popularity starting five years ago…"

He went on, but my ears wouldn't let me listen any longer. My eyes wandered past everything to a window on the outside of the room where

I saw other, more-normal-looking people arising from the lower level and leaving the building through the back. There was something else happening in the building, and I wanted to check it out. Against my will, my mind wandered back to the conversation in front of me, and I was suddenly bearing witness to attempted highway robbery.

"And with all of the effort I put into it, four ninety-nine is a steal. What do you think?"

I couldn't help but butt in. "She thinks we have to go. Thanks anyway." Grabbing Helen's hand, I pulled her back out toward the front desk.

"Hey, I really liked that piece!"

"Trust me. It was bad."

Back at the front desk, I looked behind the counter at the chalkboard where the day's events were listed, but everything below the art show was smudged.

"Find something you'd like to purchase?"

I ignored the mustachioed man's ridiculous question.

"What's happening in the back of the building?"

"Oh, that's not related to the show. Just some people from the neighborhood that share the space with us."

"Can we go back there?"

"Well, I think their meeting just ended, but the two organizers usually hang around afterward. You can take the stairs at the end of the hallway. I'll keep your PEDs, so don't forget to pick them up here on your way out."

We headed through the building to the stairs, then stepped down slowly into the dank basement. The lighting was dim, and the smell went from nostalgic to earthy. At the bottom, we came upon what appeared to be the back of a large room filled with rows of chairs. Up front, an older woman in a familiar model auto-chair swept the floor and a still-older man facing away from us looked at a hologram while swiping through an old-fashioned netphone. The hologram image's title was a bit jarring.

GENTRIFICATION: HOW COMMUNITIES ARE BOUGHT AND SOLD.

The virtual progression of images must have been telling the story of how Marktown went from working class to poor to rich in a matter of a few decades. Helen was still watching it when I headed up front to talk to the man.

He acknowledged me without even turning around. "Art show's upstairs."

"I wouldn't call that art."

Turning around to catch a glimpse of me out of his peripheral vision, he clearly didn't trust me. He finished flipping through the netphone, tapped it a couple of times, and the hologram switched to a slow, rolling reel of old photos of what must have been his dog before they were outlawed. I remembered from my virtual sessions that the breed was German Shepard, and judging by the size of the beast, I could understand why those laws were made. As large as the dog was, her name was funny to me, but before I could finish the humorous thought, the man snapped off the reel and finally turned around.

"And who are you?"

Helen walked up next to me as I responded, "Oh, sorry, sir. I'm Ryan. And this is Helen."

"How may I help you Ryan and Helen?"

"We 're interested in the history of Marktown."

Eyeing us both, he inquired.

"Is it some school project, or are you two reporters?"

"Oh, no. We've just never been to this side of town before, and we like getting history firsthand."

"Humph. Well, there's not much to tell. People with jobs lived here decades ago. The jobs left. The people who could leave, did. Those who couldn't, lived hand to mouth until they were forced out years ago. This group is comprised of the only ones left from Old Marktown, as we call it."

I needed to move things along. "Maybe you could help me find information on a person I've heard about—a former alderman."

He nodded. "You mean the Padre."

"Yes. How did you know?"

"He's the one that started the whole prosperity-and-opportunity bullshit before he snitched and got himself killed."

"What do you know about him? Before he was alderman?"

His right eyebrow went up. "Well, he was just a guy from the neighborhood. That's how he got elected. The old bootstraps-and-hard-work mantra."

"Didn't he run a gang?"

The man's face stiffened almost as if it was in pain, and I couldn't tell if it was fear or something else. The old woman stopped sweeping and rolled over next to him. The purr of her motor was nostalgically calming. That comfort instantly dissipated when she questioned me.

"Is this some kind of joke?"

I shook my head. "No, ma'am. An honest question. I heard rumors."

Her right eyebrow went up and she looked around, clearly flustered, then peered up at the man. "Allen, let's take our guests to the back room."

Helen grabbed my arm as if to say, *Let's get the hell out of here*, without words.

I shrugged her off because, while the old man was large, I figured I could handle him, and I wasn't too worried about the woman in the auto-chair.

The man extended his arm toward a narrow concrete hallway. "Follow us."

We walked down the hallway until we came to an open, thick metal door. They entered first, and we followed. After we entered, they shut the door with a clank behind us. Allen walked around a large table in the center of the room, the woman following in her auto-chair. They motioned us to sit down in the chairs on the other side.

The woman then spoke up with a bit of angst in her voice. "We don't know nothing. We never saw nothing."

"Why did you bring us back here to tell us nothing?"

Allen glared as if to try to read us better, then chimed in. "You don't work for his former employers, do you?"

"The Padre's? No. We're just local history buffs, is all."

He looked at the woman, and his expression broke. "I think they're okay, Sonya."

Her eyes got wide as she questioned him. "Are you sure?"

"No, but I'm tired of acting scared every time someone brings him up. What more can they do to us?"

I interrupted their side conversation. "Did the Padre run a gang?"

"Look, Ryan, the Padre was a flawed individual all the way up to his death."

Feeling like I needed to move the discussion to more specifics, I looked at Helen, then back at them. "He sold human organs on the black market, right? He made a lot of people disappear. Did he have any way to fake his death?"

Again, they both looked at each other, partly frightened, partly angry.

Through her teeth, the woman asked again, "Who the hell are you?"

"You wouldn't believe me even if I told you. But I just know things about this neighborhood. Plum Street used to be Main. The Sock Emporium used to be a Pete's Hardware. The fancy bistro next to it used to be a Stella's Waffle House with the best fried chicken you ever had. And the Padre used to be a crime lord. How did he get elected alderman?"

Stunned didn't begin to describe the looks on their faces. In front of them was barely more than a kid who clearly wasn't from the area, giving them a trip down memory lane. They sat blinking back their shock for what had to be ten seconds, then looked at each other a moment longer.

Allen finally spoke up. "Uh, well, the word on the street was that a job went south, and his bosses took away his power. They 'made' him alderman because they still needed his network for processing their products."

The warehouse job. That must have done him in. "What happened after his plea deal?"

"He hung around the neighborhood for a few weeks, and then his body was found in the river. Had to have been his former employers getting back at him for snitching."

"Is there anyone who could give me more information on the Padre? To confirm his death?"

Allen glared at me and pointed to Helen. "Son, if you're not careful, she's going to be confirming your death. You don't mess with people like the Padre, even if they are dead."

"Trust me. I know. Is there anyone?"

They looked at each other and sighed in unison.

Sonya responded, "I guess there's Junior, his son."

"The police officer?"

Sonya nodded. "The police *chief*."

Even more surprised than me, Helen interjected, "Your chief of police is the son of a former crime lord?"

Sonya grimaced. "Crazy, I know. Junior was a street cop for years, and everyone assumed he was a mole for his dad. But he went out of his way to bust the Padre, and then publicly denounced him afterward, when he didn't have to. It really gave him respect in the neighborhood. Some of us were even saying he should have run for the alderman position, but he declined, saying that he loved police work too much. It turned out to be a good move for him as he steadily rose through the ranks." Sonya's tone seemed conflicted, weaving back and forth between disappointment and pride, but it was probably the anxiety of Helen and my strange, unexpected visit.

"Thanks, Sonya, Allen. We'll stop bothering you now."

"To be clear, you didn't hear anything from Allen or Sonya."

"Of course. Thanks again."

Helen and I left the room and walked down the long hallway. On our way past the room with chairs, the images of the dog on the hologram flashed through my mind again, and for a moment, I thought something about it was as familiar as it was odd.

Who names their enormous dog R—?

"What are you thinking?" Helen interrupted my thought as we headed up the stairs.

It was silly anyway. "I need to speak with Junior."

"Why? The Padre's dead."

We grabbed our netphones on our way out and headed for the bullet stop.

"He might be dead, but I don't think Charlie will be satisfied without proof."

"Ryan! You heard them. You're dealing with some dangerous people. Why would you put yourself in harm's way, digging up the past?"

For the first time, I could actually feel Charlie's force welling up inside of me, and I didn't fight it.

"I would do anything for my family."

CHAPTER 23
IF ALL ELSE FAILS

I WOULD DO ANYTHING FOR MY *family*.

The air was as cool and crisp as I could ever remember, with the subtle aroma of leaves burning in the distance on every waft. Intense rays from the sun relentlessly poured over every inch of the scenery, giving the outside an overexposed look. The occasional cottony, cumulonimbus puff stretched across the sapphire sky, allowing gazers to interpret the shapes like naturally occurring Rorschach tests. Neatly groomed, forest-green Kentucky blue provided the perfect contrast to the spotless, gray sidewalks lining the area. Pockets of colossal oaks with deep red, bright orange, and dull brown leaves dotted the landscape, confirming that the season was in full swing. It had never been more evident that the imperfect perfection of the outdoors knew no bounds.

I drifted aimlessly in awe like being lost in space until the surrounding din finally offered me a buoy halfway back to reality. There was the obnoxious blare of a car horn, no doubt a bad driver getting the attention of a worse driver. The loud, quiet hum of a lawnmower doing laps across a yard could be heard from somewhere behind me. Across the way, an ill-trained miniature terrier incessantly yapped as she dragged her owner toward anything that moved. To my front left, I heard the almost rhythmic, and all the more annoying, thud-thud of a soccer ball being booted against a cement wall. If all of that wasn't enough, just past the playground, there was the tinny dribbling of a basketball in between the metallic swooshing chain net and ritualistic male howls, grunts, and groans. Sponging up all of the nuances of suburban life, part of me questioned living in the city.

"Are you okay, Charlie?"

Shaking my head, I snapped out of it. "Yes. Sorry."

On the playground, Lucy darted under the spiral blue slide, feverishly chasing some local kids trying to make one of them "it." Next to me, Joey happily gulped and murmured while gently slapping Sarah's breast as he nursed. Everything confirmed the perfection of everything else.

"What if we left the city? Moved out here?" In that moment, it felt like the most logical question I could ask.

"And where would we live?"

"You and the kids could stay with your folks while I figured something out. Maybe we could buy a house. Who knows?"

"Charlie...you heard the doctor. The kids and I being away from the city for too long is risky. Why would we take the chance?"

She was right. I only worked four or five nights a week with the Padre, and some of those nights were just prepping for the next job. So, with the little time and energy I had left at odd hours, I'd read everything I could get my hands on about spotted lung. Bizarre from the day it was discovered, scientists and doctors couldn't agree on its origin. There were two index cases in two completely different geographical locations thousands of miles apart. In both instances, the exact same strain of the virus was contracted, making it baffling and unclear who the actual patient zero was.

Patient Zero A was an older German business man visiting Hong Kong to settle a major corporate deal. Distressed by his cough, the local doctors simply diagnosed him with bronchitis. He closed the deal in spite of his fading health, and was allowed to fly back to Berlin the following week. He died a month later, but not before the disease spread quickly throughout Germany and other parts of Europe.

Patient Zero B was a poor Argentine corn cultivator for a large corporate farm. Losing his job when his sickness became apparent, he visited a free clinic a day later where all of the patients and staff soon contracted it. A Cuban doctor on the staff was the one who instituted a quarantine of the entire clinic until World Health Organization (WHO) specialists swooped in. They ran countless tests, and when similar reports came from Europe, it didn't take long for them to connect the seemingly unrelated dots.

It wasn't until a year later that a breakthrough was made where they discovered potent drugs that would "neuter" the virus, rendering it incapable of spreading to new hosts. But the problem was still two-fold. Not only could they not cure or prevent the disease, but more importantly, only people with money could afford the drugs, which left much of the population at risk. Ironically, after treating 80% of the infected in Europe, WHO declared the epidemic under control only to turn around and confirm the first case on North American soil the same day. The industrial parts of the Northeast were hit first, and in a couple months, it made its way through the Rust Belt and around the Great Lakes.

European treatment facilities were located in or very near the cities in which their infected acquired the disease since most countries didn't have the space or resources to move people far distances. However, North American doctors deviated from that blueprint, rounding up all of the infected and quarantining them away from their homes and work places. They were taken to the countryside where it was assumed that the fresh air would provide them relief as they were treated and studied. Instead, pain, suffering, and a considerable number of potentially preventable deaths ensued until doctors realized the virus had a peculiarity about it that had never been seen before in any other disease.

Spotted lung made its hosts "addicted" to pollution, with a particular preference for the pollution in the cities in which they became infected. In that sense, the virus was that much more fascinatingly adaptable, and all the more gut-wrenchingly terrifying as it moved from population to population. If the smog in a city was mainly produced by factories, the infected would flock to the industrial areas to breath in the dirty air. Large cities that had yet to ban old cars with exhaust systems had a major issue with people blocking traffic. Looking to relieve the pain in their lungs, they would walk into the streets at stoplights, stand in front of exhaust pipes, and inhale deeply. Some would get so high that they'd pass out on the road.

Once doctors acknowledged those idiosyncrasies were important to the overall treatment of the patients, they began bringing the research facilities back to the cities. That was right around the time the federal government passed the Spotted Lung Containment Act, where treatments to contain the disease were mostly or entirely subsidized. After that, the medicines and equipment to fight the virus advanced tremendously, but so too did the price hike that actually outpaced the subsidies three- or fourfold. The best equipment would allow the infected to live in their homes, go to work, and lead relatively normal lives until their symptoms got worse. Still, it was recommended as a precautionary measure that they stay in the cities where they'd caught the disease. But I was in denial, looking for anything to help my family, so I didn't want to believe the truth.

"I know. But the air is cleaner out here. There's more grass and trees. That's gotta mean something. It's just tough for me to believe that a virus, something so tiny, can manipulate the people it infects to stay in one place."

Sarah shook her head. "Even if we could move, you know I'll be starting back at work in a few months. I'll be damned if I'm going to commute into the city every morning."

"I heard they're installing solar panel roads and test driving high-speed busses from the suburbs all around the city. You might only need to drive for a year or two, and then that might be it."

"Mom!"

Our conversation was interrupted along with Joey's feeding as Lucy zoomed in to talk to us.

Sarah turned to her. "Yes, Lucy?"

Heavily breathing, Lucy put her hands on her knees.

"Honey, how are you feeling?"

"I'm tired. But I'm good. Bradley's getting ice cream with his family. Can we get ice cream too?"

"We'll be going back to Grandma and Grandpa's here in a little bit, and we'll see if we can get some ice cream then. Before you go back out there, take two breaths off your inhaler."

Watching Lucy play, talk, and grow like a normal kid made me think that she would be all right. But I knew that wasn't true. We had settled on the older-model equipment and less effective medicine, but having worked a few jobs for the Padre, we could already afford the better stuff. The problem was that I had yet to tell Sarah I had quit the line, and where the sudden influx of money came from.

"So, honey, there was something that I have been meaning to tell you."

Sarah nodded to me as she puffed on her inhaler.

"I'm sure you saw the numbers in our bank account. They're looking pretty good. Well, I wanted to use that toward the best for the kids and you, so you can feel better."

Still catching her breath from the inhaler, her eyebrows went up in curiosity. "Yeah, what happened with that? You take on a side job? Spades promote you?"

"Not exactly. It's something I meant to tell you earlier, but I didn't want to worry you."

"Charlie. What is it?"

I could hear the doubt in her voice.

"You remember my buddy Sam who I told you about? Well, he got me a job working for a man in the city."

"What man? What job?"

"Promise not to get mad?"

"Dammit, Charlie! Spit it out!"

Joey popped off the breast to see what the commotion was, then glared at me just like his mom as if to say, "Just tell her already so I can get back to eating!"

I took a deep breath. "I do odd jobs for…the Padre."

"What the hell! The guy from all the stories we heard growing up? Isn't he a gang leader?"

"I'm not sure what he is, but it's nothing I can't handle. With the money he's paying me, it doesn't matter. How else are we going to afford to keep you and the kids healthy?"

"You know things will get easier when I go back to work, right?"

I shrugged. "What if you're too sick to work? What then?"

She shook her head and exhaled hard. "We'll figure something out!"

"Sarah, I've seen what the damned disease can do. One minute, you feel fine. The next, you're out of breath to where you can't even talk. Mrs. Reno was a mess for a couple years as she slowly faded away."

"This is ridiculous. Nothing justifies working for a scumbag. You need to go back to Spades and beg for your job back!"

Joey whined a bit, then stared at me again, echoing Sarah's concern.

"I can't go back. The night I quit, the line manager cussed me out and said I'd never be welcome there again."

"Dammit, Charlie! It's like the marines all over again. Without so much as talking to me, you make a big life decision, and there's no turning back. At least the marines were honorable. But this? An illegal job? What if you get arrested? Or worse?"

"The Padre's son works as a cop, so we're always one step ahead of them. And we still take a lot of precautions."

She turned from livid to upset in an instant. "One night I go to bed with an honest line worker. The next morning, I wake up next to a criminal working with corrupt cops and worse. I'm more than disappointed in you, Charlie. I'm disgusted. I'll never be okay with this."

Sarah's words stabbed me right in the heart. Throughout my life, I had always felt like other people's bad decisions had made my life worse. But I never thought I'd be on the other side. Part of me hoped she would come around, but she was as stubborn as she was smart, so I knew it wasn't likely. It wasn't a long-term job, in my eyes anyway, so it was probably a good thing that she wanted me out as soon as possible. And I was sure the Padre would be understanding of my sick family.

"Okay, Sarah. Once you're back at work, I'll find something else. In the meantime, I'm going to get us the best equipment money can buy."

Scowling, she handed Joey to me to burp while she packed up our things. "Lucy! Time to go!"

As we headed for the car, Sarah wouldn't even look at me. Driving back to the in-laws, the silence in the car was palpable.

Lucy, perceptive as she always was, chimed in. "Mommy, Daddy, since you're both mad, does that mean we're not getting ice cream?"

Sarah snapped back before I could say anything. "Ask your dad. He's got all the money."

"Your mom and I are just figuring things out. We can all get ice cream after dinner."

"Yay! Thanks, Daddy!"

When we arrived at her folks' house, Sarah jumped out of the car and slammed the door. She jerked the back car door open and grabbed Joey, then headed straight in. Unbuckling Lucy, I held her hand as she jumped from the car.

She held on tighter after landing on the grass. "Daddy?"

Moments like that made fearing for her future that much harder. "Yes, sweetie."

"What's going to happen to us since we're sick?"

Struggling to keep it together, I tried to calm her concerns. "You remember the machine at the hospital that helped you breathe?"

"Yeah. It was scary at first, but it did make me feel better."

"We're going to get one for your room. Joey's room too."

She smiled. "Does that mean we're going to get better?"

"Yes. It's going to help a lot."

"Good, because I don't like being sick."

"I know, sweetie."

Even with the new job, the feeling of helplessness was ever present. There was no guarantee that the medicines and equipment would do anything but prolong the inevitable. Still, if buying time was the best we could do, I wasn't going to spare any expense.

Lucy and I entered the house and were immediately hit by the delicious aroma of Tammy's famous lasagna. Having a higher degree in chemistry, Sarah's mother made the kitchen her laboratory and produced some of the best food I had ever had. It didn't disappoint as everyone but Sarah ate their fill, barely leaving room for the ice cream treat I had planned.

Phil must have realized his daughter was unhappy, and I was sure it was his paternal instinct that led him to know I was involved in some way. He turned to me as Tammy cleared the table and said, "Charlie, join me for a beer on the porch."

We headed out and cracked our beers almost simultaneously while we stood looking out into the dimly lit neighborhood.

Phil spoke up as I took my first swig. "I'll be honest with you. I never thought anybody would be good enough for Sarah. Maybe it's a father thing. I don't know. But you definitely fit into that category when I first met you, 'not good enough.'"

Since he was more like a father to me than any other man had ever been, I wasn't offended by his comments, but hung on his every word as he sipped his beer.

"But you made her happy, and you always seemed like a nice guy. That's all it took for me. When you were left for the war, she talked about you almost every day. 'Lucy has Charlie's eyes,' 'I hope Charlie's doing okay,' and so on. That's why you got Tammy's and my blessing to marry."

Taking a breath, he turned to look me in eye. "Now, whatever's happening between you two, you may not want to admit you're wrong. Hell, you might not even *be* wrong. But *she* thinks you are. Dead wrong.

So, you need to decide whether her thinking that is more important than keeping your house together."

"What if trying to make things right will also tear us apart?"

A subtle smirk came across his face. "Then have a backup plan when the choice you make is undoubtedly the wrong one."

The conversation quickly divulged into small talk, but the wisdom in Phil's words had an instant impact on me, and I knew what needed to be done. The family and I wrapped things up at the in-laws and headed back to the city. Both kids were out like lights by the time we merged onto the expressway. It was the little break from the day that Sarah and I both needed, and I couldn't pass up the opportunity to talk to her.

"You know I love the kids and you, right?"

She shrugged at first, but then dropped her shoulders and sighed. "I know you do, Charlie. But that doesn't mean you can do whatever you want. We're supposed to be a team."

"You're right about a lot of things. The job is dangerous, and bad things could happen. But since I can't quit anytime soon, I need you to promise me something."

"Okay."

"If the time comes, and you know it's bad, don't think twice about me. Just do what's best for the kids and you."

The look on her face professed that she was going to yell at me, but she muted her anger. "Charlie!"

"I know it's not fair, but it's the only way we can be prepared for the worst. Just promise me you won't wait for me. Just make sure our family is safe."

"Dammit, Charlie!" she said through her teeth.

"Promise, Sarah."

"Fine. I promise. But it's such bullshit."

"I know, and I'm sorry."

Getting home, I carried Lucy to her room as Sarah did the same with Joey, and then we met back in the hallway.

"I have a small job to do tonight, so I'll be home later."

She just gave me the stink eye and shooed me away. Before I left, I went out to the balcony. Obtaining my wallet from my back pocket, I opened it and pulled out a business card that was given to me by my discharge sergeant. It was bizarre that such a service existed, but it was especially strange that I would be taking advantage of it. It seemed like the perfect solution given the situation.

PLAN B.

The title on the card was followed only by a phone number, and I dialed it on my way to the car. It rang five times, and then the call disconnected. Wondering if the sergeant had lied or if they had gone out of business, I was about to dial the number again when my netphone buzzed with a message.

GATHER ALL OF YOUR PLAN B MATERIALS AND BRING THEM TO THE COORDINATES IN THE FOLLOWING MESSAGE.

Another buzz, and I had a destination. I stepped to the edge of the balcony and looked over at the long planter that was there. Putting my hands in the dirt, I pulled out a plastic bag containing a large sum of cash that I had withdrawn and hidden since my first few checks from the Padre. I went back inside the house and grabbed my dog tags off the key rack. Next, I sat down with a piece of paper and a pen and began writing.

Sarah,

If you're reading this, that means I will not be coming home anytime soon, if ever. Enclosed is $200,000 in cash and another note explaining what to do next. Like you promised, don't think twice about the contents of the note. Just make sure our family is safe. I'm sorry. I wish I could have been a better husband and father. I love you all.

—Charlie

Note 8001: You are safe. Use the cash to continue taking care of the family.

Note 8002: You are not safe. Take the kids to the location provided in the package, and they will instruct you on what to do next.

Apparently, many veterans returning from the war were putting themselves and their families in harm's way, so an underground business found a niche market for delivering packages and hiding people should the right number be called and passcodes entered. Bundling everything up, I went down to the car and headed to the location. Turning down the street where I would ultimately drop everything off, I noticed movement in my peripheral in the passenger seat next to me. To my surprise, it was Ryan, in my body, sitting next to me. But for the first time, I wasn't shocked at seeing him, but curious instead. Having gotten a glimpse of his world and seeing him in my body made me think he was somehow from the future, and if that was the case, that he might be able to help me in a couple of ways.

"How do you keep appearing like that?"

"I don't know."

"Do you know what I'm doing?"

"Yes."

"Will you do some things for me?"

"What?"

"Can you find out what happened to my family?"

"How?"

I held up my phone and showed Ryan the number for Plan B.

"Find them. Give them the codes ninety-two-thirty and eighty-O-two. They should be able to help you after that."

"Okay, Charlie."

We pulled up to the building. Ryan took a good look at it and turned to me. "What if your family is—"

"I just need to know."

Ryan nodded as he responded, "I'll do my best."

"Thanks, and another thing, Ryan."

"Yes?"

"Can you find out what happened to the Padre?"

He shook his head. "He hasn't been heard from in years. He might be dead."

"But I need to know for sure if he's alive and, if so, where."

"Okay, Charlie. I can do that for you."

"And Ryan?"

"Yeah?"

"Be careful. You don't know these people or what they're capable of."

CHAPTER 24
THE PRICE OF A MEMORY

"Be careful. You don't know these people or what they're capable of."

Helen's fear was understandable, but my well-being was the least of my concerns. I had to figure out the right way to convey that to her. "It's tough to describe. Before migrating, all I could think about was getting my legs. I spent countless hours dreaming about walking, running, jumping! Hell, I was extremely excited about going to the bathroom on my own. But ever since I discovered Charlie and all his memories, it really is my new obsession, for better or worse. I almost feel like a writer or musical producer who gets stuck on a notion and is almost forced to put all their effort into creating something. Well, for me, it's seeing this Charlie thing through. Otherwise, I just go back to the boring old life of Ryan Carter, and that's getting more and more distant. I'm getting used to the idea that there's something more out there for me. For us, Helen."

"I had the same thought last night. Even triathlons seem boring compared to this stuff. But can you just promise me something?"

"Sure. What is it?"

"Keep me involved—somehow, some way. Maybe we can sit down and map out everything you know before you make your next big moves."

"That sounds like a great idea. As much as I have always dealt with things internally, this is too important to keep in. After I find out more today, we can have that sit down."

We hung up and I quickly got myself ready for the day. It had been a week since I'd spoken with Mom, so I arranged for us to have a nice lunch.

I had something specific I wanted to discuss with her anyway. She insisted treating me to a hearty Italian meal to make sure I was eating enough, so we met at a fairly upscale ristorante. It was a strange feeling seeing her after it had been so long. Prior to the migration, the longest I had been away from her was a few days at time for longer hospital stays.

"How's empty nesting coming along?"

Her initial casual demeanor dissipated as her face lit up with a smirk. "It's awful! There's still moments where I'm doing nothing and suddenly get alarmed that I forgot to check on you."

I couldn't help but chuckle as she went on.

"And I continue to buy and make too much food. Looking in the fridge this morning, I realized I'm running out of room with all of the leftovers."

"Oh, Mom. I'm sure it will get better as time goes on."

"Yes, I'm sure too. Though, on a positive note, I've started crocheting again. Be prepared. I'll be shipping you a new blanket every month."

"Can't have enough warm blankets! Winter is coming."

The conversation was a welcomed break from all of the seriousness surrounding Charlie, but I knew eventually I would need to ask for her help.

"How are you doing, honey? You had me send that anonymous message to that number, and then you message me that you lost your job. Is everything okay? If you need credits…"

"No, don't worry. They were going to run me out of that place one way or another. I still have a enough credits left over to get me through the month, and if that changes, I'll let you know."

"Don't be afraid to ask for anything."

"Well, there was something. About sending an anonymous message…."

"Yes?"

"Can you show me how? There's someone I need to contact, but I need to be discreet."

She shook her head in complete disagreement. "Ryan, I only helped you because you said the person was in trouble. You could get hacked, or even spend a long time in jail if you get caught."

"I know that. But it's…too important and sensitive for you to get involved anymore. I don't want anything bad happening to you."

She squinted at me as she tried to figure out what was going on. "What is it? Are you in danger? Let me help you, Ryan."

"All I can tell you is that it's related to my migration."

Anger washed over her face in an instant. "I knew it! They screwed it up, didn't they? Are you okay? Oh no! Are you dying?"

Her volume disturbed the people sitting at the nearby tables. I smiled and waved them off.

"No, Mom. I'm more than okay. I just need to look into some things. I'll promise to be as safe as possible."

She sighed hard, revealing how much she would begrudgingly say the words that were about to come out of her mouth. "Fine. If you're going to go get yourself in trouble without cluing me in, I guess I can't stop you. Come by the house tonight, and I'll show you what I know. But please don't get yourself into too much trouble, Ryan. It's bad enough that I only talk to you once a week now."

"Mom, I know it's tough to process, but I'm not that helpless boy anymore. I can take care of myself, and I truly believe that I'm finally doing that."

"And you need to understand that a mom's worry never goes away."

Her comment forced me to nod and smile. "I guess you're right, Mom. Thanks."

We finished lunch and headed outside to say our goodbyes.

Mom looked up at me, then paused for just a moment. "It's hard to believe. My little boy is in this big man's body. It's literally like you grew up overnight. So, if you're wondering just how hard things have been on me, just keep that in mind."

"I know. For what it's worth, I think you've done a great job, and I really appreciate it."

"Of course, Ryan. Now, make sure you call me more!"

"I will, Mom. I love you!"

"Love you too, sweetie."

We parted ways and the timing couldn't have been better. I had received a message from Tony the previous night that he wanted to have a "routine follow-up" to our last meeting. I bulleted to ADG and headed straight for his office.

"Hello, Ryan! How are you?"

"I'm doing well, Tony."

"Hey, I figured we'd take a walk before our session officially starts. Come with me."

We headed into the migration area and went straight for Genesis labs where hosts were grown from cells to the age and specifications set forth by the migrators, depending on the package they purchased. The labs were off-limits to anyone scheduled to complete a migration within a twelve-month period. Apparently, it caused stress in migrators from years ago who would get attached to a particular host as they went through the process, only to be disappointed if that host had to be swapped out later. Instead, in preparing for the procedure, we were shown a virtual simulation of the process, which made it less personal and easier to handle. Tony and I approached the security doors where a guard stood outside.

"Alex! How are you?"

"Great, Tony. Did you see the game last night?"

"Yeah! Heartbreaker. But that's how the season has been going."

"I was sure they were going to win too. I lost five big ones on it."

"That's too bad! Glad I didn't have any skin in the game. Anyway. I wanted to take this post-migrator into the lab."

"No problem. Let me just have both of you scan in."

The guard tapped a button, then Tony and I took turns thumbing the ID reader. The doors opened up to a bright-white and sterile-looking environment. Laid out like a museum exhibit, there were informative, interactive stations for each major development stage of a host.

Starting with a series of microscopes, Tony motioned me to take a look at the artificial-conception stage. Watching the exact second the synthesized sperm penetrated the synthesized egg was fascinating. After watching a couple of conceptions, I lifted my head and read the sign above.

Q: WHY NOT SKIP CONCEPTION AND JUST
CREATE HOSTS FROM SCRATCH?

A: EVEN WITH ALL OF OUR TECHNOLOGY, NOTHING
HAS BEEN ABLE TO EFFECTIVELY RECREATE THE
SIMULTANEOUS COMPLEXITY AND SIMPLICITY OF
NATURE'S WAY OF CONCEIVING HUMAN HOSTS.

Moving on, we made our way to the zygote stage, where we were presented with holograms that we could touch and move to gain a better understanding. It was at this point that any remaining genetic manipulation would occur. Above was another sign.

Q: WHY DOES FURTHER GENE MODIFICATION
HAPPEN AT THE ZYGOTE STAGE?

A: OUR SYNTHESIZED SPERMS AND EGGS ARE JAM
PACKED WITH VARIOUS GENETIC TRAITS. IN ORDER TO
ENSURE THAT A HOST IS AS CLOSE TO SPECIFICATIONS
AS POSSIBLE, WE MUST INCLUDE SOME TRAITS WHILE
POSSIBLY EXCLUDING OTHERS FROM PROGRESSING.

Thirdly, we came to the fetal stage, where there were more holograms and more information.

Q: AT WHAT POINT DO YOU KNOW IF A HOST IS A
CLOSE-ENOUGH MATCH FOR A MIGRATION?

A: ONCE GROWN TO A FETUS, WE ARE ABLE TO
RUN VARIOUS COMPUTER GROWTH MODELS TO
MATCH THE HOST TO THE CLOSEST REQUEST.

Next was the gestational-completion stage, where the baby would be ready to be born had it been grown in utero. Additionally, the brain was developed enough to require neural inhibitors to stop cerebral development from occurring. It was described as a "switch" that was inserted to "turn off" the acquisition of knowledge, memories, and personality traits. Later, the switch would be flipped on in preparation for a migration.

Q: DO THE NEURAL INHIBITORS HURT THE HOSTS IN ANY WAY?

A: COMPLETELY UNAWARE, THE NEURAL INHIBITORS
ARE A PAINLESS, HUMANE WAY TO KEEP HOST
MINDS CLEAN OF IMPURITIES, MAKING THEM
IDEAL FOR OUR MIGRATION PROCESS.

Finally, we came to a forest of test tubes of various sizes, each showing a host in the latter stages of development. Examples of newborns, infants, toddlers, adolescents, teenagers, and young adults were all present, suspended in the crystal-clear preservation liquid. The last Q and A was there as well.

Q: WHAT'S THE OLDEST HOST THAT CAN BE PURCHASED?

A: THE OLDEST HOST TO TAKE PART IN A SUCCESSFUL MIGRATION WAS THIRTY-FIVE. HOWEVER, HOSTS THIRTY-FIVE AND OLDER PRESENT UNIQUE CHALLENGES IN THE MIGRATION PROCESS, AND THUS, THE CURRENT UPPER LIMIT IS THIRTY TO BE SAFE.

Having seen all the phases firsthand, all of my pre-migration excitement came flooding back. Watching the creation of life was nothing short of amazing, and seeing each step of host growth in all of its glory reminded me of the miracle that was mind migration.

"What do you think?"

I was certain that Tony could sense my glee.

"I'm just really happy I went through the process. It's been a crazy ride and a lot of hard work, but it's been totally worth it."

"Good. Let's head back to my office for more meditation to further your progress."

Back at the office, Tony again held up the holo-pad with a message for me to place my phone on the couch and meet him in the gardens.

"Okay, Ryan. Please lie down and just let your thoughts drift into the silence."

I was only out in the gardens for a minute when Tony appeared, saying, "We have to be careful. If the wrong people find out about what we're doing, we'll both be in big trouble."

"Trust me. I understand."

"Good. Now, I wanted to show you the Genesis labs so it was fresh in your mind when I tell you what I've found."

"What is it?"

"Each host has a sixteen-digit sequence ID that is a result of their very specific development at each of the stages we just saw."

"Okay."

"For practical purposes, the numbers are unique. Due to nano-nuances in the development after conception, even identical twins result in a different sequence ID. This ensures that every host can be tracked from the moment they receive a number until they finally pass away. If you recall the waivers you signed, you will be 'donating' your host back to ADG after your time is up, for analysis, cataloging, and ultimately, disposal, so that your host is never used again."

All of the information was nice, but I was getting a little impatient. "What are you getting at, Tony?"

"What I found is…" Passersby caused Tony to look over his shoulder, lower his voice, and lean in closer. Looking back at me, his voice trembled just a bit. "…your host might be a duplicate."

"What!"

"Shhhhh!" He grabbed me by the shoulders and looked me in the eyes. "I was searching the sequence database a few weeks ago when I noticed that your host matched that of an anonymous host from almost a decade before ADG completed its first migration."

"Why would they have records going that far back?"

"That's the thing. They don't. The next time I logged in to look again, the older data was gone and everyone in the company received a message that there was a temporary glitch in the system, resulting in a bunch of invalid records."

I shrugged, trying to figure it all out. "So, could it have been a glitch that let Charlie into my host's mind?"

"I'm not so sure. With the problems you're experiencing on top of the weird glitch, I'm wondering who or what your host really is. If your host never had neural inhibitors or they malfunctioned, I have no idea what kind of irregularities that would cause."

"What do you mean?"

"Let's just say it's starting to validate the things you've told me about Charlie. It even has me questioning what actually happened to Amanda Robinson. A record with her name appeared on the list as well as a very strange entry prior to hers."

"What kind of entry?"

"It looks like there may have been someone who migrated before Amanda."

"But all of the stories…"

"All of that stuff was always just rumor. Even the people I worked with who were familiar with her case didn't have direct contact with her." Tony looked around and took a deep breath. "Unfortunately, I've done enough snooping the last couple of months, and don't want to press my luck. I'll be laying low for a while before trying to dig any further. You can still come to me for real therapy sessions, but we can't speak about this topic for some time."

I didn't care that he needed to take a break. I was just happy he was helping. "Thanks, Tony. Sometimes it just seems like Charlie is some kind of imaginary friend of mine since no one else can see him. But the more I discover, the more I push further into the depths of my mind, and the more he was—the more he *is* real. I have to see it all through."

"I'll keep doing what I can to help you. Now, let's head back in."

Back in the office, I grabbed my phone, and sat for Tony to wrap up our "session."

"Now that meditation is over, I wanted to remind you of something, Ryan. As time goes on, you'll experience important dates in your host—birthdays, anniversaries, holidays, and other significant days. They may seem a little strange because you'll be able to do more things to celebrate and honor those days. I encourage you to push yourself to use as much of your new abilities as you can during those times. You may find that you actually feel more like your true self in the end."

To my surprise, I had completely forgotten about that advice from post-migration therapy. My birthday was coming up, and I hadn't even contemplated what to do since I was so consumed with Charlie.

"As always, Tony, I really appreciate all that you've done for me."

"My pleasure, Ryan. You take care now."

I strutted out of the office and through the halls of ADG, a silly confidence welling up in me as I reveled in Tony's findings.

I'm not crazy.

It was probably the most positive thought I had had in a week or more as I exited ADG and headed for the bullet. My last errand of the day was to search for the building Charlie had shown me.

Plan B.

My recollection of the building was fuzzy, and the city looked a lot different from what I remembered. I wasn't even sure if the building actually existed based off my dream, and even if it had, there was no telling if it was still around. Regardless, I was drawn to uptown to start my search, and getting dropped off right in the middle of the busiest intersection, I walked around for many blocks. After thirty minutes without luck, I stopped on a street corner to gather myself and pulled up a holo-map of the area. I had covered about 80% of the area, and still, nothing stood out to me. Regardless, I felt like I was close, so I just needed to keep looking.

Speaking into my phone, I said, "Show me the map from twenty years ago," and the holo-map morphed itself back in time. Gone were most of the skyscrapers, and in their places were much smaller buildings and businesses. Glancing around, I noticed that even the streets had been reconfigured to some extent.

"Walk me through the streets that don't exist anymore."

At street level, I walked through a virtualization of the city back then, complete with people in period-trendy clothes and cars with exhaust systems. The faces of the walking commuters looked noticeably happier than those from my time, and I wasn't sure if that was added as part of the simulation or was just accurate. Looking around, I began to get jealous as I saw more and more delicious-sounding East Asian eateries that no longer existed.

"What happened to those restaurants?"

Before my phone could respond, sadness overcame me and I tapped the button to stop the last command. While I had never visited the area, I read about it while doing research in school.

Near the end of GIP, many East Asian immigrants and even some citizens were rounded up and either deported or jailed indefinitely on suspicion of supporting extremists. In reality, they were targeted because of alleged sympathies toward FPR. News headlines steadily grouped FPR in with the extremists, even though it was generally known that they were bitter enemies. Still, in response to the sweeps of East Asians, the locals rose up with protests and marches, successfully paralyzing the city for several days. That was when the mayor declared a state of emergency and federal troops were brought in to squelch the rebellion. Demolition of all foreign-influenced businesses soon followed, along with the reforming of the roadways. After all of the reconstruction, local law enforcement advertised that an "uprising" in that part of the city could be contained and dispersed within two hours of forming. It seemed more threatening than comforting. Deep in thought, I was still gazing at the old map when I thought of something.

"Overlay the present map on this one."

The visual in front of me fluidly transformed to provide a cross-reference. All of the current buildings had replaced older buildings—except for one. It appeared that one of the towers I had passed was built atop an older building. A specialty shop was the first floor to some office suites. Doubling back, I reflected on how it did seem a little out of place compared to its surroundings.

The sign read Paul Robyn: Living Memories.

As I opened the door, the warm fragrance of flowers blew onto my face from the meticulously designed, neatly organized room. The space had an elegance the likes of which I had never seen, with tasteful paintings spaced in satisfying intervals on the walls, strategically placed indoor plants, and a few obscure but somehow appropriate sculptures. The whole building was much smaller than I would have anticipated based on the size from outside.

A mature woman in a blood-red dress approached me. "Hello, sir. Is there something I can help you with?"

"Sorry. What kind of business is this?"

"Oh, you haven't heard of us? Allow me to introduce you to our services." She lifted her arm, signaling me to head toward the center of the room as she walked next to me.

"For humans, time is finite. We only have so many breaths to take, only so many beats from our hearts. But a memory. That is something that can be timeless so long as it's preserved."

"Interesting."

"Yes. At its core, a memory is simply data. But we offer so much more than the digital interpretations of someone's mind."

We approached the far end of the room, and she tapped a button next to one of the better paintings, prompting it to flip into the wall. A first-person hologram appeared of a man standing at the altar of what appeared to be his wedding. The other groom made his way up the aisle to meet him. They said their vows and kissed with the audience cheering ever so loudly. It was a pretty powerful scene of happiness.

"Virtualizing someone's memories allows those moments to be eternal. To the people who our clients give access, they are able to view each snapshot as many time as they like."

"Wow."

"If having your memories live on for friends and family doesn't interest you, we also have our business package that allows memories to be permanently stored for various applications—trade secrets, litigation, and a host of other things."

The whole concept was more than interesting, but I needed to see if she had any information on Plan B.

"I'm actually here on a whim. I found a note from a friend of the family who passed away years ago. It had a number on it, and it said, 'Plan B.'" I noticed the slightest grimace on her face. "Does that mean anything to you?"

"I'm sorry, sir. But I have no idea to what you are referring."

"Are you sure? I have the number. I just wanted to finally put his memory to rest, and so I thought this might be the place to do it. Please. If you know anything…"

Hesitating for another moment, she tapped the wall to flip the painting back, and without a word, she started walking back to the front of the room.

Following, I pried. "Plan B does mean something to you, doesn't it? Can I give you this number?"

"Sir, like I said, I am unfamiliar with your Plan B." Her words contradicted her actions as she held her hand out, looking for me to give her something.

I keyed the number into my phone and handed it to her. Pressing a button on the wall, an old-fashioned computer keyboard appeared, and she began typing.

I was startled as the floor on which we stood began to move and the entire corner of the shop rotated into the wall.

"What the—?"

With a jolt, the floor stopped moving in a dimly lit room.

I couldn't contain my confusion. "What is this place?"

The woman placed her index finger to her lips, shushing me, and then pointed to the far side of the room. There was a series of numbers on the wall. Hearing her type again, I was staring at the wall as a single number popped out on the far-left side. It almost seemed like a mailbox. Looking back at her, she leaned toward the mailbox, cuing me to go take a look.

I proceeded trepidatiously toward the container protruding from the wall without so much as a clue as to what I would find. Closing in, I could finally make out the number *9230*, and gulped hard as I peered inside.

Surprisingly, the metal box was completely empty except for an old scrap of paper, and I whispered to myself, "They got the money and the note." Then I gingerly grabbed the note and held it up in the dark room.

> Charlie,
>
> If you're reading this, do not ever come looking for us. We're better off without you.
>
> —Sarah

Tears began to rush down my face as Charlie erupted from me. "I can't believe I threw it all away!"

CHAPTER 25

TRIAL BY FIRE

I CAN'T BELIEVE *I* THREW IT *all away!*

Sitting next to my public attorney, I sulked in regret, thinking about the bad decisions I had made. Even if I was innocent on some of the charges, the trial about to begin was surely rigged with lies and trumped-up charges. Having never seen a courtroom in person, the one I was in appeared much smaller and a lot less fancier than the ones in the movies. It almost looked more like a multipurpose room with cheap, low carpeting and generic furniture. Too ashamed to turn around, I could hear and feel the menacing crowd growing behind me. The place probably only held a hundred people or so, but it didn't matter. I felt like the whole world was against me.

I had lost some weight while I'd rotted in my cell, but the dress suit they had arranged for me was still a half size too small, and it was just my luck that the wide-open room was somehow suffocatingly muggy. The sweat soaking my shirt forced me to recall my time in the desert, where that was the norm. Hell, there was even a mob of locals behind me that wanted my head. But the humidity combined with the certainty that my fate was sealed made it different enough from my service time so that I didn't even feel comfortable in my own skin, much less my snug suit.

"All rise for the honorable Judge Donaldson. Case 41024290 to begin: *The People versus Charles D. Rios.*"

A rumble overtook the room as the crowd followed the instructions of the court officer.

An older, black-robed man appeared from a doorway next to the bench and addressed the room before sitting down. "Thank you. You may be seated." Judge Donaldson cleared his throat. "This court is now in session. In *The People versus Charles D. Rios* and on the five felony counts, twelve misdemeanors, and twenty-two citations, how does the defendant plead on each?"

Looking like his first day in court, my lawyer gingerly stood up from his seat. With zero confidence, he began rattling off each plea as he and I had discussed. "Not guilty, not guilty, not guilty, not guilty, not guilty...."

Knowing full well what the result of the trial would be, I could have saved everyone a lot of time and energy by pleading guilty to all counts. But then the prosecutor would have had much more time to get curious as to why I had access to the car and who I worked for. If I gave them any leads on that, it would further incriminate me and border on snitching on the Padre. As much as I hated him, I knew snitching wouldn't hurt the Padre, while it would only make my life exponentially worse. Most importantly, though, drawing the whole thing out in court meant that I wouldn't be completely forgotten in some maximum-security prison where I would be ripe for getting taken out. Instead, I'd be in a holding cell during the trial as well as leading up to sentencing.

The prosecution had it out for me. "Your Honor, we feel the defendant is a threat to public safety. We want bail set at five million."

My spineless public defender had at least enough guts to contend. "Your Honor, given my client's clean record and veteran status, we feel that bail should be set no higher than five hundred thousand."

But the judge didn't hesitate. "Given the number and severe nature of these crimes, I'm erring on the side of caution. Bail is set at five million. Trial will begin on the first of next month. Court dismissed."

While I was unfazed by the judge's decision, it seemed to hit my lawyer pretty hard. Poor guy. It almost seemed like he would be the one sitting idly in a cell for the next few weeks. Fortunately, the time went by relatively quickly, and I was back in court hearing the opening statements.

"Good morning, ladies and gentlemen of the jury. On the day in question, the defendant, Charles Rios, manually drove around town in a large steel-framed car at speeds unsafe by anyone's standards. Clearly unstable, he continued menacingly driving this way until he spotted a car with innocent pedestrians getting inside. It was at that point that Mr. Rios consciously made the decision to speed up even faster and crash into the defenseless car, killing one occupant and severely injuring the others. It is my duty over the next several days to present the obvious evidence that will lead to your easy decision to convict the defendant on all accounts. Thank you."

If my fate wasn't sealed before, it was after the comments from the prosecution. There was no way my timid lawyer was going to give anywhere near as convincing of a speech. While he wasn't great or even good, I was pleasantly surprised by his performance.

"Ladies and gentlemen of the jury, thank you for taking the time to fulfill your civic duty. I am Lee Jenkins, and as you know, opening statements are meant to give you an introduction to the case at hand. The prosecution decided to interpret the facts to make their case seem that much better. I will present the facts in a way that show Charlie Rios is a troubled veteran who, in spite of his mental issues, still managed to maintain a clean record leading up to the alleged crimes for which he is in the court today. Throughout this trial, I will prove all of this to you, and the only verdict that will make sense is not guilty on all accounts. Thanks again."

"The prosecution can call their first witness."

"The prosecution calls Anthony Rodriguez to the stand."

One of the Padre's bulbous goons came thudding from the audience, up to the stand, and swore on the Bible that he'd tell the truth.

He didn't.

"I was walking down the street when I noticed one of those old-fashioned Cadillacs speeding. I couldn't take my eyes off of it as it passed me, and it seemed to speed up once it got the green car in its sights. The window was down a bit in the car, and I even heard him screaming, 'I'm going to get you,' right before totaling the car. If he hadn't been knocked out by the crash, I would have been scared for my life."

"Thank you. No further questions."

"The defense has the floor."

"Mr. Rodriguez, let me remind you that you're under oath. Do you have netphone coordinates proving that you were at the location you said you were?"

I thought my amateur of a lawyer was onto something. But I was wrong.

"Yeah. I gave that to the prosecutor."

"Okay. What were you doing walking down the street?"

"I was headed to the grocery store to pick up a few things for the day."

"Mr. Rodriguez, according to court records, you live on the complete other side of town. Why were you walking where you were to a grocery store so far away from your home?"

"Objection, Your Honor. Irrelevant."

"Your Honor, it's possible that the witness planned to be in the area when the defendant allegedly committed the crime for which he is charged. He may be fabricating what he saw to help convict my client."

"Sustained. The witness himself is not on trial."

"Then I have no further questions, Your Honor."

A couple other doctored witnesses took the stand, and their stories were mostly the same. There were two other people who seemed to be legitimate witnesses, but they were either told to keep their stories consistent or had gotten wind of the Padre's involvement. It was definitely an open-and-shut case for the prosecution. That was when things changed—not in the case itself but in the way in which I remembered it. Mr. Jenkins, who hadn't been worth his weight in salt for most of the trial, stood up and said something that sent chills running down my spine.

"Your Honor, I'd like to call some character witnesses to the stand."

"Very well, counselor."

But there never were any character witnesses in the real trial. I certainly didn't know of anyone who would vouch for me, and Mr. Jenkins never asked. Yet apparently that was where the trial was headed, and what was about to transpire would shake me to the core. Mortified didn't begin to describe the emotions that overtook me as the name left Mr. Jenkins mouth. In complete disbelief, I waited for the so-called character witness to make his way to the stand before I could even acknowledge was what happening.

"Mr. Reno, do you swear to tell the truth, the whole truth, and nothing but the truth, so help you God?"

"I do."

My scumbag of a lawyer, who was apparently in on framing me, approached the witness stand. "Mr. Reno, do you know the defendant?"

"Yes, I do."

"How would you describe Mr. Rios as a person?"

"He's hardworking and dedicated. I took him from an orphanage known for housing some of the worst kids in the state, but raising him was one of the easier things I had ever done. He listened closely and did the chores I gave him. And even the few times he questioned me, he changed his tune once I presented him with the logic of the situation."

"So, you'd say Mr. Rios was a good kid growing up?"

"Absolutely. Which is why it was so shocking that he turned out to be such a vindictive ass who stops at nothing to hurt people he believes have wronged him. When I needed him most after years of depression and suicidal thoughts from losing my wife, he treated me like a plague. I provided him a safe home with food on the table for eight years, and all I asked was that he earn his keep. And like I said, he did. But his good behavior was all a lie. He was plotting against me from the day I saved him. It got so bad that by the end of high school, he even hit me, an old, broken man, because he didn't work hard enough to get good grades. And to this day, he blames me for all his shortcomings. A pathetic man and a terribly ungrateful person. He deserves to rot in prison, or worse."

I couldn't hear any more of his lies. "You bastard! You said kids were only good for their cheap labor!"

The gavel came down hard two times. Thunk! Thunk! "Order in this court! Order!"

Mr. Jenkins didn't stop. "Isn't it true that, after all the things you did for him, he didn't want anything to do with you? He legally changed his name back to the name of the parent who abandoned him?"

With fire in his eyes, Mr. Reno looked dead at me. "You're damn right. In the end, he's a really sad, confused, and dangerous person who has no place with the general public."

"No further questions, Your Honor."

I felt like a professional boxer had socked me in the gut. It was tough to breathe through it all, and as bad as it was, nothing could have prepared me for who would come next.

"Your Honor, the next character witness."

"So be it."

Turning around to see who would be coming to the stand, I jumped up and blurted, "Sarah! No! You can't be here! You need to be in hiding with the kids!"

The court officer darted in my direction to restrain me, and the gavel attacked my ears even louder than before.

Thunk! Thunk! "Mr. Rios! Either you maintain the order in this court, or I will add contempt to your laundry list of charges."

Being slammed back into my seat by the bailiff, I watched as the woman I loved headed up to swear on the Bible. What I thought was going to be a rigged trial that would come and go turned out to be the longest and worst nightmare I had ever had.

Mr. Jenkins began his questioning. "Please state your name for the court."

"Sarah Cunningham."

Her last name is no longer hyphenated with mine? Trying to rationalize it even though it hurt, it made sense if she were trying to distance herself from me.

"Ms. Cunningham, do you know the defendant?"

"Yes. Intimately. I fell in love with Charlie in high school. He was such a sweetheart, going out of his way to let me know how much he liked me without the slightest creepy vibe. I had secretly thought he was cute, but it was his personality that really attracted me to him once we started talking. It wasn't long before I knew he was the man I wanted to be with for the rest of my life. But things started to change after I left for college."

"What would you say changed in him, Ms. Cunningham?"

"Well, we had a plan to be together in college. I lived up to my end of the bargain by settling for a state school when I had a shot at an Ivy League university. But then I came home after one year away, and Charlie had just pissed away all our hopes and dreams."

"So, based on your relationship with Mr. Rios, would you say he's a good person?"

"In a word? No. He's a foolish man who makes terrible life decisions without thinking of the consequences."

"Do you think he would be capable of committing the crimes with which he is being charged today?"

"I was surprised he didn't do worse. And sooner. He had been running with the Padre for a while, and I knew it would catch up with him. I told him it was a bad idea the day he told me. Mind you, he told me after several weeks of breaking the law, doing who knows what for blood money."

Popping from my seat, the bailiff had already began attacking me again as I blurted out anything to get her to stop. "Sarah, no! You'll put the kids in danger! Stop!"

The gavel, piercingly loud, assaulted my ears to nearly the breaking point.

"This is the last warning you'll get, Mr. Rios. Now, you'll sit down and you'll listen to everything these witnesses have to say, or we will lock you away and no one will ever hear from you again."

Mr. Jenkins went on. "So, you're saying that Mr. Rios was part of a larger criminal conspiracy?"

"Yes. Dirty money from dirty people. If I could have done it all over again, I would never have gotten mixed up with the big-headed football player in high school. The only good things to come from our relationship are our children, and he even tried to ruin them. The world is better off without him."

It was too much for me to take. If I had had a bridge to jump from, without question, I would have. But it was around that time that something else came to mind. In my darkest hour in that court room, I remembered being that low before. Only it wasn't a feeling from the past, but a feeling that somehow felt like it was coming from the future.

My cell. The chain mechanism opening and closing the door. The sheets. The metal hook. It was all rushing back to me. *I did end it all! I can remember my last breaths. I can remember my life flashing before my eyes. So, I had to be in some kind of hell where I was reliving the worst parts of my life.*

"I have no further questions for this witness, Your Honor. But I would like to call to the stand my last character witness."

"You may proceed."

"Ryan Carter, please make your way to the front of the court."

My thoughts began to race as I tried to recollect who Ryan was and what he represented. If I was indeed in hell or some twisted nightmare, he seemed to be someone I could trust, someone who would help me. Maybe he was the best attempt of my subconscious at creating something positive amidst all of the negativity that swirled throughout my mind. As terrified as I was at the testimony from Mr. Reno and Sarah, I was a lot less on edge anticipating what Ryan had to offer. But then a seed of doubt started to grow in me. Something didn't add up about how Ryan had all of a sudden started to appear in my thoughts and memories. He appeared out of nowhere in the weirdest wheelchair, and the next thing I knew, he was in my body. I started to wonder if he was a red herring trying to get me to drop my guard so my emotional underbelly would be exposed to make for an easier evisceration. I began to question whether he could be trusted, and then I answered my own question.

No one can be trusted.

I was on my own, and no matter what Ryan said, I would need to stay strong. He said his oath and sat down.

"Mr. Carter, do you know the defendant?"

"Yes."

"How do you know him?"

"It seems like I've known him his whole life. All of his thoughts and memories, I've been there for all of it."

"So, you would say that you have a good idea of who he is. Correct, Mr. Carter?"

"Absolutely. As much as anyone."

"Can you describe Mr. Rios for the court?"

Ryan shuffled in his seat and sighed. "Charlie is a complex man. When he was younger, his folks moved around so much that he never really developed a concept of home. Unfortunately for him, it was when he was abandoned at the orphanage with troubled boys that he learned a definition of home and even of family. But unsurprisingly, those definitions were flawed, and they only got worse when Mr. Reno swiped Charlie up from the boys' home."

I found myself nodding as Ryan went on, but I was still cautious that things could turn at any moment.

"He was indeed a slave to the Renos. If you take a castaway with a head full of bad ideas and work him to death, it usually ends up very poorly. Miraculously, Charlie stayed afloat in life and in school. Then he met Sarah, which further saved his life. She gave him something good to work for, so much so that he made a difficult, albeit rash decision to join the marines. But he did it because he concluded that it was the only way for him to pull his own weight in the long run."

Mr. Jenkins encouraged Ryan to keep talking.

"After everything he experienced overseas, a lesser man would have acted out more. Instead, he came home to the woman he loved. Even with doubt in the back of his mind, he loved her. He happily, if somewhat awkwardly, took on the task of being a new father to his four-year-old, whom he'd never met. He worked terrible jobs for awful pay to make ends meet."

Ryan turned and looked directly into my eyes for the rest of his speech. "But then his whole family got sick. And the pressure to make more money overcame Charlie. In spite of his best efforts, society at large didn't provide Charlie a good means to get his family through tough times. It was only then, in one of his most desperate hours, that he finally caved in and looked outside the legal job postings for something better. Obviously, the job wasn't better morally or ethically, but better financially. Charlie's only concern at that point was to pay for his family's treatments."

"Thank you, Mr. Carter. That will be all."

"No, it won't be."

In disbelief, my eyes widened as Ryan continued in defiance of Mr. Jenkins.

"Say what you will about Charlie. Call him all the names you like. I've seen the things he's dealt with. I've seen the way he's handled life. And while he's made his fair share of mistakes, he could have turned out ten times worse. Had he not stayed strong his whole life, we wouldn't be here because of a car accident—which was just that. An accident. We might be here because he finally snapped back at a world that tried at every turn to cast him aside. He could have planned, orchestrated, and seriously harmed many, many more people. And instead, he did what any of us could ever hope for in his situation."

Ryan had me on the edge of my seat with tears ready in my eyes.

"Charlie did his best."

And there it was. The deepest sob of my life overtook me, and I lost all ability to stay guarded against Ryan or anyone else, for that matter. If someone was waiting to hit me with a deathblow, they had their chance right then. It didn't matter because for the first time in my life, I felt completely understood. I felt validated in all of the experiences I had ever had and could feel the weight of the world dissipate from my shoulders. I admired Ryan for his kind words as he turned his head to the audience and a look of extreme confusion washed over his face. Concerned, I hesitated for just a moment before I looked back to see what the matter was.

With distress in his voice, he called out to the person that he saw. "Mom? What are you doing here?"

Turning around, the face of the woman in the crowd became clear. Apparently, it was Ryan's mother, but why did she look so familiar? Then I remembered. She was there when I was in the wheelchair, when I was seeing through Ryan's eyes. That must be where I knew her from. But the more I thought about her, the more I realized that she was there for a much more important reason.

Still troubled, Ryan inquired, "Why is she here, Charlie?"

I responded with the only thing that made sense to me.

"I think we were meant to be together, Ryan."

CHAPTER 26

HOW FAR FROM THE APPLE TREE?

"I THINK WE WERE MEANT TO be together, Ryan." Helen looked up at me with a goofy grin on her face, breaking the seriousness of plotting out everything I knew about Charlie.

While I wasn't really in the mood, she was gushier than usual, so I smiled back and played along. "Oh yeah? Why's that?"

"Well, we both grew up paralyzed. We're both very smart people. We both mind migrated. So, it's pretty obvious. We're a perfect match."

"Didn't you make fun of me for thinking that since we were both in auto-chairs, we probably had something in common?"

"Yes. But it was coincidental that we actually had things in common."

"Okay. Well, I won't argue. You're great."

"*We're* great, Ryan!" she quickly corrected me.

"We are. Now, about this Charlie situation." I pointed back to the virtual character map on the wall, and her gaze followed.

"Right, can you do a quick summary for me and try to place the dreams chronologically?"

I tapped the different parts we had entered and began lining them up. "Let's see. Charlie's bad childhood goes first. Then there's Mr. Reno. Next, Sarah."

Helen's face became very serious at the mention of Charlie's wife. "Did you have to bring her up?"

"I'm just—"

She broke into laughter and punched me in the shoulder. "I'm only joking. I get it now. So, what's next?"

Part of me knew it still bothered her, but I moved on without much reaction. "Then the marines. The Padre. Then jail. And the dream I had last night."

"What happened in that one?"

"It was different from the other dreams. I think Charlie memories are blurring with mine. We were in a courtroom where there were people that he knew taking the stand. But then I took the stand, and it was the strangest thing. I saw my mom in the audience."

"What do you make of it?"

"I don't know. Maybe she represented safety."

"Does Charlie scare you?"

"No, not anymore. Instead, I'm scared *for* him. Because I know how it all turns out."

I moved the trial to the end of the current timeline, then queued up another map item. "How's that?"

I hadn't thought much about the end for Charlie in a while, but it became clear in the last several days. I began typing onto the map item, then moved "Charlie's Suicide in jail" to the end.

Helen gagged. "Ugh. That's morbid."

"Yes, but the more I think about it, seeing his suicide was a turning point for him. And for me."

"What makes you say that?"

"It was the night of Cameron's speech when I had that dream. Ever since then, I've felt a connection with Charlie, and it helped me get through all of the doubt surrounding my mind migration."

"Now that you mention it, I did notice a change in you right around that time—confidence that you had never really shown. I just thought you were full of yourself since you're in a new, hot body."

"Very funny."

"So obviously the suicide was the end for Charlie, huh?"

"I guess. I haven't had any dreams that take place after that. But he clearly wants his story to keep going through me."

"Then what's the end game? What does Charlie want?"

"Well, that much I know for now. He wants proof that the Padre is dead."

"Then what?"

"I'm hoping I'll know when I get there."

Helen tilted her head down so she could give me that you're-full-of-crap look. "How's that conversation going to go down? 'Hey, Chief what's-your-name, I heard your dad was a crime lord turned politician who snitched and got murdered. Mind if I poke around?'"

She was right that I hadn't really thought it all out. Still, I knew things about Junior that he'd likely not want to get out.

"I mean, he was a crooked cop, at least for some time."

"What the hell, Ryan! You think blackmailing a cop is going to get you very far? You're going to get yourself arrested or killed. I think tomorrow morning is too early to meet him. You need to call it off."

I pulled out a large hunting knife I had gotten from the local Happy-Mart. "I'm not calling it off.

As pissed as I thought she would be, she only rolled her eyes. "Do you even know how to use that thing?

"No, but Charlie does, so I'm hoping that means something."

She scrunched her brow in disbelief and didn't say a word.

"Look, Helen, we talked about this. I could definitely use your help, but if it's too much for you, I understand."

She shook her head. "I knew I wouldn't be able to talk you out of this, and since I can't come with you, I did the next best thing. I stopped by the used-tech store and picked this up for you." Helen handed me an old-fashioned earpiece.

"Yuck. I can only imagine whose ears this has been in."

"Don't be a baby. You're going to wear this when you meet with the Padre's son. I'll be able to hear you within five kilometers. You'll be able to hear me."

"Okay."

"If things go south, let me know and I'll give you a ride. I'll borrow my dad's auto-car."

"Helen, I don't want you near him and me if it's dangerous."

"Relax. I have this covered. He's got the latest model, so it's legal to send it without a passenger."

It felt good that she had my back even if she was right that the whole plan seemed completely nuts. In that sense, we were in fact perfect together, so I figured it was my turn to break the tension.

"Thanks, Helen. You're turning out to be quite the girlfriend."

Her head nearly exploded. "Girlfriend? Girlfriend! Uh, you still haven't officially asked me out. So, you need to pump the brakes with all that 'girlfriend' talk."

"Oh yeah? What if I don't want to pump the brakes?"

"Well, then I guess you'll just have to ask me out. Right now. Go ahead. See what happens."

"Okay, fine. Helen, will you be my girlfriend?"

She smiled even bigger than before. "No! You're crazy. How will I know if I'm with you or Charlie?"

"Helen!"

"Just kidding. Of course, I will be your girlfriend, Ryan." She accompanied her positive affirmation with an exaggerated wink.

We both leaned in and had another one of those passionate kisses that I couldn't get enough of. With our relationship finally settled, we finished discussing how the meeting with Junior would go with the occasional flirting glance to keep things loose. We both agreed that I needed to be safe, and so the anonymous phone call that I'd leave would have Junior meeting me just outside of Marktown in the alleyway of a fairly busy street right before rush hour. Ideally, I'd ask him about his dad, see what he knew, and then walk away. But it would be naïve to think it would be so easy.

Having worked all day as a lead generator at NTE and putting in the few hours with me, Helen was exhausted. "I'm going to catch some winks. I don't suppose I can talk you into coming with me."

"I'm going to be sending the message, and then I'll come right back. Though I doubt I'll be able to get much sleep tonight."

"Too bad. I was thinking we could have a little fun to celebrate our first night together."

Still getting used to being active in the bed, I had too much on my mind at that moment to give even an average performance. "Definitely a rain check on that one."

"Suit yourself. I'll get up with you in the morning to see you off. And Ryan?"

"Yes?

"Don't go getting yourself killed."

"I'm liking living way too much to go and do something like that. Now go get some rest."

After Helen disappeared down the hallway, I threw on my sweater and headed for the door. Mom had shown me that the key to sending an anonymous message was actually pretty simple. Bundle the text, the number it was intended for, and five hundred credits to the Anono domain on the Darknet. Apparently, there was honor amongst thieves on that domain because the next hacker up would grab the request and process it while keeping the sender completely anonymous. At least, that's how Mom described it. She had emphasized that if the authorities were *listening* for the message or if I ran into a rogue hacker who lacked the aforementioned honor that I could be in big trouble, but it was worth the risk to find out more about the Padre.

"Ernesto Guerrero Jr. I am an old friend of your father's. I haven't seen him in years, and I'd like to know where he is. Meet me at 5:30 AM in the alleyway on Waveland between Madison and Kent. Please come alone."

With the message fully typed out, I paused to think for a moment. If I hit Send, it would put into motion a lot of things that I wouldn't be able to control. The more I mulled it over, the more doubt crept into my thoughts. Maybe Helen was right to wait another day. Maybe I needed more time to get everything in order. All of it reminded me of the sad mantra from my childhood.

I just can't do it.

It might as well have been a lifetime ago, given how different things had become for me. It was weird thinking about that pitiful paraplegic kid dragging himself around the house. Then I realized I was starting to become just another entitled walker like many of the people I had resented in my life. That wasn't how I overcame I-just-can't-do-it to complete the mind migration. Embracing who I was and fully tapping into the abilities that I did have had been the key. I knew then that was how I would get through everything ahead of me, and in that moment, I became certain. With all my might, I pressed down on my netphone. Fifteen seconds passed, and I received a reply message from the Anono domain.

"Your analog message was successfully sent."

That was it. There was no going back, and it felt great. Riding high on my accomplishment, I walked back to the apartment. Figuring I wouldn't get much rest that night, I grabbed a bottle of Bobby Brüce from the fridge and headed for the balcony to wind down.

Dim streetlights provided the perfect backdrop to relax, and I noticed that the smell of the city was tame that night. In one motion, I plopped down into the patio chair, cracked off the cap to my beer, and took a big swig.

"Ahhhhhhhhhhhh!"

In an instant, the cold, smooth libation made the world that much more bearable. Placing it in the drink holder on the chair, I took a deep breath and involuntarily reflected on everything I had been through. I realized that as hard as it had been growing up and as difficult as the mind migration was, I'd had it relatively easy. Meeting Charlie had made it obvious that there was an extremely complex and dangerous world out there—one where politics, economics, and power were all that anyone cared about. My mom had done an amazing job of sheltering me from it my entire life, and had it not been for my mind migration, I might have gone on living in my little bubble. Instead, it appeared that all my life struggles up to that point were nothing compared to the trials and tribulations that lay ahead of me. I couldn't help but liken it to one of the places I had always wanted to visit.

Tapping my netphone, I flipped to the virtual reality application. "Show me the base of Mount Kilimanjaro, real time."

At the west base of the massive, snowcapped peak, my view of the morning sun was completely eclipsed. Seeping around the titanic mound, brilliant light glistened off the fresh morning dew on the tall, wild grass. Peering up, my eyes followed the various trails that hikers had taken while attempting to conquer the colossal pile of earth. Nicknamed the "Walk-Up" mountain, it was probably not a coincidence that I was obsessed with it. Still, less than half of the people setting out to scale it actually ended up on the highest summit. In that sense, the challenges ahead of me were just like that.

Charlie and people like him were cut from a different cloth than me. They could handle covert meetings, fights, and running for their lives. But I hadn't so much as slapped another person, much less confronted someone about their murderous father. Helen was right to question me. What if the Padre's son wasn't cooperative? What if he was hostile? And even if I discovered that the Padre wasn't dead and I could locate him, what would I do next? It was clear that I could no longer wander innocently forward on my journey, or I might not live to see it through.

Leaning back in the chair, I tried to calm myself down by brainstorming ways to handle the situations sure to follow. My thoughts swirled, considering the permutations of how things might turn out. Soon my eyelids began to get heavy, and before I knew it, they closed. Violent memories coursed through my mind as I settled in.

A knife fight with an extremist. Shooting at drugged-up buyers trying to steal the product. Punching a giant man—the Padre—in the eye. Bashing a machinist with a hammer. Getting beat down by jail guards. With each flashback, an anger grew in my chest. None of the fights that I recalled ended up being any good for anyone. The war was a disaster. The Padre ruined countless lives, and Charlie decking him was only so he could get away. The poor machinist was in the wrong place at the wrong time. And those bastard jail guards had nothing better to do than rough Charlie up. They weren't even working for the Padre, or they wouldn't have left Charlie alive.

It became clear the fights that lay ahead of me had to be different. I wouldn't be randomly attacking anyone who crossed me. My battles would be for a man who had been wronged his entire life, and though he'd made mistakes, he'd deserved much better than he was given. My fight was for justice, and anyone who got in my way would feel the righteous indignation of a good man scorned.

"Don't worry, Ryan. I'll teach you the ways."

Charlie's voice had become a beacon of peace for me, and I knew he had something in store to help prepare me. Then I heard another voice.

"Ryan. Ryan!"

Popping out of my seat, I was ready for anything. I was frozen for a moment until my eyes finally focused enough to see Helen.

"Ryan, it's four-twenty-five AM. The next bullet leaves in twenty minutes, and you'll want to be on it."

Helen, again, had my back.

"Whew. Thanks."

"What happened last night? I was worried as hell when you weren't in bed."

"I must have passed out in the chair."

"It's cold out here. Let's get inside."

Closing the balcony door behind me, a rush of confidence overtook me. "I had a dream, Helen. Everything's going to be okay."

"Did it have something to do with 'beating it out of him if he didn't tell you?'"

"Yeah, how did you—?"

"You were talking in your sleep. I thought you were awake when I first went out there."

"Well, yeah..."

"Don't go beating anyone unless it's absolutely necessary."

"But what if—"

"Ryan!"

"Okay!"

I grabbed my knife in its case and put it in my waistband, grabbed a bandana for my face, and then I kissed Helen on the cheek.

Her face scrunched up. "Maybe you should brush your teeth before the meeting!"

"Maybe you should shut up!"

Leaving the apartment, I bulleted three blocks from the alley with about fifteen minutes to spare. Scoping out the surroundings, I needed to be sure that Junior was coming alone or else things could go south really fast. I walked to the perimeter and looked high and low, not seeing anyone or anything out of the ordinary. I placed the bandana over my face and made my way to the spot. Entering the alley, I was pleased with the location I had chosen. To the left, there was the rear of a flea market that had God knows what in its dumpsters. To the right was a laundromat, already busy spewing the scent of fabric softener into the air. Still, the surrounding area was quiet, making it perfect for the meeting. As I tried to settle on a place to stand to wait for the Padre's son, a ruckus came from the other end of the alley.

"Shit!"

It was just garbage collectors rumbling in their massive truck.

Shaking it off, I turned around to find him already moving towards me from the alley's entrance.

I had to take control of the situation. "Stop right there."

He stopped.

At twenty meters from me, I could see that his frame wasn't as massive as his father's and figured it was likely due to being in better physical shape. Regardless, he was anything but small. Otherwise, it was clear that he was his father's son. He had successfully mimicked the Padre's appearance with his goatee and slicked back hair.

"Did you come alone?"

He nodded.

Anticipating his response, I asked a silly question. "Where can I find your father?"

His expression didn't change even a little. Standing silently, it was as if he didn't hear a single word I said. "I said, where can I find—"

A huge, black auto-truck, the only vehicle legally allowed to still use gasoline, made a fast, wide turn to enter the alleyway.

"Junior, watch out!"

He reached for his gun as he turned toward the screeching tires.

I could tell he wasn't going to get it out of the way in time, so I dashed in his direction. As he turned his sights back to me, the barrel of his gun was nearly pointed right at my head. Just before he could get a shot off, I dove at him at such an angle as to knock him out of the way of the auto-truck swerving back and forth into the alleyway.

Laying on the ground, he yelled, "Run!" He popped up and grabbed his gun.

I was already moving toward the same goal, and we both sprinted out of the alleyway. I could hear the truck peeling out, no doubt turning around to chase us. To lose them, we headed right onto Waveland and down the street. The squealing tires of the truck exiting the alley added to my terror as I ran faster than I ever had before. Junior motioned for us to take the next left onto Kent, and then a right into another alleyway. Another thirty meters, and we ducked into a small, rear parking lot with buildings on three sides. Backs against a building, we looked around the corner, and sure enough, we had lost the truck. We both struggled to catch our breath. I stumbled toward a parked car, realizing quickly it had to be Junior's unmarked police auto-car.

Junior grabbed me by the arm, twisted it hard behind me, and slammed me up against the car.

"Ow, dammit!"

"Who the hell are you, and why are my father's old goons after you?"

I tried to stay in character even though I was still winded and my arm was hurting like hell.

"Ah! I told you, I'm his friend."

He twisted my arm harder and pressed more of his bodyweight against me.

I thought he was going to dislocate my shoulder.

"I haven't heard shit about my father in years. Then, out of the blue, I get an anonymous message to meet one of his...'friends.' My father had business partners, and he had thugs that worked for him. He never had so much as a single friend. So, I'm only going to ask you one time. Who the hell are you?"

"Okay, okay. I'll talk. Just...let me go."

He patted me down, then grabbed the knife from my waistband and chucked it across the ground. He gave me one last oomph against the car, then backed away from me while simultaneously pulling out his piece and pointing it at my face.

Having never had a gun point at me until that day, for a moment, all I could do was swallow hard and hope he didn't have an itchy trigger finger.

"Spit it out."

I said the first thing that came to mind. "Okay! I used to work for him. He screwed me over on our last job, and I just wanted to get back at him."

"No. No. You run like a scared bitch and clearly can't fight for shit. I don't believe you ever worked for him."

My mind raced as I tried to figure out a way to prove that I knew his father without getting into the strange details. Only one thing came to mind, and I had to give it a try. "Lord, please provide us with your protection as we attempt to complete the job that has been put in front of us. Please provide us with buyers who are of sound mind and soul and ready to make a deal. Please ensure, should something happen, that our resolve is quick and our aim is steady. We ask this in the Lord's name. Amen."

The life drained from Junior's face as he slightly lowered his weapon. "How the hell do you...?"

I was surprised it worked so well, but had to move things along before he started asking real questions, and I didn't want to let on that I knew his father was dead. "I told you. I knew your father years ago. I can't get into the details. I just need to know where he is."

Still in shock, Junior looked around aimlessly, dropped his weapon to his side, and sighed hard. "You get to a point in your life where you think the past is behind you—like you really got through it all and things can only get better from then on. And then a message like yours brings it all rushing back."

Taking a couple steps toward me, his expression changed to one of concern.

I shuffled back against the car to be safe.

"You just got out of the pen?"

I nodded.

"Damn. You must have had it bad in there. What should I call you?"

Scrambling to think of an alias, a random name popped into my head. "Joey."

"Okay, Joey. My father's been dead for twenty years. Any revenge you want, he already got, tenfold."

"Shit. How'd he die?" I could have gotten an Oscar for my performance.

"Bullet to the head, then he was dropped in the river."

"You saw him for yourself?"

"Yeah, I worked his case even though I was told not to. No one was going to stop me from seeing his dead ass and making sure it wasn't another one of his schemes." He let loose a breathy snicker, and then a seriousness returned to his face as he took a deep breath. "Growing up, everyone assumed that I would follow in his footsteps. I even entertained it in my late teens. I felt powerful having people respect—*fear* me the moment they knew who I was."

Junior cleared his throat. "But once I realized what kind of business he was running, I was disgusted. I couldn't stand to be involved in any of it, and struggled with depression for a while before I figured out how to live with who I was, how to reconcile what my father was doing. That's when I applied to the police department, and I'll never forget the look on his face when I told him."

"I can definitely relate to dad issues."

"Yeah? Poor us, right? I knew I would never get anyone's pity being his son, but I had it bad as a kid, and it only got worse as I got older. I guess it didn't help that I got on the other side of the law."

Knowing what I knew, I couldn't hold my tongue. "So, why did you cover for him when he was running a gang in your neighborhood?"

Pain washed over his face with just the slightest hint of anger. But he quickly went back to a softer look. "He held my mother hostage for my betrayal and said he would hurt her if I ever caused trouble for him. But honestly, he was still always one step ahead of us anyway. Even though he had Mom, I never once broke the law for him."

"Damn."

"It wasn't until one of his biggest jobs fell through that I took advantage. He was picked up by the metropolitan city police and temporarily booked. I went straight to his complex, muscled his thugs, and rescued my mom."

"Good for you."

"Yeah, but once he got out and was given the alderman position, we butted heads for years until he finally slipped up and we busted him for real. I thought for sure he was going down, and that would be it. But he weaseled his way out of that, too. Luckily, it wasn't long before his business partners finished the job."

The meeting was going nowhere, so I had to do something to get more information. "Did you have the case files? Any business partners listed?"

"Yeah, it's been public information for years now, why?"

"Great. I'd like to have a conversation with his associates."

Junior seemed like he was mulling it over. "Hell, it's your life. But know this. If you do what I think you're going to do, you'll end up right back in the pen, or worse."

"I get it."

"And before you do anything stupid, just ask yourself, 'Is he really worth it?' It was the only way I was able to live with myself for years."

"Will do. Thanks, Junior."

He got into his car and pulled off.

I grabbed my knife and gathered my thoughts.

Charlie, I'm going to need your help on this one.

CHAPTER 27

BETRAYAL NEVER COMES FROM ENEMIES

"CHARLIE, I'M GOING TO NEED your help on this one," the Padre croaked from the backseat while exhaling his thick cigar smoke toward the windshield.

"Sure thing, boss. What did you need?"

"One of the jobs I did—before your time—it didn't go over so well."

"Okay."

"I'll need you to drop me off at a safe spot for about a week."

"No problem, boss. When?"

"Tonight. Let's stop by my place, and I'll grab a few things, then we can head out of the city."

That night's job had been the smoothest. The buyers were prompt, said all the right things, and left immediately after the exchange. Having bought ourselves an extra hour's worth of time, I didn't mind helping the Padre out in a pinch since he'd been so gracious to me and mine.

"I don't mean to pry, boss, but these jobs seem so routine to me already. What went wrong?" I could hear him taking a big drag off of his Cuban as I asked the question.

With a puff in my direction, he responded, "Let me tell you a little story." He pushed his cigar into the ashtray, and the sizzle was accompanied by more smoke making it a little hard to breathe as he started his tale. "I've always been fascinated with large predatory animals, and as you could have guessed, dogs are particularly interesting to me. It's a little-known fact that human evolution was directly impacted by wolves that scavenged on the food and scraps of prehistoric people. At some point, someone decided to repeatedly test these remarkable creatures, and thus began the age-old practice of dog training. It wasn't long before once-vicious wolves were tamed pets entrusted around even the weakest human children, sick, and elderly. This was because the strongest adults established themselves as pack leaders, and the wolves obeyed."

The Padre took a deep breath. "But that only split the species into domesticated and wild. To this day, there are still feral wolves that would do anything to survive. Pack-oriented killing machines created by thousands of years of natural selection and God's will. They could take down prey much larger than themselves with cunning and ferocity."

He cleared his throat. "But even large wild predators like wolves lack reason. They don't have true ill intent. They just work off of instinct. Still, doubt was cast on that well-known fact in India about twenty years ago. The native Indians living around the West Bengal area began to notice a strange phenomenon. The largest male and smallest female Indian wolves began to show up dead throughout the grassland. At first, the thought was farmers, but quick examinations of the carcasses showed that their bodies had been mangled like meat at a butchers' school and had no spear or bullet holes. The natives were baffled, and even the wildlife experts that were brought in couldn't quite figure out what was happening. It wasn't until a person—one of the Indian's greatest hunters—was killed that local authorities finally stepped in."

Breeeeng!

The Padre took the call without even pardoning himself from the story. As the backseat lit up from the hologram, I refocused on the road and estimated that we were about ten minutes from the Padre's complex.

"Yes, I know the facility isn't fully operational, but they can still run the tests on me. Now, wait until I get there for more questions." The Padre grunted in disapproval at the call, then hung up. "Sorry about that, Charlie. Now, where was I?"

"An Indian was killed."

"Ah, yes. Local law enforcement originally declared it a normal animal attack due to the lack of evidence to conclude otherwise. It took one of the detectives and a wildlife specialist to really see what was happening."

Breeeeng!

"Dammit!"

Tapping his netphone hard, he answered the call, and after a little conversation, got pissed again. "That will have to wait until next week. Don't call again until then!" Hanging up, he made small talk. "Just when you're trying to take a vacation, that's when everyone needs you."

"Five minutes from your place, boss."

"Thanks, Charlie. Now onto what they found."

Breeeeng!

"Ah, to hell with it. I'll tell you later."

We pulled up to his complex just as the Padre ended his latest call, and he rocked himself out of the car. Leaning my head back, I tried resting my eyes a little while I waited for him to come out. After a couple of deep breaths, a deep relaxation overcame me, and I could feel myself begin to slip into a light sleep.

"Charlie!"

Startled, I popped up and grabbed the steering wheel, ready to drive in a moment's notice. "Yes, boss!"

"No, Charlie. It's me."

Turning to my right, there sat Ryan in the passenger seat of the black Cadillac. Again, he was in what appeared to be a copy of my body, but that didn't nearly concern me as much as what his presence meant for the job I was on.

"What? You can't be here, Ryan!"

"But I am, Charlie. I need your help with something."

Shaking my head, my curiosity got the best of me. "Help with what?"

"You're taking the Padre to a safe place. I need to know where it is."

Peering over Ryan's shoulder, I could see the Padre exiting his place with suitcases in hand, heading for the car. "Look, you can't be here when he gets in, or we're both dead."

"That's something I've been meaning to tell you, Charlie."

"What?"

"This isn't real. I mean, it *was* real. But we're actually just in a memory."

"What do you mean it's just a memory?"

"All of this. It's your memory."

"Then how are you here? I don't remember knowing you before... before...well, I actually don't remember when we met. But I know you never came on jobs with me. And why do you always look like you're in my body?"

"I don't know everything yet, but I can explain what I do later. Right now, I'm trying to figure out if the Padre had any business partners that could have helped him fake his death. I have a list, but it doesn't mean much to me. When I thought hard about it, this is the…this your memory that came to mind."

More than confused, I couldn't believe that what was happening in that moment was actually in the past. While it felt real enough, there was an odd sense of déjà vu coming over me the more I thought about it, but that brought me more bewilderment than comfort. Considering I didn't have a better explanation or plan, I just tried to roll with it.

Lumbering to the Cadillac, the Padre popped the trunk, dropped in both of his bags with a thud each, and swung around to the back door. He flung the door open and dropped onto the seat, causing the car to rock up and down as usual. Terror welled up from my gut to my throat thinking about Ryan as the Padre got settled.

"Who the hell is this?"

Swallowing hard, I put faith in what Ryan had told me. If it was all in my head, I called the shots. "Don't worry, boss. He's with me."

The seconds of silence before his response seemed to take forever.

My heart was beating out of my chest, and I blinked at least a dozen times, waiting for my brains to be blown out onto the windshield.

"Now, Charlie, you have to tell me when you're going to bring guests along. Hello, friend. What's your name?"

"Ryan."

"Well, Ryan, you can call me Padre."

"Nice to meet you."

I exhaled with relief that Ryan was right. We must have been in a memory or dream or something for the Padre to be okay with him being in the car. It made me delve deeper into my memories of Ryan, and I recalled him being good to me in the…past. Then something else came to mind about him, something that I needed to discuss with him as soon as possible, but it would have to wait until after I dropped the Padre off.

"Charlie, take the Kennedy out to the interstate and head west."

"No problem, boss."

"Now, back to my story. Don't worry, Ryan, I'm just getting to the good part."

Ryan nodded in acknowledgement.

I was still weirded out by the whole situation.

"The detective and wildlife specialist began mapping out the killings—the wolves and the Indian. All autopsies showed that each one occurred roughly two days apart, but what was more telling was the geographical locations of them all. It turned out that they made a perimeter five miles in diameter with the body of the Indian near a major road. It was pretty clear that whoever or whatever was doing it was marking their territory."

The Padre lit his Cuban again, clouding up the car.

Ryan began to cough, and in my peripheral, I could see him turn back to get a good view of the Padre. But it was the look on Ryan's face when he faced back forward that was concerning. Still, I let the memory play out as the Padre continued his story.

"The local authorities sent in a heavily armed group, including the detective and wildlife specialist, and they discovered smaller perimeters with more corpses—some animals but a couple of missing locals. Closing in on what had to be the epicenter, they were strategically attacked by small groups of not only wolves but wild dogs as well. Like an army sending out coordinated battalions, they were under siege for the better part of a day trying to push forward. Losing more than half their party and running low on ammo, the detective and wildlife specialist miraculously survived through the battles. But what they went on to find was nothing short of astonishing and horrifying."

The Padre cleared his throat. "The wolves and dogs were trying to stop the group from reaching a sinkhole that had opened up in a thick patch of trees. When the party tossed a flare into the sinkhole, a bloodcurdling growl-into-bark replied, sending everyone but the detective and the wildlife specialist running for their lives. They were left to discover the largest gray wolf ever documented. Standing nearly a meter and a half at the shoulder, with a jet-black coat, the hauntingly enormous beast revealed itself from the sinkhole with fresh, ruby-red blood on its lips. Without hesitation, the detective fired the last three shots from his revolver into the alpha male, but that only made him angry. He jumped five meters, pounced on the detective, and in one motion, bit completely through his neck, sending his head tumbling. That left only the horrified wildlife specialist behind to take on the nightmarish creature. In astonishment and terror, the wildlife specialist was paralyzed from shock as the monstrous canine bared down on her. That was where things took a turn. With her giant head, the mammoth wolf motioned the wildlife specialist to leave. It took a minute for her to overcome the shock and actually run away. It took her even longer to figure out what the hell had happened. The specialist was allowed to survive to tell others what she had seen and bring back more meals for the hell hound."

"Damn, boss. What happened after that?"

"The country's army was sent in to dispatch the beast. The only known specimen of *Canis lupus giganticus* was killed and brought to the wildlife specialist for autopsy. It was over seven feet in length and weighed nearly three hundred pounds, which didn't include the fifty pounds of cow in its gut. But the most telling part was what they found in the sinkhole."

"Oh?"

"He kept trophies of his human kills. The femur bones of more than thirty missing Indians ranging from the west side of the country all the way to the east where he made his den. The theory was that the freakishly large wolf got a taste for Indian blood and made his way across the country until he found a place where he could consistently get his fill."

As much as I thought he was embellishing the story, the last part rang a bell.

"No shit, boss! The veterans that were in my squad in Pakistan used to tell the 'Man-Eating Wolf' story to new recruits trying to get them to piss their pants."

"Oh, it's more than a story, Charlie. It's the truth."

He cleared his thought. "So, what happened on the job you asked? As human-like as *Canis lupus giganticus* was, it had one big flaw. He underestimated his enemies and got complacent at the top of the food chain. To remain alpha male, that's not something you can do. So, after I provoke buyers who renege on deals, I don't stick around to see what happens. These buyers know where I stay, so it's the perfect time to watch from a distance while they spin their wheels, and I handle other business. You always have to have a backup plan, Charlie."

I had to admit I was mildly impressed. "You've thought of everything, boss. Five minutes from the interstate."

"Thanks, Charlie. I'll be messaging you the coordinates to our destination now."

Obtaining my netphone, I glanced at the coordinates before flashing them to Ryan. "Got it?"

"Yes.

The rest of the drive was fairly quiet as we made our way out of the city and toward the rural expanse. Plush forests lining the interstate illuminated by intermittent street and headlights were a welcome break from the concrete jungle to which I was accustomed. The small towns we passed seemed quaint, and my mind began to wander, thinking about what it would have been like to grow up in one of them—a place where everyone knew everyone else and all the kids went to the same local schools. I could feel an involuntary grin sweep across my face as I fantasized about a simple, rustic life without all of the urban complexities that had become normal to me. Then the smile slowly melted away as I remembered the true reality outside of the city. My musings were nothing but a romanticized version of years gone by. The problem in the country was the same as—no, much worse than—the city.

Jobs.

Decades ago, major businesses would prop up clusters of small towns in areas like the ones we drove through. Factories, insurance companies, tourist attractions, and the like would employ the majority of residents across miles and miles. The only alternative was to get a service job—food, lodging, and the like—to support those businesses secondarily. Regardless of their near monopoly on labor in those areas, it wasn't enough. With very few exceptions, most of those companies moved in what became known as "The Great Corporate Migration," to the cheapest places they could to set up shop—the South and other countries. They hired remote workers at minimum wage to handle as much work as possible while underpaying most of the skilled labor in the area since they were the only places within a reasonable commute. All of that left many of the major stretches between cities destitute.

Random methamphetamine labs thrived for a couple of years until they couldn't supply their product cheaply enough to the dirt-poor population. Hundreds of rail-thin, chalk-skinned, toothless addicts aimlessly wandered the countryside as their bodies slowly gave out. The old stories said that if you traveled far enough away from the expressway and turned off your car, you could hear the faint moans of meth heads dying. I had to physically shake my head to stop the morbid line of thought, and fortunately, we were close to the location.

"Ten minutes out, boss."

"Okay, Charlie. Once you exit, you'll make a right, and after a few miles, you'll see the road fork to the left with construction signs saying that a road is closed. It isn't."

"Got it, boss."

Leaving the interstate, I followed the Padre's instructions. We cut through a heavily wooded area when the road split. Driving around the sign, I made a slight left onto a gravel road, and the fluid suspension of the car lent itself to a smooth ride.

I looked at Ryan. "You getting all this?"

"I am. Thanks."

After a winding half kilometer, we came to a small parking lot, and in front of us was a building under construction lit up by security lights across the top. There were already two other Cadillacs in the parking lot, and I drove past them so I could get the best spot next to the building. I got out of the car and headed for the trunk to get the Padre's bags, and Ryan, scoping out the surroundings, slowly followed.

The Padre than emerged from the car.

"What is this place, boss?"

"Let's just say a great mind is a terrible thing to waste on a bad body." He headed into the building.

Ryan swung around and pointed at the custom sign for the company that owned the building as he read, "Oceanic Laboratories: Where Dreams Become a Reality."

Suddenly, time stood still for everyone but him and me.

"I figured it out, Charlie!"

"What is it?"

"I know where the Padre is in my…time."

"He's still alive?"

"Yes. I met two people in Marktown. One of them was a man with pictures of an old dog. A dog named Ruby just like the Padre's ring! The Padre must have mind migrated into the man's body after his plea deal."

"Whoa, he mind *what*?"

Ryan pointed to the building in front of us. "This place was the first to try putting the mind of one person into a different body. I always heard stories about how they failed with humans and scary stuff happened. Now I don't know what to believe."

I couldn't stop my eyebrow from going up when I began to connect the dots. "This mind...migration. Is that how you ended up in my body?"

Ryan nodded. "Like I said, there's a lot for us to discuss. Right now, I just need to know how to go after the Padre."

Looking Ryan up and down, I wasn't so sure it was a good idea even if he was in my body. "From what I know, you don't seem like the 'going after' type. Weren't you in a wheelchair?"

"Yes, but I'm hoping your...abilities will help with that. Maybe you can even teach me."

A sigh forced itself out of me, and I knew that as much as I wanted to mentor Ryan in all things stealth and combat, it didn't feel right knowing what I knew about him...about us. "Before we do that, there's something I need to tell you."

Ryan shook his head. "What's more important than catching the Padre?"

"Trust me, you're going to want to know this."

"Okay."

I cleared my throat, and as I searched for the right words to say to Ryan, tears welled up in my eyes. "Since I became aware of my thoughts again, it seems like vengeance is all I've known. But the last thing I want is for you to get hurt for me, without knowing everything. Before you make any rash decisions about the Padre, I need to share something with you—something that recently became clear to me. I need you to know who I really am."

Ryan's puzzled expression broke into one of more confidence as he responded, "I know you, Charlie. I know everything about you."

"That's the thing. You don't. What I am about to tell you—show you— has been buried in my mind as deeply as I could put it. I think the best way to communicate it to you is through a letter I wrote while I was in jail. It contained everything I wanted to say to the person I wronged the most in my life. It's important to me that you hear it before you decide what you're going to do."

Again, confusion overcame Ryan's face. "Okay, Charlie. Let's hear the letter."

As I pinpointed the memory in my mind, Ryan and I were whisked away from the building parking lot in a blur and reappeared together in my holding cell. Sitting on the edge of my bed with a pen in my shaking left hand, I began writing the letter on a small table. The shame from that moment was still fresh in my mind. As disappointed in myself as I felt writing it, I felt even worse reading it to someone close to me. Each word was more and more painful, but I knew it all needed to come out, so I persevered.

"Words will never be able to convey just how sorry I am. Hurting you is one of the biggest regrets of my life, and I am certain that me rotting in a cell for the rest of my life or even getting the death penalty will bring you very little solace. As far as people go, I know that I am as low as they come. It only makes sense that you would have these thoughts, and I am here to tell you that they are valid.

"You may be looking for some kind of explanation for why it all happened. I could go into the details about my childhood and how I was mistreated starting at an early age. But I know it's a tired story that you will have no concern for. I could bring up all of the traumatic experiences I had while serving in the military where I saw countless dead bodies of people I knew. Though I know it doesn't excuse what I have done. The line of work that I chose was always meant to be temporary. I just wanted to make enough money to get by, and then I would quit. But as each job came and went, I had to dig deeper and deeper to compromise my morals. Sure, I didn't get involved in the shadiest aspects of the work, but I knew. I knew what I was part of. I knew that I played a vital role in a horribly corrupt operation, and I kept on enabling it until it was too late.

"In a twisted way, it's fitting that I finally paid the price on the day that I decided to quit. However, it shames me more than anything that others were hurt in the process. If I could do it all over, I would have stayed working the backbreaking line job I had, and would have been content to barely make ends meet even if that would have made things tough at home.

"In closing, I want to let you know that I have tortured myself enough these last few months so that there is only one more logical thing for me to do. I'm going to give you the thing that you undoubtedly seek and unquestionably deserve. By the time you read this letter, you will have justice, and the world will be a better place. Sincerely, Charles Rios."

"Charlie, I know you felt like you let Sarah and the kids down. I was there for all of that."

"No, Ryan. That letter wasn't to Sarah."

In an instant, I queued up the memory of that fateful day. I was at the wheel, Ryan was in the passenger seat, and we had just gotten away from the other black Cadillacs chasing us. I eyed my mirror, and it seemed like I had lost them. I turned completely around to be sure they were nowhere in sight. Exhaling hard, I thought that I might actually have gotten away until I finally turned back around.

"Charlie! Watch out!"

Slamming on the brakes, I was too late.

Crash!

Waking up on a stretcher, I was being wheeled along the side of the road with Ryan walking by my side. As I was being lifted into the ambulance, Ryan and I caught a good glimpse of the parked car. It was totaled so bad that it was difficult to tell if it was green or gray. Then a cold feeling washed over me as I peered down to see a pool of blood below the wreckage.

Someone was in that damned car!

Immediately after that heartbreaking realization, screaming came from the paramedics near the car I had smashed. "Cut this damn thing open! Late-term female in the backseat with a strong pulse!"

I could only make out a piece of what he was saying as the doors to my ambulance started to close, but one look at Ryan's face was enough.

Ryan turned back to me with piercing eyes. "This is bullshit!"

CHAPTER 28
THE HOUSE THAT LIES BUILT

"THIS IS BULLSHIT!" FURIOUSLY TEARING into the closet, I chucked shirts, pants, and dresses all over the room.

"Ryan! Calm down! What's going on?"

"Stay out of this, Helen!"

I was working my way to the back where there was a stack of boxes in the lower right corner. I snatched the top one and flung it out onto the floor. I dropped to my knees and went to work flipping through random trinkets from my childhood—a childhood of countless lies. Chucking that box aside, I dove back into the closet for the next.

"You're making a huge mess! Wait until she gets off work so we can have a talk with her."

Hurling the next useless box with all my rage, I stood up to get in Helen's face. "This is between me and my mom! She doesn't get to hide the truth from me any longer! There has to be proof somewhere around here, and I'm going to find it before she gets home!"

Box after box, I dumped the contents out and pushed through the piles, trying to find anything of significance. Coming up in vain each time, the ire was only growing in me. After reaching the last box and on the verge of exploding, I darted past Helen, into the hallway for some air. Struggling to catch my breath, I headed downstairs to gather my thoughts on where to look next. At the base of the stairs, I glanced over at the front door and something caught my eye. The virtual reel was flipping through old pictures. I ran over and lifted it from the table, then waited patiently for confirmation as it rolled.

"There it is! The son of a bitch car was green!"

"Ryan, you wouldn't tell me why you're so angry at your mom on the phone. At least tell me what's going on now!"

Still livid, I tried to calm myself enough to explain what Charlie had shown me. "My mom was in serious accident in the car from this picture."

"How serious? She's not permanently injured, right?

"No. She wasn't. I was!" My body went cold, having clearly stated the truth for the very first time in my life. The frenzy that had overcome me for that last hour almost instantly waned into deep sorrow. Tears began to pour from my eyes as I collapsed to my knees.

Helen was near enough to catch me from falling on my face, and she held me as tightly as she could. After a minute of me sobbing, she finally pulled away just a bit. "You were with her? Isn't she too young for you to be with her."

Gathering myself enough to talk, I stood up and wiped my face with my sleeve. "That picture must have been months before. I wasn't just with her during the accident. Mom was pregnant with me."

I could almost see the gears turning in Helen's head.

"That means you weren't paralyzed from a birth defect."

"Exactly! That's why I'm so pissed, because it's all I've ever known about my disability."

"How did you find all of this out?"

"As crazy as it sounds, Charlie showed me."

"What! The Charlie inside of you?"

"Yes. One of the first flashbacks I had with Charlie was of the job where he tried to quit working for the Padre. It ended in a high-speed chase where Charlie took his eyes off the road for just a second. *He* crashed into Mom's car."

Shock washed over Helen as she tried to process it all. "How in the hell?"

"I know. At first, I was in denial, thinking that our memories were blurring together. But the more I've thought about it, the more it makes sense."

"But it *is* crazy. Why not just talk to your mom to clear it up before jumping to conclusions?"

"Imagine the one person you've trusted your whole life turns out to be the biggest liar you've ever known. No, I need proof, or she might try to keep the lie going."

Suddenly, a light bulb went off in my head. Mom had always kept a storage room in the basement locked up, saying that she didn't want me going in there. Since the stairs had no lift to get down there, I never thought twice about it. But that room would have been the safest place she could keep anything related to the accident without me knowing.

With my original fervor returning in full force, I threw the virtual reel across the room and bolted downstairs to the storage room. Discovering the cheap padlock standing between me and the truth, I scrambled to find something to deal with it. Across the room, there was a sizable, rusty plumber's wrench on the workbench. I sprinted to pick it up, gripped the wrench tightly, and headed back to the padlock.

Clank!

But it only bent slightly.

"Dammit!" Panting hard, I gave it another strike.

Clank!

The padlock was holding on by a thread. Then a hand grabbed my shoulder, and I instinctively turned around ready to bludgeon someone over the head with the wrench.

"Ryan!"

Helen stumbled back in disbelief that I was prepared to strike her down.

Realizing my fanaticism and trying to catch my breath, I dropped the wrench, and the sound of it unevenly bouncing off the concrete floor rippled throughout the basement.

I felt to my knees, deflated. "I'm sorry, Helen. I wasn't prepared to find out that my entire life has been one big lie after another."

"Ryan, this is unacceptable. Until you talk to your mom, you're just getting worked up! You're going to hurt someone."

Turning back to the storage room, I reached for the lock.

"Ryan!"

"What?"

"I bet this is the key. It was on a hook by the workbench."

Still trying to catch my breath, I used the key on what was left of the lock, and it popped off the door. I reached for the handle, trying to prepare myself for what I would see, assuming it was going to be pretty bad.

"Ryan, sweetie!"

For the first time in my life, chills of rage covered my whole body when I heard the words that had been said to me thousands of time. Completely unable to feel any kind of affection for her, I needed Mom to know just how hurt I was and that I wouldn't tolerate any more lies. I wanted to curse and yell and throw things at her because of how unfair it all felt. But instead, all I could do was turn around slowly as she continued to talk.

"Before you go into that room, let's go for a walk."

It was tough to maintain my anger when I finally made eye contact with her. Even if she lied about everything, she had always been there for me.

"But I need the truth, Mom."

"That's what I need to tell you."

Helen, understanding the importance of the moment, headed upstairs. "I'll go get your room cleaned up, Mrs. Carter."

Outside, the day was as gloomy and cold as the conversation Mom and I were about to have. We made our way to the sidewalk and headed down the street.

Mom let out a big sigh. "I assume you know about the accident based on how the house looked."

"I do."

She nodded and gave me that mom-look, like she was about to tell me a story. "Before it happened, I was just a young soon-to-be mom, worried about everything that could go wrong with a natural pregnancy. Somewhat of a hypochondriac, I must have gone to the doctors at least ten times before I even got to the third trimester. The miracle of life was inside of me, and I didn't want anything to ruin that."

She cleared her throat. "Having never been in a car accident in my life, it seemed like a cruel twist of fate that the day I would go into labor was the same day it happened. I got into the car, focused entirely on my contractions, and the last thing I remembered was the loudest crashing noise before I blacked out. I woke up two days later, and the doctor told me what had happened. I had to be restrained in my hospital bed trying to get up to find you. To calm me down, they assured me that the operation on your spine was successful and that you were stable in recovery. But I didn't truly believe them until I saw you in the NICU."

She paused for a moment. "Staring at you, so little and innocent, lacking the words to describe just how unfair everything was to you, I made a decision at that moment. We were going to move on. I refused to let the events before your birth hold me...hold *us* back."

As bad as it all was for her, I couldn't just accept her side of the story. "But you didn't just withhold information. You created a whole series of half-truths to support the one big lie that you told me when I was younger. Now, I have no idea if anything you have ever told me is true, Mom."

We continued walking down the street until we reached an intersection where Mom made us turn right onto a side road.

"You're right. What made it easier was that an anonymous donor paid for all our medical expenses, and after the initial reports in the newspapers, the local media outlets stopped reporting on it. I guess when I decided to look forward, I also completely blocked out the past. Lies were easier to believe than the truth. I came up with a story that made no one at fault for your situation—a simple genetic mishap."

"But you went to great lengths to make that lie seem as real as possible! I remember asking about it so many times."

"Yes, you were a curious child, so I had to fill in the blanks for it all to make sense. As you got older, I debated telling you what really happened countless times. But once you got Auto, you became less interested in the past and more interested in exploring the world. Part of me thought it was all finally behind us. That feeling got even stronger when you became dead set on your mind migration. Without knowing it, you were determined to overcome the last major fallout from the accident. As much as I said I was against it because I didn't want to lose you, I was also secretly really proud of you for going through with it because it meant I could move on."

Stopping at a corner for the signal to cross, several bullet-busses sped by, blowing our hair and clothes about. Once we received our walking cue, we crossed.

"But, Mom, that's bullshit!"

"Language! I'm still your mother."

"Sorry. It's just not fair because you got to move on while I was living a lie."

"Again, you're right. That's why I wanted to tell—*show*—you everything before I apologized. Let's keep walking. It's just up ahead now."

We approached an expanse of open land with high fences surrounding it. I looked up at the sign above the archway and read aloud, "Northwest Cemetery." Peering down and across the expanse beyond the fences, I finally noticed all of the headstones and other sullen landmarks.

Winding a half kilometer into the graveyard, Mom finally stopped us at a very particular plot. "Here it is." She pointed down to one of the dirtier headstones.

As I read the name out loud, my mouth became agape. "Ryan D. Carter. What the hell?"

"I didn't want you to see his pictures before I told you. The day you became paralyzed inside of me was the same day I lost my first true love."

My whole world was being turned upside down, and it was hard to bear. With my mind spinning, I tried to piece it all together.

"Wait. So then, Dad—who was Jim?"

"I met Jim about a year after you were born. Having a paralyzed one-year-old and struggling with postpartum depression, PTSD, and a whole slew of other mental illnesses, I was surprised that anyone would want to be around me, much less fall in love with me. But Jim did. He did, and he also cared deeply for you."

"Then why did he leave us when I was six?"

Tears began to stream down both of our faces as she furthered the story.

"That's actually why we split up. Jim was an amazing father figure. He made it clear that he thought it wasn't fair to you, growing up thinking that he was your father. But even after six years, I was still really messed up from everything. Clinging to the lie, I told him if he didn't agree with my decisions that he could leave. I didn't think he would, but he did."

As Mom's crying intensified, a cold drizzle began to fall on us.

Still no words came to mind to accurately describe how I was feeling as we stood staring down at my father's headstone.

My disability.

My father.

Jim.

After standing silently in the frigid rain for what felt like several minutes, Mom finally asked the obvious question. "How did you figure it all out?"

The words froze me in my mental tracks. *How in the hell am I supposed to tell her about Charlie?*

302

While I was far along in coming to terms with my situation post-migration, it would be wild trying to explain it to Mom. I could try to explain the dreams I had during the mind migration—my earliest memories of Charlie. Or maybe it would have been better to start from the point where Charlie and I officially met—around the time of the Cameron Walsh speech. Going over the different ways to tell her, attempting to verbalize it to her of all people just sounded so crazy. I quickly found myself becoming humbled the more I thought about it, and it wasn't long before I came to the exact same conclusion that she did all of those years ago. As hypocritical as it made me, I couldn't utter the full truth to her in that moment, and I also wasn't justified in staying angry at her.

"There was an old news clipping I came across, then I saw the picture of the green car by the front door. Combined with some of my earliest memories of X-rays, it made sense that my spine was never deformed but severed."

She nodded through her tears. "I am truly sorry, Ryan. It shames me having lied to you for so long. I know you'll always question the things I tell you from now on, and rightfully so. But I swear to you that you now know the whole truth."

"I think I get it, Mom. It'll take me some time to fully grasp everything from today, but you were put through a lot at a time when you should have been focusing on giving birth and taking care of us. You're still my mother, and I still love you."

Leaning in, I gave her the tightest hug, and we just held each other for a few minutes as the rain picked up.

"I still want you to see the room downstairs. As strange as it sounds, I made the room so that I would never forget, and I would go in there from time to time to remind myself what we'd been through."

We made our way back to the house where we found Helen anxiously wondering if we had made amends.

"Well?"

"Well, what?"

"Shut it, Ryan. Are you two okay?"

"We're good, and you were basically right!"

"Yes! I knew it! Wait. What was I right about?"

"I didn't know the whole story. We can talk more about it later. Were you able to clean up my mess?"

"Her room looks good as new."

"Thanks. If you don't mind, I'm going to spend some time downstairs with my mom. I'll call you later."

"Sounds good. See ya, Ry."

"See ya."

Mom and I headed for the basement, and she let me open the door to the room. Stale air filled my nose as we entered together, and she flipped the light switch.

I turned slowly around in a circle twice to take it all in. The room was laid out like the old-fashioned crime labs I had seen in those cop shows. Photos, newspaper clippings, printouts, and drawings were all organized across the walls, and near the far edge of the room was a large rectangular table that had books and other papers on it. The entire left side of the room was dedicated to my real father.

Looking at the pictures, I could definitely see the resemblance. He had been a tall man, and it was obvious that he'd worked with his hands. Near the end of the wall, there were pictures that had to have been taken weeks and days before the accident. Some were from what had to be my baby shower, and it put a knot in my throat, making me want to break down in tears again. My mom and dad looked so happy together in every picture. The very last photo forced a question to fall out of my mouth.

"Is this from…?"

"The day of the accident? Yes. That's me when my contractions started. I told your father we should wait at home as long as possible, but he was so worried that he insisted we get in the car and head to the hospital as soon as we could. That was part of the problem. I thought that, had I just tried a little harder to convince him, we'd all be a family to this day."

"Mom, you can't blame yourself for the unknown. You were in labor. That's enough."

"I've told that to myself thousands of times. But it doesn't make it any easier to accept."

I turned to the back wall with the table and began looking at the pieces of old newspaper. The headlines unveiled the story that I had come to know that day.

PREGNANT COUPLE TARGETED WITH MANUAL
CAR; SUSPECT IN CUSTODY.

UPDATE ON TARGETED, PREGNANT COUPLE: MAN
DIES; PREGNANT WOMAN SURVIVES, MINOR INJURIES;
NEWBORN SURVIVES, IN SERIOUS CONDITION.

TARGETED WOMAN, STACY CARTER, AND BABY LEAVE
HOSPITAL, SAYS: "I JUST WANT TO GET ON WITH MY LIFE."

Next, there were hand drawings and some notes scribbled onto what looked like journal paper.

"What are these?"

Mom took a step toward them and nodded. "From the trial of the man who crashed into our car. As much as I wanted to just move on, I had to go to the trial to make sure he wasn't able to do to others what he had done to us."

"Did you know much about him?"

She didn't answer right away, but instead reached for something under one of the books on the table. I was overcome by confusion at what she revealed. "This is the only picture I have of him."

It was like looking in the strangest mirror seeing his face in real life, and I couldn't help but wonder.

"Did you ever meet him? Or talk to him?"

"Yes. Charles Rios was his name. He was a deeply disturbed man."

"What do you mean?"

"He pled not guilty to crimes that he obviously committed. When he took the stand, he hid behind the Fifth Amendment for most of the questions. When he finally did answer questions, he was short, vague, and not helpful. It seemed like he had given up all hope."

"Oh?"

"He was a veteran, and must have gotten really messed up when he served overseas."

"Sure."

"I almost felt a little sorry for him until…"

"Until what?"

"Never mind."

"Mom. You said you weren't hide anything from me anymore."

"It's not that. It's just…it was a horrible thing. It's hard for me to even think about, much less show to my son whom was deeply affected by it. But I did say that I would tell you everything moving forward, and I meant it."

She reached into her pocket, obtained yet another key, and approached the table. There was a locked drawer off to the right. With a couple of clicks, it was unlocked, and she pulled it out. With a trembling hand, she reached inside and obtained a single piece of laminated paper.

Dear Stacey Carter,

Words will never be able to convey just how sorry I am. Failing to kill you all is one of the biggest regrets of my life, and it was worth trying even if I ended up rotting in a cell. As far as people go, you're as low as they come. It only makes sense that I would have these thoughts, and the more I know about you, the more I know they're valid.

You may be looking for some kind of explanation for why it all happened. I could go into the details about how you're antiwar and antitroops. But it's a tired story that you will try to deny. I could bring up all the freedoms I protected while serving in Pakistan where I saw countless bodies of people I knew. Though you'd still try to excuse what you have done.

I just wanted to make someone pay for the criminal behavior of the so-called protesters. I knew you were a part of it. I knew that you played a vital role in the whole movement, and I wanted you and everyone else to pay.

In a twisted way, it's fitting that you finally paid the price on the day you were going to bring another ungrateful mouth into this world. However, it shames me more than anything that I only killed one of you. If I could do it all over, I would have driven faster.

In closing, I want to let you know that I have tortured myself enough these last few months knowing I let you survive. I refuse to live and let the kangaroo court convict me against the justice that I sought. By the time you read this letter, I will have ended it all in disgrace, and I hope that you never get the fake justice you preach about to your friends.

See you in hell,

Charles Rios

My blood boiled reading the real letter that Charlie had sent to my mother. He had been lying to me all along. He was the one who ruined all of our lives, and it was time that I settled things with him once and for all.

For my father.

For my mother.

For me.

I used all of my mental power to dig into my mind and find Charlie, and my grip on reality began to slip. I could feel my body shake and my eyes roll back into my head, and with all of my might, I screamed at the top of my lungs.

"You're going to pay for this, Charlie! You hear me?! You'll pay!"

CHAPTER 29

WHAT DOESN'T KILL YOU

"YOU'RE GOING TO PAY FOR this, Charlie! You hear me?! You'll pay!"

Awaking to pure black nothingness, a familiar voice was distorted to a shrill as it echoed painfully loud throughout the open space.

Flick!

The spotlight from before popped on and shone brightly onto me.

Flick!

The other spotlight appeared a hundred yards away or so.

It was Ryan, and even from my distance, I could tell he was furious.

"You're going to pay for this, Charlie! You hear me?! You'll pay!" He yelled again with even more ire in his voice, but there was no echo that accompanied it the second time.

It was clear as day, and so too was it clear that the time had come for me to show Ryan the last things that I had to offer him.

"You're right to be angry, Ryan."

"You're a liar and a murderer!" he screamed.

I could feel his visceral emotions. When someone goes mad like that, they tend to not think about their actions so much, and they live off pure adrenaline. That was exactly what I needed to see my plan for Ryan through.

"Now that you know the truth, Ryan, there are some other things I need to show you. Things you're going to need to know."

"Don't say another damn word!" Shaking his head, Ryan made a move. With me in his sights, he put his head down and bolted. Quickly getting to top speed, even the spotlight had trouble keeping up with him as he blazed across the abyss.

At the rate he was going, he would collide with me in a matter of seconds, but something told me that it wasn't the time or place to fight. "No, Ryan. Not here. Not now."

I tightly closed my eyes and thought of the best setting to begin engaging Ryan. The sounds of a violent wind and crackling electricity began to fill the emptiness around us, and I felt a vortex encircle me. The weight on my feet lessened and lessened until I was finally lifted up into the infinite void. I focused all my mental power on going deep into my memories to get to where we needed to be, and a tear in the black space allowed it to happen.

After just a moment, the intense commotion around us began to fade, and I felt the vortex gently lowering me back down until my feet felt something firm below. Eyes still closed, I relished the cool breeze blowing across my cheek and the warmth of what had to be the sun on my brow. An early spring scent was in the air, and while part of me thought it was nostalgic, another part of me hated where I had taken us. Upon opening my eyes, I was anything but surprised to see the field behind Mr. Reno's house.

Looking down, I was in my eighteen-year-old body, wearing my favorite t-shirt and jeans. It was just before I was going to leave for the marines, and I was already in pretty good shape. I found Ryan standing twenty yards away, looking identical to me.

He charged, closing the distance between us while yelling, "Everything is all your fault! You ruined my life! Now I'm going to erase you from my mind so that you can't hurt anyone else."

"Yes, Ryan. Channel your anger and attack me!"

He put all of his force behind a right hook toward my cheek.

Narrowly dodging his fist, I knelt down and left jabbed him in the gut, knocking the wind out of him. "Pitiful, Ryan!"

He stumbled back, then gathered himself, and even more livid, came back with a left uppercut toward my chin.

I leaned back making him miss, then landed a right jab to his neck, causing him to gasp even more. "That's not going to get it done, Ryan!"

Trying desperately to breathe, he doubled over. Through his hate, he inhaled deeply, looked up, and shot me a dirty look. Next, he took his first step right for me with his head down. Like a bullfighter, I took two steps to the right and out of his way, sending him tumbling to the ground. It was clear that I had learned more about fighting at Gates as a kid than Ryan had learned his entire life, and that just wouldn't do.

"You find out that I killed your father, ruined your mom's life, and paralyzed you, and all you can do is swing and miss? If you're going to beat me, you'll have to do better than that."

"Screw you!" Popping up he offered more swings and more misses.

He received more counterstrikes from me.

"Ow!" Out of breath, Ryan stopped flailing and just looked at me with fire in his eyes.

Above, thick black clouds began to cover the entire sky, and our battle was momentarily darkened. Intermittent lightning strikes in the distance provided a strobe light effect that gave each of us a clear glimpse every few seconds.

"To defeat your enemies, you must fight them where they are weak. If this truly is my mind we're in, you should know what I'm going to do before I even do it. Use that against me."

A bit of confusion leaked through the anger on Ryan's face as he tried to decipher my advice. Finally, with a scowl, he nodded in my direction and shut his eyes tightly. He began to shake violently as he concentrated hard to find the knowledge and skills that I possessed for hand-to-hand combat. A red radiance enveloped him, and I could feel my presence getting weaker the stronger his glow became. Then the light around him dissipated, and he opened his eyes. Our stares couldn't have been any more intense.

With an unmistakable newfound confidence, he took the first step toward me to resume our fight. "You bastard!"

His blows came in rapid-fire and with much more precision, not allowing for any rebuttals.

Left jab at my eye.

I blocked.

Right hook at my jaw.

I dodged.

Swinging back kick to my ribs.

Landed.

"Oomph!" Stumbling back, I was impressed by his decisions, but knew

I needed to continue antagonizing him to bring out his best. "Is that all you got?!"

Without missing a beat, he came at me with a flurry of quick punches, knees, and elbows that I was able to block or dodge. Finally, he put everything he had into a massive roundhouse kick to the side of my head.

"Ahhh!" The force of his foot flipped me head over heels, and I hit the ground with such an impact that I bounced twice, then lay there for a moment.

Ryan stood over me. The little bit of light that was creeping through the clouds was completely eclipsed by his silhouette. The flash of the lightning strikes compared to the boom of thunder meant they were very close, and I knew that our time in that place in my mind was about to be up.

"This is for being one of the Padre's thugs!" With a heavy foot, he attempted to come down dead center on my face and end it all.

Harnessing my mental power, I focused on another time and place for the next phase to begin, and the vortex returned, sucking both of us up into the black infinity and dropping us elsewhere.

We both opened our eyes, and we were standing twenty feet apart in the sandy hills of Pakistan. As always, it was arid and blistering hot, but the thunderclouds from the field had followed and the thunder roared. Sensing the change in my clothing, I looked down to find that I was in my camo fatigues and armed with my trusty knife. Again, we looked identical with blades already drawn.

With a piercing glare, I did my best to rile him up again. "What are you waiting for?"

Dagger pointed, he sprinted toward me, again attempting to end it all.

With a loud clink of my blade against his, I diverted his stab, then shoved him to the ground. "More of this silliness, Ryan? Come on!"

Getting up, he lunged at me again, but with more control, and we sparred for several seconds.

Tink.

Tink.

Tink.

After parrying one of his swings, I caught him with a left hook in the mouth, staggering him back.

Ryan spat blood at my feet, and surprisingly, a maniacal grin swept across his face. "You won't hurt anyone anymore, Charlie. I'm taking you out!" He took a giant leap back and closed his eyes again.

He entered his meditative state much more quickly this time, and a brighter orange aura encapsulated him. His shaking was much less intense as I felt my essence being drained. He was learning, I was dying, and I couldn't have been happier.

"That's it, Ryan. Take my energy and use it against me."

In one motion, his eyes opened, and he dashed at me, swinging the knife with much more accuracy. The scuffle was highlighted by the repeated contact of metal on metal.

Tink.

Tink.

Tink.

Following Ryan's last attack that I repelled, he kneed me in the ribs and head butted me back. While I was still reeling from the blows, he pounced at my face with his knife, and it took everything I had to dodge the point of the blade, but the razor-sharp edge still managed to slice a sizable wound into my cheek.

Backhanding his thrusting arm, I was able to knock the weapon from his hand. He followed that move with an elbow to my temple, dropping me to the ground and nearly causing me to lose consciousness. I purposely remained on the ground as Ryan grabbed his knife and again stood over me, determining my fate. Thunder and lightning boomed all around us as he firmly gripped the handle of his knife with both hands and raised both of his arms up above his head.

He began the motion down, aiming right for my skull. "This is for my father!"

Tapping into my dwindling strength, I commanded the vortex to swoop us away through the void to yet another time and place. A calmness came over me as we shifted between locations, but it was only a few seconds before we were plopped down in the rotting old steel mill where I had seen the vile product the Padre had gotten rich from. We were both dressed in my normal, dark work garb and both armed with my favorite 9mm.

Thunder and lightning rumbled just on top of the building, causing the whole structure to shake.

Finally making eye contact with me again, Ryan fired a shot in my direction while he dove behind some rusty machinery. Instinctively leaping behind a wall, I got out of the way just in time for his bullet to whiz past my head instead of into it. Getting to my feet, I peeked around the corner, and I could see Ryan's head sticking out from the machinery enough to get a clear kill shot had I wanted to. Instead, I aimed at the metal plate below him and pulled the trigger.

Ping!

Ryan ducked down but popped out only his gun to return fire.

Pop! Pop! Pop! Pop!

"You're wasting bullets, Ryan! That's not how you get vengeance."

"Go to hell!"

Eyeing a heavy piece of metal within my reach, I grabbed it and chucked it across the room.

Clink, clink, clink...

It worked. Ryan rolled out from his cover and emptied his magazine in the direction of the noise, giving me the opportunity to sprint from my position and kick the gun from his hand. As a surprising counter, he grabbed my foot, dropping me to the ground beside him. Climbing on top of me and holding me down, he reached over my head for the gun. We were both shaking as he tried to impose his will on me, and I resisted all the more. He inched closer to my gun, and I used what energy I had left to hold him back while working to free my other hand.

Getting impatient, he lunged for my weapon, giving me just enough space to hurl him off of me while never losing my weapon. As I popped up, he scurried to grab his gun and then disappeared through a door into the dark maze of the steel mill's maintenance area.

Keeping up my guard, I slowly followed behind him. I entered the hallway where the walls were a finely meshed fencing with various doorways to the equipment that used to drive the whole operation of the place. Ryan could have been lurking in any of them, so staying low, I weaved back and forth from wall to wall, pointing my weapon in each of the openings, ready to fire. He had to have gone deeper into the mill since I wasn't able to find any sign of him.

"What are you hiding from, Ryan? Don't you want me dead?"

Suddenly, it felt like the life was being sucked right out of me as I stumbled into an open room between hallways. I could make out a bright yellow glow from one of the corners, and I knew what Ryan had gone there to do. The thunder and lightning felt like they were inside the building at that moment, and I knew we were getting close to the end.

With my vitality being drained down to nothing, I dropped to my knees and watched the yellow glow dissipate. A lightning strike came down directly on Ryan, and between my long blinks, I watched him vibrate as energy left my mind and entered his. He was finally ready to exact his revenge, and from the darkness I heard his final words.

"This is for me!"

Pop! Pop! Pop! Pop!

Thunder and lightning exploded through the ceiling of the mill, causing the ancient building to groan. Numbness overtook my body as I watched chaos reign when the whole structure started to fold in on itself. With my remaining energy, I made the vortex take us to our final destination.

This time an overwhelming silence swooped in, and the smell of the woods filled my nose as I was placed onto the ground. I knew exactly where I was. It was night, and I was behind the Oceanic Laboratories building.

Ryan was in the parking lot screaming my name. "Charlie!"

That was when I communicated with him in the only way I knew he would listen. Snap!

"Charlie!"

Snap! Then I used an inner voice to communicate with him. *Be quiet or be dead.*

Waiting to hear his angered yelling, all I heard was the wind, so I continued talking between our two minds. *Your surroundings are as important as the enemy. Never get caught in the open without a plan.*

I could hear slight movement just in front of the building.

Focus on deliberate, fluid motion, like an animal.

There was more obvious rustling, so I moved swiftly through the shadows in his direction, and cracked him in the jaw.

"Ow!"

By the time he fought through the pain to look for me, I was already out of sight again.

Control your breathing. Exhale in tandem with your movements.

I blinked, and he was no longer in the location where I had stuck him. *Good. Approach the enemy from behind, and strike without hesitation.*

Hearing the faintest footsteps behind me, I moved just in time to sweep his legs, slam him in the chest, and disappear back into the darkness.

"Ahhh!"

"That won't do, Ryan. Now, live in the shadows. Strike from behind. No hesitation."

Again, he vanished from the ground, and a moment later, I heard the sound of Ryan's fist through the air as he landed a pulverizing kidney shot to my back. Before I could writhe in pain, he had already gotten his forearm around my neck and was squeezing the little life that I had left out of me.

"Good, Ryan! As I get weaker, you should get stronger."

Blinking as the end became eminent, everyone I had loved and wronged flashed before my eyes.

Sarah. Lucy. Joey.

"I'm sorry."

Ryan. Stacy. Ryan.

"I'm sorry."

I used the last bit of energy I had to send off a message to Ryan, and then everything turned to nothing for the last time.

"No! I can't breathe!"

An intense flash of light whited out everything around me, and I squinted, trying to keep my view. Pictures from the past appeared in front of me. Charlie playing as kid. Charlie in high school, courting Sarah. Charlie fighting the war. Charlie being a father and husband. Charlie working for the Padre. Charlie in jail. Charlie committing...

Before I saw the end of Charlie, my perspective faded to black. Having seen Charlie's entire life in an instant, I forgot all of the rage I had just felt for him and became aware that I could no longer feel his presence.

To be sure he was gone, I called out to him in the abyss. "Charlie! Charlie?"

But there was no answer.

"Charlie! Where are you?"

Not only was there no response, but I couldn't even feel his essence around me like I always had since the migration. And in being alone for the first time in my mind, it was strange. I thought I would feel relief and happiness. I thought I would feel independent and free. Instead, there was a certain emptiness that didn't bring me any comfort. Quite the opposite, an intense melancholy quickly overcame me.

Looking around the black space, I wondered what would be next for me. It wasn't a second later that, similar to before I encountered Charlie, my mind began to spiral like an unplugged drain. My thoughts began to slip away as a throbbing migraine set in. God-awful, unbearable agony overflowed from my mind as my reality was sliding into the infinite darkness.

Whoosh!

Blurry at first, I wiped my eyes only to be shocked half to death. I was back in Auto, sitting at the ID reader, and Atlas the Ant was ready for me.

"Greetings, Ryan! Thanks again for your investment in Atlas Digenetics with your purchase of a standard mind migration and host package. You've come a long way to get to this point, and the next phase of your journey begins with your acceptance of the terms and conditions that were laid out in your migration contract. To review the terms and conditions, please say 'Review' or tap the Review button on the hologram below. Otherwise, simply say 'I accept' or you can press the Accept button."

More than confused, I felt like I had awoken at the end of some cheesy movie where the whole story was just a dream. But the more I took in my surroundings, the more I understood what was happening wasn't exactly real.

"Do you accept, Ryan?"

Without any other obvious choices, I went along with it. "I accept."

"That's great!"

Instead of rattling on about my migration specialist, something else appeared. It was a letter to me.

Dear Ryan,

From the moment I first sensed your presence within my mind, I was not only in disbelief but genuinely afraid. Afraid was never something that I liked being for too long, so I needed to settle it one way or another. I wasn't sure if you were friend, foe, or something different altogether. It wasn't until I stumbled upon some of your memories and thoughts that I realized who and what you are.

In many ways, we were very similar people. Just like you, I spent so much of my time lost in thought that while it was depressing and lonely at times, it was all I knew. You too were a kid who had been dealt a bad hand but had a great attitude and strong work ethic.

After realizing this, it felt safe to reveal my most vivid flashbacks. For better or worse, they all surrounded the unanswered questions that plagued me throughout my life, right up until the end. In hindsight, it was pretty selfish of me to do so, knowing that they might pique your interest. I don't know if it was your morbid curiosity that was driving you or if you truly cared for me. Either way, in spite of the intense confusion and fear that I felt in you the entire time, you pushed forward. You put your own safety on the line to help me. In re—remembering the darkest parts of my life, I came to the depressing realization that I was much closer to you in the time we were together than anyone in my previous life. From my childhood to the marines to my family life to my time as a thug for the Padre, you were there for it all, albeit in memory only. Regardless, you brought an innocent, objective lens to it, which was a perspective that I didn't believe existed in the world outside of young children.

When I chose to take my own life in that jail cell, I did so thinking that would be the end. Not just the end for me, but the end of all the suffering I had caused, not just for you and your family, but also for Sarah and my family as you saw in the Plan B box. But I also felt like I had no other options. When I awoke to your energy and discovered it was more than just a dream, I felt like I had been given a second chance—one I didn't want to squander. You helped me make that wish come true. You helped me confirm that my family got as far as Plan B, and I cannot thank you enough.

I also cannot apologize enough for dramatically changing the course of your life. As fate would have it, I turned out to be the dealer of the bad hand you had to overcome your entire life. Looking through our eyes, I saw the letter your mom received with my name on it, and I want to be clear: That was not the letter that I left in my cell before ending it all. My only guess is that it was something the jail

317

manifested to cover their tracks. I assure you that the letter I read to you was the truth. I was sincerely sorry when I wrote it. I was even sorrier when I realized exactly who you were.

Finally, I don't really understand how our two minds came together and how you came to be in my body, but regardless, you're ready to take on anything. In our last moments, when you fought me with everything you had, I was actually preparing you, should you decide to go after the Padre. It's a good thing too, because you really wouldn't have stood a chance without those skills. Obviously, it would have brought me great joy to see the Padre suffer the same fate that he imposed on so many others. But after I showed you who I truly was, I forced myself to come to peace, believing that won't happen. Still, I really feel like you have a stake in my vengeance. Had it not been for the Padre, all of our lives would have turned out much differently, and likely, much better. That said, it is your decision to make, and yours alone. No matter what you choose, I couldn't have asked for anyone better to occupy my body. Use it as you see fit and have a great life, Ryan.

Sincerely,

Charlie

"That bastard." Tears had begun flowing halfway through Charlie's letter, and by the time I finished, I was bawling like a baby. Part of me had known what I'd read at Mom's was a lie, but I was so angry after everything I had learned that I was looking for any reason to release my rage.

Regardless, I felt completely justified in hating Charlie for everything he'd done. Even if the Padre had set things in motion, Charlie had been the one who'd gotten my family involved. And with that, it struck me as strange that, when I attempted to focus on the hate that I thought I felt for Charlie, I came up empty. There was no hate there. Instead, there was a bit of respect for how he'd handled himself as long as I'd known him.

So, finding myself at another crossroads just as I did when I first discovered Charlie, he was right that I had a decision to make. While it might have been one of the toughest decisions of my life, I knew exactly what I need to do.

"Wake up, Ryan! Wake up!"

CHAPTER 30

HELLO DARKNESS, MY OLD FRIEND

"WAKE UP, RYAN! WAKE UP!"

I jumped out of bed startled, and it was too dark to see. I could sense Helen was not next to me, and heard a commotion near the doorway.

"Helen! Where are you!"

Her muffled scream came from the hallway and the faintest sound of a fist cutting through the air came from behind me. My instincts kicked in. Ducking just in time, I slipped under the punch, and feeling the presence of a body next to me, I gave it a hard elbow to what had to be the ribs.

"Oomph!"

Thrusting my knee up toward where dark figure's head had to be, I could feel the exact moment when I made contact with his front teeth. As the figure reeled back from that blow, I followed with a powerful punch to the neck, and he gurgled to the floor in agony.

"Helen!" But I couldn't hear her anymore, so I darted down the dark hallway.

Her next scream came from the direction of the balcony. "Ryan!"

"Helen!"

I zipped into the living room and flinched at the click of a cocking gun from the corner. Time slowed down, and without thinking, I went into a sliding motion.

Pop! Pop!

My momentum brought me to the wall just a meter from the intruder.

With all of my might, I kicked him in the kneecap, dropping him to his other knee.

Even though he yelped, he was still able to swing his massive fist and crack me in the jaw.

"Ah!"

As much as it hurt, I instinctively came back with a punch to his chest, but he was a big man, and it hardly did any damage. Realizing I was catering to his strengths with close combat near the floor, I popped up and tried to kick him in the face when he grabbed my supporting leg and dropped me back down onto my back. Kneeling above me, he then balled both his fists together and, with all his might, tried to come down on my face to crush my skull. I dodged to the left, then to the right, and as he pulled back for a third attempt, it became apparent that I had to end the fight quickly or his size advantage would be the end of me.

With his next attempt to bludgeon me, I countered with a calculated strike to his right temple that made him go limp and slump over.

Pushing the lug off of me, I sprung up. Helen screamed from outside. Darting out to the balcony, my still-adjusting eyes were blinded by the streetlights while I was trying to see where they were taking Helen.

"Ryan! Listen with your ears!"

Finally able to focus, I heard Helen's last scream from below. I peered over the railing and saw the big door to the black auto-truck slam shut just before it squealed its tires and sped off.

"Shit!"

I was about to follow down the fire escape when I realized that not only did I need transportation, but I had no clue where they were going. Remembering that Helen had borrowed her dad's car, I ran back into the apartment and into the bedroom. I kicked the gasping man still on the ground and grabbed my netphone from the nightstand. It had the startup program to the car. Then I remembered what Helen had last screamed.

Listen with my ears?

Opening the drawer to the night stand, I was first presented with my hunting knife, which I instantly grabbed. Moving some other things around, I found the radio to the earpiece. I didn't have much time to catch up to them, given its five-kilometer radius, so I dashed out of the room, onto the balcony, and down the fire escape. I slid down the hand railings, back and forth until I hit the ground. I darted across the street and started the auto-car from my netphone. The driver's side door opened and I dove into the seat. I pressed the ignition button, and the seatbelt strap shot around me as the auto-driver slowly pulled out of the parking space and presented a navigation hologram followed by the vehicle's annoying voice.

"Where would you like to go, sir?"

I tapped instructions into the hologram, and the car headed in the direction of the auto-truck. Then it became painfully apparent to me just how slow auto-drivers went—I was losing precious seconds to catch Helen. Looking across the dashboard, I saw the manual override button. I remembered what to do from driving as Charlie, and knew I had to take my chances.

Pressing the button hard, the auto-driver first warned me, "Caution, sir. Manual driving is a dangerous endeavor. Please reconsider. Otherwise, press manual override again."

More than pissed, I pressed the button with my fist. With a surge, the dashboard transformed to present a steering wheel and two pedals appeared on the floor. I gripped the wheel and hit the accelerator hard, and I was off with a screech. Then I switched the radio on, and through the choppy reception, I heard Helen trying to give me clues.

"Why the hell are you taking me across the city? What do you want with me?"

"Lady, if you know what's good for you, you'll shut your mouth."

"Screw you, asshole. If you're taking me to Marktown, my boyfriend will find us. He knows your little neighborhood through and through."

"It would make my night for him to follow us. I'd love to see what the boss will do to him. Now, shut your damn mouth!"

For the next few minutes, I could only hear the sounds from her pocket. I had to think hard about where they were going. Marktown had changed a lot since Charlie's time, and it didn't make sense for them to go to the old building where we saw the art show.

After twenty minutes of driving, I entered the neighborhood, and fortunately, voices started coming from the radio again.

"Juan and Marco haven't checked in since we left that place. You think they're all right?"

Helen butted in. "I bet Ryan beat their asses, and when he gets to this big house on Spruce Street, you're next."

"Hey, why the hell do you keep talking like that?"

The muffled sounds of them patting her down culminated with what had to be them pulling the earpiece out of her pocket and crushing it.

Click!

Then nothing, and my gut dropped.

A big building on Spruce street? The Padre's old complex!

I picked up my speed just a little and made all of the turns that would get me there as fast as possible. Pulling just a kilometer from where the Padre's complex used to be, I parked the car. I hopped out of the car and made my way one hundred meters across the street to get within line of sight.

They had knocked down the "ghetto" mansion and replaced it with a legitimate one, but upon further glance, it was much more. The Padre had built a three-story, brick suburban fortress, and it would be tough to infiltrate.

Weaving in between the street lights, I made my way into the yard of the neighboring house, pretty confident that eyes were on me right away. I assessed the front door, knowing it would be foolish to enter that way, so I looked through the narrow path between the neighboring building. I saw the black auto-truck parked under the garage overhang and thought I should head back that way, when I realized something.

It was uncomfortably quiet up and down the street. Something wasn't right. Still, I didn't have a choice but to move forward. Sneaking along the edge of the other building, I got about ten meters in when a giant shadow appeared from behind the building in front of me, and I didn't have to turn around to know someone had come around the house to follow me. Being so close to Helen, I wasn't messing around anymore, and I pulled out the hunting knife.

Both of the guards simultaneously charged in my direction, and I didn't have much time to figure out the best way to deal with them. Jumping as high as I could, I kicked off the one building and then off the other, getting just high enough to come down, knife in hands, into one guy's shoulder as I landed behind him.

He squealed like a stuck pig.

A slight nausea set in as I felt every centimeter of my blade impale the flesh of another human.

The other guard took advantage of my distraction to land a decent shot to my eye.

The force of his punch sent me stumbling back several meters. Fortunately, I had kept my hand on the knife that was in the other goon and it pulled out as I fell back. It took a moment to get my vision back after the blow, but when I did, it was just in time to catch the other thug rushing at me. He was too big to out muscle, so I let him get within a meter of me, dropped to a knee, and pointed my weapon at his gut.

Thud!

He toppled over me but not without taking all twenty centimeters of the knife to the midsection, and he quickly went into shock from the wound. Wiping some of the gore off of me as I got up, I finally made my way toward the backyard.

I was ready to turn the corner when I heard a single footstep and intuitively ducked down to catch the next guard by surprise. When his gargantuan frame appeared, I hesitated for just a moment before trying to stab him in the chest. That split second turned out to be the difference, and he batted the knife from my hands before I made contact. Panicking, I rolled to the ground and popped up behind him to get him in a choke hold.

Charlie's words echoed in my head. *"As he gets weaker, you should get stronger."*

The only problem was that this guard didn't seem to be getting weaker. Instead, he reached over his shoulder and grabbed one of my arms. Before I could react, he effortlessly flung me into the backyard some ten meters away, and I painfully bounced a couple times off the ground. Stunned, I looked up to watch him pull a gun with a silencer from the holster and point it at me.

I scrambled to get away. The sound of a shot fired pierced the air.

And then everything went black.

"Wake up…Ryan…wake up." A familiar voice rang in the distance.

When I opened my eyes, I was surprised to see nothing but darkness, and I called out. "Hello?"

"You've come too far to fail, Ryan."

"Charlie? Is that you?"

"Remember what I taught you."

"I remember, Charlie, but what if I fail? What if I just can't do it?"

"You can do anything you put your mind to. And, Ryan?"

"Yes?"

"Never give up hope!"

Then a flash of light wiped away the darkness. Regaining consciousness, my head was groggy, but I otherwise felt fine. I opened my eyes, and the brightest light accosted my pupils. I half-expected to relive Charlie's old warehouse memory, and then jump up from the ground to run away from the Padre's goons in a Cadillac. Only this time, I awoke to the real world, relieved that the shot I had taken wasn't fatal at all. But the reprieve was short lived when I took in my surroundings. A makeshift hospital room with curtains all around and a hanging light above. I tried to sit up, and was denied by thick straps holding down my upper and lower halves to a medical table. Before I could further assess the situation, I overheard talking somewhere on the other side of the curtain.

"The new sedative worked well. Once the test results come back, we'll confirm each of their statuses."

The woman must have been talking about Helen and me.

A man responded, "Good."

I recognized his voice.

Then footsteps made their way in my direction, and fear began to grow in me. Fingers poked through an opening in the curtain and ripped them open. It was Allen, from the basement at 'art' show, as I had suspected.

He walked to the foot of the table. "You're finally awake. Good."

"Where's Helen!"

Before he could respond, she screamed from somewhere across the room. "Ryan!"

"Helen? Are you okay?"

Only silence. Then they must have gagged her.

"Dammit! I swear, if you hurt her…"

"I assure you, she's fine. You'll both be fine for now."

Still angry, I fired back, "What are you going to do to us, *Padre*!"

A maniacal grin slowly crept across his face, and my stomach began to sink. Then the familiar hum that had calmed me for a decade slowly filled the room as Sonya, in her auto-chair, appeared next to Allen.

"We'll be getting to the bottom of how you found us. But there's one thing you got wrong. *I'm* the Padre."

While I was caught off guard, it didn't change the situation. I turned my glare to him. "What are you going to do to us?!"

His face was even more sinister than Allen's, despite his façade of an elderly woman. "Oh, Ryan. Sometimes it's better to be lucky than good. Last week, when you found us at the community center, I almost had Allen kill you both for talking like fools. Then it dawned on me that you might help me get back at my son. Frustrated when that plan failed, I was about to put a hit out on you again when I had another revelation."

The Padre's grin was pure evil.

"You see, the bodies that Allen and I occupy are wearing out, and we were about to start the long, drawn-out process of finding new hosts. Then, you found us. And I must say, it'll be nice to get out of this old hag's body. She barely made it through the original procedure, leaving me in this damn mechanical chair. It'll be nice to get into a spry, young man's body."

Words couldn't begin to describe how I felt. They were going to wipe our minds and migrate into our hosts, and who knew how the hell that would turn out. Wherever Charlie was, it would be the worst kind of hell for him to have his body do the bidding of the Padre.

Then I remembered something. "Helen and I are already in hosts! You can't migrate another mind into these bodies!"

They both let loose an evil cackle.

The Padre continued to snicker as he spoke. "Why? Because those silly *laws* say so? Those were nothing more than a placebo to appease the public. In fact, having already completed a migration, you're the perfect candidates for us. Now, I don't feel like waiting to scan your minds, so why don't you just tell us how you found us?"

In that moment, I felt more helpless than at any point in my childhood. The Padre seemed invincible in Charlie's time, and that only seemed truer as I lay there on that medical table. If he had it his way, he'd migrate into new bodies until the end of time, an undying source of evil. If there was anything left for me to do, any cards left to play, I had to scramble to do it before it was too late.

Then, it hit me. Looking the Padre right in the eye, I revealed my secret. "Charlie sent me."

The Padre's gaze didn't flinch even a little as he stared through me.

My focus didn't waver either. As the seconds passed, I thought he was just going to kill us and find other hosts when things took a turn.

"Ha ha! Charlie? Charlie Rios! He's been dead for years. That coward took his own life in jail before I could get to him. So, stop bullshitting. How did you find us?"

If Helen and I are going to die, I might as well cast some doubt into their minds to haunt them for as long as possible. "You're right, Padre. You *are* lucky. After Charlie struck you down at the warehouse, he lost your thugs on the road. If he didn't get in that accident, he was going to hunt you down."

The confident expression on the Padre's face disappeared for the first time that night. His brow shot up, and he barked at me. "You work for the Brazilians! Those bastards!"

"Wrong! I thought you were a little aggressive on the Korean job. That's probably what set them off."

Squinting in disbelief, the Padre's jaw dropped. "How in the...?!"

He leaned within centimeters of my face, and it was clear that he hadn't given up his cigar habit.

With him that close, I couldn't help but to pile it on. "You were also a little rough with the product on the Russian job. I think that's why the compressor failed."

"It can't be..."

Jolting the Padre's attention, an alarm sounded and red lights lit the place up.

The guard from the backyard walked up next to Allen and acknowledged the alarm in a robotic voice. "The perimeter has been breached."

The Padre just continued staring at me. "But you can't be...Charlie. He's...dead."

"Sir, the perimeter has been breached."

I smiled and delivered the final blow. "And if you would have just let me know about the 'pilot' job, I could have made arrangements."

Clearly in shock, the Padre slowly rolled back from me.

The mechanical guard chimed in again. "An auto-car just arrived in the parking lot."

Snapping out of his stupor, the Padre turned to the guard. "Show me holo!"

The guard pulled up a holo-pad and flashed it on. It showed the same auto-car Junior had driven after our meeting, and he was parking at some abandoned building. In the corner of the holo, I could just make out the deteriorating sign.

Oceanic Laboratories! That's where we are.

Anger came over the Padre's face. "My damn son wants to bring the fight to me. Well, I'm tired of his bullshit. Release the auto-hounds!"

"Yes, sir."

The robotic guard tapped some buttons on his holo-pad, and then the hologram disappeared. I thought the Padre was going to turn his sights back to me, but a ruckus broke out in the same direction where Helen had been. Allen and the robot guard darted through the curtains behind me. Based on Allen's face, he wasn't very happy. The Padre spun around my table to turn toward the distraction, and I was ready to call out to Helen to add to the disruption when my attention was instantly drawn to the back of the Padre's auto-chair. His model was the exact same as Auto.

The battery is prone to flare ups!

Then memories from Charlie kicked in, and I knew exactly what I needed to do. But based on the sounds behind me, a scuffle must have broken out near Helen. The obvious thuds of punches, and finally, a small explosion had me worried to death.

I fought my straps like hell to get free, to no avail. "I swear to God, if you hurt her!"

The Padre, still taking in the situation, didn't even have a chance to respond when my concerns were more than put to rest.

"Ryan! Where are you!" Helen's voice was moving, and that could only mean one thing.

She is free! "Over here, Helen!"

With Junior coming, the alarm sounding, and Helen loose, it was the right amount of chaos to overwhelm the Padre.

"God dammit! Can't I get any decent help around here for once! Do I have to do every little damn thing myself?!" From a compartment in his chair, he pulled out the hand cannon with the dog skull insignia on it and put it on his lap, then engaged the auto-chair to change directions.

The familiar hum moved around my table, toward Helen. As he turned the corner near my feet, I was able to stretch my right foot out just enough to hook the battery wires known to be faulty. He only had to drive another half meter before the electrical surge kicked in and sparks began to fly.

"What the hell?!" He spun in circles, chasing the mini-firework show coming from the back of his chair.

Helen stormed through the curtains behind me. "Ryan!" She darted to my table and pressed the button to release the straps.

The sparking Padre finally saw what was happening and reached for his gun. "You little shits! We'll find other hosts who are not such a pain in my ass."

"Helen, get down!"

We both dove behind the other side of the table as shots rang out.

Bang! Bang! Bang!

Only it wasn't shots but small explosions from the Padre's auto-chair battery.

"Come on, Ryan! Let's get out of here." Helen pointed to the set of double doors labeled Exit.

"No! I have to make sure he dies." Peeking my head above the table, I saw the Padre catch fire in his chair.

His agonized screams filled the room. "Nooooo!"

Bang! Bang!

Boom!

More mini-explosions followed the big one, and he was thrown from the chair, through the curtains. As delighted as I was at seeing the Padre suffer, I was just as terrified when the blowout spewed flames across the room. The curtains erupted, encircling Helen and me in the makeshift room.

The Padre, still burning, began slowly crawling away, through the burning wall of curtains.

At first, I thought he was trying to get away, but then I saw where he was headed. Just meters beyond the flames were more than a dozen oxygen tanks. Something had to be done or the whole place would blow up before we could get out.

"Dammit, Ryan! We have to go."

I hoped Charlie would make an appearance in my mind and help me figure out the right thing to do, but he was nowhere to be found. If we were going to get out of there, I had to act fast.

Popping up, I darted around the table.

"Ryan, stop!"

I dashed toward the Padre.

He rolled over with the dog skull gun in hand, the barrel pointed right at me.

I threw caution to the wind, and leaped into the air. Sailing the remaining distance was the longest seconds of my life. An unquestionable certainty overcame me.

This is all about to end.

Pop! Pop! Pop!

I dropped on top of the Padre, and as I waited for the pangs of death to overcome me, I heard Helen scream.

"Ryan, no!"

Fearing the worst, I rolled off and onto my back, quickly realizing my chest was actually burning from the cinders on the Padre and not bullet wounds. I kept my eye on the Padre while rolling to put my burning clothes out, but the only motion was from the flames consuming his body. The larger fire grabbed my attention again, and it was growing exponentially larger by the second.

Helen ran in my direction, then dove onto the ground in front of me and pointed at the double doors.

Junior!

He had shot the Padre and was still pointing his gun in our direction.

I waved, and he dropped the weapon to his side, then motioned for us to follow him.

I turned to Helen. "He's all right. Let's get the hell out of here!"

We jumped up and ran toward the exit. Junior covered us, though he had already made short work of the few guards that were there. We hurried through the short maze of hallways on the second floor, and we hit the stairwell and raced down the two flights.

A loud bang shook the entire structure and debris fell from the ceiling.

"Hurry!" Junior yelled.

We sprinted through a few more hallways at ground level until another explosion rocked the foundation on which we stood and more rubble fell from above.

Junior pointed ahead. "That's our exit!"

Not having had a moment to really check on Helen, I looked over as we ran and realized that we had been holding hands since we left the burning room. Most importantly, she looked all right. I looked back, and with the main entrance in sight, we sprinted like mad and burst through the doors. Outside was the same parking lot from Charlie's memory, only decayed from age and neglect. It was also littered with the remains of what must have been the auto-hounds.

"Over here." Junior ushered us to his car.

Helen and I flung the door to the backseat open and jumped in.

Hopping into the driver's seat, Junior started the car, turned the wheel hard, and slammed the accelerator to the floor. The car peeled out and raced through the parking lot, toward the woods.

A flare-up in the rearview caught my eye, followed by the loudest explosion I had ever heard. The building was completely obliterated. Only flames and a rolling cloud of smoke remained.

I couldn't resist confirming the obvious. "No one could have survived that."

Junior chimed in. "Let's hope not."

I turned to Helen. "You okay? How the hell did you get free?"

"Honestly? I called your name, and then blacked out. When I came to, I was standing over Allen and the other guards, and they were in pretty bad shape. That's when I called your name again."

I shook my head, but in that moment, I couldn't bring myself to delve into what it might mean.

"Blacked out? Well, I'm just glad you're okay."

She nodded. "How are you, Ryan?"

"I'm fine."

We naturally leaned in together to hug and kiss. Pulling back after a moment, there was something else I wanted to know. "How'd you find us, Junior?"

He slowly peered up into the rearview, and I caught his slight grin.

"Well...*Joey*...I was really close to catching my father...Sonya...when you messaged me. I offered five times the credits on the Anono domain for them to reveal your contact information, and within minutes, I got it. I kept an eye on you for several days, but thought it was a dead end. Then gunshots were reported at your apartment building, and I drove up just as you were pulling away and followed from a distance. I almost lost the auto-truck from Spruce Street to the lab, but then I found the road through the woods."

"Well, that was one hell of a hunch. Thanks for coming."

"It was nothing. Anything to get back at my father."

Silence overtook the car as the night was finally catching up to all of us, and there was nothing left to say.

I looked in the rearview and stared at myself, thinking about how far I'd come. A paralyzed kid. The migration. Meeting Charlie. Helping to avenge all of the named and unnamed victims of the Padre. It had already been a wild ride, but part of me knew it was still just beginning. As the thought ran its course, I could feel my mind expanding rapidly in a way that I had never felt before, and the slightest pain came over my right eye as the pupil began to glow a bright white. I trembled a little as the most nostalgic presence from within made itself known, then I let loose a breathy laugh.

I whispered, "You're forgiven, Charlie."

THE END

DEAR READER,

Thank you for reading *Between Two Minds: Awakening,* my very first novel. As it got closer to becoming a published book, my obsession shifted from writing it to that of feedback from people like you. When you have a minute, please return to the website where you purchased your copy and submit a review—good, bad, or indifferent. It would mean a lot, and ultimately challenge me to make subsequent books that much better for you.

Thanks again!

ACKNOWLEDGMENTS

A loving thanks to my parents, siblings, and wife for being my guiding lights throughout life and this novel.

A very special thanks to Debra L Hartmann and her team at IAPS for providing end-to-end editing and design work of the utmost quality. My debut novel wouldn't be what it is today without your cordial guidance every step of the way.

A special thanks to:

- My teachers, coaches, and friends from Hammond, IN. You all shaped me in many ways as a person and author.

- The students and football players I mentored as a teacher and coach. Your willingness to work hard and chase your dreams inspired me to become an author.

- My teammates in data migration and software development. My time with you inspired much of the story behind this novel.

ABOUT THE AUTHOR

D. C. Wright-Hammer is an avid storyteller with a passion for fantasy and science fiction. Currently, he is a certified scrum product owner at a large software company, and formerly, taught engineering and technology to high school students. He also has a passion for multimedia including music and video.

To stay on top of all of his latest content, visit hammerstonecreative.com and follow him on Facebook at facebook.com/dcwrighthammer and Twitter @dcwrighthammer2.

CPSIA information can be obtained
at www.ICGtesting.com
Printed in the USA
LVHW08s0507021018
592117LV00021B/135/P